FADING

e.k. blair

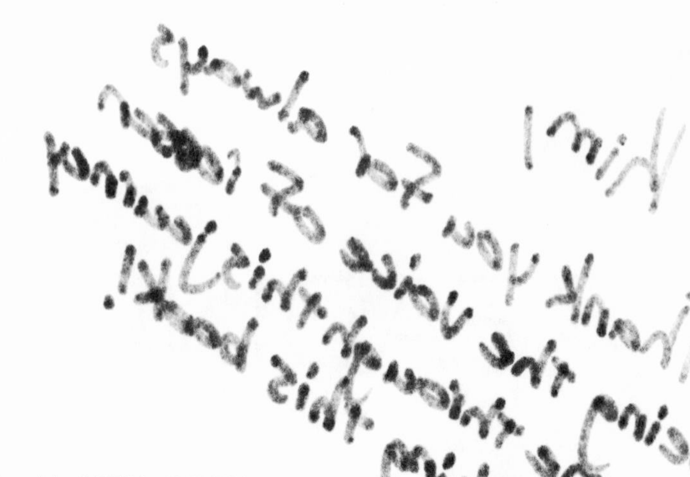

Cover Design by Sarah Hansen, Okay Creations

Editing by Lisa Christman, Adept Edits

Interior design by Angela McLaurin, Fictional Formats

Photography by Maxim Malevich

ISBN: 978-0-578-12543-5

For Gina

I've never been more pleased, and it's all your fault.

"And though she be but little,
she is fierce."

~William Shakespeare

prologue

“What do you mean they cancelled? They’ve been on the books for weeks.”

“I don’t know. I didn’t take the call, but we’ve gotta fill that slot in the next couple of days. Classes at U-Dub started today, so this weekend is gonna be busy as hell.”

“Shit!” I pause for a second, frustrated as fuck. “It’s too late to do anything about it tonight. I’ll make some calls tomorrow and try to get another band booked. Oh, hey, if those fuckers call back, tell them to find another bar to play.”

“Right, boss. You heading out soon? It’s past midnight already.”

“Yeah, in a little bit. I need to finish this paperwork and I’ll be gone. Go ahead and go.”

“See you tomorrow, man.”

“See ya.”

I try working on the inventory supply sheet that I need to get in to our liquor distributor, but my mind is elsewhere. I really need to call Gina and tell her to not come over tonight. She’s starting to become so damn clingy. I can’t stand chicks like that. The last thing I need to deal with is her needy shit. Gavin had warned me about her, but fuck if I listened. I was just looking for a one-night thing, but her stopping by my place and calling me all the time is getting annoying.

A clatter outside snaps me out of my thoughts. I look down at my watch to see it's nearing one in the morning. *Shit.* When I start packing my things up to head home, I hear more commotion from outside. I shake my head knowing it's probably just some drunk guys heading back home from a party. People are always cutting through the back alley.

I start locking everything up and make my way downstairs to the back door. "Crap," I whisper to myself, realizing I left my cell in my office. Walking back up the stairs to my office, I grab my phone off my desk. Then I hear screaming. A girl screaming.

"Fuck!"

Bolting out of my office, I quickly run downstairs to the back door and out to the small employee parking lot in the alley.

"God, please! Stop!" a girl shrieks.

Before my mind can process what I'm seeing, the bastard smashes his fist into the girl's face.

Adrenaline courses through my body, and I run. Yanking the guy off her, I start slamming my fist in his face over and over. I completely lose control of myself and relentlessly whale on him. My knuckles start to burn as the flesh begins to split open. He manages to get a few swift hits to my jaw and ribs, which allows him a quick moment to work out of my grip and flee.

Before I can charge after the guy, I catch a glimpse of the girl. It doesn't take but a split second for me to refocus. She lies there, completely unconscious, bare, with her clothes ripped off of her. My stomach clenches and my chest tightens as I slowly approach her and kneel down on my knees. Too scared to touch her, I take off my shirt and cover her naked, battered body. Her face is scratched and covered in blood and dirt. The side where the fucker's fist landed is already starting to swell and bruise, and her knees are ripped open and covered in gravel. My heart pounds and my gut is in knots.

I pat my pockets for my cell but it's not on me. I must have dropped it as I ran out here. Not wanting to leave her, I look around and spot her purse. I lean over and grab it in search of her phone. When I find it, I swipe the screen and dial 911.

As I sit next to her, she lies there, breathing peacefully. Whatever is running through her head right now has to be a million times better than the hell she's going to wake up to.

What the fuck just happened? I stare at her. I don't know what else to do. She is so small, and when I look at her tiny hands, there is bloody flesh under her nails. *Shit.* I notice a little heart tattoo on her lower hip that is still exposed. Sliding the shirt over a little to cover it, I finally hear the sirens.

"Thank God," I whisper.

chapter one

"Where did you meet this guy?"

I stare at my hazel eyes reflected in the mirror and apply a little mascara to my already dark, thick lashes. "I ran into him at the country club."

"What the hell were you doing there? You hate all those pretentious tartlets," she says with a dramatic eye roll.

"I know, but my parents wanted me to meet them for brunch."

"How did that go?" Kimber asks.

I turn around to face her, "Oh you know, the usual. Mom is still up my ass for majoring in dance. Thinks I'm throwing my life away. I swear to God, the woman has got to get a life and stop trying to control mine."

Lying on my bed while I browse my closet for something to wear, Kimber says, "Ugh, forget about her. So tell me, is this guy hot, or is he a loafer-wearing, country club douche?"

Sliding on my favorite white pants and grabbing a sleeveless navy blouse, I shoot Kimber a smirk. "Hot, no loafers, clean cut, and a total mama's boy. So yeah, a bit of a douche."

"Seriously? Why did you agree to go out with him?" She rolls off of my bed and starts rummaging through my shoes. Kimber is like my sister. I met her my freshman year when we were randomly paired together to share a dorm room. She's very outgoing and has a flair for dramatics. Although her sense of humor can be a bit brash, her heart is sincere. After our freshman year, we ditched the dorms and moved into this house, which her parents own. The past three years have really bonded us, and I couldn't imagine my life without her.

"Because my mother was standing right there, and I just didn't want to deal with any more of her nagging. So, he asked, I said yes. We are just going out for a drink, that's all. No biggie."

"Here, wear these shoes."

"Thanks," I say as I slip on my gold Tory Burch sandals. I run a brush through my long, thick brown hair and give myself one last look in the mirror.

Smearing on some lip-gloss, I make my way toward the kitchen. When I grab my cell off the bar to check my texts, I see I have one missed call from Jase. I met Jason around the same time I met Kimber. I immediately connected with him and can tell him anything. I love Kimber, but for some reason, I'm able to let all my walls down with Jase.

There's a knock on the door, and I yell for Kimber to answer it. Quickly, I type out a text for Jase.

Heading out for a few hours. Come by later. Dying to see you.

Tossing my phone in my purse, I walk into the living room to meet Jack.

"Hey, Jack."

"Hi, Candace. You look great," he says, and I hear Kimber let out a tiny snort. I shoot her a look over my shoulder and mouth '*be nice*!'

I hop into Jack's car and we head to Prescriptions, a trendy upscale bar in downtown Seattle. Jack parks and then swiftly makes his way to my door to open it for me. Taking my hand, he helps me out of his small Audi.

When we walk inside, the bar is dimly lit and scattered with sleek leather couches and leather-upholstered coffee tables. The main bar runs along one of the walls and is made of a rich chocolate wood. Spanning the length of the wall behind the bar of lit-up bottles is a solid black chalkboard with the word 'Prescriptions' written across it with all the drinks listed below in a unique, artistic script. As we settle onto one of the couches, a waitress comes by; Jack orders a beer, and I order a glass of red wine.

Lifting his knee, he angles himself toward me on the sofa and asks, "So, how come I've never seen you at the country club before? I see your parents often, but never you."

"Not my scene, I guess. My mother serves on a few committees, so she practically lives there."

Jack narrows his dark blue eyes at me, and the edge of his mouth lifts into a slight grin. "You don't get along with your mother, do you?"

"It's complicated," I sigh. "We have very different views on life. She's really into appearances. Looking the part. Playing the role. I just don't see the point."

The waitress arrives with our drinks, and I take a generous sip of my wine. I can't help but notice how sexy he looks as he tilts his head back to take a drink from his bottle of beer. *Maybe I was wrong; maybe he's not a douche.* I let out a small giggle at my thought.

"What's so funny?"

"Oh, nothing. Just thinking about how maybe I had gotten the wrong impression of you the other day." I take another sip of my drink. "So, Jack, tell me about yourself."

"What do you want to know?"

"Hobbies? Major? What do you plan on doing after you graduate?"

"Well, I play on the lacrosse team, and I'm studying Political Science." He takes another swig of his beer and clarifies, "I'm pre-law. So after this year I plan on going to Stanford for law school. What about you?"

"I'm a Fine Arts major. Ballet. Another thing my mother doesn't approve of."

"So, what are your plans after this year?"

"Auditions, I guess. I mean, I'd like to dance professionally for as long as I can. Eventually I want to teach."

We fall into easy conversation as we continue to talk and get to know each other better. He seems genuinely interested in what I have to say. Jack isn't the typical guy I go for; he's a frat boy and comes from an upbringing such as myself, but he's really nice and for the most part, seems down to earth.

I tend to have a lot of first dates with guys but never find myself in a relationship with any of them. I don't really know the reason for that; maybe I just haven't found anyone that I care enough about to keep around. I'm not a slut by any means, far from it. I've only slept with one guy, my high school boyfriend. We dated off and on for over a year and wound up having sex the night of our graduation. I was young and stupid, but that was three years ago, and I haven't heard from him since that night.

After a couple of hours pass easily, I excuse myself to the ladies' room. I wash my hands and search my purse for a hair tie. The wine is starting to make me feel warm, and I need to get the hair off of my neck. I have always wanted short hair, but as a dancer, it needs to be long enough to secure in a bun on top of my head. So for now, I have long, thick, dark brown hair with natural golden highlights that hangs a few inches below my shoulders. When I finally find a hair tie, I quickly sweep my hair up into a ponytail.

When I return, Jack stands up and holds out his hand for me. "You ready to go?"

"Yeah," I say as I slide my hand into his.

Jack parks his car in front of my house, and once again, jumps out and opens my door for me. He walks me up to the front door and says, "I really had fun with you tonight. How about we do this again?"

"Umm, yea. That would be nice," I say as he leans in and lightly brushes his lips against my cheek. My neck heats, and I feel slightly embarrassed by the gesture.

"I'll call you so we can set something up."

"Okay, that sounds good. Thanks for the drinks. I had a really nice time."

"Me too. Goodnight, Candace."

"Night, Jack."

I watch him walk back to his car, and I turn to open the door. Instead, the door handle jerks out of my hand, and I stumble to my knees inside the house.

"What the hell, Kimber?!"

Nodding her head towards the door, she questions, "Mmm hmm...what was that all about?"

Pushing myself off the floor to stand, I look at her with an annoyed expression on my face, "What was *what* all about?"

"Him kissing you on the cheek. Lame." She scrunches up her nose in disgust. "Who does that?"

"God, whatever. And you didn't have to watch him kiss me. I swear your voyeurism knows no limits."

"Well?" she continues, staring at me with her way too

curious, blue eyes.

"Ooh, leave me alone," I sigh. "I might have been wrong about him. He's a pretty decent guy. I think we might try and get together again. We'll see." I walk to my bedroom to change clothes, and Kimber follows me. She lies across my bed while I put on a pair of cut-off sweat shorts and a cami.

I watch Kimber as she stares up at the ceiling in deep thought with her wavy blonde hair fanned out around her. Kimber is beautiful, and she knows it. She's fit but has been blessed with feminine curves, where I have more of a straight, lean body. Typical ballerina form.

Still staring at the ceiling, she says, "Shit, Candace, do you realize that we are about to start our senior year, and I have yet to come across any decent husband material?"

I bust out into a fit of laughter. "Is this the crap that is constantly floating through your head?"

"Well...kinda. I mean, I have never had to work a day in my life, and I'll be damned if I have to work after we graduate. I mean, if I had a job, when would we ever hang out?" She gives me an evil smirk.

"You're crazy, but I love you so much." I lay down behind her and give her a tight hug.

"Hey, girls," Jase's voice booms through the house.

I jump up, run to the living room, and give him a big hug. Kimber quickly follows me and steps in for her hug while I take the two wine bottles out of his hands. I walk to the kitchen to grab a corkscrew and some wine glasses. When I return to the living room, I set everything down on the coffee table and make myself comfortable on the floor. Opening the wine, I pour myself a glass while I watch Kimber and Jase talk as they sit together on the couch. Jase is a very attractive guy. He has a hard, athletic build, and his skin is lightly tanned. He wears his thick, brown hair, which has turned more of a blond over the course of the summer, lightly gelled in a messy faux-hawk. His eyes are a unique shade of light gold that stand out against his dark lashes.

"So, how was your trip to San Diego?" I ask.

Jase finishes pouring his glass and says, "It was good. I hung out with friends, went out to a few bars, and saw some bands. You know, the usual visit home."

I take a sip of my wine and smile, "Well, we're glad you're back."

"You have no idea how happy I am to be back," he says with a straight face, and I can see a hint of tension in his eyes.

"Man, was it that bad, Jase?" Kimber asks.

"It's just not home to me anymore. Plus, I missed you bitches," he laughs, and his mood instantly shifts. "So, what have I missed?"

I get the feeling that Jase is hiding something about his trip back home. I look at him as he is downing his glass of wine faster than usual. Yep, he's definitely hiding something. I'm pulled out of my thoughts when I hear Kimber speak up.

"Well, Candace is dating a douche from Mommy and Daddy's country club," she says as she winks at me.

"I am not!" I say. "We went out for drinks. That's all."

"Are you seeing him again?" she asks even though she already knows the answer.

"You're seeing him again?" Jase questions, scrunching his eyebrows together. "Wait, who's *him*? Who are you seeing?"

"No. I mean, yes. God, really, it's no big deal."

"Must be if he's getting a second date," Jase says as he takes another drink. "Is that where you were earlier? On your date?"

"Uh huh," I nod.

"Where did you guys go? You never told me," Kimber

asks as she folds her legs underneath her.

"We went to Prescriptions."

"I love that place," Kimber says. "Anyway. New subject. What the hell are we doing this week before classes start back up?"

"I have some serious studio time I need to put in. I also have to work."

"You always keep yourself so busy," Jase says. I don't even try to make excuses because he's right. I just shake my head and take another sip of my wine.

After a while, Jase and Kimber decide to watch some trash TV. I move to the couch and lie down with my head on Jase's lap while we all watch MTV. As he combs his fingers through my hair, it isn't long until I doze off.

I wake up to the feel of my bed dipping down and I smell wine. Jase lies behind me and wraps his muscular arms around my waist. I nestle back into his warm chest.

"Did I wake you?" he whispers.

"Yeah, but it's okay," I mumble quietly. "What time is it?"

"Around two. You passed out, so I carried you in here and hung out with Kimber for a while longer."

"Is she asleep?"

"Yeah, and snoring like a beast." We both laugh quietly at his words.

I roll over in his arms to face him in the dark, even though we can't see each other. I lay my head on his chest, and he wraps one arm around my waist and the other cups the back of my head.

"So, why did your trip really suck? I know something's bothering you."

Jase lets out a long sigh before saying, "I told them."

I wrap my arms tighter around him. "What did they say?"

"They threw me out."

My heart breaks and a quiet tear escapes my eye and rolls onto his bare chest.

"I'm so sorry. Why didn't you call me?"

"I don't know. I was embarrassed, I guess. I haven't told anyone what happened. I don't want the pity."

"You know I don't pity you, right?"

"Yeah," he whispers and kisses the top of my head.

"I'm sad because I love you. When your heart hurts, so does mine. Your pain is my pain."

We lie there together holding each other as my heart breaks to sync up with his already broken one. I love Jase. He's my best friend. We have a deep connection that runs through us and links us together. He has had a lot of pain in his life. He had a sister that was two years older than him. They were extremely close, but she died in a car crash the night of her senior prom. His parents still refuse to touch her room, like they are expecting her to come home one day.

Jase was extremely confused with his sexuality in high school. He said he didn't want to be gay and figured if he just slept with enough girls, maybe he would start to feel differently. So he slept around. A lot. He told me that growing up, he felt trapped as if he was living a lie—silently suffering on the inside as he held on to his secret. Until he came to college, no one ever knew he was gay. I'm happy he finally told his parents though. He needed to free himself of the secret he had been keeping from them. I hate that they turned their backs on their own son and would just toss him out of their home like he didn't even matter to them.

"You know this is your home, don't you? Right here with me. Kimber and I are your home. And we don't give a shit that you like guys."

Jase kisses the top of my head, and I grip my arms tighter around him.

"Jase?" I whisper.

"Yeah, sweetie?"

"I love you."

"I love you, too."

chapter two

I wake up to the smell of bacon and coffee. “Thank God.” I roll out of bed and make my way to the kitchen where Jase is cooking breakfast. Just another reason why I love him so much: he loves to cook, and I love to eat.

“Hey, lovely,” he says to me over his shoulder as I pad into the kitchen.

I walk over to the stove where he is scrambling some eggs, and I lift up on my toes to kiss him on the cheek. “Morning,” I say, then stroll over to grab a mug, and I begin to pour myself a cup of coffee. “What time did you wake up?”

“Early. I didn’t get much sleep. Couldn’t seem to clear my head.”

I lean back against the counter and give him a side stare. It kills me that he’s hurting so much. He peeks up at me and catches me staring.

“Don’t.”

“Don’t what?”

He continues to whisk the eggs, “Don’t look at me like that.”

“I’m not. I’m sorry,” I say as I walk over to sit at the bar. “So, what are you up to today?”

He turns around, dumps a portion of the eggs onto a

plate, and takes several slices of bacon before setting it down in front of me.

"Not much. I need to pick up my books for my classes, and then I was going to hit the gym for a couple of hours. What about you?" Jase sets his plate on the bar and sits down next to me.

"Work," I say as I take a bite of my bacon. "I have to work all week. I also need to go up to the studio to get in some solo time before classes start."

We continue to eat in silence for a few minutes. When I finish my breakfast, I look up at him and tease, "My ass thanks you for the bacon." Winking at him, I walk around to the other side of the bar and rinse off my plate.

"God, you guys are up early," Kimber says as she walks into the kitchen with her eyes squinted as if the morning light is too much for her to bear.

"It's nine. Hardly early, Kim," I say sarcastically.

She grabs the box of Lucky Charms and pours herself a bowl, barely opening her eyes to do so, then sits on the barstool next to Jase. He stares at her with a smirk.

"Whaa?" she says with a mouthful of milk and a magical leprechaun concoction of cereal and marshmallows.

"You have this kickass kitchen to cook in, but you continue to eat like a six-year-old kid," he says, shaking his head and laughing.

"This shit's good," she says, using her spoon to point and emphasize her beloved breakfast cereal.

Jase and I laugh at her. I walk over and pour myself another cup of coffee before heading to my room.

"I'm going to hit the shower and get ready for work. I'll see you guys later."

"See ya," they both say in unison.

The weather is oddly nice today, so after I'm dressed, I decide that I will just walk to work. I've been working at

Common Grounds, a local coffee house right off campus, for the past two years. I don't need the job for the money; I just like having the responsibility.

I pull out my phone as I walk to check my messages, and I notice I have a missed call and voicemail from my mother. Already annoyed, I go ahead and listen to her message.

Candace, I was hoping to hear all about your date with that young man from the club. I surely hope you didn't already screw this one up. It's your senior year and you should be taking your future seriously. I just heard Maggie's daughter got engaged to the Garrison's son. Well, anyways, I have a lunch date with the ladies, so I need to go. Please, call me back.

Deleting the message, I drop the phone into my bag. Of course she would think anything that didn't work out to her liking would be my fault. She's so unbelievable. I only wish I could have a decent relationship with her, with both of my parents, really. I know I shouldn't have those expectations, but I can't help hoping, that maybe one of these days things will change.

When I arrive, I am greeted with the familiar aroma of freshly ground coffee and muffins. I love working here. Everyone is really nice and my boss, Roxy, is great. She's in her early thirties and is extremely eccentric, with long, choppy colorful hair—purple this week— a pierced nose, and tattoos. She's always there for me when I need solid advice.

Roxy is working the espresso machine as I round the counter to grab my apron. I tie it on as she finishes with her customer.

"Is it just us this afternoon?" I ask as she is handing the customer his change.

Walking over to me, she sits down on a stool. "Yep. Brandon had to take care of some issue with his scholarship. But it's been pretty dead so far."

I pull up a stool and sit beside her.

"How was breakfast with your parents the other day?"

"You know, just the same old crap. Nothing ever changes. I don't understand my mother and why she just can't be happy for me. I keep holding on to the hope that she'll change, but I'm starting to get tired. If it wasn't for my father, I would probably never even see her." I look away from Roxy and focus on my hands. "God, that sounds horrible, huh?"

"No, hun, that sounds honest. Don't apologize for your feelings. You're allowed to be angry with her." Roxy stands up and walks back over to the espresso machine to make herself a drink. Talking over the loud grinding and hissing she asks, "So, did you do anything fun last night?"

"I kinda had a date," I said, peeking at her over my shoulder.

"Oh, yeah? How did that go?" She walks back over to her stool, sits down, and takes a slow sip of her drink.

"Fine, I guess. We just grabbed a couple of drinks. He said he wants to hang out again, which I guess would be okay. I mean, I might as well enjoy another date before the quarter starts and I get too busy."

Roxy shakes her head at me. "You take life too seriously, you know? You need to let loose and have some fun. You're never going to get this time back, Candace. Just enjoy it. Be young and carefree."

I know she makes a good point. I tend to have a hard time letting myself be free. I mean, I go to the occasional party with Kimber, and I go out on dates here and there, but mostly, I'm dancing, studying, working, or hanging out with Jase. I've been in college for three years, and I have yet to do anything crazy. Roxy is right; I'll never get this time back. After this year, I'm going to be focused on my dancing and trying to make it into a career. I need to relax and not take life so seriously all the time.

"Yeah," I sigh. I stare out at the front of the shop that is covered in floor to ceiling windows. I breathe in a deep breath and say, "Maybe you're right."

"I know I'm right. Every school year you get sucked into your classes and dance. You keep yourself so busy. Let go. Just for a moment—let go. Be a little spontaneous."

I stare her straight in the eyes.

"Just try," she says.

I'm not sure what it is about today that makes me actually listen to what she is saying. Maybe it's the fact that I am still irritated with my mother's crude voicemail. I've heard it all before, but this time, I feel it seeping into me. Roxy is right. What the hell was I doing? Kimber is always out having the time of her life while I have my head buried in books. I'm always striving to be perfect, but I know I will never be that in my mother's eyes. I try to do my best in school and with dance. Maybe if she sees how others look at me, she might start to appreciate me. She might even start to like me. *Screw it.*

"Let's go next door," I say as my lips start to turn up into a grin.

"Huh?"

"Come on. It's dead in here. Let's close up for an hour." I hop down from my stool and start taking off my apron.

Roxy gets an approving look on her face and smiles. "Hell yeah! No way I'm gonna give you even a second to back down. Let's go."

Next door to the coffee shop is the tattoo parlor that Roxy's boyfriend works at. We both yank off our aprons, and

Roxy locks up.

The buzzing of tattoo guns fills the shop. The walls are painted black, and they are covered in tattoo flash. I don't even look because I already know what I want. I have thought about getting a tattoo in the past but was always too scared.

"Hey, Rox," Jared says as he walks up to the counter. "What are you guys doing here?"

Jared and Roxy have only been dating for a few months, but they are head over heels for each other.

"Candace wants to get a tattoo, and I need you to do it fast before she chickens out."

"I'm not going to back out," I say to her.

Jared looks at me surprised. "A tattoo, huh? Well, you're in luck. My next appointment isn't for another hour." Jared comes around the counter, takes my hand, and walks me back to his station. I hop up onto the table and he asks, "So, what are you wanting?"

Clasping my hands together nervously, I look down at him. "I'd like a tiny heart on my lower hip."

"Easy enough. Just lay down and relax while I get everything set up."

As I lie on the table, I suddenly get nervous wondering if it's going to hurt. I close my eyes and try to relax. Taking a few deep breaths, I feel Roxy grab ahold of my hand. I open my eyes and look at her.

"I can tell you're freaking out," she says.

"Just a bit. Does it hurt?" I ask as I eye the tattoos on her arms.

"Nah," Jared says as he wheels over to me on his stool. "Unbutton and pull down your pants a little."

Nervously, I do as he says.

"You ready?" he asks.

I look at Roxy as she gives me a reassuring look that

reminds me of the conversation we had a few minutes ago. I want to do this. I need to do this.

"Absolutely," I say.

I feel Jared's fingers press down on my hip as the gun starts buzzing. The pricking of the needle stings slightly on the sensitive area, and I pinch my eyes shut.

"You doing okay?" Jared asks me.

Opening my eyes as I start to numb to the sensation, I look down at him. "Yeah, it's actually not as bad as I thought."

"Well, I'm just about done."

"Really?!" I say, surprised at how fast it was.

Roxy lets out a soft laugh, "Candace, It's just a tiny-ass heart. How long did you think it was going to take?"

"Done," he says and he rolls away on his stool to grab a mirror and then rolls back. He hands it to me, and I hold it up, staring at the reflection of my new tattoo. It's a simple black outline of a heart. Small and discreet.

"I love it, Jared. Thank you."

He rubs on a glob of cool ointment and adheres a bandage over it. I grab his hand as he helps me sit up.

"Here," he says and hands me a sheet of paper. "This will tell you how to care for the tat as it heals. If you notice anything unusual going on, call me."

I nod and tell him, "Will do. Thanks again."

Roxy grabs Jared around his waist to give him a hug. "Come over later?"

"Yeah, I get out of here around six," he says before leaning down to kiss her. "See you girls later."

"Bye," we both say as we head back over to the coffee shop.

Holy shit! I cannot believe I just got a tattoo. My act of rebellion is thrilling, and I like the energy that flows through me. I could get used to this excitement.

chapter three

"I still can't believe you got a tattoo, and I'm still pissed that you did it without me," Kimber says.

"Honestly, it was a spur of the moment thing," I say as I sit on the floor and unpack my dance bag. I have been living in the studio for the past few days. Classes are about to start, and I want to make sure I'm prepared and on top of my game. Kimber had been upset when I told her about my rare act of rebellion, but she's since calmed down.

"I am so excited that you are coming out with us tomorrow. I'm not sure what has gotten into you, but I like it," she says as she sits on my bed and watches me as I rub baby powder into my pointe shoes and hang them on a hook in my closet to air dry.

I start stripping off my sweaty clothes. "I don't know. Roxy just finally got through to me, I guess. She's right; it's time to start having a little bit of fun."

I hear my phone chime, and I walk over to my desk to read a new text.

"Who's that?" Kimber asks.

"It's from Jack. I haven't heard from him since we went out last Friday."

Kimber jumps off the bed and is quickly hanging over my shoulder to read his message.

Got plans tomorrow night?

For some reason Thursday nights are big nights to go out around here. The bars and clubs are always packed.

"You should ask him to come with us," she says as she smacks my bottom and walks out of my room.

I sit down at my desk and text him back.

Going dancing at Remedy with some friends. You should come!

Remedy huh? What time?

Around 10:30.

Meet you there?

Yeah. See you then.

I hop up from my chair, excited about seeing him tomorrow, and throw on some clothes. I make my way to the kitchen to fix a salad. While I'm chopping some veggies, my phone begins to ring. I pick it up to see that it's my mother. *Crap.*

"Hey, Mom."

"Hi, darling. Look, there is a banquet this Saturday, and I am being recognized for my contributions to the Children's Foundation. I need you to be there," she demands.

I know she only wants me to attend for appearance's sake. One supportive, happy family. It's such a lie.

"I can't, Mom. I have to work that night."

"Well, take off," she says as if it's no big deal.

"I can't ask off work three days in advance. It doesn't work that way." I get so annoyed by her lack of consideration.

"Christ, Candace," she barks at me. "This is important. I don't even know why you have that little job."

"I like working, Mom. I'm sorry, but I just can't go," I say in the softest tone I can manage because I know she's about to flip. This is so typical of her.

"I swear, I don't know how to deal with you. You are such a selfish little girl. Here you are, playing around in college on your father's dime, and you can't even choose a respectable major. It's quite embarrassing. Then, when I ask you to do something to support me, you blow me off for some trivial job you don't even need. Where is your loyalty to this family?"

My face heats and I slam the knife down on the hard granite countertop. "Support you? You always want me to support *you,* Mother. What about supporting me? Shit, Mom, you have never once attended any of my shows. I work my ass off. You have no clue what it is I am doing here. I'm sick of this shit. I'm never going to be good enough, am I? What do you want from me? Please, just tell me so I know exactly what I need to do to make you fuckin' like me!" Disconnecting the call, I throw the phone across the counter. I am beyond pissed. My heart is racing, and I try to slow my breathing so I can calm down.

"What's with the screaming?" Kimber asks softly, knowing I rarely ever lose my temper.

My eyes begin to sting, and when I turn around to look at her, the tears start to fall. I feel so hopeless. I've fought with my mother my whole life, and I have no idea why she is the way that she is. She knows exactly what to say to me to set me off. I know it's only a matter of time before my dad calls to smooth things over and make excuses for her.

Kimber walks over and wraps her arms around me. "What happened?"

I let go of Kimber and wipe my face with the backs of my hands. “My mother. She went on another one of her tirades and thought it would be fun to belittle me. She just set me off, and I couldn’t hold it in.”

“Want to tell me about it?”

“Not really. I think I’ll just take a quick shower and call it a night.”

“You sure?” she questions me with concern.

“I’m sure.”

Kimber heads back to her room, and I bag up the vegetables I was cutting and put everything back in the refrigerator. I can’t even think about eating when I am this upset. I pick up my phone and decide to turn it off for the night so I don’t have to hear it when my father calls. After a hot shower, I start to relax. I know I should probably check to see if my dad has called, but I don’t have the energy to deal with it tonight.

Waking up the next morning, I’m surprised that I’m still pissed off about the fight I had with my mother. I throw the sheets off of me and walk over to my dresser. I pull out a pair of cutoff knee-length sweats, sports bra, and a loose fitting grey tank top. I get dressed, grab my dance bag, and throw in my pointes. After brushing my teeth and pulling my hair up in a messy bun, I go to the kitchen to grab a breakfast bar. I toss a couple bottles of water and an apple into my bag and make a cup of coffee to take with me. Throwing my bag across my chest, I head out to my car.

When I walk into the studio, I drop my bag onto the floor. I walk over to the stereo, plug in my iPod, turn up the speakers, and hit play. I sit on the floor with my legs stretched out, and I lower myself between them and begin to warm up my muscles. The melodic strains of Yann Tiersen's 'Comptine d'un Autre Ete' fill the room as I begin to stretch.

Feeling warm and loose, I grab my bag. I start taping my toes and stuffing my toe pads with new lamb's wool. Sliding on my pointes, I lace the ribbons around my ankles. This is what I love about ballet—the familiar rituals.

With the music filling the room, I grab the barre and begin to work. I start the very methodical routine: pliès, tendu, degagè. Feeling my muscles stretch, I continue to work the rest of the exercises, freeing my mind of all my stresses, and focusing on nothing but my turnout, posture, lines, and movement. Hearing the box of my toe shoes thudding against the worn wooden floor and the gliding of the shredded satin as I work my feet is soothing. I love this feeling of pure focus. Sometimes it's nice to shut out the world and be completely immersed in dance, feeling like there is no life beyond the walls of this studio. It's freeing.

After an hour or so, I end my barre work with grand battement, working on my high kicks. As I finish, I begin to feel slightly light-headed. I sit down and grab my water, downing it in just a few seconds. I remove my shoes and tape, lie on my back, close my eyes, and breathe. I know as soon as I walk out of here, the stress of my mother will creep in. So I just lie on the floor.

After leaving the studio, I sit in my car and call my dad. I just want to get it over with. I talk to him on my drive home and the conversation is the same as always. I apologize to him for my outburst, and he makes excuses for my mother. The conversation couldn't have ended any sooner. I was done with it.

'The Edge of Glory' by Lady Gaga is blaring

throughout the house while Kimber and I get ready for our night out. I'm looking forward to seeing Jack, which is a bit odd for me because I never really take that much interest in guys.

I pick out a pair of cute white shorts, a sleeveless satin hot pink top with a white Moroccan pattern, and a pair of nude pumps. My hair is down in soft, wavy curls. I apply some lip-gloss before Kimber and I head out.

We arrive at Remedy, and the place is already packed. Kimber and I walk in and find a few of our friends sitting at a small group of couches that are set off from the dance floor. We make our way over to greet everyone. When I find Jase, he takes my arm and drags me to the bar with him.

"You thirsty?" I ask sarcastically.

"Not really. I just saw Mark," he says as we slide onto our barstools.

"Isn't that the hottie you used to see that plays guitar?"

"Exactly." He eyes me with a serious look. The bartender approaches, and Jase orders us four shots of tequila and two beers.

I shoot him a questioning look and say, "Okay, spill it. Clearly you're into getting drunk, so tell me what happened."

The bartender sets the drinks down in front of us, and Jase slides two of the shots and a beer my way. We clink our tequila shots together and down them quickly.

"He caught me kissing his roommate," he confesses.

I start laughing at him and take a swig of my beer. "You can be a slut sometimes, you know?"

"Trust me. I know," he says and hands me the second shot. We sit there for a while and continue to talk and laugh. Warm arms wrap around my waist, and I turn my head to see Jack standing behind me. He looks good in a pair of worn jeans and a simple black V-neck shirt.

"Hey, Jack," I say. When I stand up, I feel the effects of

consuming the shots so quickly. Plus, I haven't eaten a lot today.

"Whoa, you okay?" Jack questions as he grabs ahold of my arm.

"Yeah, just stood up too fast." I turn to Jase and introduce the two guys to each other. When I sit down, Jack does as well and orders us another round of beers.

"So, what did you do today?" Jack asks.

"I spent the morning at the dance studio to get in some practice. Then I came home and took it easy for the rest of the day. You?"

"Been harassing the new pledges at the frat house." He laughs and takes a drink of his beer.

I sneak a quick glance at Jase and roll my eyes. Frat guys were never my thing. Maybe it's their arrogance, but I didn't catch that about Jack when we went out the other night.

Jack leans in close to my ear and whispers, "You wanna dance?"

Taking my hand in his, he helps me off the barstool, and we make our way to the crowded dance floor. I start to move to the beat of the music that blasts throughout the club. 'Push It' by Garbage is playing, and I lose myself in the sea of people dancing around me along with the flashing lights and loud music.

Jack is behind me, and I feel his arms as they slide across my stomach, underneath the hem of my top. He moves in sync with me as I dance to the rhythm of the song. I can already feel drops of sweat trickling down my spine, and it must be the tequila that is making me feel bold when I reach up behind me and wrap my hand around the back of his neck. I feel the stubble on his jaw as he glides his chin along my damp neck and takes a soft bite. *Shit, that's hot.*

Turning me around in his arms, I can see the heat in his

darkening eyes. I rake my fingers through the hair on the back of his head as he pulls my hips tight against him, and he leans down and covers my mouth with his.

I'm not sure what has come over me. Since my conversation with Roxy, I have been a little bit bolder with myself. But here, in the middle of this dance floor, kissing Jack, is pretty damn bold for me.

Jack and I continue to dance through a few more songs when we decide to take a breather and get a drink. We walk over to our section and sit down on one of the couches. I take a long drink of my beer and nearly choke when Kimber suddenly yanks me off the couch.

"I've gotta piss," she says to me while looking at Jack.

"You're such a lady." I smirk at her and give Jack an apologetic look. "I'll be right back," I say to him. He nods back at me while stifling a laugh.

Kimber is nearly dragging me to the bathroom. As soon as she closes the door behind us she says, "What the hell was that shit on the dance floor all about, hooker?"

I start laughing. "What are you talking about?"

"What do you even know about this guy?" she questions.

"Well, nothing. I guess that's what makes it kinda fun," I say as I lean in to look at myself in the mirror. I lick my finger and swipe it under each of my eyes in an attempt to fix my makeup. "And why are you always spying on me?"

"Hey, can't blame me for watching. It was hot."

We both start laughing, and I shake my head, feeling a little embarrassed about the indiscreet show we gave her on the dance floor.

Kimber and I walk back, and Jack is laughing about something with Jase.

"What's so funny?" I ask as I make my way to sit in between the two of them.

Jack grips my thigh, giving it a little squeeze. He leans over and kisses me behind my ear and whispers, “I can’t even remember now that you’re here.”

I look at him with a tiny smirk and shake my head. Sometimes Jack will say things that seem a little too fast, too soon, and it makes me feel slightly embarrassed. I turn away from him and ask Kimber how much longer she wants to stay.

She looks at her phone and says, “It’s a little after one. I guess we can think about calling it a night if you’re getting tired.”

I look at Jack and give him an undecided shrug.

“Why don’t we finish our drinks, and I’ll drive you home,” he says.

“Okay.”

Kimber jumps up, “Great, well then I’m heading out. If I’m asleep when you get home, wake me up.”

“I shouldn’t be out too late, but I will,” I say to her.

Kimber winks at me, then leaves. Jase says his goodbyes as well and heads out shortly after Kimber. I finish my beer and lean against Jack with his arm wrapped around my shoulders. We talk about what we have been doing the past few days. Most of our conversations are pretty easy, even though we don’t seem to have a whole lot in common. But, it feels good to be next to him, so I don’t really care what we talk about.

I’m pretty tired on the drive home. Leaning my head against the cold window, I close my eyes. It has been a crazy night for me, and I’m feeling a little confused about Jack but try not to think too much. I’m always thinking too much. When I feel the car start to slow, I open my eyes and roll my head to the side to face Jack.

It's now raining outside, and the trickling against the car is loud. Jack and I stare at each other in silence. I have missed having the affection of a guy, so I don't object when he leans in to kiss me. He touches the side of my face, and I wrap my hand behind his neck. His kisses are passionate and eager. I part my lips slightly, and he slides his tongue in my mouth and caresses it with mine. Grabbing my hips, he pulls me over the console and on top of him. With my legs straddled on either side of him, I can feel how turned on he is. He has both of his hands buried in my hair as he deepens our kiss. I am totally lost in him.

A soft moan escapes my lips, and I pull away. Suddenly, I'm thinking again as I look down at his flushed face. *What am I doing?* This isn't me. I don't act like this and especially not with guys I don't know and hardly care for. *Stop thinking, Candace.* I lean down and press my lips against his and we begin getting lost in each other again. Well, that's not true. I can't get lost because I can't stop thinking about how this is wrong. I'm only leading him on.

I manage to break our kiss and rest my forehead against his. My eyes are shut because I'm too embarrassed to look at him. As he runs his hands down my back, he whispers, "It's okay, Candace."

Pulling back, I look into his dark blue eyes. "Sorry," I whisper back and slowly shake my head.

"Can I see you again?" he asks as he continues to run his hands slowly up and down my back.

I know I should be honest with him and say no, but my hormones answer, "Yeah."

He reaches his hand behind his seat, and I wonder what he's searching for. He grins at me as he hands me an umbrella.

I laugh softly, "Thanks."

"Come on. I'll walk with you."

"No, it's fine. Don't worry."

He lifts up and plants a chaste kiss on my lips. "I'll call you, okay?"

"Okay," I say as I climb off of his lap and out of the car.

I make my way inside the house and slip off my heels.

"Kim, you awake?" I whisper loudly as I walk into her room.

She rolls over in bed and says, "Yeah. Come here, I want all the dirty details." She sits up and turns on the lamp that's on her nightstand. I walk over, sit down next to her, and let out a long sigh.

"I think he likes me."

"So, what's the problem?"

I look over at her, then flop back onto the bed and stare at the ceiling, "The problem is, I'm only trying to have a little fun, but it feels wrong. There is just nothing there, yet I keep kissing him, and I'm only leading him on. He asked to see me again, and my stupid mouth said yes."

Kimber lays down next to me, "So, see him one more time, and just tell him. Honestly, Candace, I think you're being hard on yourself and making this a bigger deal than it actually is."

I turn to face her. "You're right."

"I always am." She gives me a grin, and then asks, "Did you kiss him good-bye?"

"More like straddled his thighs, grabbed his hair, and let him shove his tongue in my mouth," I say, and then I burst out laughing as I cover my heated face with my hands.

"You little hooker!"

I jump off the bed, still laughing. "Good night, Kim," I say in a singsong voice as I head to my room.

"Night, slut!" I hear her yell down the hall.

chapter four

I'm working in the back, restocking supplies, when I hear Roxy shout for me from up front. I stop what I'm doing, walk to the front counter, and see Jase. I spoke to him the morning after our night out at Remedy. He ran into Mark out in the parking lot and ended up talking to him for a while and Mark decided to give Jase a second chance.

"Hey, Candace," he says as he leans in to give me a peck on my lips. "I've been trying to call you."

"Oh, sorry. I was at the studio this morning and let the battery drain on my cell, and I never remembered to plug it in to recharge," I said. "I'll go do that now before I forget again." I run into the back and grab my phone and the charging cord. When I walk back up front, I plug it in by the register.

"So, I wanted to see if you and Kimber could get together with Mark and I later tonight?" Jase asks while he's leaning against the counter.

"I'd love to, but I'm working late tonight. How about tomorrow afternoon?" I ask. "We can do a cookout at our house."

"That sounds great. I really fucked up with him, and I want to make it right. Plus, I want you guys to meet him."

Resting on my elbows, I look up at him and say, "Of

course, Jase."

"Great, I'll call him and let him know," he says, then leans down to kiss my forehead. I smile up at him as he turns to leave.

I notice my phone automatically turns on once it gets enough life in it. Picking it up, I swipe the screen to look at all my missed calls and texts. I see I have a missed text from Jack, and I tap to open it up.

You free Monday night? Frat house always throws a huge party after the first day of classes.

"What are you reading over there?" Roxy asks as she is steaming some milk for a customer's drink.

Looking up at her, I say, "I'm reading a text from Jack. He wants me to go to some party, and I'm not sure how to respond." I look back down at his text and stare.

After Roxy finishes up with her customer, she walks over to me. "What do you mean 'you don't know how to respond'? What's going on?"

I lift my arms off the counter and step away to face her. Crossing my arms in front of my chest, I say, "I need to distance myself from him. I think he wants more than I do. I mean, I don't want anything, so..."

"Just tell him you can't go. Or go, and tell him later that you just don't have time for a relationship right now," she says.

I pick up my phone to respond.

What time?

I walk over to pour myself a cup of coffee when I hear my phone chime.

"That was fast," I hear Roxy say.

"No kidding." Walking back to my phone, I set down my mug, and tap on his message.

Pick you up around 10?

Okay, I'll see you then.

Miss you.

"Shit," I mumble quietly and set the phone down, wanting to pretend I didn't see that last text.

"What are you 'shitting' about?"

I take a sip of my coffee and then toss Roxy my phone. Sitting on my stool, I watch her closely as she reads through the texts. I notice her eyes get big, and I know she finally reached the text that is starting to make me panic slightly.

"Okay, it's not that—"

"You know I don't do well with this stuff. I never make it to date number two and now this guy says he misses me." I feel my heartbeat start to quicken and, yes, that is definitely panic I am feeling. I don't deal with intimate relationships well at all. In fact, I'm pretty closed off emotionally with guys. I've never had any closeness with my parents, then the one guy I thought at least liked me in high school turned out to be just another asshole. I feel like I'm emotionally moronic.

I look up to see that Roxy is laughing at me. "It's not funny!"

"It actually is a little bit," she says. "Relax, don't respond. He probably won't even notice. Guys are stupid anyway."

I hope she's right. I hope he isn't sitting there waiting for me to text him back to say that I miss him too. I don't like opening myself up like that.

The next day, Kimber and I get ready for the cookout. I'm in the kitchen preparing the burgers for the grill, and Kimber is chopping up veggies for a salad. Jase has never bothered to introduce us to any guys in the past, so I know he must really like Mark. I don't know much about him aside from the fact that he plays guitar for a local band.

"Hey, Kim, has Jase ever talked to you about Mark before?" I ask as I pound out another hamburger patty.

"Not much. He was pretty pissed off at himself when they broke up, so I figured he had really cared for him but didn't realize it until they split." Kimber slides the salad in the fridge then opens a bag of chips to pour in a bowl.

"Hmm..."

"What?" Sheeyes me as she pops a chip in her mouth.

I walk to the sink to wash my hands. "Nothing." I shake my head. "Just curious."

"We're here," Jase calls out.

I walk into the living room and give him a hug.

"Mark, this is Candace," Jase says as I pull away.

I turn to Mark, "Hey! It's great to meet you. Come on in. We're in the kitchen getting the food ready," I say as I start walking towards the kitchen.

"Hey, Jase," Kimber says with a mouth full of chips.

Jase looks at Mark then back at Kimber. "And this crazy girl is Kimber."

"Nice you meet you guys," Mark says with a grin.

Mark is good looking with an athletic build similar to Jase's. He has dark brown hair and striking green eyes.

"Will one of you start the grill?" Kimber asks the guys.

"Yeah, I can do that," Mark says, and Kimber leads him out back.

Jase and I grab the food and head out behind them. We are lucky to have a large backyard with a nice patio that is covered with a pretty white pergola. We have a table that seats six and off to the side, several chairs that circle around a fire pit. There is a small bar area with a built in grill that we only used when there were guys over to start it up.

Most students our age live in smaller houses or apartments, but Kimber's parents own this house. They bought it when they were having the house built that they live in now.

"This is a nice place you have," Mark says.

Kimber flops down in a chair. "I suppose," she says with a sigh.

I roll my eyes at her and look at Mark, "Please, just ignore her dramatics."

Kimber looks at me and laughs.

"Hey Jase, will you run inside and grab the case of beer that's in the fridge and bring it out? There's a cooler next to the door that already has ice in it," I say.

"Sure," he says and he walks inside the house.

I walk over to Mark who is standing next to the grill and hand him the plate of burgers. "So, Mark, are you in college too?" I ask

He grabs the plate from me and starts placing each patty on the grill. "Yeah, I'll be graduating after this year." He closes the lid and we both sit down as Jase walks over and hands us all beers.

"Same here," I say. "What are you studying?"

Mark takes a swig of his beer, "Same as Jase: Architecture." Looking over at Jase, he adds, "That's how we know each other."

We continue getting to know Mark and having good conversation. I really like him and we corner off for the majority of the night, talking and laughing, while Kimber and

Jase drink and talk about who knows what. It's nice to have a relaxing evening with friends.

After cleaning up, it was starting to get late, and we decide to call it a night. I have an early class in the morning, so I need to hit the sack.

"It was so good to meet you, Mark," I say as I walk him to the front door.

"Same here," he responds.

I lean over and give him a hug, "You're welcome anytime, and you don't need Jase with you to stop by." "Thanks," he says.

Kimber and I say our good-byes to the boys and they head out. Walking to their car, Mark holds Jase's hand and leans in to kiss him on the neck. When I close the door, I look at Kimber. "I love seeing Jase like that," I say.

"Like what?" she asks.

"Happy and comfortable," I say as I lean against the door.

Smiling at me, Kimber says, "Me too. He told me about his trip home."

"Sucks, huh?" I say as I push myself off the door and start walking towards the back of the house to our rooms.

"Yeah," she says and she follows me. "I love you, Candace."

I turn to her, surprised by the affection behind her words.

"I know I tease you a lot, but I just wanted to say it so you know," she says.

"I love you too, Kim," I say as I wrap my arms around her tightly. Kim and Jase are like family to me. They both love me and support me the way family should.

We pull apart and head to our separate rooms.

"Good night," I say.

"Night, hooker."

I shake my head and laugh as I close the door behind me.

chapter five

So far my classes have been uneventful. It's the first week, so I don't expect much until at least next week. I just left my Methodologies class and I'm on my way to the studio for my Ballet Technique class. When I walk through the double doors, I am greeted by a few of the girls.

The dance program here at the University of Washington isn't huge. You're in classes with the same people every quarter. I've been with these girls for three years, and even though we all see each other every day, I don't hang out with any of them outside of classes and studio. Everyone is pretty competitive, so I prefer to keep it strictly professional and not mingle outside of school.

This year will be exceptionally competitive because of our senior capstone, which is a self-choreographed solo. Only two solos will be selected to perform during the final production at the end of the year. It's an important performance for graduating seniors because there will be lots of agencies in attendance. Getting a solo can mean having a job after graduation.

Everyone is scattered around the studio, taping up their toes, banging new pointes on the floor to break in the box, stretching, and a few are even quietly chatting. I keep to myself and start taping my toes. The past three years that I've spent here have been good. I tend to get lead placements in dances, standout solos, and duets with the male dancers. We combine with the guys on Tuesdays and Thursdays for an extra hour on top of our normal two-hour class.

I look up and see Andrea Emerson walk in. She's our instructor for all technique classes, and she is hardcore. She has no patience for inconsistency and expects perfection. She's tough, but she's the best. I feel a little nervous upon seeing her, even though I put in studio time at least three days a week over the summer. If you are off your game, she will let you and everyone else know it.

Ms. Emerson is a seasoned dancer who has made a decent name for herself throughout her career. Although she is in her fifties, she can still dance like the pros. She has an intimidating look about her. She always wears her long blonde hair up in a tight bun with a black leotard, white tights, and a sheer black wrap skirt. She always has a stoic look, and in three years, I have yet to see her break a smile.

She claps her hands twice, and everybody goes in search for their place on the barre. We all look the same with our hair secured in buns on the tops of our heads, black leotards, white tights, and our pale pink pointes. The classical music of a piano comes through the speakers and fills the room. I place my left hand softly on the barre and wait for the signal to begin our exercises.

The routine never changes. I've been doing these exercises since I was eleven and was in my very first ballet class. It was my mother who first signed me up for ballet. She never imagined that I would want to make a career out of it, but I have always loved dance. The freedom you can find within the strict boundaries of technique makes me feel alive. I am happiest when I am dancing.

I work gracefully through the ninety-minute routine, and when we come to an end, Ms. Emerson calls for us to gather in the front of the room. She begins to talk about our solos for the year.

"Things will be different this year. Instead of you choosing your piece of music, you will be drawing it out of this basket. There is a different piece on each CD. You will randomly choose your CD and that will be the song that you will use to choreograph your final routine. Don't forget ladies, this could be the beginning of your career, and for some of you, the end," she says.

I slowly make my way up to the large, weathered black wicker basket. I look down at the pile of discs that have the potential to launch me forward or drown me. Picking the wrong song could be disastrous. I close my eyes and pull out a CD, all the while praying to the dance gods to bless me with the perfect piece of music. I stare at the blank disc as I make my way over to my dance bag that is lying on the floor. I sit down, shove it in my bag, and start to remove my pointes.

I walk out in the warm August afternoon and slide into my white Infinity coupe, setting my bag on the passenger seat. I take out the disc and push it into the CD player, turn up the volume, and hit play. I close my eyes as I wait for the music to start. I can barely hear the strings of a violin at first. They slowly and quietly begin to build with the low, deep hum of a cello followed by a dark, melodic piano. I recognize the piece as Clint Mansell's 'Lux Aeterna'.

This is an extremely dark piece of music. My stomach hollows and I feel anxious. I have never danced to, yet alone choreographed, anything this dark. I was hoping for something feminine and delicate, not this. All I can picture is Natalie Portman's psychotic character in 'Black Swan' as she bleeds out on stage. When the song comes to an end, I turn off the stereo and drive home in welcome silence.

I don't want to think about what I just heard. Instead, I try to focus on clothes. *Yes, clothes. Think about clothes,*

Candace. Sorting through my closet in my head, I try to think about what I'm going to wear to the party tonight. It doesn't take long for my mind to fill with dread when I think about being honest with Jack and letting him know that I'm not looking for anything with him. And based on the music I just heard, my year is fucked. I am going to be living and breathing dance if I'm expected to choreograph a masterpiece to that song.

I wake up from my nap, and even though I took a shower when I got home after dance class, I decide to hop in for another. The bathroom fills with steam, and I open the glass door to the shower. I try to calm my nerves as I focus on the water beating against my back, but I don't think anything will take away these butterflies in my stomach. I give up on the shower and step out. I wrap a towel around me and see Jase fiddling around on my computer when I walk into my bedroom.

"What are you doing?" I ask while I walk over to my dresser and open the top drawer.

Staring at the screen, he says, "Nothing really, just messing around. I just finished my last class and thought I'd come chill with you."

I pull on my underwear and start to slip on my bra when he turns to look at me.

"You going somewhere?" he asks.

"Yeah, there's a party at Jack's fraternity tonight, and he asked me to go."

Jase leans back in the chair and sarcastically says, "You sound thrilled."

Grabbing my hair dryer, I look back at him. "It's just...I'm not into him aside from kissing. We have nothing in common, and I feel nothing towards him."

Jase grins at me.

"This should not be a surprise to you, Jase," I say.

"Nope, no surprise at all. Typical Candace, devoid of all things emotional. Well, except for me." He gives me a big smile then turns back around to the computer, and I flick on the hair dryer.

I see the lights of Jack's car pierce through the large windows in the living room. I grab my purse and yell at Kimber from across the house. "Jack is here. I'll see you later."

"Bye, sweetie, and good luck," she hollers back.

By the time I open the front door, Jack is already walking up to the house.

"Hey," he says, reaching out his hand for me to take.

Holding hands while walking to his car feels weird to me. I know it probably shouldn't since the last time I saw him I had my legs spread across his lap, but I guess it was the fact that I knew I was going to end things tonight. I feel like I'm being deceitful by holding his hand.

He opens my door and I slide into the car. When Jack gets in, he leans over to give me a kiss. I make sure to keep the kiss short. The silence is a little awkward as we drive to his fraternity house. I stare out the window and watch the streetlights pass.

"Is everything okay?" he asks.

I turn my head to look at him and say, "Uh huh. I'm just a little tired, that's all. I had three classes today plus my studio." With my head lazily leaning against the headrest, I continue to stare at Jack. I think about Jase's words back at the house: *Typical Candace, devoid of all things emotional.*

Do I purposely avoid relationships or is it simply because I just haven't met the right person yet? Maybe I should try and give Jack a chance. Maybe that's it. I never see a guy long enough to give him a chance. Maybe if I gave him time, I might wind up really liking him.

I snap out of my thoughts when I feel Jack's hand run up my thigh. He cocks his head to the side and gives me a little smirk. I smile in return.

"You're beautiful when you smile," he says and then returns his gaze to the road ahead.

I don't say anything. I simply sit there with my head resting on the seat.

I can already hear the music as we pull up to the house. Jack pulls around to a small parking lot behind the house. We get out of the car, and the muffled music and voices become clearer the closer we get. Jack opens the door and there are throngs of people everywhere. It's a two-story house and the stairs are covered with students who already seem to be drunk. Everyone is shouting over the loud music to make themselves heard. Jack's warm hand grabs mine, and he gives it a squeeze as he leads me back to the kitchen where he is greeted by a bunch guys that are slapping him on the back and grabbing his hand the way guys do. He doesn't introduce me, which is fine; I'm feeling slightly uncomfortable. I look around and watch a group of girls that are sitting at a table playing some sort of drinking game with a few guys. The rest of the room is filled with people talking and laughing loudly. Everyone is drinking and having a good time.

"Want a beer?" Jack asks.

"Yeah, that sounds good. Thanks." Jack walks away to fetch our drinks, and I'm left alone. I lean back against the center island and continue to watch the drunken girls as they giggle and act stupid. Looking at them, I'm starting to feel underdressed. Most of the girls here are wearing little skirts and dresses with nice heels. I feel a little awkward in my black retro Vans tank top, worn tattered jeans, and a pair of black Chucks. I tried dressing it up a little by adding a fitted red and black flannel that I left unbuttoned, with a vintage gold necklace. But these girls look like they have a particular goal in mind for the night.

Jack returns with our drinks, and I take a long, slow drink. Wrapping his arm around my waist, he moves to stand in front of me. When he leans in and kisses me below my ear, I quickly move my head back.

"What's wrong with you tonight?" he snaps with his eyebrows knitted together.

I try and lessen the tension as I smile and say, "Nothing, I'm just a little uncomfortable, that's all."

Jack sets his beer down and places each hand on the countertop on both sides of me, locking me in. "Relax," he says in a soft voice.

But I can't. He backs away, takes my free hand, and walks us out to the main room where people are dancing and hanging out.

"I'll introduce you to a few people," he shouts over at me.

We walk over to a group of people and Jack introduces me. There are a couple girls that I have seen around campus, and we are able to strike up a light conversation. I'm not sure how much time has passed, but my head is starting to hurt from all the loud music. The girls suggest we go hang out outside. I let Jack know, and I leave him there with his buddies while I head outside with the two girls. We find a few chairs and sit down. They are carrying on a conversation while I rest my head back and close my eyes. I am somehow able to drown out the noise and focus on the light breeze that's sweeping across my face.

"You tired?"

I open my eyes to Jack's voice, and he is kneeling down in front of me with his hands on my knees. I look at him and nod my head. He stands up, takes my hand, and starts walking me back into the house. When he takes me upstairs, he leads me into a dark room with a couple full-sized beds.

"What are we doing in here?" I ask him and he moves to sit down on one of the beds.

"I figure we could just hang out and relax away from all the noise. Is that all right?"

I walk over to him and sit down. "Yeah," I say, and then I turn to look at him. "I'm sorry I'm being a drag. I've just had a long day."

"It's fine, Candace," he says as he lies back on the bed.

I shift and lie down next to him and close my eyes. My head is starting to throb with an oncoming headache. We just lie there in silence, and the peace feels really nice. Jack brushes his hand over my cheek, and my eyes flutter open. Leaning over me, he looks in my eyes, and I can smell an obscene amount of liquor on his breath.

"Jack," I whisper as he leans down and presses his lips against mine. I know this is wrong, and he has clearly had too much to drink, but I find myself getting caught up in the moment. I run my hand up the back of his neck and start kissing him in return. He rolls on top of me, and the weight of him presses me into the bed. Our kisses turn frantic, and my breath quickly becomes labored. He runs his hand across my stomach, hooks it into the waistband of my pants, and gently tugs down. I feel my stomach knot up, and I push away.

"I'm sorry," I say, closing my eyes tightly. "I shouldn't be doing this."

"What the fuck, Candace," he spits out, and when I open my eyes, I see the irritated look on his face. "What's the problem? It's like one minute you're all over me, and the next, you're pushing me away. You pulled this same act the other night."

I push back against his chest, but he doesn't move. "I'm sorry, I'm just a little confused. I don't want to lead you on, but—"

He crashes his mouth against mine and starts kissing me again. *What the hell is he doing?* I push against his shoulders, but I'm only pushing myself deeper into the bed. I feel his hand run up my inner thigh and between my legs. I gasp for air, but I feel like I can't get enough into my lungs. I jerk my head back and forth and manage to roll onto my side. The weight is gone. Taking a deep breath, I look at Jack who is sitting on his knees in the middle of the bed.

"What the fuck is wrong with you?" I shout as I stand up on my shaky legs.

Laughing at me, he says, "You can stop with the good-girl act, Candace." He says my name like it's dripping in disdain. He climbs off of the bed and starts walking towards me. "I just can't figure you out, and it's starting to frustrate me. I like you, but I get the feeling like you're playing me."

"I'm not. I'm just...I don't know. I just don't think this is going to go anywhere," I say as I stare at the floor.

Jack tightly grips my shoulders with both of his hands, pushing me backwards. I stumble a little when we hit the wall. My body turns cold, and I feel the skin on my neck prickling. I'm getting nervous, and my heartbeat quickens. *What is he doing? Is he pissed? Shit, I just want to leave.* I just want to go home and pretend this night never happened. It's been weird from the start, and it's only getting worse.

"Oh, no? And why's that? You must think it's funny to lead me on. Is this how you get your kicks?" He is inches from me when he speaks, his breath hot on my face.

My shoulders are trembling under his hands, and I feel

the lump in my throat growing bigger, which is making it hard for me to breathe.

"I'm not jerking you around, I swear. Listen, I'm not good at this stuff. It's not you." My voice is shaky, and I hate that.

He pushes his body up against me and buries his face in my neck. I gasp for air and let out a whimper. I don't want to cry, but my emotions are all over the place right now. He thrusts his hips against mine, and that is my undoing. Tears flow down my cheeks, and I'm pushing my hands against his chest, but he won't budge.

"Jack, stop! What are you doing?" I am freaking out as he completely smothers me. Fisting my hands, I start smashing them into his chest, trying to get him off of me. I can barely see through my tears, and I wind up punching his lip. He takes a step back and wipes his mouth. It's bleeding. He looks up at me with a murderous glare, and I know he's about to lose it. I bolt for the door and run.

My heart is pounding against my ribs, and I struggle to breathe as I run down the stairs. Bumping shoulders with people in the crowded living room and stumbling over my shaky feet, I find the door that leads out to where Jack's car is.

I notice I don't have my wristlet purse that has my cell phone in it. There is no way I'm going back inside though. I quickly decide to just walk home and deal with the purse situation later. It won't take long for me to get home if I cut through behind a few buildings. I walk fast and try to grasp what just happened, but I can't clear my head enough to focus. My heart is starting to slow, and the tears return. I am overwhelmed, and I think it is so much more than what just happened with Jack. Confusion doesn't even begin to describe my current state of mind.

"Candace! Wait!" I hear Jack's voice calling from

behind me.

I turn to see my tiny gold purse clutched in his hand, but fear creeps over me, and suddenly, I don't care about the stupid purse anymore. I run.

I run fast.

I hear his feet pounding against the ground, and I know he's running after me. *FUCK!* I will my legs to move faster but they won't. My throat is on fire, and I can't breathe. I don't turn around to see, but I know he's close. My whole body is burning with panic. Quickly, I cut behind a building and suddenly feel an intense stinging as the side of my face slides against the pavement. Jack is flipping me over onto my back while I desperately claw my nails into the road, pleading to break free from his grip on me. The flesh on my cheek burns as he slaps me across the face. I can't see. *Why can't I see?* I force out a weak scream and am instantly muffled by his hand.

"Shut the fuck up," he violently snarls in my face.

I can barely make out his face with the tears that flood my eyes. I squeeze them shut because they are burning intensely. My body is weighed down, and I can't move beneath him. I'm not sure what's happening, but the terror rushing through me is frightening.

He reaches down, rips open my jeans, and starts yanking on them. I try and kick my legs uncontrollably, but he's sitting on them. Somehow, he manages to pull them off of one of my legs, as he releases his hand from my mouth.

"Plea-hease. Stop!" I scream, and he quickly clamps his hand back over my mouth. I desperately try to bite him, but I'm too frantic. I'm sobbing and barely breathing. It takes everything I have to choke out any sounds. But, it's no use. I hysterically pound my fists as hard as I can against him, but he won't stop. *God, please stop!*

Grabbing the neck of my shirt, he jerks down, tearing

the soft worn fabric too easily. With everything I have in me, I try to lock my knees together, but he's so much more powerful than me when he knees my thighs and forces them open. Consumed by rampant fear, I fight as hard as I can, screaming against his hand. I feel him pulling my bra down, and my breast begins to burn. I'm in such a panic when I realize that he is biting me. Shrieking in desperation as the pain shoots down to my belly, I dig my nails into his arms in response to the pain.

"Bitch!" He shouts through clenched teeth as he pulls back and backhands me across my face. The blood pools in my mouth, and my body heaves as I begin to choke on it through my cries. *Somebody help me!* The fabric of my underwear cuts into my skin and stings when he rips them off of me. "You're not gonna fuckin' tease me anymore, bitch."

He pins my wrists above my head with his large hand, and my body shakes in horror when I realize that I'm completely helpless. *God, please don't do this!*

I manage to let out another choked sob as I frantically try to jerk my body from underneath him, but my muscles are so weak, and the weight of him is too much for me to fight. He's so heavy on me. I wail when I feel a sudden burn as he violently rips and pounds into me. My whole body locks up.

What's happening?

Is this happening?

God, is this happening?

Is this really happening?

My head falls to the side, and my body goes limp aside from the involuntary twitches from each of his assaults. I focus every ounce of strength I have left on the corner of the dumpster that's next to me. It's painted dark blue, but maybe it's a lighter blue during the daylight. I can tell it's been painted five or six times...I can see every layer. It's chipping away, and the dark grey metal from underneath is exposed. The line along the chipped paint is ridged and there is a thin vein of white between the blue and grey. Gritty dirt clings to the wheel, and the wheel lock is beginning to rust. The dumpster is worn and full of dents... one... two... three... four... five... six...

I snap out of my thoughts when Jack grabs my chin and forces me to look at him. "Tell me you like this," he taunts, and my sobs are excruciating as I feel his body jerk into mine, and he stills himself, grunting loudly.

He yanks his pants up and starts running his hand down my naked torso. *What else does he want from me?*

"You're nothing but a cunt," he lashes when he abruptly jabs his fingers inside of me and then spits in my face.

I begin to yell and thrash my body, fighting to escape. "God, please! Stop!"

He lifts up, and suddenly, I see a flash of light that is devoured by darkness and silence.

chapter six

Where am I? Why can't I see? I hurt.

I try and move but something is holding me down. I feel my body rattling on something hard, and I sense that I am moving.

Am I dreaming? I'm so confused. What's happening?

I feel like I'm in a car or something, but I can't move.

Why can't I move?!

I'm panicking. I can feel it, feel my heart beating harder and louder.

Open your eyes, Candace. Focus—open your eyes.

"Miss?" I hear a man say.

Someone's here. Help me! Wake me up!

"Try and relax, Miss. We're almost there."

Where? What's happening? Someone fucking help me!! Where am I?!

Sheer fright shoots through me, and I feel the strain in my eyes as they start to open. I squeeze them shut immediately because they burn. I start to feel my body come to life and wriggle my wrists, but something is holding them down. I'm terrified and turn frantic as I keep trying to free my arms. The wriggling quickly turns into erratic jerks. I'm strapped down and I'm terrified.

"Help me! Get me out of here!" I shriek out in a hoarse voice. I try to move my head, but I can't. I feel something is wrapped around my neck preventing me from moving.

"It's okay, we're almost there. You're in an ambulance. You were knocked unconscious. We're on our way to the hospital."

I try and open my eyes, but they still sting. I blink several times when I feel a damp cloth cover them. I start crying at the calming feel of the cool wet cloth. He presses it down gently on my eyes and forehead, then wipes softly.

"Try opening your eyes," the man says.

I do as I'm told, and he wipes one more time. After a few seconds the sting starts to subside.

"You have a lot of dirt and sweat that has gotten into your eyes."

Blinking a few more times, I start to focus on the man hovering over me. I keep trying to move, but I can't get my limbs free.

"Just try and relax," he says in a soothing voice. "You are strapped down to a backboard and are wearing a neck brace until we can assess your injuries."

I stare up at the bright white light that is above me in the cab of the ambulance and focus on my breathing.

What just happened? Is this even real?

"Miss, how do you feel? Can you tell me if anything hurts?" he asks.

How do I feel? I don't know how I feel. I don't even know what the hell just happened. I feel scared and numb. I feel everything and nothing all at once. I feel like this is a dream—a very, very bad dream that I can't wake up from. I don't understand. I'm so confused. Fear and misery rip through me and create a new emotion that I can't even begin to describe. My heated tears roll continuously down the side of my face as I remain staring at the white light.

"Miss?"

"I don't know," is all I can manage to say, my only

attempt at a response to his very confusing question.

I move my eyes downward to look at my body, and I am covered in a grey wool blanket. Suddenly, I remember that I am naked beneath this blanket. Embarrassment wells up inside of me, and I begin to sob uncontrollably.

"I want to go home!" I choke out. "I want to go home!!" I barely recognize my own voice. The panic I hear in myself is frightening.

We stop abruptly, and the smell of fresh air envelops the ambulance as the doors to the cab open. As I am rolled out, I watch the white light move up and over the top of my head. I want to cover my face with my hands, but they are still strapped down. I start choking on short breaths between sobs. *Where are they taking me? What's going to happen?* I feel completely out of control, and I live for control.

There is a lot of noise and people chattering while I am being wheeled into the hospital. I'm finding it hard to hear what they are saying over my crying and heaving breaths. But the whole world stops moving when I hear that unmistakable word. *Don't say that word.* I can't move. I can't blink. I can't do anything. This isn't me. This can't be me.

I am wheeled into a private exam room, and there are several nurses moving around and checking the IV that must have been put in place while I was unconscious. My legs and arms are finally unstrapped, but I no longer feel the need to move. I just lie there. Still. One of the nurses stands by me and asks, "Ma'am, my name is Allie. I need to ask you some basic questions. Is that okay?"

I nod my head.

"Can you tell me your name?"

I look at the nurse and she looks to be in her thirties. She's pretty, with a short blonde bob and almost emerald eyes. Her scrubs are green, which make her eyes appear extremely vibrant. She has flawless makeup, especially her black eyeliner. The stethoscope's cord that hangs around her neck is hot pink, and I figure that outside of work, she must have a flair for style. I don't really know, I'm just imagining.

I feel my hand warm, and I look down to see that she is now holding it. I look back up at her green eyes. "Candace," I whisper.

Taking her hand from mine, she starts writing on the clipboard she is holding.

"Last name?"

"Parker."

She continues through the questions as she fills out my chart with all of my information. When she finishes, she tells me that she is going to call another nurse who handles cases like mine to come in and talk with me.

"Would you like to call anyone?" she asks me.

I shake my head no. I don't want to talk to anyone. How would I even begin to explain this?

"Would you like me to call someone for you? Sometimes it's easier if you have a friend here with you."

Looking up at Allie, my eyes begin to fill with tears again. I do want my friend here. I want him here so badly, but I am so embarrassed. What will I even say? All I know is that I want Jase here.

"You'll call for me?" I ask, my voice shaky.

"Of course," she says softly.

"Jase. You can call Jase," I say. I give her his number, and she leaves the room.

I am only alone for a few minutes when a doctor wearing a white coat enters my room, along with another nurse who is carrying a white cardboard box. She sets it down on a table, walks over to me, and stands next to the doctor who is holding a steel box clipboard and is looking at it intently. When she looks up at me, she says, "Hello, Ms.

Parker, I'm Dr. Langston. I am ordering a CT scan to rule out any evidence of a cerebral hemorrhage and a set of x-rays to be certain you don't have any fractures or broken bones."

I hear her words, but nothing makes sense to me. So I just lie there while tears stream down my temples and into my hair.

She sets the clipboard down, walks over to me, and assesses my face. She shines a small flashlight into each of my eyes then steps away as she puts the light back into the pocket on her white coat.

"This is Julia, and she is the Sexual Assault Nurse Examiner for the hospital. She's going to talk to you while we are waiting to run those scans, okay?" She says this all so matter-of-factly, and I'm not sure how to even react, so I just whisper, "Okay."

Dr. Langston proceeds to walk out of the room and closes the door behind her.

"Hi, Candace," Julia says in a soft, pleasant tone. I wonder if they teach everyone here how to talk to people like me, because they all sound the same. Gentle, as if they could break me with their words. "I need to know if you want to complete a sexual assault evidence kit examination."

I feel my heart rate pick up and anxiety kicks in. "I'm sorry. What?" I ask.

"A rape kit," she says. "It is an exam that is used to collect DNA evidence." She continues to talk to me and goes into more explanation, but her voice becomes distant. How is this happening to me? I don't know what to do. I look back at Julia to see her looking at me, and she's no longer talking.

I shake my head and say, "I don't know. I...I don't know."

"How about if we just talk? Can I ask you a few questions about what happened tonight?"

"Okay," I say unsurely.

She picks up her clipboard and pen, and then asks, "Do you know who did this?"

I hesitate before answering, "Uh huh."

"Can you tell me his name?"

"Why? What's going to happen?" I'm extremely nervous, and I'm not sure how much I should say.

"Nothing will happen unless you want to press charges."

"I don't," I immediately say. God, I don't want anyone to know about this.

The door slowly opens, and Allie pops her head in as she quietly says, "Jase is here. Would you like me to send him in?"

"Does he know?" I ask. "Did you tell him?"

Stepping in, she closes the door behind her. She walks over and sits down on a chair that's next to me.

"No. All he knows is that you were brought here by ambulance," she says softly.

"I don't know what to say." I look at Allie with a pleading expression on my face. There is no way I can tell Jase. I mean...I want him to know, I just don't want to be the one who tells him.

Nodding her head, she says, "It's okay. We will help you. Would you like me to bring him in?"

"Can you talk to him? Alone?" I ask. I don't want to hear what she is going to say, and I definitely do not want to see his reaction when she tells him.

"If you want me to, I will. How much do you want me to tell him?"

"Everything," I say softly.

"Okay. I'll be back in a few minutes." Allie stands up and makes her way out of the exam room.

I let out a sigh, and Julia continues asking questions about what happened. I don't tell her Jack's name, but I go ahead and tell her everything that happened tonight, starting from my house. She asks me to go into detail about the attack. She wants to know every part of my body that was touched, all the places his saliva could possibly be, and the questions seem to go on forever.

I look up when the door opens again, and Jase is there. I fall apart when I see the horrified expression on his face, and he rushes over to me and wraps my head in his arms. He keeps kissing the top of my head and repeating that he loves me as sobs wrack through my body. I slowly start to calm down, and the tears begin to subside. Jase sits down and looks at Julia.

"So, what's going on? Is she okay?" he asks her while holding my hand.

"We have just completed the written account of the assault." She looks at me and continues, "The next step, if you choose, is to complete a physical exam to collect evidence. We can do this whether you choose to press charges or not."

I look at Jase and shake my head, not knowing what to do.

Jase looks back at her and asks, "What's the exam?"

The nurse picks up the same white cardboard box that I saw her walk in with. "This is the rape kit. There are sixteen different pieces of evidence we collect. You are in total control of the exam. You say 'stop,' we stop. I will explain each step as we go so you know exactly what to expect."

"How long will this take?" I ask.

"It can take around four to six hours."

"What?! No," I say to her. I look back at Jase with wide eyes and sternly repeat, "No."

"Candace, I really think you should do it. I get that you're scared right now, but maybe in a few days you might feel differently about this." He turns and asks Julia, "If she does this exam, then what?"

"If she decides to press charges, we will hand over the kit to the police. If not, we keep the kit here. If she changes her mind about prosecuting, then at that time, we will hand the kit over to the criminal lab."

Jase squeezes my hand, "I'm right here. I think you should do this, sweetie." I have never seen this look on Jase before. I know he loves me, and I can trust him. I nod my head, and I fight back the tears that are threatening to spill over.

"Since the doctor has ordered a CT scan and x-rays, we will need to wait until after those tests are run. When you get back, we will begin the exam." She gives me a concerned look as she continues, "I want to let you know what to expect when you are taken for those tests. The nurses and techs will refrain from touching you as much as possible. I want you to try and stay calm and still. They will move you to and from this gurney by lifting the sheet that is underneath you. Okay?"

Nodding my head, I respond, "Okay."

"The scans shouldn't take that long, but your friend will have to stay here."

I look up at Jase before looking back at Julia, and ask, "He can't come with me?"

Shaking her head gently, she says, "No, I'm sorry."

Jase assures me that it will be okay, and all I can do is trust him. But I'm scared to be alone, even if it is for a little while. Feeling like I have lost control is making me very upset, when Dr. Langston returns to tell me they are ready to take me back.

When I am wheeled back into the exam room, both

Julia and Jase are there waiting for me.

"You okay?" Jase asks as he comes to stand next to me.

"Yeah."

Julia picks up the white box and opens it, pulling out several white envelopes and lays them down on one of the stainless steel carts that are in the room. "We are going to start by collecting your clothes, okay?"

"Okay."

She walks to the private bathroom, and when she comes out she says, "Candace, I need for you to carefully remove all of your clothing, including your jewelry. I have laid down a large sheet of paper that is there to collect any evidence that may fall off of your clothes or body. Just stand on the paper while you undress, hand me each article of clothing as you remove it, and I will place each piece in a separate evidence bag. There is a hospital gown hanging on the door that you can change into."

"Do you want me to leave?" Jase asks.

I grab onto his arm tightly, "No. I don't want to be alone."

Jase nods and helps me off of the bed. I clutch onto the wool blanket that is still covering me, and I walk into the bathroom. I hand the blanket to Julia and step onto the paper that is lying on the floor. I look down at my body and start to cry. My shirt and bra are ripped and hanging off my shoulders. I quickly notice that I am bare from the waist down.

I jerk around and frantically ask, "What happened to my pants?"

"The EMTs collected them. We already have them."

I nod and look up at Jase as my body trembles.

"It's okay," he reassures me.

I slowly remove my tattered clothing and hand each piece to the nurse. The paper beneath my feet crumples with every movement as if it's taunting me as a continuous reminder of the misery I feel. The last item I remove is my necklace, and I watch as it is placed inside a ziplock evidence bag. When I turn to pick up the hospital gown, I catch my reflection in the mirror. My body freezes as I observe the face staring back at me.

My left eye is bruised and swollen and the whole side of my face is scratched and covered in dried blood and dirt. My eyes are bloodshot and puffy from all the crying. I hardly recognize myself. I turn away from my image in the reflection, slip on the hospital gown, and step off of the paper.

I walk straight into Jase's arms, and I let him hold me for a while as I hear Julia moving around the room. Jase rests his chin on the top of my head and runs his hands up and down my back. My arms are clutched tightly around his waist as I bury my face in his chest.

"Candace," I hear Julia say softly, "whenever you are ready, I need you to have a seat on the exam table behind the curtain."

I slowly pull away from Jase and lean the top of my head against him as I stare down at my bare feet. I realize I have no clothes here, and I look up at Jase and say, "I don't have anything to wear."

"When the nurse called me, she told me to bring clothes with me. They are in my backpack," he says.

I walk across the room and sit on the exam table, never letting go of Jase's hand. I go into a haze when the nurse begins to explain each procedure. I just nod my head as I feel cold metal digging under my finger nails; I don't watch anything in particular because I don't want to see what's happening. Everything feels like it's miles away from me. She begins swabbing my neck, my ears, my mouth, my breasts, my thighs.

When I lie back on the table, she begins to take samples. My body is being poked and prodded—everywhere. Turning my head, I begin to zone in on a tiny piece of thread that is beginning to unravel from Jase's shirt. I focus in on the tiny little holes that the thread used to occupy that are now hollowed.

I suddenly become very cold. My knees begin to quiver, and my heart is pounding. I look down and over my knees. I see Julia's lips moving as she is talking to me, but I can't seem to focus in on her voice. I watch as she opens yet another white envelope and pulls out a small black plastic comb. Jerking my feet out of the stir-ups, I clumsily shuffle myself back on the table and sit up. Pure panic. That is all I can feel. Panic.

"Enough!" I shout. I feel like I am losing control of myself, and I desperately want everything around me to stop. "Get out!" I yell at Julia as she looks at me in shock. I can almost taste the venom in my voice. "Stop touching me, and get the hell out!"

"Candace. Calm down, sweetie," Jase says. His eyes are wide, and I can tell he is freaked out.

"I'll be right outside," the nurse says, and she quickly places the sealed envelopes in the box and leaves the room.

I draw my knees up to my chest. "I want to go home."

"What happened?"

"I want my clothes, Jase," I say as I look him straight on.

He doesn't say a word; he simply walks over to his backpack that is lying on the ground next to the chair. When he picks it up, I see the door crack open.

"Candace, Detective Patterson needs to ask you a few questions," Allie says. "Can I send him in?"

"Can she at least get dressed first?" Jase answers for me.

"Of course," she says, and she gently closes the door behind her.

Jase walks over to me and sets the bag in front of me. Grabbing it, I walk into the bathroom. I pick up a hand towel that is folded up on the cold sterile counter and turn on the faucet. I soak the towel in warm water and begin to clean my face. I suck in a tight breath between my teeth at the stinging of the opened flesh on my face. I do my best to wipe the grime off. Taking a new towel, I pat my face dry. I slip off my gown and start putting on my bra and underwear. When I finish dressing, I walk back into the room, and Jase is standing next to some guy. He appears to be around my father's age. He is tall and fit with short greying hair. He's wearing charcoal slacks and a navy button up dress shirt with the sleeves rolled up toward his elbows. I notice a shiny gold badge that is clipped to the waistband of his pants. He looks up at me and takes a step forward.

"Ms. Parker," he says. "I'm Detective Patterson. Do you mind if I ask you some questions?"

Shaking my head slightly, I ask, "Right now?"

"Yes, ma'am."

"I've already told the nurse everything. Why can't you just ask her?" I am so exhausted and am starting to lose my patience. I just want to leave. "Look, I don't want to press charges or anything like that, so..."

"Ma'am, I know this is difficult, but there's a good chance we can catch this guy and the fact that we have a witness--"

"What?" I interrupt him.

"Yes, they called the police."

My mind is in overdrive, and I feel myself shutting down. "I just want to go," I say, barely whispering.

"Well, if you change your mind, here is my card. You can call me at anytime, okay? You might find that you feel differently once a little time has passed." He steps towards me, pulls out a card from his back pocket, and hands it to me. I don't even look at it before shoving it into my pocket. He takes a step back and nods his head, "Well, thanks for your time." He turns to look at Jase and reaches out his hand. Jase shakes his hand and gives him a nod in return.

As Detective Patterson is leaving, Allie comes back with a tray of bandages, ointment, and other small items I can't quite identify.

"I'm just going to clean up and bandage these cuts for you, okay?"

I silently nod my head and return to the table to sit down. I watch her as she washes her hands and puts on a pair of sterile latex gloves. She starts cleaning my wounds and covers them up. Once she is finished, she asks me if I want to take the morning after pill. My eyes dart to hers as I quickly try to think if I really need it. I feel my stomach hollow out, and I suddenly turn cold. *He didn't use a condom. Christ, he didn't use a condom.*

I whisper softly, "I think so." I can hardly move, let alone speak.

I hear Jase mutter an obscenity, and when I turn my head to look at him, he is sitting in the chair with his head in his hands.

"Okay, I will put in the order for that, and we can also take a few other preventive steps to safeguard against STDs," she says as she lays her hand on my knee. She gives me a reassuring look, and all I can do is continue to nod my head like an idiot.

About an hour later, Jase has his arm around my waist

as we leave the hospital and head to his SUV. He unlocks the car and opens the door for me. He helps me up into the seat and shuts the door. I watch him in a daze as he walks around the front of the car and climbs into the driver's seat. I start to feel the anxiety build in my stomach at the thought of going home. I know when I get there I'm going to have to explain all of this to Kimber. God, I don't want anyone to know. I just want to pretend like this never happened. I want to hide from this nightmare.

"Can I spend the night at your place?" I ask as I stare at my fidgeting hands in my lap.

He reaches over, takes my hand, and gives it a squeeze. "Of course."

chapter seven

I walk into Jase's apartment, and without a second thought, head straight toward the bathroom. I feel completely filthy, and the urge to scrub every inch of my body overwhelms me. I don't say a word to Jase as I close the door behind me. Reaching into the shower, I turn on the water. Purposely avoiding looking at myself in the mirror, I start removing my clothes. The bathroom quickly fills with steam. I open the large glass door and step into the scalding hot water. Standing underneath the showerhead, I let the water pelt against my body. I brace both of my hands against the wall of slick tile and let my head fall down. My face is hot, and I know I'm crying even though I can't feel my tears as they mesh with the water running down my face.

Time is frozen as I stand here in this position. My chest aches, and my whole body feels broken. My stomach burns, and I swear to God I can start to feel my soul begin to break. Piece by piece I begin to lose myself. My chest is crumbling into painful shards of what used to be me. Violent sobs wrack my body, and I slowly collapse on the wet tile beneath me. Sitting there on my knees, with one hand on the floor balancing myself, and the other pressed against my chest, I try desperately to gasp in breaths between my wails.

I know I am no longer alone when I feel arms wrapping around me and a heavy chest on my back. Jase holds me tighter than anyone has ever held me, and I begin to cry harder. I sit here, on the bottom of the shower, and everything I know about myself, everything I love, everything I am begins to fade.

My tears run dry, and Jase and I sit in silence under the water. He loosens his hold on me, and I continue to rest on my knees—frozen. Jase takes the body wash and starts to rub it into my skin. All of my energy has disappeared, so I don't protest; I just let him take care of me.

After he washes my hair, I open my eyes and look at him for the first time. He is soaking wet in his gym shorts and t-shirt. He turns the water off and strips out of his clothes, leaving them on the floor of the shower as he steps out. Wrapping a towel around his waist, he grabs another and drapes it over my shoulders as he helps me stand up. He walks me over to the toilet and sits me down.

"I'll be right back," he says as he walks out of the bathroom. When he returns, he is wearing a pair of dry gym shorts and is carrying a handful of clothes for me. Grabbing a hand towel, he kneels down in front of me and starts wiping my face. I look into his eyes, and I can see the worry in them. I reach up and rake my fingers through the wet hair on top of his head and grip tightly as I drop my head and begin to cry again.

"I'm so sorry," I manage to say through my tears.

He takes my hand from his head and kisses it. Leaning his forehead against mine and holding my face between his two hands, he says, "You...don't you ever be sorry for this."

We sit like this for a while before he dries me off and helps me put on one of his shirts and a pair of his boxers. We walk to his room and slide into bed. Wrapping me in his arms, I lay my head on his chest and listen to the rhythmic sound of his heartbeat. I release a silent prayer that when I wake up, this will have never happened—it will have only been a horrendous nightmare. I hold on tightly to that prayer as my eyelids become heavy, and I slowly drift into a restless sleep.

I jolt awake and can hardly catch my breath. My hands are shaking, and when I look up, I see Jase on his knees next to me.

"Are you okay?" he asks, looking completely freaked out.

"I don't know," I say. I'm really confused, and my heart is pounding. "What happened?"

Jase lets out a deep breath as he falls back on his heels, sitting next to me. "You were having a nightmare. You scared the shit out of me, screaming and thrashing around."

"I'm sorry. I don't even know what I was dreaming about," I say as a slowly lie down on my side and try to calm my erratic breathing.

Lying down facing me, Jase asks, "How are you feeling?"

"Numb," I answer and close my eyes. Maybe I cried out all the emotions I had, because I can't seem to feel much right now. When I open my eyes, Jase is staring at me with concern written all over his face. I really wish he wouldn't look at me like that; it makes me feel weird, like I'm suddenly different now. I know that I am, but can we just pretend that I'm not?

"What time is it?" I ask.

He rolls on his back, reaches over to his nightstand, and swipes his phone. "It's almost three in the afternoon," he says as he rolls back to me.

"Three?"

"Yeah, we didn't even leave the hospital till after five

this morning," he says, and then reaches his arms out as a request to hold me. I scoot over and allow the embrace. He kisses the top of my head before asking, "Do you want to talk about it?"

I haven't spoken one word to Jase about what happened last night. I'm not sure I can. But I know that I don't want to. I swallow hard against the lump in my throat and simply shake my head. How am I supposed to talk about it? What do I even say?

The tears start to well in my eyes; the tears I thought I no longer had. It's hard to fight them with the tightness in my throat. Jase must feel my body trembling when he kisses the top of my head and whispers, "I'm sorry, sweetie. I didn't mean to push you."

As the tears spill over, I silently curse my unanswered prayer. I try hard not to cry, but it only makes my body jerk as I try and hiccup the sobs back. Jase moves one of his hands up from my back, cups my head, and whispers in my ear, "Please don't hurt yourself like this, Candace. Just let it out. It's just me here."

I shove my head harder and deeper into his chest as a desperate attempt to hide. Hide from the cloud that is suddenly looming over me. He tightens his grip on me, and I let it out. I lie against his chest and just cry. I cry like a baby—helpless. I'm so desperate for someone to save me. To make it all go away.

The heat of Jase's bare chest against my wet, teary face suddenly makes my skin burn. I push back off of him and cup my cheek, unable to stop the free-flowing tears. He removes my hand and looks at the cuts on my face.

"I'll be right back, sweetie," he says as he jumps out of bed. I hear him in the bathroom, and when he returns, he's holding a large square bandage and some ointment. He sits on the bed in front of me and starts tending to the scratches on my face. Once he is done, he adheres the bandage to my cheek, then walks to his closet, and throws on a t-shirt.

"You hungry?" he asks.

"No," I say as I shake my head and lie back down. "I just want to go back to bed."

Walking towards me, he says, "You really should eat. Just try."

I lie there with my eyes closed. "Please, Jase."

He doesn't say another word. He simply crawls back into bed behind me and holds me until I fall asleep.

Drifting in and out, I'm finding it hard to shut my brain off. Every time I close my eyes I picture Jack on top of me. The more I try and fight the thoughts, the more vivid they become. He's right here with me, right here inside my head. I close my eyes again, and I can hear the ripping of my shirt as Jack fists the fabric. I quickly sit up in the bed and grab my breast where he bit me. I can feel the sharp pain shooting through me again. *Why can't he leave me alone? Why can't I get away from him?* My gut is in knots, and I am shaking. I jump out of bed, run to the bathroom, and empty the contents of my stomach into the toilet. Since I haven't eaten in over a day, there's hardly anything left in me. I begin dry heaving painfully. My whole body is convulsing, and tears are streaming down my face. I close my eyes, and I see Jack's murderous glare as he's ripping off my underwear. I hear frantic screams. My mind is in overdrive, and I can hardly focus, but the screams are piercing. I cover my ears and shuffle back into the corner on my bottom. I have no idea where all the noise is coming from, but it's scaring me.

Suddenly, the bathroom light turns on, and I see Jase run to me. He falls to his knees in front of me and grasps onto my wrists that are against my face. His lips are moving, but I can't hear him over the screaming. I try and focus on his lips to make out what he is saying, and his voice begins filtering through. I can hardly hear him when he says, "It's okay." I continue to focus and the more I do, the more I can hear him and less of the screams. "It's okay, Candace. I'm right here." He pulls me to him and slowly rocks me back and forth. The swaying feels soothing in the madness around me. As he whispers, "Shhh," into my ear, I realize that those screams I heard were coming from me. *How can I be so disoriented?* Terrified by what just happened, I feel myself being lifted off the floor. Jase scoops me up in his arms and carries me to the couch. I bury my head into his neck, fully embarrassed by what has just happened. I can barely comprehend it.

Setting me down, Jase walks into the kitchen and comes back with two bottles of water and a box of crackers. He twists the cap off of one of the bottles and hands it to me.

"Drink," he says.

I lift the bottle to my lips and take a slow sip. The water burns along my scratchy throat as I swallow it down.

I shift uncomfortably on the couch. My whole body is sore, and my back is badly bruised and scabbed over. It makes it nearly impossible to not think about what happened. I wish I could ignore it, but I can't because I hurt...*everywhere*. Sometimes when I move, I can feel the pain from his intrusion, and I want the throw up.

"What just happened?" he asks.

"I don't know. It felt like a nightmare, but I was awake," I say and take another drink.

Jase rests his elbows on his knees and clasps his hands together. Letting out a sigh, he says, "You scared the shit out me. I know you don't want to talk, but maybe..." He trails off as my phone rings.

"You have my phone?" I ask.

Standing up and walking to the kitchen bar, he says, "Yeah, the nurse at the hospital gave me your purse." He picks up my gold wristlet purse and hands it to me. I pull out my phone and swipe the screen to see that I have a few missed texts and a missed call from Kimber.

"Who was it?" Jase asks as he sits back down and starts opening the box of crackers.

"Kimber," I say, fiddling with my phone.

"You should call her, she's probably freaking out and wondering where you are," he says, as he eats a cracker.

"Maybe later." I set the phone down, lay my head back, and stare at the ceiling. I just want to hide here for a while longer. Maybe forever.

"She probably knows you're with me. She sent me a text earlier asking if I knew where you were. I figured you didn't want her to know just yet, so I didn't respond."

I let out a sigh, roll my head to the side, and look at Jase. I don't want Kimber to ask me any questions, but I know there is no way around that. One look at my face and she's going to flip. I can't hide all the cuts and bruises. I look like hell.

Jase holds a cracker up to my mouth and when I open it, he shoves the cracker in and gives me a smirk. Chewing it up, I turn my body and lie on my back with my head in his lap. I stare up at him and say, "I don't want anyone to know."

He looks down at me, starts brushing through my hair with his fingers, and says, "I know, but she's going to know that something happened. She's going to want to know how you got all these bruises."

"I don't know what to say."

"Why can't you tell her? You know she wouldn't say a word to anyone."

"I just can't. Even the way you look at me now is different." I sit up and turn to look at him. "It makes me feel weird. It just reminds me that it happened, when all I want to do is forget." I pull my knees up to my chest and lay my head on the back of the couch again.

Jase puts his hand on my knee and says, "You know you can't do that. It did happen."

The tears roll down my temples. "But why?" My voice is shaky as I speak. "I don't understand what I did that was so wrong."

Wiping away my tears with his thumb, he says, "You didn't do anything wrong."

"Then why did this happen to me?" I turn my head and look into his eyes, desperate for answers I know he doesn't have.

He shakes his head, and his eyes start to rim with tears. "I don't know, sweetie. But I do know that you didn't do shit to deserve this. This isn't your fault."

"But maybe it is. I mean, I really led him on when I had no intentions of..."

Jase cuts me off me off and snaps, "You mean Jack did this?!"

My whole body turns cold. *Oh shit! What is he going to do?* I quickly sit up and turn towards him. "Jase, you can't say anything," I plead in a stern voice.

"Christ, Candace. I thought it was just some random asshole. Why didn't you tell the police? Why didn't you say anything?"

"Because I can't. Everyone would know. Everyone, including my parents."

Jase rakes his hand through his hair, and I can tell he is pissed, which upsets me. I don't want him to be mad at me.

"Fuck," he spits out. Looking at me, I can see the rage in his eyes, and I start to panic. "I'm gonna kill that fucker."

"Jase!"

"What the hell happened?" he demands.

"Don't."

"Candace, you have to tell me."

"Please, don't." Slowly shaking my head, I begin to cry. I'm scared. Scared to talk. Scared of what Jase might do. Scared that people will find out.

Jase stands up and walks out to the balcony, slamming the door shut behind him. I sit in his living room, alone in the silence. The sun is starting to rise and Jase is leaning on his arms against the railing. I know he is pissed at me, which kills me inside. I can't stand to see him so mad and upset. I get up and make my way to his bedroom, leaving my phone on the couch.

I must have fallen asleep because when I open my eyes the room is bright. I sit up and look down at Jase who is sleeping next to me. I slip out of bed and make my way to the kitchen to get some water. I look at the clock and see that it's almost nine in the morning. I'm not too worried about the classes I missed yesterday or the ones I will most likely miss today. It's only the first week, so I know that classes are no more than discussing expectations for the quarter. But I'm worried about the fact that I missed my studio yesterday. I haven't looked at my face yet, but hopefully the swelling and bruising has gone down enough that I can attempt to cover it with makeup.

I open the fridge and grab a bottle of water. I twist off the cap and down the whole thing in a few large gulps. My head is throbbing slightly, so I begin to make a pot of coffee when I hear Jase come out of the bathroom. Scooping the coffee grounds, I look up at him as he walks into the kitchen. I don't say anything because I am unsure of his mood. I hope he understands where I'm coming from and isn't still mad at me.

He walks straight to me and turns me to face him. Cupping my cheeks with his hands, he says, "I'm sorry."

I can't find any words, so I simply nod my head. I notice his eyes are puffy and bloodshot before he pulls me in to hug me. I wrap my arms tightly around him and squeeze. It hurts to know that he must have been crying when he was out on the balcony earlier this morning. I press my head against his chest, and we just stand there, clinging to each other.

chapter eight

I sit nervously in Jase's car as we drive to my house. After coffee this morning, we decided that I would stay at his place for a few days. I emailed all of my professors and told them that I had gotten sick and wouldn't be attending class for the rest of this week. None of them seemed to mind. Knowing that I have always been dedicated to my classes in the past, no one even questioned me, not even my dance instructors.

I let out a sigh of relief as we pull up to the house and see that Kimber's car is gone. Giving Jase a kiss on the cheek, I thank him before hopping out and walking over to my car. We agreed that he would go in and get my things in case Kimber showed up. As I slide into my car and turn the key, guilt begins to wash over me. I feel like I'm lying to Kimber by avoiding her, but Jase is the only one who knows, and I'd like to keep it that way.

I call Roxy while I drive back to Jase's apartment and tell her the same thing I told my professors. I ask if I could have a few days off, and she doesn't even hesitate. Lying to everyone feels horrible, but I just can't tell them the truth.

Pulling up to the apartment, I hear my phone chime. I pick it up and read Jase's text.

Got everything you asked for and more. On my way now.

Thank you so much. See you in a bit.

I am in the bathroom putting more ointment on my face when I hear Jase walk in. Wiping off my hands, I make my way into his bedroom where he is unzipping the bags that have my toiletries, clothes, textbooks, and dance gear.

Looking up at me, he says, "I grabbed more clothes than what you had asked me to."

"Thanks," I say as I walk over to the bed. I start unpacking, hanging up my clothes, putting my makeup and other toiletries in the bathroom, and throwing my books and dance things in his closet. Jase sits on the bed and watches me as I move around his room. When I turn and look at him over my shoulder, he has that look in his eyes. The look I can't stand. The look that reaffirms the fact that I need to keep this private.

"Stop," I say.

"What?"

I walk over and sit down next to him on the bed. "Stop looking at me like that."

Lowering his head to stare at the floor, he says, "You know Kimber is going to flip when she comes home and sees that a bunch of your things are gone."

"I know," I sigh out as I lie back on the bed and close my eyes. "What am I going to tell her?"

Lying back and turning his head to look at me, he says, "We'll figure it out."

As we lie here, staring at each other with no words, Jase holds my hand and laces his fingers through mine. This simple gesture comforts me in a way that only Jase can do. We have always been very affectionate with each other, but it has never felt weird. It was our natural chemistry from the moment we met our freshman year. And now, I feel like he is my only lifeline.

I lift up slightly and rest my head on his chest, and he wraps me in his arms. We decide, without spoken words, to remain in bed for the afternoon and nap. But just before I am about to doze off, I hear someone enter the apartment. Before I can sit up, Mark appears in the doorway of the bedroom.

I notice a shift in his eyes as he says, "Oh my God."

I think for a moment that maybe he is upset that I'm cuddling in bed with his boyfriend, but that thought is quickly replaced with anxiety when he asks, "What the hell happened to your face, honey?"

Shit! I quickly try to cover what he has clearly already seen with my hands. Turning to Jase, I see he is already sitting up next to me, looking at me with the same worry that I feel. Mark's eyes dart back and forth between Jase and I as we sit there, not knowing what to say because we never got around to discussing it.

"Um, hey. I'm sorry, but could you give us just a minute?" Jase asks.

Mark looks at me and then back at Jase before responding. "Yeah, man. Sure, I'll just be in the other room."

Mark turns and closes the door behind him, giving Jase and me some privacy.

"Shit, I'm so sorry," I say as I rake my fingers through my hair.

"What for?"

"I don't know, for having your boyfriend see us in bed together."

"Don't worry about it. I talk about you all the time. He knows how we are; it doesn't bother him," he says, reassuring me. He shifts his body to face me and continues, "Candace, I don't know what to do here. I just got back together with Mark, and I can't lie to him."

I stare at him for a long while. We sit there, looking into each other's eyes, and we don't say a word. I can't be selfish with Jase; I love him too much, and I know how happy he is to be with Mark again. But I can't help to be terrified out of my mind. I lower my head and look down before I hesitantly nod.

Lifting my chin with his finger, he says, "Mark would never say anything. He isn't like that, Candace."

I am so scared and begin to cry at the thought of anyone else knowing. Jase wipes my tears and leans his forehead against mine.

"Don't cry," he whispers.

"I'm so embarrassed."

Pulling me into his arms, he sighs, "I know you are, sweetie, but you shouldn't be."

He continues to hold me as my crying grows stronger. I bury my head in his neck and let it pour out of me as I feel him slowly rocking me back and forth. I don't know how long I've been crying when I feel the bed dip down next to me and another hand on my back. I know that it's Mark, and now I'm even more embarrassed that I can't even look up. So I just stay there, in Jase's arms, and cry.

As the tears start to slow and my body grows tired, Jase slowly pulls away. Fixing his eyes on mine with his eyebrows knitted together, I feel the bed shift again. I turn my head to see that Mark is kneeling beside the bed in front of me. I look down at him as he stares at me with nothing but concern. I'm no longer crying, but the tears keep falling, and I don't know how to stop them.

He takes my hand before speaking. "Who did this?"

It's pretty obvious that this didn't happen by some accident by the way I was just sobbing for what felt like an hour. I can't find any words though. I no longer feel the intense anxiety; I feel defeated. So, I just continue to stare at him.

Jase clears his throat before I hear him say, "Um...Candace was attacked Monday night."

Hearing those words knocks the air out of me, and I lower my elbows to my knees and hide my face in my hands. Jase never takes his hand off of my back, but I now feel two more hands on my legs.

"What happened?" Mark asks.

I hear Jase let out a long sigh, and I start shaking my head in my hands. I know he's about to say it. I'm scared to hear the words I know are coming any second. My body turns cold, and I tense up as I try desperately to hold onto the sob that is threatening to escape my chest.

Jase slides his hand up my back to my shoulder and squeezes tightly.

"She was raped."

I feel Mark's forehead fall to my knees, and the pain I was trying so hard to contain suddenly rips out of me, and I can do nothing but sob. My body begins to jerk when it becomes difficult to breathe.

The three of us sit there and cling to each other. How the hell did this become my life? I am not a weak person. I am strong and hold my emotions tight. I hardly recognize the weakness that is pouring out of me. Defeat. I am so tired and worn out. Exhausted.

I wipe my eyes with the backs of my hands as I take in a slow shaky breath and let it out slowly. Looking up, I see Marks eyes staring into mine.

"I won't say anything, if you were worried about that."

I nod my head. "I'm so tired," I say, not knowing what else to say really.

"I told her she could stay here for a few days," Jase tells Mark. "She doesn't want anyone to know, and if Kimber saw her face, she would question her."

"I think that's a good idea," Mark responds, then looks at me and says, "I know we don't know each other that well, but I am here if you ever need me. I feel like I know you well by how much Jase speaks of you. The both of us are always here for you."

I nod my head and say, "Thanks."

We sit in the living room and eat a late lunch. After my embarrassing breakdown, Mark offered to go and pick up some Chinese food. While he was gone, I took another quick shower. I have been taking a lot of those in the past few days. There's something about the hot water against my skin. It makes me feel clean, but only for a short while.

"I've gotta get out of this apartment," I say as I pick up an egg roll and take a huge bite. With my emotions running on high and the lack of sleep, my hunger finally caught up with me.

"Okay. What did you have in mind?" Jase asks.

"I don't know. Some place quiet."

"Why don't we go to my house? Change of scenery," Mark says while twirling a fork full of lo-mein.

I look at Mark and say, "Perfect."

We sit there quietly and continue to eat our greasy food when I hear my phone ring. I walk over to the bar and see that it's Kimber calling. Suddenly nervous, I let it continue to ring until it goes to voicemail.

"Who's that?" Jase asks.

I turn around to look at him and answer, "Kimber." Before I can set the phone down, it chimes with a text from her.

I'm starting to wonder if you're mad at me. Where's your stuff?

I don't respond. Instead, I turn my phone off and leave it on the counter.

"The more you ignore her, the worse it's gonna get," Jase says, picking up his plate and walking into the kitchen.

I watch him as he starts to rinse off his dish in the sink. "Drop it, please. Can we just forget? Just for today?"

The truth is, I don't want to drop it just for today. Call me the Queen of Avoidance, but I hate dealing with issues head on. I get really anxious and nervous, so I tend to just ignore and let things slide. But I know this isn't going to just disappear. And Jase is right: the longer I wait, the worse it will be. I just don't have it in me right now.

After lunch, we hop into Mark's car and head over to his house, first stopping to pick up some beer at the store. I stay in the car with Mark while Jase goes in. I'm very self-conscious about the scratches on my face, so I'd rather avoid public places.

Mark lives right off campus in a small house. After the fiasco with his roommate and Jase, Mark kicked him out and got another roommate. Mark assured me he wouldn't be home though.

The patio in the backyard is surprisingly large, so we decide to relax outside and drink for the afternoon. I'm not in the mood to talk, so I just listen to Mark and Jase. I begin to tune them out as I start on my second beer. Sitting back in my chair with my eyes closed, I enjoy the heat of the sun on my face. I keep dozing in and out of a light sleep, and I can faintly hear the boys talking about Mark's band and how they just got a new gig to play this weekend at a local bar. I have never heard them play before, but they seem to be popular around UW.

"Hey, Candace?"

Squinting my eyes against the bright sun, I look over at Jase. "Kimber just texted me."

Closing my eyes again, I say, "We're pretending, remember?"

And with that, the subject is dropped.

The next few days pass in a bit of a haze. Jase has classes during the day but stops by to check on me when he can. I spend most of my time in bed trying to sleep. Nights are rough. Something about the darkness. I have been having nightmares—bad nightmares. Jack is constantly in my dreams, tormenting me. I wake up in a state of confusion, screaming and crying; often having to run to the bathroom to throw up. I know I'm freaking Jase out, but he stays calm and holds me while I cry until I fall into another fit of sleep. He suggested that I call my doctor to see about getting on a sleeping pill. I will do just about anything to get Jack out of my head to get some rest. I'm exhausted, and it shows in my eyes.

By Sunday, the scratches on my face are hardly noticeable, which is a relief because I have to work this evening. I decide to go to the studio since I know it will most likely be empty, and I can have the place to myself. I haven't danced all week, and I'm hoping that being back in the studio will make me feel a little more normal. Before I leave the apartment, I put on some makeup just in case I run into anyone. I am able to cover up the light scars on my face pretty well now that the ugly scabs are gone.

I breathe a sigh of relief as I pull into the studio's parking lot and see that it's empty. I head inside and proceed with my normal routine. Once my pointes are tied up and I'm stretched, I plug my iPod into the stereo system and decide against the barre for some much needed center work. I start going through various adagio and turn combinations. As I begin working the floor, I am relieved when my mind begins to emancipate, as it always does when I dance. All I think about is my turnout, posture, port de bras, and lines. Gliding through my movements and hearing the thuds of my pointes against the wooden floor are therapeutic in a way. I listen to the music that fills the room and move through several combinations that I know by heart and repeat them over and over. I don't want this serene feeling to end, so I keep repeating the combinations. I feel surprisingly flawless for being out this past week, and I continue making my way through the different combinations.

A crash of thunder quickly brings me out of my euphoric state. I walk to one of the windows and look up into the sky to see dark clouds rolling in. I decide to pack up and head back to Jase's before the storm hits. Taking off my pointes, I powder them and my feet before sliding them into my flip-flops. I sling my bag over my shoulder, run out, and hop into my car. When I turn the key, I look at the time on my dash and am shocked when I realize I've been dancing for over two hours. I don't know how the time slipped away so fast.

As I drive, reality slowly starts creeping back in, and the weight in my chest returns. The thunder continues to rumble, and I feel like the weather fits my mood perfectly. The clouds open, and the rain begins to crash down on my windshield. I turn my wipers on high, but I struggle to see the road ahead. I pull into one of the empty parking lots on campus to wait until the rain lightens up. While sitting in the car, I listen to the rain beating violently against the steel.

For some reason, I get the urge to get out of my car. I open the door and step out into the rain. Closing the door, I lean against the car, and within seconds, I'm drenched. The beating of the raindrops against my delicate skin feels good, almost painful in a way—but good. I lean my head back and feel the pellets as they strike my face. I enjoy the biting sensation. With my eyes closed, I just stand there, wishing I could live here, in this vacant lot, alone, focusing on nothing more than the stinging pleasure of the storm as it batters me. Knowing that this will soon end, that the sun is lingering behind the clouds and I will be faced with the hell that is my life, my body slides down the side of my car, and I sit in a puddle of water on the dirty ground and cry.

Why didn't I fight more? Why did I just lie there? I am constantly replaying that night in my head, wondering what I could have done differently. What happened at the party that made his mood suddenly shift? I know that I led him on, and I shouldn't have. If only I could have just been honest with him from the start. Now I'm constantly haunted by his eyes, his voice, and the feel of his hands clamped around my mouth, keeping me from screaming.

He took so much from me. He took everything that wasn't his to take. I had only been with one guy, and that experience was far from a loving one. Preston was drunk off of keg beer, and the whole thing lasted less than a few minutes before he passed out on top of me. Why is this my life? Why did I allow this asshole to take all that was good in me? I feel like nothing.

When the rain lightens up, I drag myself off the ground and slide back into my car, leaving puddles of dirty water on my leather seats. I drive the rest of the way in a complete daze, feeling drained and emotionally exhausted.

I wander aimlessly into the apartment and head straight to the bathroom to strip out of my soggy clothes and grab some towels. I wrap one of them around me and lie down on the floor, enjoying the cold tile against my face.

I savor the numbness I currently feel and drift off.

chapter nine

After my unexpected nap on the bathroom floor, I'm finishing up my makeup and getting ready to go to work. I have managed to pull myself together as much as possible to try and resume my normal routine, but the knots in my stomach won't seem to go away. I am nervous about seeing Roxy. I'm not sure what I will say if she notices the healing scars on my face. I think I have done a pretty decent job with my makeup, but I'm still nervous.

Walking out of the bathroom, I grab my purse and jacket then head out. Luckily, Jase hasn't been home today. I really needed the alone time. He and Mark are spending the day together, but they said they would be here when I get off work in a few hours.

Before I pull out of my parking space, I swipe my phone to see how many more missed calls and texts I have from Kimber. Her texts have turned rude and so have her voicemails. I really can't blame her though. Jase told me she came over the other afternoon when I was out running errands with Mark. She was pissed off and demanded to know where I was. Again, I told him to drop it, but I could tell he didn't want to. I don't want her mad at me, so I decide to finally send her a text.

Hey, I promise that I'm not mad at U. Just needed a little time away. Will explain later. Love U.

If only I knew what the hell I was going to explain. I know I have to resolve this quickly because I will be going back to our house in a few days, and I really don't need any more awkwardness.

Mark and I have been spending time together when he isn't in class. I can see why Jase loves him. They are alike in many ways, and we have bonded pretty effortlessly. He's wanted to stay over, but I am too embarrassed for him to witness the nightmares that seem to come every night.

As I drive to work, I listen to music and try my best to act normal. I'm not even sure what that is anymore, but I desperately crave it. I feel different, and I don't like it. When I pull up to Common Grounds, my nerves intensify. I haven't seen any of my other friends all week. Only Jase and Mark. Will Roxy be able to see right through me? Will she ask questions? My heart is racing, and I start taking slow deep breaths to calm myself. Getting out of my car, I walk straight in and towards the back to put my things away and get my apron. I pass Roxy, and she is busy helping a customer. When I reach the back room, I take a minute to try and pull myself together.

I take one last look at my face in the small compact mirror that's in my purse before walking back out. Looking around, I notice that the place is dead. I really wish we were busy so that my interaction with Roxy would be limited. I'm nervous and want nothing more than to get back into my car and drive to Jase's apartment. I walk slowly to one of the stools by the front counter and sit down.

"You feeling better?" Roxy asks.

Nervously, I lift my head and answer, "Yeah, thanks," hoping she can't see what I am hiding under my makeup.

"That's good. I missed having you up here." She walks over to sit beside me and continues, "So, I never did hear what happened with Jack."

My body turns cold when she says his name, and I blurt out, "What do you mean?"

"The party? You telling him you weren't interested?" she questions. "How did it go?"

"Oh, um...yeah, it was fine," I say, stumbling over my words and hoping that will be enough to satisfy her, but I know that it won't. I really want to be left alone right now. Maybe being normal isn't what I want because all I want to do right now is run back to the bubble I just came out of. It's safe there. No questions.

Roxy chuckles and says, "That's all I get? Girl, you were freaking out. Seriously, what happened?"

I suddenly feel my ears heat, and before I can stop myself, I snap at her, "Nothing, I already told you. Can we drop it?"

I immediately feel bad, but I can't do this. I stand up and walk straight back to the bathroom to try and compose myself. I lock the door behind me, and the tears are back. I quickly wipe them away and rest my hands on the sink. Staring at my reflection in the mirror, I start thinking about what excuses I could use to get out of here. How am I supposed to do this? I spend a few minutes settling my nerves before returning.

"I'm sorry," I whisper as I sit back down next to Roxy.

She slides me a coffee and says, "Here. It's okay. I won't mention it again."

"Thanks."

After about an hour, the place starts to pick up, and I enjoy the much needed distraction. It's been a little tense and uncomfortable as Roxy and I struggle for conversation. But now the place is full, and there is a line of customers. Roxy is working the register while I move about quickly, making various versions of lattes and espressos.

When the line dies down, I finally get a chance to lift my head and realize that it's dark outside.

"What time is it, Rox?" I ask while I begin wiping down the counters.

"A little after ten," she says over her shoulder as she is replacing the receipt tape in the register. When she finishes, she walks over and starts helping me wipe down the machines. We are both silent as we clean up and prepare to close.

When eleven o'clock rolls around, we shut everything down and lock up. Before I can head toward my car, Roxy pulls me in for an unexpected hug. The gesture makes my eyes prick with tears, but I quickly blink them away. When she pulls back, I can see concern in her eyes, and I know that she knows something is going on. How could she not? I have been acting weird all night.

"Have a good night, okay?"

"Thanks, you too," I say, trying to avoid eye contact.

We both walk to our cars, and in an attempt to make this less weird, I look over my shoulder, and in a fake perky voice, I say, "See you Tuesday!"

"Yeah, see ya."

When I walk into the apartment, Jase and Mark are in the kitchen cooking dinner. They have music playing loudly, so they don't hear me when I enter. I stand there and watch them move around the kitchen, flirting with each other. Jase approaches Mark while he's standing over the stove and wraps his arms around his waist, kissing him on the neck. A part of me feels a little sad—envious. Maybe I'm just not meant to ever have that. When Mark turns around to look at Jase, he sees me.

"Hey!" he says excitedly. "We're making Italian

tonight. You hungry?"

"Yeah, a little," I say, walking toward the bedroom. Why am I suddenly feeling sad? I wish I could get a hold of my emotions. I should be happy for Jase and Mark, not pitying myself. God, I am so selfish.

Closing the door behind me, I toss my purse on the floor. Walking across the room, I sit on the edge of the bed and take a moment to myself to just be sad. I need to get it out now before going back out there. I am sure the boys are sick and tired of my depressing moods.

I hear the creak of the door opening while I'm sniffing and quickly wiping away my tears. I really don't want to put a damper on the evening, so I paste on a smile before looking up to see Mark walking in the room.

"Hey, what's up?" I say in a fake cheerful tone, pretending that I wasn't just crying.

He closes the door and starts walking over to me. "What's wrong?"

I watch him as he moves across the room and sits down beside me. He places his hand on my knee and gives a light squeeze. "Nothing, just a weird day at work. That's all."

With a friendly smirk, he teasingly says, "You lie."

Not wanting to pretend, I just confess what's got me in my mood. "You're right," I softly chuckle. "Honestly, I love you and Jase, so don't take this the wrong way, okay?"

"Okay."

"I see how happy the two of you are, and I can't help but wonder...why not me? I know it's selfish, but..."

I don't finish, when Mark cuts me off and says, "You are *not* selfish." Shifting on the bed, he turns his body to face me. He looks extremely serious as he stares into my eyes. "I know what you're thinking, but stop. You will have that, I promise. Look, I can't even imagine how much everything sucks for you right now, but this does not define you."

Tears rim my eyes when Mark rests his hands on my shoulders and repeats himself sternly. "This doesn't define you." Leaning in, he kisses my forehead, and the tears slip out. He takes his thumbs, and wipes them off my cheeks. "It doesn't, okay?"

"Why does it feel that way? Maybe you believe that, but..." Looking down, I shake my head before looking back into his eyes. "None of this makes sense to me."

Tucking a lock of hair behind my ear, he says, "One day, this pain will make sense to you." He pulls me in for a hug, and I try to believe his words, but it all sounds too good to be true.

I pull back and attempt to lighten the mood as I grin and ask, "So, what are you boys cooking for me?"

Mark smiles, but I clearly see the concern in his eyes. "Jase is the one who is doing everything. I'm not much of a cook. I'm trying to look helpful, but all I'm doing is stirring the pasta." Laughing, he stands up, grabs my hand, and pulls me off the bed. "Come on, let's devour the bruschetta while we admire Jase's sexy ass moving around the kitchen."

I smile, thankful for the humor, and say, "Absolutely."

Walking into the kitchen, Jase strides over to me, pulls me in for a hug, and gives me a quick kiss. "Hey, sweetie. How was work?"

"Weird at first, but it wound up being a busy night, which was good," I say as I walk over to the wine rack and select a bottle of Nero d'Avola. I uncork the bottle and pour three glasses of the floral Italian wine. As Mark and I settle at the bar, Jase picks up his glass and stands next to us. No toast is needed when the three of us clink our glasses before drinking.

Mark and I sit, chitchatting, while Jase slices up a baguette for the bruschetta. This is exactly what I needed tonight: a relaxing evening with my guys, good food, and wine.

"So, what are you cooking?" I ask Jase as he's stirring a few pots on the stove.

"Lobster tortellini, vodka sauce, pan-fried asparagus, and roasted garlic bread," he says as he moves around the kitchen.

"God, that sounds good!" I look over at Mark and ask, "Hey, didn't your band have a show last night?"

"Yeah, we played at Blur. It was a great gig; the place was packed."

"I've never been there before," I say.

Jase looks over his shoulder at me and jokingly says, "Candace, you haven't been anywhere." He chuckles and then adds, "You should really hear them play sometime. You'd like their sound."

The conversation halts when there is a knock at the door. Mark walks over to open it, and my stomach sinks when I see Kimber standing in the doorway. I jump off the barstool, and Jase is immediately by my side.

"What the hell is going on?" she asks. She is pissed, and understandably so. Walking in, she throws her purse on the couch, and with her hands on her hips, she continues, "You two have been avoiding me all week, and I have no clue what I did to piss you guys off!"

"We're not pissed at you," Jase reassures her, but by the look on her face, she's not buying one word. "Candace just wanted a little time away, that's all."

"From me? I'm supposed to be your best friend?!"

I've seen Kimber worked up before, but not like this. She is visibly not only pissed, but I can tell that her feelings are hurt as well, which hurts me in return. It's not my intention to hurt her at all. I love Kimber, and we have never had secrets between us until now.

"Why won't you talk to me?" she demands.

"I'm sorry," I say, as Mark heads back into the kitchen. I walk over, sit down on the couch, and quickly think of any reason to give her. She moves to stand in front of me, and I know she is waiting for an answer. Nervous, I start to speak again, "Jack and I got into an argument at the party. I was upset, he was drunk, so I called Jase to come pick me up."

Jase butts in and adds, "I suggested she stay here in case he showed up at your house. That's all."

"So why couldn't you just call me and tell me?" The look in her eyes is calling *bullshit* on our lie.

"I didn't want you getting involved. You can sometimes overreact, and I just wanted everything to die down without any drama. It's no big deal, and I haven't heard from him. It's over, so can we just drop it?" My hands are sweating; I hate even mentioning his name. I really want this conversation to be done with. I look up at Kimber, and she is shaking her head at Jase and me.

"Bullshit!" she snaps as she grabs her purse off of the couch and heads for the door.

Jumping up, I say, "Kimber, wait. Please don't be mad at me. I'm coming back home this week. It's not a big deal, please don't make it into one."

She takes a step towards me and says, "You're the one who made it such a big deal when you decided to avoid me all week. We have always been honest with each other, but if you really want me to believe your story, then fine. I believe you." With that, she turns her back to me, walks out, and slams the door behind her.

chapter ten

"Are you sure everything is all right?" Jase asks as he is helping me unpack my bags.

After my fight with Kimber, I stayed a couple more nights with Jase. It was nice to have him there when I got home from classes on Monday. I didn't think returning to school would be as stressful as it turned out to be. I didn't miss much, so I wasn't stressed about that part. I guess it's more paranoia than stress. Truth is, I am terrified of running into Jack on campus. I know the likelihood of that happening is slim, considering I have been here for the past three years and our paths have never crossed before, but I can't help constantly looking over my shoulder while I walk around campus. The feeling consumed me every day, and when I got back to Jase's apartment, he was there when I broke down from all the panic I was trying to keep bottled up all day. He had asked if I needed him or Mark to help out by trying to meet up with me on campus, but none of our schedules matched up enough for it to be possible.

"Yeah, Jase. I can't stay with you forever, and you and Mark don't need me around all of the time." I start piling my dirty clothes in the hamper and get a load of clothes separated to wash. In all honesty, I don't want to be here. But I feel like a burden to Jase. He keeps assuring me I'm not, but I know he and Mark really want some privacy. I don't blame them. Plus, I haven't heard from Kimber since Sunday night when she showed up at Jase's, so my being back here at the house is unsettling.

Tossing my empty bags in the closet, Jase asks, "What time do you get off work tonight? Do you want me to meet you afterward?" I know he's worried about me since my new feelings of paranoia have surfaced. He met me yesterday after I got off work to simply walk me to my car and follow me home. But I really don't need him to keep doing that since I always walk out with Roxy or another employee.

"I close tonight, so I'll leave around eleven, but you don't have to meet me there. I'm working with Roxy, so I won't be alone," I say as I grab the basket full of clothes and walk out of the bedroom. I dump the basket off in the laundry room before heading to the living room. Jase takes his bag, and I walk him to the door. "Thank you."

Looking at me, he asks, "For what?"

"Everything." I barely get the words out when I feel the tightening in my throat. I'm not really good at expressing how I feel, but I wish I could because everything Jase has done for me this past week and a half has been beyond anything anyone has ever done for me. The compassion and love he gives me every day means the world to me.

"Sweetie, I feel like I haven't done nearly enough," he says. But he has. He couldn't have done anything more.

I shake my head and start to cry. He knows me well enough that no words are even needed. He pulls me in, and we hold each other tightly. I press my head into his chest, and the tears keep coming. Jase combs his hand through my hair while I cling to him.

"You keep the key to my place, okay. Come over anytime you need, even if it's the middle of the night."

Nodding my head, I pull back and look into his eyes. I lift up on my toes and give him a quick kiss. "I love you."

"I love you, too," he responds as he opens the door. "Text me tonight when you get home."

"Okay." Shutting the door behind him, I walk back to get my laundry started and to start reading for one of my classes.

As soon as I get into my car, I pull out my phone and text Jase to let him know that work was fine, and I am heading home. Kimber had classes all afternoon, so I didn't see her before I left for work, but I know she will be there when I get home.

Roxy is starting to get a little concerned about me. She keeps asking me questions and wanting to make sure everything is all right. I try assuring her that everything's fine, but I know she doesn't believe me. I can't blame her really. Just like at school, I keep fearing that Jack is going to walk through the doors at work. Every time the little bell over the door rings, the anxiety builds in my stomach, and I know Roxy notices.

Pulling up to the house, I see Kimber's car out front. I didn't tell her I was coming home today. Walking inside, I make my way to the kitchen to grab a bottle of water before I go to my room. I see Kimber sitting at the bar when I enter.

Looking up at me, she says, "Hey, I didn't know you were coming back today."

"Yeah," is all I manage to say as I open the fridge and grab a water. The silence is very awkward, and I just want to go to my room and not deal with this tension between us. "Well, I'm really tired, so I'm going to head to bed."

"Yeah, okay," she says quietly.

I really hate that things feel so strained between us, but I am not sure what to say to her. She knows I'm lying to her, and I feel bad for that but not bad enough to tell her the truth.

I brush my teeth and slip on some sleep shorts and a tank top before taking my sleeping pill that the doctor prescribed to me. Since I started taking them, I haven't had any more extreme nightmares. I lie down in bed and grab my phone off the nightstand to text Jase one more time. I've gotten used to sleeping with him in the same bed, so lying here alone feels strange, almost scary. I've been clinging to Jase as my life support lately, and not having him here with me makes me wish I was back in his bed, in his arms—not alone.

Goodnight. I miss U.

Miss U too. Did U see Kimber?

Yeah. Didn't really say much. It's awkward.

I'm sorry, sweetie. Hopefully it will get better and things will get less weird for you guys.

Maybe. Is Mark with you?

Yeah.

Tell him I said HI. Love you guys.

We love you too.

2 weeks later

Things are still tense with Kimber. We hardly even talk anymore aside from the civil greetings when passing by. I keep apologizing, but she is still mad at me. I wish we could move past this and go back to the way it used to be. But I'm beginning to think that the way it was is the way it will never be. Things are starting to get a little more comfortable at work. Roxy has never mentioned Jack again since that first night back. I've been having issues with being alone at night, so I have been spending a few nights a week with Jase. Either he comes over or I go to his apartment. Once I'm asleep, it's pretty restless. Lying in the dark, waiting for sleep to come, is the hardest part. Every time I close my eyes I am back in the alley, on the ground, with *him*.

Ms. Emerson, my dance instructor, has been making my life hell lately. I never miss a class; in fact, I have been clocking in a lot of after hours studio time. My moves are flawless, but she is on me about feeling the dance. She keeps telling me that she's watching a perfect dancer, but I'm dead. There is nothing behind my movements. The problem is, I don't know how to fix that because frankly, I feel like I am wasting away. But when I dance, it's the only time my mind feels free of the pain that is constantly consuming it.

4 weeks later

Kimber found my sleeping pills. She needed to borrow my hair dryer when hers bit the dust. While she was in my bathroom, she saw the bottle that I had accidentally left out. When she kept questioning me, I told her I was taking them because the stress of school was keeping me up at night. I don't know whether she believed me or not, but it really doesn't matter since our relationship seems to be drifting further apart.

I fought with my mother this morning when she called to bitch at me for not being a better daughter and returning her phone calls. I hadn't spoken with her or my father since the blowout about me not attending the banquet that honored my mother. Every time either one of them calls, I just let it go to voicemail, but this time I answered. My lack of conversation ticked my mother off, and she went on another one of her tangents about how childish and disrespectful I am. I didn't argue back. I didn't have the energy, so I just sat there and let her say everything she needed to say. If it wasn't for her pushy attitude, I would have never agreed to go on a date with Jack, and none of this would be happening. I know what he did isn't her fault, but I hate her for it anyway. So when she finished lecturing me on her expectations, I simply disconnected the call without saying anything.

6 weeks later

Yesterday was a horrible day. My mind has been consumed with flashbacks, and the stress finally caught up to me. After dance class, I came home. Kimber was still on campus, so I thought I would take a quick nap before having to go into work. I woke up screaming, and I couldn't calm myself down. My heart was racing, and I must have been hallucinating because even though my eyes were open, Jack was right there with me, muffling my mouth with his hand and ripping my clothes off. No matter how much I fought, he wouldn't stop. I huddled down in my closet and tried shielding my eyes from the images of him, but he was there too. With me in the dark. I felt like I was going to die. The pounding of my heart made my chest hurt, and I could barely breathe.

I managed to call Jase when I started to calm down. He came over right away and sat with me in my closet while I sobbed uncontrollably. It seems that no matter how hard I try to let go of it all, Jack finds a way to creep into my head and remind me of everything I want to forget.

I decided to go ahead and go into work, even though Jase wanted me to call in sick. But I really needed the distraction. It was a busy night, so I didn't have much time to think about anything other than making lattes. In fact, I barely even noticed the taunting bell above the door, which usually has me in a constant state of paranoia. The busier I keep myself, the less time my mind has to wander. So when I am not at Common Grounds, I'm buried in schoolwork: dancing and studying.

8 weeks later

Jase has been trying to convince me to see a therapist. He believes my erratic behavior is post-traumatic stress disorder. The last thing I want to do is talk, so I brush him off and pretend like it's no big deal whenever he brings it up, which is often. All I need is a little more time to pass, and things will get easier. I keep telling myself this every day, but so far, nothing has changed. I can do nothing but hope that one day I will wake up and things will be different.

Ms. Emerson told me to report to her office this afternoon at three o'clock. I have never been to her office before; I hadn't even been singled out in class like I have been lately. She's constantly barking at me in class, telling me to *feel* more. I can only imagine that this meeting will be more of the same.

When I pull up to the studio, I take a deep calming breath before getting out of the car. Feeling nervous as I walk into the building, I head down the hallway to all the instructors' offices. When I reach her closed door, I take a few moments before lightly knocking on the door.

"Come in," she says loudly, and I slowly open the door and peek my head in. "Ms. Parker, please, have a seat," she says as she motions to the large leather chair with weathered nailheads.

Sliding my purse off my shoulder, I plop it on the floor next to the chair before sitting down. I look at Ms. Emerson as she folds her hands together on top of her desk and clears her throat.

"Ms. Parker...Candace?"

"Please, call me Candace," I answer as I fidget with my watch.

"I can't help but notice a decline in your performance lately, and it's beginning to concern me."

"Oh..."

" I've never had to worry about you in the past, and frankly, I never thought I would be needing to have this conversation with you, but..." She backs her chair away from her desk, stands up, and walks around, leaning against the desk as she now stands directly in front of me. "Is there something going on? Something that has caused this sudden shift with your dancing?" Her voice softens when she questions me. I'm surprised by her tone of empathy.

Shaking my head, I say, "No. I'm not sure what's causing this struggle." Only I do. And the knowing causes me to swallow back hard and fight to keep the tears from pooling in my eyes.

When I look at Ms. Emerson, I see the concern. An emotion I thought she couldn't possibly possess. My body betrays my act of strength when I feel my chin start to tremble as the emotions build inside my tightening chest.

Slightly tilting her head to the side, she pushes, "You sure?"

There is no way I can speak right now, so I simply nod my head.

She pushes herself off the desk and sits down next to me in the matching leather chair. Shifting her body to face me, she continues, “Dancers like you don’t often walk through these doors. When I first saw you three years ago, I knew I was seeing something special. You are destined to have a successful career, and I’ve never had to worry about you. You breathe this.” Hearing her words, I lose my composure and let the tears escape. “But it’s almost November, and your time here is limited. Whatever *this* is...we need to fix it. I see perfection, but I no longer feel the passion in you. I feel emptiness.”

Agreeing with her last statement, I nod my head and say, “I’m sorry. I don’t...I don’t know what to do to fix this.”

She reaches over and covers my hand with hers. “Whatever is making you shut down, allow it to come to life inside of you.”

Her words are my greatest fear. Would she be telling me this if she knew? I know I have to find another way—I have to.

“I believe in you, Candace. I wouldn’t have called you in today if I didn’t.”

I am taken back by her candidness, and I know she isn’t saying this for my sake. She means it. Wiping my tearstained cheeks, I say, “Thank you.”

She stands up, and I lean down to grab my purse before doing the same. As she walks back behind her desk, I make my way to the door. Holding the door handle in my hand, I turn over my shoulder and assure her, “I’ll fix this.”

“I know you will,” she replies as she sits down.

chapter eleven

Wrapping my plush black scarf around my neck, I head out the front door into the brisk and rainy October evening. It's Halloween, and everyone at work wanted the night off to go to various parties, so I volunteered to work. Roxy will be there for a little bit, but I will be working most of the night and closing by myself. It should be pretty slow with it being a Wednesday and also a party night. Most people will be opting to drink liquor rather than coffee.

When I arrive, Roxy and her boyfriend, Jared, are the only ones in the shop. Sporting her new flame-red hair, she looks up and says, "Hey, Candace! How was your day?"

Shaking off my wet jacket, I say, "Busy. I've been trying to choreograph that solo I told you about." I shrug off my coat and scarf and hang them on the coat rack by the front doors.

"Hey, Jared," I say as I approach the counter.

"Haven't seen you in a while, girl," he says.

"Yeah, I've been keeping busy with school."

Eying my backpack, he says, "I see."

I sling my backpack off my shoulder and drop it on the floor behind the counter. "I figured it'd be dead tonight, so I thought I could get some reading done for my classes."

Roxy walks up to me, leaning against the counter, and

asks softly, “You sure you’re gonna be okay here by yourself?”

“Roxy, I’ve worked alone before. No biggie.”

“Yeah, but—”

Interrupting her, I repeat, “No biggie, Rox,” giving a slight nod and looking her in the eyes. I know exactly what she’s thinking, but I just want her to drop it. We both realize I haven’t worked alone since she’s been noticing my strange behavior these past couple months. She knows something is up, but I tend to cut her off every time she starts to insinuate concern.

I walk over to the espresso machine and begin making myself a double shot latte.

“It was nice seeing you, Candace,” Jared shouts over to me while I’m grinding the coffee beans.

“You heading out already?” I ask.

“Yeah, I gotta run.” He turns to Roxy and asks, “I’ll see you in an hour?”

“Yep, meet you at your place,” she replies before kissing him.

I turn around, not wanting to look at how happy they are and focus on steaming the milk. I add a pump of vanilla flavoring and quickly wipe down the counter before turning back around. When I do, Jared is walking out. Leaning against the counter, I blow on my hot drink before taking a slow sip. Roxy is staring at me, and I can read her thoughts clearly. I know she doesn’t want me here alone, and she is worried. Before she can say a word, I try to place the focus on her, not me.

“So, what are the two of you doing tonight?” I ask.

“A friend of ours is in a band, and they are playing a show at The Crocodile.”

“That’s a huge gig,” I say excitedly.

Roxy and I start talking about her friend’s band, and

before I know it, she's grabbing her things and getting ready to leave. A part of me is starting to feel jittery, and it isn't the caffeine. The thought creeps into my mind: *What if he comes in tonight?* I have never seen him here in the past, and to my knowledge, he has never been here, but it still makes me nervous.

"You okay, hun?" Roxy asks as she stares at my hands that are tightly clenched together.

Immediately, I loosen my grip as I feign a smile and say, "Yeah, fine. Must be the two shots of espresso, that's all." Truth is, I'm not okay, but I need to be. I need to function and be able to go about my daily routines without freaking out. The only way I know to get to that point is to keep forcing myself.

"Okay," she responds in a weary tone. I assure her I'm fine and tell her to not worry about me and have fun. Before walking out the door, she turns around and says, "Call me if you need anything, or...just call me, okay?"

Waving at her in mock exasperation, I say, "Just go."

It's a little after ten o'clock and the rain is now pouring down outside. The evening has been pretty slow as predicted. Only a handful of people are sitting around drinking coffee, visiting with friends, or studying. I have been able to get a decent amount of reading done and am now finishing up some research for a paper I need to write by next week.

My heart skips a beat, as it does every time the bell above the door rings. I look up to see a guy with dark, wet hair walking in. I hop off my stool and walk over to the register to meet him.

"Hey, what can I get for you?" I ask.

Looking at the drink list on the wall behind me, he says,

"Uh, just a twenty coffee. Black."

Roxy didn't feel like she needed to give her drink sizes any special names like other coffee establishments, so it's simply a twelve, sixteen, or twenty.

"Easy enough," I say, and before he can look up at me, I am over pouring him his cup of coffee. When I return, he is typing something into his phone. "That's one ninety-three," I say as I slide the drink towards him.

Looking up at me, he hands me a five, and I open the register to get him his change. I feel him staring at me, and when I shift my eyes up, sure enough, he's staring at me with a confused look on his face.

"Everything okay?" I ask as I hand him his change. He doesn't take his eyes off of me, and I'm starting to freak out inside. I can feel the rate of my heart as it increases, and I nervously ask, "Anything else?"

He finally blinks and shakes his head as he says, "Um, no. No, that's all," never taking his eyes off of me.

Who the hell is this guy? I take a few steps back and accidentally kick the barstool I was sitting on, and it makes a loud scratching noise against the floor. He turns around and starts walking out but looks back over his shoulder at me a couple times before finally leaving.

Panic shoots through me, and my breathing becomes erratic. Does that guy know me? Does he know Jack? My paranoid thoughts start to overtake me, and I quickly announce to the few people who are still here that we are closing immediately. My voice is trembling, and it doesn't take long for the place to empty out. As soon as the last person leaves, I lock the doors and turn off the outside lights. I walk back behind the counter, scared, not able to slow down my pounding heart. Sitting down and pulling my knees to my chest, I once again feel defeated and hopeless as the tears start to fall.

As soon as I get home, I take a sleeping pill, strip off my clothes, and lie down in bed. I hate that I have become so weak and can't get my shit together. It shouldn't be like this. I shouldn't be feeling this miserable every day. It's been two months, and I know I am stronger than this pathetic girl that lives inside of me and is consuming me.

It's sometime in the middle of the night when I wake up to Kimber loudly stumbling through the house. She's giggling, and I hear a guy's voice before her door slams shut. *Great.* I am just about to fall back asleep when her moans echo though the walls. My stomach knots up when the guy starts grunting out her name.

I can't take this. I am a mix of emotions: pissed, disgusted, jealous, and scared. Throwing the covers off of me, I grab my coat and slide on my Uggs. I need to get out of this house and away from what's going on in Kimber's room. So, I grab my keys and leave.

Quietly, I slide my key into the lock and open the door. Shutting it softly behind me, I walk through the living room while stepping out of my boots and tossing my coat on the couch. When I open the door to Jase's room, I see he is alone. *Thank God.* I pull back the covers and slide in behind him. It isn't long before he rolls over and wraps me in his arms. It is then when my stomach finally unknots, and I fall asleep.

"So what happened last night?" Jase asks when I walk into the kitchen.

Pouring myself a cup of coffee, I walk into the living

room, which is adjacent to the open kitchen, and curl up in a blanket as I sit on the couch. Jase walks in and sits next to me, propping his feet up on the coffee table.

"Kimber brought some guy home last night, and the pervert wouldn't stop shouting her name," I say.

Chuckling, Jase asks, "Who was it?"

"I have no clue. I was asleep until they came stumbling in and woke me up." I take a sip of my coffee before adding, "It was gross!"

Jase cocks his head to the side and says, "It's not gross, Candace."

"It's gross," I insist before taking another sip of my coffee.

Jase just laughs at me, but I can't help it. Hearing those two last night was disgusting.

"Anyway, new subject. How was last night?" I ask. Ever since Mark's band played at Blur, they have become somewhat of regulars and played another gig there last night.

"It was fun. You really should've come with us."

"I told you, I had to work," I say.

"Nooo, you volunteered to work," he responds and gives me a smirk.

I have been avoiding going out with Jase and Mark. The thought of going anywhere aside from my normal spots, where I feel a little safer about not running into *him,* scares me. So I stick to school, work, and home.

"You live in a bubble, Candace," he says and then grabs the corner of the blanket that I am under and pulls it over his lap as he scoots up next to me. "You need to get out."

"I am out."

"You're not. I always know where to find you because you have the same routine every week. It never changes." He drapes his arm around me and pulls me closer. "I'm worried about you."

Sighing, I respond, “You don’t need to be. I’m fine.”

“Don’t pull that act with me. I know you’re not fine. It’s been two months, and you are no more fine than you were back in August.” Kissing the top of my head, he continues, “I worry because I only know what you tell me. But I wonder how much this really consumes you that you hold in and don’t tell me about. You won’t do anything to help yourself.”

Taking my coffee mug out of my hand, he reaches over and sets it on the end table. I hate that he’s right. I hate that I am stuck. I hate that I am scared. I hate everything about my life. Every day is so goddamn hard, and all I can do is just focus on going through the motions just to get to the next day, which is the same thing all over again. But, it’s all a façade. Truth is—I’m drowning.

“I’m constantly scared,” I confess to Jase, and his arms tighten around me. “I’m scared I’m going to see *him.* And I know this sounds absolutely crazy, but...most days...” I stop in my thought, my almost confession, which might make Jase drag me straight to a therapist if I tell him. So I lay my head on his chest and take a deep breath when he says, “You can tell me.”

“I feel like I’m going to die.”

The place is packed when I walk into work Saturday morning. Brandon and I are busy trying to keep up with the drink orders while Roxy deals with the customers. Brandon and I hardly ever work together because our schedules at school are opposite of each other. He’s on a soccer scholarship and is a year behind me. He’s laughing about something when I accidently knock the iced mocha I just made all over me.

"Crap!" I grab a towel and start wiping the sticky drink off my arms and hands.

Brandon is laughing at me, and I shoot him a mock 'go to hell' look. "Go clean up, I'll take care of this," he tells me, and I holler to Roxy that I'll be right back.

Luckily, most of the drink spilled on my apron. I wash my arms in the sink and wipe down one of the chocolaty brown spots on my top. When I walk back out, the line is down to only two people. Roxy decides to move off the register and make drinks, so I take her place.

I look up to take the last customer in line, and there he is. The guy from the other night. Only this time, I'm the one staring and not speaking.

"You okay?" he asks, and I snap out of my daze.

"What can I get for you?" I ask. He looks at me intently, which makes me nervous and orders the same drink that he had a few days ago. I turn around and walk over to pour his cup of coffee when Roxy sides up next to me and whispers, "Who's that guy?"

"I don't know, why?"

"Well, he's hot, and he can't seem to take his eyes off of you."

I peek at him over my shoulder and catch him staring. Turning back to his coffee, I snap the lid on and whisper, "He's creepy."

Roxy laughs, and I walk back over to the register. "One ninety-three," I say as I hand him his drink. When I give him his change, in a moment of bravery, I ask, "Do I know you or something?"

"I don't think so. Why?"

I notice his striking eyes. They are almost clear with a slight hint of blue. I don't think I have ever seen eyes that color before. Shaking my head, I say, "You stare." *What was that, Candace? You stare?* "I'm sorry, that was rude of me,"

I quickly apologize.

Not acknowledging my apology, he asks, "You go to school here?"

"Yeah."

Taking a step back from the counter, he thanks me for the coffee and leaves. I don't know what to make of the exchange we just had, but decide not to give it anymore thought.

"What did he say?" Roxy asks.

"Nothing really. Just thanked me for the coffee," I say as I walk over to Brandon and help him finish wiping down the counters.

When I get home and pull into the driveway, I notice a red Jeep in front of the house. Walking in, I expect to see Kimber, but she must be in her room. I grab a bottle of water and an apple from the fridge, and when I start heading to my room, Kimber is walking out of hers and shutting the door behind her.

"Hey," she says when she turns around and sees me.

"Whose car is out front?" I ask.

"Oh, that's Seth's car." She says this as if I should know who Seth is. I give her a confused look when she clarifies, "The guy I've been seeing."

Nodding my head, I softly say, "Oh," when she walks off. I turn around and walk into my room, closing the door behind me. How could I not know she's dating someone? Sadness washes over me at the realization that Kimber and I are hardly friends anymore. She has a boyfriend, and I had no clue. I just figured that guy she brought home with her the other night was a one-night stand. I never thought I would drift so far from my best friend. How can we live in the same house and not know each other at all? What's worse—this is all my fault.

chapter twelve

The night is cold and misty, and Mark and I are sitting by the fire pit in my backyard roasting marshmallows while we wait for Jase to come over. I am curled up in a blanket as we sit and eat our sugary treat and share a bottle of red wine.

"Where's Kimber?" Mark asks, as he stabs another marshmallow onto his skewer.

Looking over at him, the only light coming from the glow of the fire, I say, "At Seth's, probably. She spends most nights over at his place, so I've been here alone for the most part."

"Does that bother you?"

"Not really...well, kinda." I grab my skewer, loaded with two marshmallows, and place them directly into the flame. I watch the glow of the fire brighten as my marshmallows ignite into a mini fireball. Pulling them out of the yellow crackling blaze, I blow out the flame on my now scorched confection.

"That's disgusting," he says while eying my bubbly, charred marshmallow.

Sliding off the burnt shell and leaving the remainder of the uncooked marshmallow on the skewer, I shove it in my mouth and crunch down. "It's fabulous," I jokingly say with my mouth full.

Mark laughs and shakes his head at me. "So...?" he

questions, still wanting a confirmation to his previous question.

I shove the remainder of the marshmallows that are left on my skewer back into the blaze to repeat the process. "I mean, I like that I don't have to feel awkward when she's around, but at the same time, it makes me sad that she's not around and that we hardly speak." Eating the last of my marshmallows, I lay the skewer down and continue. "It hurts. Kimber has never been serious with a guy, and now she has a boyfriend I know nothing about. She's seems really happy, and I wish I was a part of it."

"So, why don't you just talk to her?"

"Because she knows I'm hiding something and lying to her. She told me that she doesn't want to be friends with someone who can't be honest." Shrugging my shoulders, I take another sip of wine and tighten the blanket around me.

"Maybe you should…"

Mark is cut off when the door opens and Jase comes outside to join us.

"Hey, guys," he says as he walks over and kisses Mark, then turns to me and kisses my cheek. "What are you guys doing out here? It's cold."

Mark holds up the half-eaten bag of marshmallows and says, "I'm fattening up your rail-thin girl over there." He eyes me with a smirk and winks.

"Good luck, fatty," I respond playfully.

Jase sits opposite me and starts, "So, I want you to come out with Mark and I Saturday night."

"Jase," I say as I slowly shake my head. I don't go out. I never go out.

"It'll be low key, promise. Spines is closing early to have a private concert, and I was able to snag three tickets for us."

"You want me to go to a concert?"

“Candace, seriously? It’s at a book and music store. It’s a private show, but forget about that. You won’t turn me down when I tell you who’s playing,” he says as his smile grows. He reaches in his back pants pocket and pulls out a ticket. He hands me the solid black ticket with two white X’s on it.

“Are you serious?” I ask as a snatch the ticket from him. “How did you get these?”

“A friend of Mark’s,” he says.

“Who?” Mark asks.

“Ryan. I ran into him at the gym earlier today. We got to talking about music, and he mentioned the show. When I told him my best friend is a huge fan of The xx, he gave me a few extra tickets that he wasn’t using.”

Looking at Jase, I ask, “Who’s Ryan?”

Mark answers for him and says, “He owns the bar that my band has been playing at.”

Holding the ticket, I really want to go, but I am nervous. I sit there quietly, staring into the bright fire, when Jase reaches over and takes ahold of my hand.

“I really want you to go. You’ll be with the two of us. Nothing will happen,” he assures me.

Looking at him, I let out a sigh and say, “I don’t know. It makes me nervous.”

“I know,” Jase whispers. “But nothing will happen. You have to start trying.”

I look back at Mark, and he shrugs his shoulders and nods in agreement. Letting out a slow breath, I turn back to face Jase. “Okay,” I say with a shaky voice. I need to do this. I know I do. I’m just scared. Paranoid really. I tell myself everyday that I need to function, so I will push down the fear that is already rising inside of me, and try.

Sitting back, Jase quietly says, “Thank you.”

I stare at the black and white ticket that lies on my desk. Every time I walk past it, I try and reassure myself that I can do this. Jase and Mark will be picking me up shortly. I walk into my closet to find something to wear. Looking around, I decide on simplicity: jeans, a long sleeved white V-neck shirt, brown knee-high boots, and my brown crew-collar leather jacket.

I hear the guys when they come inside the house and shout, "I'll be out in a sec. I'm just finishing straightening my hair." Taking a huge gulp of the wine I've been sipping, I look at myself in the mirror. My eyes look a little glassy, but I'm not surprised. I've been drinking since I got home from work a little bit ago, hoping the alcohol will help calm my nerves.

I turn off my hair straightener, grab my cell, and slide it in my pocket along with my ID and credit card, and I walk through the house to the living room where the guys are.

"You look great," Jase says with a smile. "You ready?"

I nod my head, grab my leopard scarf that is lying on the couch, and tie it around my neck before walking outside. I don't say much on the drive; I just listen to Mark and Jase talk about school and football. When we arrive at Spines, a trendy book and music store, I begin to panic when I see all the cars.

"I don't know about this," I say quietly.

The guys get out of the car and Mark opens my door. Holding his hand out for me, he says, "No worries, okay?"

I slide my hand into his and step out of the car.

When we walk inside, there is a gathering of around one hundred or so people. There is a bar set off to the side that is serving drinks with tables and chairs scattered about.

The lights are set low and there are candles everywhere. I stay with Mark, still holding his hand tightly, as Jase goes to the bar to get us drinks.

Mark and I browse through the section of vinyl records. Flipping through them and admiring the artwork on the old cardboard cases, I am starting to feel a little more at ease. Jase finds us and hands Mark and I each a bottle of beer.

“Come on, they’re about to start playing,” Jase says. We walk over, and decide to stand next to another group of people by a low shelf of books. I set my beer down and lean my elbows on the bookcase as Jase and Mark stand on either side of me. I watch as the band takes the small stage that has been set up for them and starts getting their equipment ready. I have loved The xx for years but have never seen them live before.

The strum of a guitar fills the dark room as they ease into their song ‘Infinity.’ Listening to the slow soothing sounds, I lean into Jase—a non-verbal *thank you.* He wraps his arm around me and pulls me in closer, and I know exactly what he is telling me with his actions.

After a few songs, I am ready for another drink. I go with Jase to the bar to get another round for the three of us. When we walk back, I see Mark talking to some guy who has his back to me. When we approach, the guy he is talking to turns around, and I nearly choke on the beer that I just took a sip of.

He looks shocked to see me as he stares at me with his clear-blue eyes. He doesn’t say anything to me, so I decide to speak up. “You again.”

“You two know each other?” Mark asks.

“Not really,” he responds as he blinks his gaze away from me.

I look at Mark and add, “He’s come into Common Grounds a couple times to get coffee. How do you guys know each other?"

"He owns Blur, where the band has been playing lately," Mark says.

"And the guy who gave me the tickets," Jase says to me before turning his attention to the guy, whose name I still don't know, and adds, "Thanks, man."

"No problem at all."

I stand there awkwardly as the guys continue to talk, so I turn my back to them and focus in on the band as they begin to play 'Missing.' I haven't heard this song in months, and it begins to affect me. What I used to consider a desperate love song now breathes new meaning when I hear the words about how the heart beats. Sadness creeps through me, and my body tenses up as I try desperately not to cry.

"Hey, let's go sit down," Jase whispers in my ear, and I am snapped out of my tormenting thoughts.

Looking at him over my shoulder, I nod, not sure if I am able to speak just yet. He lowers his head and looks me in the eyes. I know he sees it—the hurt—so I quickly shake my head and give him a reassuring grin that I've got this under control. He takes my hand and leads me to a table where Mark and his friend are already sitting.

Taking a seat and setting my beer down, I say, "I'm sorry, but I never caught your name."

Giving me a half smirk, he says, "Ryan. Ryan Campbell."

I give him a slight nod and introduce myself. "I'm Candace." Eying his cup of coffee, I add, "Ever drink anything besides coffee?"

"I work a lot of late nights," is his vague response to my question.

"So, Ryan," Jase says, "Candace will be graduating this year as well. She's a dance major."

What the hell is Jase doing? I look over at him and give

him a snide look, but he just grins at me.

"Dance. What kind?" Ryan asks.

"Ballet," I say and then take another sip of my beer.

"Can't say I know anything about that," he responds with an honest chuckle.

"It's okay. Nobody ever does."

"So, I take it you're the best friend who loves this band," he says as he nods his head towards the stage.

Feeling odd about this interaction, I reply with a simple, "Yeah." I start to feel the need to close myself off. It feels weird talking to someone new. My life is very secluded, and I like it that way. It's safe. So being here, out, listening to music, talking to a new person, suddenly makes me want to run back home.

I know I can do this. I have to do this. I reach under the table and rest my hand on top of Jase's leg, in a way, using him as my anchor while I try to pull my thoughts together. He looks over at me as he lays his hand over mine and gives me a reassuring squeeze. I keep repeating in my head: *Get it together, Candace. Just function.* I say it over and over in a desperate attempt to will it to happen. I tell myself to act normal, but I'm not even sure I know what that is. I push the uncomfortable feeling aside, knowing that nothing will happen because Jase and Mark are both here with me. Everything is fine.

I'm peeling the label off my beer bottle when Ryan starts to talk. "So, Candace, what do you plan on doing when you finish school?"

I look up at him and take a deep breath before answering. "I hope to dance professionally while time allows. Not sure where that will happen. New York was always the plan, but I'm not so sure now." Why did I just tell him that? *Please don't ask why.*

Looking over at Jase, he and Mark are lost in their own

conversation, not paying any attention to Ryan and me.

"I love New York. You ever been?" Ryan asks.

"Yeah, several times. It's a great city. I actually lived there the summer before my senior year of high school. I had a scholarship to one of the conservatories in the city."

"So, your parents just let you live there alone for the summer?" he asks with a hint of concern in his eyes.

"Umm, yeah. My parents are...well, not your typical involved parents," I say.

"Sorry."

I shrug it off, and we continue to talk about our love of New York City. I'm surprised with how easy it is to talk to this new person. He's laidback and makes me feel comfortable.

Time continues to pass pretty effortlessly as we talk. Mark and Jase are engrossed in their own private conversation about who knows what.

"What are you two talking about?" Mark asks, when his conversation with Jase has died down.

"New York City," Ryan answers.

When I hear the band begin the intro to another one of my favorite songs, I excuse myself to walk over to the bookcase where we were standing earlier so that I can listen and enjoy the song. A few moments later, Jase, Mark, and Ryan join me. Jase is on one side of me and Ryan stands opposite. Leaning forward, resting my elbows on the bookcase, Ryan lowers himself next to me, and I instantly feel Jase's protective hand on my back.

I shift my eyes slightly to look at Ryan, and he is watching the band. I know I shouldn't be looking at him like this, but I find it intriguing that he doesn't make me feel scared. He turns his head and catches me staring at him. Cringing inside, I try and play it off by giving him a slight grin and refocusing my attention back to the band. When they announce their last song for the evening, Jase leans into my ear and whispers, “Mark and I will be right back.”

Looking at him curiously, I ask, “Where are you going?”

“Don’t worry about it. We’ll be back in a second.” He kisses me on the temple, and gives me a reassuring nod before he turns and walks off with Mark.

Standing here alone, next to Ryan, we listen to The xx play an extended version of ‘Intro.’ The languid plucks of the guitar are soon interlaced with the ever thumping of the bass drum. The song begins to intensify into a fusion of haunting and seductive sounds. I push back off the bookcase while Ryan remains leaning on his elbows. I watch him. I shouldn’t be, but I am. His hair is a rich dark brown that falls slightly over his ears. He has a strong, well-defined jaw and a muscular frame that is evident through his dark grey shirt. Looking back at me over his shoulder, a small lock of his hair falls over his forehead. *What am I doing?* I take a step back as he pushes himself off the bookcase and looks at me. Turning around quickly to walk away, I run smack into Mark’s chest.

Tripping over my own feet, he catches me and asks, “Whoa, everything okay?”

“I wanna go,” I say softly so that no one can hear me but him.

Clutching both of my arms, he looks back at Jase and gives him a nod. When Jase walks over he asks, “You ready to go?”

“Hey, man. It was good seeing ya. We’ll catch up later this week,” Mark says to Ryan.

I turn around as Ryan approaches Mark and they give each other a tight handshake as Mark slaps Ryan on the side of his shoulder. “Catch you later,” Ryan says before holding his hand out to me. “I’m glad I ran into you again,” he says.

Sliding my hand into his, I say with a slight hesitation, “Yeah, it was nice.”

As Jase and Ryan say their goodbyes, I walk out into the drizzly, cold night and take a deep breath. Jase walks out, hands me my coat, and I shrug it on before getting into the car.

“What was that all about?” Jase asks me.

Leaning my head against the window, I quip, “You tell me. Where the hell did you two run off to?”

Turning around in his seat, he adds, “Just thought you two should talk without Mark and I around.”

“Why?”

“Just got that feeling. You two kept staring at each other with that look.”

Sitting up, I ask, “And what look would that be?”

“Candace, the guy is hot. You know what look he’s talking about,” Mark adds as he drives back to my house.

“Doesn’t matter,” I say as I lie back against the seat.

“What do you mean it doesn’t matter?” Jase asks.

I shake my head and stare out the rain-covered window.

“Candace?”

“It just doesn’t matter, Jase. It’s wrong.”

“It’s not wrong for you to find someone attractive.”

Turning my head to look at him, I say, “Yes, it is.”

I feel the car slow down and can see that Mark is pulling into a random parking lot. He turns the car off, steps out, and opens my door. Sliding in next to me, he shuts the door behind him. “Stop punishing yourself.”

I open my mouth to speak, but he immediately cuts me off and repeats slowly, “Stop punishing yourself.”

Facing me, Jase adds, “Nobody says that you can’t enjoy life. You can. You should. You just won’t allow yourself.”

“How can I feel like that after what happened? It

feels wrong."

"It's not wrong," Mark says. "You need to let yourself feel happiness and not run away from every good feeling that comes over you."

"It doesn't feel right."

"Why?" Jase asks.

"Because...it makes me feel cheap—dirty." My stomach is in knots talking about this. I don't want to be talking about this. I never want to talk about this.

Mark places his hands on my shoulders and looks me straight in the eyes. "You aren't either of those things, not even close. What happened doesn't make you cheap or dirty or whatever else you're thinking. It happened, and you have been punishing yourself ever since."

"Candace," Jase adds, "He's right. You can't keep doing this to yourself. You can't keep taking this wound and ripping it further open beyond repair. You have to try and leave it be, and allow it to heal."

"I don't know," I say.

"I'm proud of you," Jase says. "I honestly didn't think you would come out with us tonight. Thought you might back out." He smiles at me, and I lean forward between the seats to hug him.

"I'm glad I came," I say as I sit back.

Mark takes my hand, kisses it, and says, "Think about what we said."

Nodding my head, I say, "Okay."

Mark hops out, gets back behind the wheel, and drives me home. When he pulls up to the front of my house, Jase asks, "You want us to stay over?"

"I'm fine, Jase. Thanks again, guys." I give them both a kiss and step out of the car. When I walk inside, Kimber is gone. I go to my room, strip off my clothes, throw on a pair of pajama pants and a cami, and take a sleeping pill before climbing into bed.

chapter thirteen

"I hate you!" Roxy shouts, a few octaves above normal, while she teasingly shoves my shoulder. "I love that band! How did you even get tickets?"

"Jase got the tickets from one of his friends," I say as I shrug my shoulders as if it was no big deal that I got to see The xx in a private concert last weekend.

"Man, I need to meet this *friend* so that I can score some tickets too."

Looking up at her while I'm refilling the coffee beans in the grinder, I say, "You have met him. Well, you've seen him."

"Who?"

Securing the burlap bag with the remaining beans, I tell her, "That guy that came in the other day, the one you said was *hot*."

Giving my shoulder another playful shove, she says, "You're kidding?!"

"Nope," I huff out as I carry the heavy bag into the back stockroom. When I walk back out, Roxy is standing there staring at me with her hands on her hips and an evil grin on her face. I roll my eyes when I walk past her and continue cleaning up before my shift ends in a few minutes. I can feel her stare when I finally turn around and snap, "What?"

"That's it?"

"Yes, that's it." I turn back around and continue wiping down the machines.

Roxy sidles up next to me, leaning her hip against the counter with her arms crossed in front of her. "Was he there?"

"Yes, Rox, he was there," I say as I continue to busy myself with cleaning.

"You're driving me crazy here. Talk to me, girl."

Turning around, I say matter-of-factly, "There is nothing to tell. We went out, ran into him at Spines, had a drink. There is no crazy story to tell."

I start untying my apron when I notice Roxy eying me with a strange look on her face. "Really? No story to tell," she says as she tilts her head toward the entrance.

I look up to see Ryan walking through the shop, heading to the counter. *What is he doing here?* Looking at Roxy, I shake my head at her as I make my way over to him.

"You're gonna get an ulcer," I jokingly say, even though I'm a ball of nerves on the inside.

He lets out a soft chuckle as he says, "I didn't come for coffee."

I look at him with slight confusion when he lifts his hand, which is holding my leopard scarf. The scarf I was wearing last weekend that I thought I'd lost.

"Oh," I say as I reach out and take it. "I thought I had lost this. Thank you."

"No, you left it on the table, but you rushed out so fast, I didn't have a chance to catch you."

Looking down, embarrassed about my sudden exit that night, I quietly say, "Sorry."

"No need to apologize."

With my apron still clutched in my one hand, I lay it on the counter and start backing away when he asks, "Are you taking a break?"

"Um, no. My shift is over."

"Perfect timing," he says with a grin. "Want to have a quick drink?"

Before I can decline, Roxy butts in and answers for me. "She'd love to."

"Actually, I..." I don't finished my sentence because I can't think of an excuse fast enough, and I am totally busted. Letting a slow breath out of my nose, I reluctantly agree. "Sure. Let me go grab my bag."

When I walk into the back room to get my purse, I'm feeling very uneasy. Heading back out, Ryan is sitting down at one of the tables by the front window. I walk over and sit down. He already has a drink for me, and as I eye it he says, "Your co-worker said you like hot tea."

Sitting down in front of him, I say, "Oh, thanks. She's actually my boss. Roxy." I sound like an idiot with my voice slightly trembling. I pick up the tea and take a long drink, focusing on the hot, floral infused liquid as it slowly heats my chest. The rain is pouring down outside, and I watch the raindrops as they trickle and twitch down the foggy glass window.

"Did Mark tell you we are heading down to Mount Rainier on Saturday?"

I look up at him and reply, "Yeah, Jase mentioned something like that to me."

"You should come with us."

The nerves I thought I had just gotten under control return. Why is he inviting me to go hiking with him?

"I don't know," I say. "I have a lot of studying I need to get done." This is my go-to excuse when I want to back out of something. But I notice him staring at me with a look that screams *I know you're lying.*

"Well, if you change your mind, we are heading out in the morning around eight."

Nodding my head, I take another sip of my tea.

"How did you know I would be here today?" I ask.

He grins at me before replying, "I didn't. I just thought I would stop by, and if you weren't here, I was just going to leave your scarf with whomever was working."

"I didn't mean for that to come out rude," I apologize.

"It didn't."

As we sit there in awkward silence sipping our hot drinks, he finally speaks and asks, "So, what are your plans for the rest of the day?"

"I have class in a couple hours, then I go to studio until five o'clock."

"Studio?"

"It's dance class," I explain.

Nodding his head, he asks, "You do that every day?"

"Yep. Two hours a day except for Tuesdays and Thursdays, which are three hours. But I tend to go in on the weekends as well for extra practice."

"That's a lot. When do you have time for anything else?"

Pressing my lips together and shaking my head, I say, "I don't"

"That bother you?"

"No...Why?" I ask.

"I don't know. When do you ever get down time?"

Down time isn't an option for me. The more occupied my time is, the less my mind tends to drift. "I don't. But I love dance, so I consider that my down time. It relaxes me."

Ryan continues to ask questions about dance and school as time begins to pass gently by. When I finish my tea, he notices and offers to get me another. I decline, knowing that I need to head home and clean up before going back to campus. He walks me out to where my car is parked and reminds me to think about the hiking trip the guys have planned. I tell him I will before getting into my car.

Storming out of the double doors of the studio, I head straight to my car, slide in, and slam the door shut. Frustrated, I grab the steering wheel and lay my head against my hands. My heart pounds fast, and I can still here the echoing of Ms. Emerson's hasty remarks in my head: *Get it together, Candace! Where is your head at?* CLAP! CLAP! *Feel it! Come on!*

I am so humiliated. I have never been yelled at like that in class before, but I feel like what she is asking for is outside of my control. My feet are flawless, I have no doubts about that, but I know what she's wanting, and I just can't give it to her. Inside that studio is the one place, the only place, where my head is free—where I am free. I don't want to lose that, lose the escape, the freedom, the nothingness.

She hammered me for nearly the entire two hours. I kept my eyes focused, but I could hear the sneers from a few of the other girls.

As I'm driving home, my phone rings from inside my dance bag. Digging through it, I grab my cell and look at the screen that reads: MOM CALLING. *Ugh!* I decline the call and let it go to voicemail then toss it back into my bag. That woman is the last person I want to talk to right now. Who am I kidding? She is the last person I want to talk to most of the time.

I haven't spoken with either one of my parents in over a month. Thanksgiving is a week away, and I'm certain that's why she's calling me. I'm dreading having to go home and spend time with them. For now, I'll just avoid her, because with the mood I'm in, there will be no way to avoid a fight with her.

Pulling up to my house, I see Kimber's car and Seth's jeep parked out front. I was hoping she wouldn't be here. I really just want to be alone right now instead of having another awkward and tense interaction with the girl who used to be my best friend—who I wish still was.

When I walk through the door, the house is quiet, and I assume they are in Kimber's room. I walk back to my room and begin powdering my pointes. I hang them up in my closet to air-dry before hopping into the shower.

As I am rinsing the last of the shampoo out of my hair, I hear the sounds that are becoming all too familiar from Kimber's room. "Are you kidding me?" I mumble in frustration. All I want is some peace and quiet to ease the stress I'm feeling.

Shutting off the water, I step out of the shower and quickly dry myself off. I throw on some underwear and a white tank top then walk into my closet to grab my black velour sport pants and matching zip-up hoodie. Standing in front of my mirror at my dresser, I shake out as much water as I can from my hair before throwing it up into a messy, loose bun on top of my head. I quickly apply some powder and swipe on my lip-gloss before sliding into my Uggs.

Hearing Kimber and Seth is making my skin crawl at this point, so I throw my sleeping pills in my purse, grab my keys, and get the hell out. I figure I can just spend the evening at Jase's apartment. I really need a little space to clear my head and relax.

When I arrive at Jase's and let myself in, I'm shocked to see Ryan sitting on his couch. I stop in my tracks and stare, unsure of what to say. *What is he doing here?*

"Hey, is everything all right?" I hear Jase ask from the kitchen.

I turn my head away from Ryan and focus on Jase. Taking a few steps further into the apartment, I respond,

"Umm, yeah...I mean no." I'm stumbling over my words like an idiot, but I am so caught off guard that Ryan is here. And then realizing that it wasn't but a few minutes ago I was in the shower and here I stand with my wet hair that's tied up in a hair tie is making my head swirl.

Jase walks around the bar with a couple bottles of beer and heads over to the couch to hand one to Ryan. "What's that mean?" he asks.

"Nothing, never mind." I let out a deep sigh and walk over to take a seat in the oversized chair that is next to the couch. I flop down and lean my head back. "I didn't know you would have company, or I would have called or something."

Laughing, Jase says, "Candace, I gave you a key so you wouldn't have to call. You can come over whenever."

"You okay?" Ryan asks me.

I turn my head to look at him, then back at Jase, whom I know is wondering the same thing. "I don't want to talk about it," I say as I shift my eyes to the TV, which is playing SportsCenter. "Where's Mark?" I ask as I continue to zone out on the football highlights that are currently playing.

"He's finishing up rehearsals with the band. He should be here shortly, then we are heading out to Malone's to shoot some pool and chill," Jase says. His cell begins to ring and when he answers it, he grabs his jacket and excuses himself to the balcony.

"So, I take it the rest of your day didn't go well?" Ryan asks.

Looking over at him, I say, "Not exactly."

Even though I was extremely uncomfortable the other night at Spines, I'm feeling a little more at ease after hanging out with him this afternoon at work.

"Don't want to talk about it?"

I shake my head and turn my attention back to the TV

when Jase walks back in.

"Who was that?" I ask

"Just Mark. He's heading over now."

"Hey, did you get a chance to think about Saturday?" Ryan asks. When I look over at him he is taking a sip of his beer.

"Saturday?" Jase questions.

"Yeah, I asked her to come with us."

I wish he wouldn't have brought this up because I know Jase will hound me until I say yes. He is on a mission to get me out more.

"Oh yeah? You coming?" Jase asks me.

Eying him, I say, "I have a lot of studying to do before finals."

"Please, we both know you are way ahead in all your classes," Jase says. "You should come. We are hiking up to the Tolmie Peak Lookout."

Not wanting to argue with Jase in front of Ryan and make him wonder why I am so anti-social, I appease him with a simple, "Fine."

When I look up at Jase, he has a big grin across his face, and I shake my head at him. Honestly, I don't really feel uneasy about going hiking. It's November, so there more than likely won't be too many people there, and it's not that often that I go to Mount Rainier. I went over the summer to go running a few times. I have never hiked to this particular lookout, but I have heard that the peak has an amazing view of the Sound.

I hear my phone ring from my purse that is sitting on the floor next to me. Reaching down, I pick it up and see that it's my mother again. I hit decline as I did when she called earlier and toss it back in my purse.

When I look up at Jase, he is giving me a questioning look, so I go ahead and answer his unspoken curiosity.

"My mother."

By the time Mark arrives, I am ready for sleep. Having been at work this morning by six, I'm exhausted. As the guys get ready to leave, I ask Mark, "Do you mind if I stay here tonight?" I feel like I need to ask Mark most of the time instead of Jase because Jase will never tell me no.

"Of course not. I was going to go back home anyway. Thursdays are early days for me, so it's better if I'm not here," he explains.

As I nod my head, he gives me a long hug, knowing that something must be bothering me or I'd just go back to my house. When we pull apart, I catch a glimpse of Ryan over his shoulder, and he is watching me with a curious look on his face. He's probably wondering why I have a key to Jase's place and why I'm sleeping here tonight. I'm sure it must look weird to him, but for me, this is my normal.

chapter fourteen

Throwing an extra set of clothes into my bag, along with a few toiletries, I go to my closet and grab my black hiking boots. It's another chilly and misty grey day, but that is nothing new for this time of year, and it doesn't stop people from being outdoors either. The plan is to hit a few of the trails before hiking up to Tolmie Peak. Afterwards, we are going to hang out at Mark's house for pizza and beer.

Today feels a little strange for me. I haven't gone out like this since this past summer. But, it also feels nice, and it is keeping my mind busy and focused. I've been warming up to Ryan as well. He blends nicely with Jase, Mark, and I. Last night, Ryan ended up hanging out with us over at Jase's. We just laid low and watched a series of 'Ridiculousness' reruns on MTV. It felt nice to laugh like that. I honestly can't remember the last time I laughed so much. Last night, even if it was just for a moment, I felt a little normal—and it felt good.

When I pull into Mark's driveway, all three guys are tossing their shoes and backpacks into the back of Mark's white Range Rover. I grab my bags, step out of the car, and lock it before walking over to Mark.

"Hey, Candace," he says as he pulls me in for a hug.

"Hey, here's my backpack," I say, and I hand it to him to put in the car. Holding up my other bag, which has an extra set of clothes and toiletries, I say, "I'm just going to run this inside and leave it in your room."

"Sounds good."

Saying 'hi' to Jase and Ryan, I walk inside the house to drop my bag in Mark's room so that I can shower and change when we get back. When I make my way into the kitchen, I run into Ryan.

"Hey," I say as he is pulling out several bottles of water. "Can you grab me one of those?"

"Yeah, here you go," he says as he walks over and hands me one.

"Thanks."

"No problem. So, are you ready?"

"Yep. I haven't been out to Rainier since this past summer," I say and then I open my water and take a sip.

"I didn't know you liked to hike."

"I like most things athletic, although the majority of that is inside the confines of the ballet studio. I mainly just run the trails there, but I've been hiking a few times as well."

Picking up the waters, he says, "You're a runner too? I'm impressed," while walking towards the door. I walk over and open the door for him when he says, "You should come running with Mark and I sometime. We've been going early Tuesday mornings before hitting the gym."

We walk out, and Ryan tosses the waters into the car. I still haven't responded when he questions, "What do you think?"

I look down before looking back at him. "I haven't been out running in a while. I'd probably just slow you guys down. It was always something I did alone anyway."

Jase comes up to me, puts his arm around my shoulder, and asks, “What do you do alone? Besides everything.”

I elbow him gently in the ribs and smile as I walk around the car and hop in the back seat. “I’m ready to go,” I teasingly announce before closing the door and putting on my seatbelt.

Ryan gets in the front with Mark, and Jase slides in next to me. For most of the two-hour drive, the guys talk amongst themselves as I doze in and out of sleep. I have been spending a lot of overtime in the studio, and last night I was there pretty late, so I didn’t get much rest.

When my body suddenly jerks out of a restless sleep, and I gasp in a loud breath, all eyes turn to me, but Ryan’s are the only ones filled with questions. Mark turns around and starts talking to Ryan to take the attention off of me while Jase undoes his seatbelt and slides up next to me, wrapping his arm around my neck. Resting my head on his shoulder, he whispers in my ear, “You okay?”

I nod my head, close my eyes, and concentrate on my breathing. I feel embarrassed, and attempt to force out the thoughts that are creeping through my head. I just want to have fun today. I need to have fun today. For the remainder of the drive, I sit in the comfort of Jase’s arms.

When we get to the turnoff, we have to drive about twenty minutes on a pot-holed gravel road to get to the Wonderland Trail that will lead us to Tolmie Peak. When we finally arrive and park the car, Mark opens the hatch, and I sit on the bumper while I tie up my hiking boots. It is lightly raining, and I pop the hood on my raincoat up and over my head. This time of year, the lower trails can become extremely muddy with the increase in rain. Ryan hands me an extra bottle of water to throw into my backpack before I sling it onto my back and wait for everyone else.

Once the guys are ready, we start making our way over

to the trailhead. Mark told me the hike should be around four hours. The terrain isn't too difficult to navigate as we start on the trail. We are all keeping a pretty decent pace and Mark is talking about the last show they played at Ryan's bar. I have never been to Blur. Jase has invited me a few times to go watch the band play, but has never pushed too hard.

A couple hours into our hike, the clouds open and it begins to rain. As we continue to trek on, the ground becomes marshy beneath our feet. I start to fall behind a little, but I yell to Jase to keep going and I'll catch up. I pull the hood on my jacket further over my head, so I don't realize that Ryan has stayed back until I almost pass him. Stopping, I look up at him, and he doesn't have his hood over his head. Rain is dripping off the ends of his hair, and it reminds me of the first night he came into the coffee shop with his rain soaked hair.

"You don't have to hang back. You can hike on ahead."

"Don't worry about it," he says as we continue to make out way through the trail. "I would hate for you to fall and hurt yourself and nobody be around."

Turning to look at him, I give him a grin and say, "Thanks."

"This shit's freezing."

I start laughing and agree with him. The rain is really cold.

After about a half hour, the rain finally lets up, and at this point, I am soaked from head to toe. I stop for a moment, take the hair tie that is around my wrist, and pull up my stringy wet hair on top of my head. Ryan walks closer to me. Laughing, he swipes his hand across my cheek, and the gesture makes me a little uncomfortable, until I see the brown mud on his fingers, and I laugh with him.

"You are covered in this shit," he chuckles, and all I can do is shrug my shoulders. You can't expect to not get dirty when you are hiking in the rain.

"Yeah, well, you're covered in it too," I say as we keep moving forward.

We manage to catch up with Jase and Mark near the incline to the peak. It's a mile hike up, and there is a light dusting of snow throughout the trek. When we reach the top, I climb the stairs to the lookout house and take in the view. I look out at the Sound and just stare. It's a breathtaking view. I walk back around the lookout, sit on the stairs, and grab a protein bar out of my backpack. Jase sits down behind me and kisses the top of my head. I look down to Mark and Ryan who are standing down below and catch Ryan looking up at us before he walks around to the other side of the lookout.

"Having fun?"

Turning my head to look at Jase, I say, "I actually am."

"Good." He wraps his arms around my shoulders, and I lean back into him as I eat my snack and rest.

"We should start heading back," he says after ten minutes or so.

"Okay."

We walk back down the stairs and find the other two.

"You guys ready to head back?" Jase asks them.

Everyone agrees, and we start the trek back down after we have all taken in the spectacular views. The walk down the peak is a slippery one from all the rain earlier. It isn't long before my feet slide out from underneath me, and I fall back into the mud.

"Crap!"

Reaching out both of his hands, I grab tightly onto Ryan's wrists as he pulls me out of the soggy mud.

"You're a complete mess."

"Yeah, I know," I say with a muddy face and now a muddy ass. I feel absolutely disgusting.

I keep ahold of Ryan's arm until we finally reach the

bottom and let go. Jase and Mark are several steps in front of us, apparently lost in their own conversation, and it's not long before Ryan and I start talking about his job.

"So, how did you come about owning a bar?" I ask.

"Just kind of fell into it. When I graduated college, the economy was starting to decline, and I couldn't find a job. So, when I found out that the previous owner of that bar was about to shut the place down, I worked out a deal with him and was able to do a slow buyout."

"You went to U-Dub?"

"Yeah, I graduated back in 2007."

"So, that makes you...?"

Laughing at me, he says, "Twenty-eight."

"What did you study?"

"Business Finance. So, it wasn't too far out of reach that I would come to own my own business."

"You enjoy it?"

"I do. When I did the buyout, I changed the whole place out and created a new vibe for it. It wasn't before long that the business was taking off quicker than I expected. At this point, the staff pretty much runs the place, and I have a trustworthy manager, so my schedule is very flexible."

"Sounds like the perfect job."

"You ever been there?"

Looking over at him and smiling, I say, "No. I don't really ever go out." I shake my head and continue, "I'm sort of a work-a-holic. Jase is always nagging me about that."

"Well, you should stop by sometime."

"Yeah. Maybe."

He laughs and says, "You're full of shit, aren't you?"

"Yeah. Maybe," I say, chuckling back at him.

Still laughing, he shakes his head at me as we continue the hike back.

When we finally reach the car, all of us are a mess, wet

and covered in mud. I grab one of the towels that is in the back of the Range Rover and attempt to clean myself off, but at this point, most of the mud has dried and is now a hard, crusty matting on my clothes and face. Not wanting to drive all the back in these clothes, I ask Jase if he brought any extra. He tells me that Mark keeps a bag full of clean clothes in the back for when he goes to the gym. I reach in, grab his gym bag, and pull out a t-shirt and athletic pants, along with a dry pair of socks. I wouldn't think twice about changing in front of Jase, but I tell Mark and Ryan to go sit in the front so that I can change. Mark laughs at me, but gets in the car along with Ryan. I quickly strip out of my soggy clothes and Jase hands me the clean ones. Once I am good to go, I hop into the back seat and snuggle up tightly with Jase to try and warm up.

After everyone has showered and cleaned up, we all sit around the living room and tune into the Washington vs. Colorado football game. Mark throws a few logs of wood into the fireplace, and I go to get a bottle of wine from the kitchen. Mark and I have the same taste in wine, so we decide to share a bottle while the other two drink beer.

"What kind of pizza do you want, Candace?" Ryan hollers to me from the other room.

While I am opening the wine I shout back, "I don't care. I'll eat anything at this point."

As I walk back in with the wine and two glasses, Ryan is on his cell ordering dinner, and Jase is already finishing his first beer and watching the pre-game show on TV. We sit around, talking about our day and begin planning our next hike and the other trails we want to explore.

After a couple hours and way too much pizza, I lie back

on the couch and laugh at Jase who has had a few too many beers and is screaming at the TV at a penalty call. Enjoying the entertainment of his theatrics, I hear my phone ring from the kitchen. Before I can get off the couch, Jase runs in and answers it with an obnoxious slur. When I stand up, he is walking my way, holding the phone out and mouthing 'I'm sorry' to me.

"Who is it?" I whisper as I take the phone from his hands, and he quietly says, "Your mother."

I walk out to the back patio when I finally say, "Hi, Mom."

"Jesus, Candace! I have been trying to get ahold of you for over a week. Why haven't you returned any of my calls?"

"Sorry, I've been busy and I guess a little distracted lately." Truth is, I have been purposely avoiding her calls. Thanksgiving is this Thursday, and she loves putting on a show at the country club. God knows the woman would never lift a finger in the kitchen, so for my whole life, every holiday dinner has been at the club.

"Well, your father and I were wondering when you were coming home?"

"Umm...I have a lot of schoolwork to get done, so I won't have much time," I lie. "What time are the reservations for?"

"That's it? You are just going to come for dinner? We haven't seen you in three months!"

Why does she do this? She always wants me to call her and visit her, but when I do, all she does is criticize me. "Mom, I'm really pressed for time, plus I am not sure when I have to work." Another lie.

"Well, that's just great! I had invited the Anderson's over for brunch Saturday morning. Now, I will have to rudely cancel."

My heart skips a beat when I question loudly, "Why

would you do that, Mother?"

"What do you mean?"

"Mom! I haven't spoken with Jack in months." God, I hate saying his name. My stomach is knotting up just talking about this. But what the hell is she thinking? Why would she invite his parents over and just assume I was involved with that asshole?

"Well, what happened?"

"Nothing, Mom. We just didn't have anything in common."

"So, you ruin yet another possible relationship. What did you say to him?"

"Of course this is my fault, right?" I yell at her. "You are unbelievable, Mother!"

"I just have to wonder why, at the age of twenty-two, you have yet to meet anyone." Her voice is like ice to me, and I lose it.

"Why does it matter? Why do you even care? I wish you would show as much interest in me as you do my non-existent dating life." My voice is harsh and loud.

"Candace. Please. This is so childish of you to always yell at me when you don't like what I have to say. I'm just concerned, that's all."

"Well, Jack's a fucking asshole! I'll see you Wednesday, Mother," I spit out then hang up before I give her a chance to respond. God, she drives me absolutely crazy.

Shoving the phone in my pocket, I sit down on one of the chairs and stare up at the black sky. I take a moment to quell the tears that are threatening and breathe. I need to collect myself before going back inside. When I do get up and turn back to the house, I see Ryan watching me through the double French doors. He opens one of the doors and asks, "You okay?"

Not wanting to let this ruin my evening, I brush it off

and laugh. "My mother's lost her mind, that's all."

"Wanna talk about it?" he asks when I walk past him.

Turning around to face him, I casually say, "Nothing to really talk about." Then I walk back into the living room and lie back down on the couch next to Jase.

"What did she want?" he asks.

"She wanted to know when I would be home for Thanksgiving."

"When are you going to leave?" Mark asks.

I watch Ryan walk back into the room and take a seat on the fireplace stoop. Looking back over at Mark, I say, "I told her I would be there Wednesday night. I'll probably leave Saturday morning." Turning my head to Jase, I ask, "When are you guys heading out?"

"Our flight leaves around noon on Tuesday," he says. Mark is taking Jase home with him to meet his parents in Ohio. Jase has been nervous about meeting Mark's parents, but I know it'll be fine. From what Mark has told us, his family is more than accepting of his sexuality. I am so happy that Mark and Jase were able to work everything out between them because they are so happy together.

"When do you guys get back?"

"Late Sunday afternoon."

I roll onto my side and ask Ryan what his plans are for Thanksgiving.

"I'm going to go spend a few days with my family down in Cannon Beach in Oregon. My aunts and uncles always come to my mother's house with my cousins for a big dinner."

"Will you be there for the weekend?" I ask.

"Nah, I'll come back home that night. My mom and her sisters spend the day plotting for Black Friday, so I always come back home and just lay low."

"Sounds like you have a big family," Jase says.

“Yeah, man, five cousins and between them they have seven little kids. I love them, but shit they’re loud,” he says, laughing.

“Must be nice though. I’m an only child with no cousins. Small family,” I say.

I wish I knew what it was like to have a family like that. I had always wished I had a brother or sister growing up. I always felt lonely. My father worked constantly and my mother was never around. Always too busy attending all of her charity functions to pay attention to me. I know now that I will never have that close family that I had always dreamed of.

chapter fifteen

I grab my last pair of shoes to put in my suitcase before driving to my parents for Thanksgiving. Kimber left Monday to go stay with her parents who live in Redmond, and Jase and Mark left Tuesday to fly to Mark's parent's house in Ohio. Everyone seemed excited for the break before they left while I have been dreading it.

I try to avoid my parents for the most part. Growing up with them wasn't easy. My mother is a social bee and is concerned more about herself and her family's image than happiness. She is a very stern and critical woman, and to please her is nearly impossible. Everything in her world has to be simply perfect so that others will envy her.

My father, being an orthopedic surgeon, was never around much. Both of my parents are influential and well-respected. But they were always so busy that I was left alone for the most part. When my mother was around, all we ever seemed to do was fight. We still do. It has always bothered her that I never participated much in her endeavors. She is involved in many charities, fundraisers, and other social events around town. I know she dreams of a daughter that would follow in her footsteps among her friends and be more concerned about my, as she puts it, 'social standing in the community.'

So now I am making the short twenty-minute drive to

Shoreline to spend Thanksgiving with my parents. I plan to leave Saturday morning so that I can have a little down time before classes start back up on Monday.

As I enter through the gates of The Highlands, I make the slow winding drive that leads to the house I grew up in. Pulling up the drive to the two-story coastal house that is reminiscent of a Hampton beach house, I park, grab my suitcase, and walk up to the front door.

When I walk in, I can hear my mother talking on the phone, and I follow her voice to the kitchen to let her know I'm here. She stands there, leaning her hip against the center granite island, in her houndstooth pencil skirt, cashmere sweater, and black pumps. She acknowledges me with a slight nod before picking up her glass of wine and walking to the living room to continue her conversation.

I drag my suitcase to my bedroom, flop my purse onto the floor, and lie down on my bed. I turn my head to look through the French doors that look out over the Sound. I have always loved this view, even as a little girl. I used to spend hours sitting up here and staring out this very window wondering what my life would turn out like.

"Candace, dear," my mother calls from downstairs, and I am snapped out of my reverie.

Making my way downstairs, I meet her in the kitchen as she is refilling her glass of wine.

"Candace, there you are. How was your drive?"

"Not too bad," I say as I take a seat at the kitchen table.

"Did your friends already leave to go home?"

"Kimber did. Jase is actually spending Thanksgiving with his boyfriend's family."

"Candace, you know how I feel about that boy," she says in her judgmental tone.

Looking at her, not wanting to begin arguing with her ten minutes into my visit, I brush it off. "Yes, Mother."

"Well, then, your father got called into the hospital, so it's just us for the afternoon. I thought we could go over to Bellevue and do a little shopping."

"Yeah, that sounds great, Mom," I say as I stand up and walk to the fridge to grab a bottle of water. If there is one thing my mother is good at, it's shopping.

Standing in front of the three-way mirror in the fitting room, I slip on a beautiful lace and tweed Karen Millen shift dress. I smooth down the pencil skirt with my hands and admire the detailing.

"How does the dress fit, darling?" my mother asks from outside my fitting room.

"It's perfect." The one thing, possibly the only thing, my mother and I have in common is our love for fashion. I have always admired my mother's elegance and flair, and thankfully, it has always been something we have agreed upon.

My mother pulls back the heavy curtain to my dressing room, holding a pair of black platform pumps. Handing them to me, she says, "Here, try these on."

I slide on the shoes and turn to her to see her approval of my outfit.

"Stunning," she says and then turns to walk back out into the store.

I carry the outfit, along with a few tops and several pairs of pants, to the register and set everything on top of my mother's selections. As the sales clerk begins to ring up our items, my mother asks, "So, did you hear about Olivia's engagement?"

Keeping my eyes focused on our clothes, I respond, "No, I didn't hear."

“Yes, to William Lewis. He just partnered with his father’s law firm. And she is heading up the new division for the Children’s Foundation.”

I am trying hard to keep myself in check. I know exactly what my mother is doing, but I am determined to let it go. I know my mother wishes I were more like the Olivias of the world.

“That’s great,” I say as I grab our bags and start heading toward the exit.

“Before we leave, let’s go to Neiman’s for a little while. Maybe we can indulge in a glass of wine at Mariposa as well.”

“Sounds great, Mom.” I could really use a glass to help with the nerves that she is beginning to pinch.

While shopping through the racks, my mother continues, “I spoke with Sheila the other day, and she told me that her daughter was accepted into Columbia’s graduate program for Museum Anthropology.”

“Mom,” I say as I eye her over the rack of clothes.

Shrugging her shoulders as if she is clueless, she says, “What, dear?”

I tilt my head to the side and give her a knowing smirk.

“Fiiine,” she surrenders.

We finish up, purchasing more clothing than necessary, and go find a seat at Mariposa. Aiming to keep the focus off of me, I ask her about how the planning is coming along for the annual Christmas party at the Seattle Golf and Country Club that she heads every year. She begins to ramble on and on about it for the next hour before we decide to drive home.

“Bunny!” my dad exclaims as I walk into the house. He has called me ‘Bunny’ for as long as I can remember. When he pulls me in for a hug, I inhale his familiar scent. Since I was a little girl, he has always worn the same clean-scented cologne. I oddly find comfort in that smell. Although my father and I are far from having a close relationship, we never fight like my mother and I. Even though my father won't go against what my mother says and will always make excuses for her, I think that on some level, he might actually understand me.

"Hi, Dad," I say with my arms wrapped around him.

When he pulls away, he takes the bags from my hands, carries them into the kitchen, and sets them on the center island. He turns to kiss my mother on her cheek and says, "So, I see you ladies had fun spending my money today."

My mother laughs at him, and retorts, "Lots of fun, honey."

"Well, I am sorry that I had to work so late. We had a few emergency cases come in, but I have all of tomorrow off to spend with you," he says as he walks up to me and kisses me on my forehead. "Come on. Let's go have a drink before heading out to dinner." He takes my hand and leads me to the living room.

We all sit down, and I instantly become invisible as my parents begin to talk about anything and everything concerning them. I sip on my wine and tune them out as I pull out my cell and text Jase.

How's your trip so far?

I only have to wait a minute before he responds.

Good. Mark's family is oddly great!

LOL! What's that like? :)
Take it you're not having a good time.

It actually hasn't been too bad. Went shopping with mom, all the while bragging about how great her friend's children are doing. As if I'm slumming it at UW.

Sorry. Just a couple more days.

I really miss you. I'm so happy for you though!

Thanks. I miss you too. Text if you need me.

"Well Bunny, are you ready to go get something to eat?" my dad asks me.

Looking up at him, I grin and say, "Yeah, let me go freshen up really fast."

I quickly shoot Jase one last text before heading up to my room.

I will. Love you!

Love you too.

Dinner last night was surprisingly pleasant, although my parents continued to talk all throughout dinner as though I wasn't even sitting there. I have learned, with them, that sometimes it is better to be invisible than not.

I am finishing getting ready for our four o'clock reservation at the club. I have been keeping to myself most of the day with a run first thing this morning and then studying in my room. No one has said anything about my avoidance, but that's nothing new.

Wearing the dress dress that I got yesterday while

shopping with my mother, I slide on the black pumps and put in a pair of pearl earrings. I take one last look in the mirror before grabbing my wool coat and going downstairs.

My parents are sitting in the library having a drink when I walk in.

"Don't you look lovely."

"Thanks, Dad," I say as I stand in the doorway. "It's almost time to go. You ready?"

"Yes," my father says. He stands up and takes my mother's hand before helping her up as well.

When my mother walks towards me, she doesn't say a word, and I wonder what's got her strung so tight. I shake it off and follow my parents out to the drive.

"Oh, hey. Do you mind if we take separate cars? I was thinking about visiting Katy after we leave the club. I haven't seen her since summer."

"Of course, darling," my father says as he opens the car door for my mother.

"Great." I walk over to my car and hop in. Katy and I grew up together and we try to see each other when we are both home from college on breaks.

When I pull up to the prestigious Seattle Golf and Country Club, I am greeted by one of the valets. He opens my door and helps me out of the car where I am rejoined with my parents. Walking in, I plaster on a smile as people begin to say hello to my parents and myself. The faces never change, only the occasions.

When we are seated at our table looking out over the immaculate greens, our waiter approaches, and I quickly order a glass of wine. Looking down at the menu card that is placed on the center of my place setting, I let out a sigh of relief that this year they are actually serving turkey instead of the dreadful duck they had last year. But of course, it's not your traditional turkey, not that I even know what that is since I have spent every holiday dinner here in this very room. They are serving a porcini-soy stuffed turkey with shallot-truffle gravy. Nothing can ever be simple.

When the waiter returns with our drinks, my father orders some hors d'oeuvres before our main course. My father lifts his glass and makes a quick toast before we clink and take our sips.

"So, Bunny, how is this school year going for you?"

"It's been really busy, but I am managing to maintain my four point GPA, which should make you proud."

I hear my mother softly chuckle as my dad says, "You know how important grades are to me, and it shows that you care. Of course I'm proud."

"Thanks, Dad."

My mother clears her throat, and I eye her when she says to my father, "She's a dance major, honey. How hard can it be to have a four point?"

Clearly she had one too many cocktails in the library back home, because she is being more bold than usual. I tell myself to let it go so that this doesn't wind up in an argument.

My father doesn't say anything when she continues, "Sorry if that came out rude, but have you given any thought as to what you will do after graduation this spring? Have you applied to any graduate schools yet?"

"Graduate schools?" I ask as I shift my look to my dad and shake my head feeling like this choice of conversation was premeditated.

"Yes, well, your mother and I were concerned about your next step."

"You know I have always planned on dancing. That has never changed."

In a much softer voice, my mother says, "We were assuming that you would be taking a more serious outlook on your future. I mean, we have allowed you these past four years, hoping you would grow out of this little ballerina dream of yours." She says this as if I'm a child with foolish dreams, like when a little girl says she wants to be a fairy princess when she grows up.

I take my time to respond when my father speaks up. "Your mother's right, dear. It's time we start making some serious decisions. Although I have been fine with letting you direct these past four years, it's time to get on track and get focused."

I look at these two people sitting in front of me. My parents. The two people that should know me the best, love me, support me, and encourage me. But they don't know me at all. My stomach twists at the realization that they have never known me. Deep down, I've known this all along, but I guess I've been fooling myself to believe that I was wrong about them. How can they be so oblivious to who I am?

"I thought you guys knew what I wanted. This was never something I have wavered on." I begin to feel my eyes sting, but I refuse to cry. Although I'm aware that they disapprove of my choice of major, I never really thought they would try to step in and change my dreams.

"You can't seriously think that you can make a respectable career out of dancing, do you?"

"Yes, Mom. I do." I snap back.

"Your mother and I just want to help you avoid having regrets."

"About the only thing I regret was believing that you two supported me," I whisper harshly. "How can you do this?"

"Honey, look at yourself. Your choice of friends is a little concerning, you don't participate in any extracurricular activities, you don't have a steady boyfriend, you never call us or visit when we live only a few miles away. I look around and see the girls you graduated high school with and they are either getting married, furthering their education, starting their careers, and I just have to wonder what went wrong?"

"Nothing went wrong!" I say a little louder than I should have. Lowering my voice, I continue, "Is it so hard for you to believe in me? To trust that I am making the best decisions for myself? And as far as my friends go, at least they understand me and love me anyway."

"Bunny, we do love you."

"No. You may think you do, but you just want me to be someone I'm not. I've never been that person. How can you not see that?"

"Candace, calm down."

"No, Mother. What did you expect? That you and Dad could just trap me here and I would willingly let you step in and take control of my future? That's not going to happen. Thank you for paying my way through college, but we're done."

"Your mother and I are not going to stop supporting you, Candace. That's not what we are saying. But this idea of yours...it's just not realistic—"

My father is cut short when my mother interrupts. "I can't deal with you anymore. I simply cannot figure you out and why you can't be more responsible. Do you know how embarrassing it is for me when people ask me what my daughter is studying in college? The looks I get when I tell them you're a dance major, knowing you have no intentions on going to grad school and finally getting a respectable degree. And your attitude is just very unbecoming lately—"

She stops talking when I stand up and throw my napkin down on the table. "What's unbecoming is *you*, Mother. You are nothing but a self-centered woman who never even put her education to use. You married rich and frolic with all the other housewives, and you justify your lifestyle with your charities, but I see right through you." I look over at my father and quickly apologize for my abrupt departure before turning my back to them and walking out of the dining room.

The tears begin to fall as I feel another part of myself breaking, a part that I have held onto so tightly with hope, hope that my parents, behind all their shit, really loved me. But I just realized that to them, I am nothing more than a tarnished accessory.

chapter sixteen

I feel lost, like I'm floating around and there is nothing to grab onto to ground me. Today did not go as I thought it would. Sure, I often argue with my mother, but today was more than another fight. Today was my realization, a culmination of everything, finally clear and right in front of my face, staring into my eyes.

After I walked out on my parents, I drove back to the house and grabbed all of my belongings. There's nothing left for me to say, and there's nothing they could say to dull the pain that's shooting through my chest. I finally see that I'm a failure in my mother's eyes and a disappointment in my father's. So, I just left.

Pulling up to my empty house, I sit in my car for a little while and listen to the rain beating against my car. I close my eyes and lean my head back on the headrest. Everyone is probably having a great time, eating dinner, and visiting with family and friends, laughing. And here I am, alone, sitting in my car in the pouring rain. Pathetic.

I step out into the rain, pull my suitcase out of the trunk, and walk slowly to the front door not caring that I am getting soaked. It's dark and quiet when I walk inside. I drag myself to my room and head to the bathroom to shower.

When I am cleaned up and in my pajamas, I unpack my bag and hang up all of my new clothes. While I am sorting through my closet I hear my phone chime. I rush over to my bed to grab my cell when I see a text from a number I don't recognize. Swiping the screen to open the message, it reads:

Got your number from Mark. Wanted to see how your Thanksgiving went. –Ryan

I hold the phone in my hand, staring at the text for a minute before typing my response.

I think we managed to fall into the universal tradition of holiday drama. :)

That bad?

Kinda. Now I'm home with no food.

It takes a while for Ryan to text me back as I continue to hold my phone and stare at the screen. I have never considered Ryan one of my friends, more of just Mark or Jase's friend that I hang out with on occasion. But being able to sit here tonight, when I feel like crap, and text him, feels nice.

Sorry, saying bye to everyone. About to head home myself.

Did you have a good time with your family?

Yeah, I did. Ate way too much. Feel like I need to hibernate.

LOL. Drive safe. Is it pouring where you are?

Not too bad. Try and have a good night.

Thanks.

Before I set my phone down, I store his number into my contacts then hop up to go rummage through the kitchen. I find an old bag of popcorn. No one went grocery shopping since we all were supposed to be gone for the week, and now there is nothing to eat. I decide to heat up the bag, get comfortable on the couch, and turn on the TV.

The chiming of my phone wakes me. Squinting my eyes against the sunlight that is filtering in through the windows, I grab my phone to see that it's almost eight in the morning and that I have a missed text from Ryan. I shift and sit up on the couch, then read his text.

I am heading out for breakfast. Wanna join?

Grocery shopping is the last thing I want to do, so with no food in the house, I type my response.

Sure. Where?

The Dish Café. 9:00?

See you then.

I hop off the couch to take a quick shower and get ready. I wasn't planning on coming back home for a couple days, so it'll be nice to hang out since I have nothing to do otherwise.

After smearing on some lip-gloss, I slide on my leopard rain boots under my boot-cut jeans. I clasp on my watch and make my way out into the rain to get into my car.

When I walk into The Dish, a small dive café, I see Ryan is already sitting at one of the tables. He looks up from his menu as I approach the table.

"Hey," he says.

Shrugging off my coat and draping it over the back of the chair, I sit down and say, "Hi, thanks for inviting me. I literally have no food at the house."

"So, what did you wind up doing last night?"

"I ate an old bag of popcorn and passed out on the couch."

Laughing at me, he says, "That's pathetic."

"My thoughts exactly," I say grinning.

"I ordered you a hot tea."

Surprised that he remembered that I like hot tea, I say, "Oh, thanks."

I pick up the menu and quickly decide on the blueberry pancakes. When I set my menu down and look up, Ryan is staring at me. I know the obvious question that must be lingering in his head is what happened yesterday that made me come home early. Before giving him an opportunity to speak, I quickly turn the focus on him and ask, "So, how was your Thanksgiving?"

"It was good. We did the typical family thing like we do every year. Mom and her sisters being loud and gossipy, cooking all day. I hung out with the guys and watched football while the kids ran around screaming and playing. My head was pounding by the end of the night."

"That actually sounds nice."

"Yeah, it is. It's not too often that everyone can get together, so when it does happen, it's fun. Crazy, but fun," he says then picks up his cup of coffee to take a sip.

When the waiter stops at our table, I tell him I want the blueberry pancakes, and Ryan orders the heuvos verdes.

"So how many nieces and nephews do you have?" I ask as I sip my tea.

"Three nieces and four nephews all under the age of five. I'm not lying when I say it's loud and crazy!" I can see by the smile on his face that he loves the kids regardless of his comments.

"So, you're an only child?" Ryan asks.

"Yeah. I have a pretty small family. My grandparents on my father's side died when I was in high school, and I have never met my mother's parents or her sister. My father is an only child as well, so it's just the three of us."

"Quiet."

"Hmmm..." I don't even want to begin to explain my family's dysfunction, so I ask, "Is your mother out with the crazy Black Friday crowd today?"

"God, you have no idea. She and my aunts go bat-shit over the sales."

The waiter comes and drops off our food. I let out a pleased sigh when he sets down my pancakes that are bigger than the plate they are served on. I pick up my fork and knife and look up at Ryan as he says, "That's a shitload of food. You gonna be able to eat all that?"

Putting all manners aside, I cut a chunk of pancake that is obscenely large, shove it into my mouth, and chew while nodding my head at him in response. His smile broadens and he laughs out loud at my gesture.

We continue to chat as we indulge in our food. Ryan is a really easy person to talk to, even without the company of either Jase or Mark. We talk mostly about his family, and I do pretty well with keeping the focus off of myself. When I can't eat another bite, I lean back in my seat and groan with the discomfort of being entirely too full. I close my eyes when I hear Ryan laughing at me and saying, "I can't believe you ate all that. You sound like you're about to die."

"You have no idea."

"You gonna be able to walk, or will I have to carry you?"

I open my eyes to look at him, when I say, "Honestly, I really need to walk this off."

"Come on, let's get outta here." Ryan stands up, throws some cash on the table, and reaches his hand out to me. We walk out into the rain, and he nods his head towards a four-door black Rubicon.

"What?" I ask as I wonder what he's thinking.

"I know you don't have shit to do today, so come on." He walks over to the large jeep that sits high on its wheels and opens the passenger door. "Come on."

I stand where I am and ask, "Where are we going?"

"I'll figure that shit out when you get in."

I can't help but laugh at his apparent love for the word 'shit.' Walking over to him, he takes my hand again to help me into the seat and closes the door behind me. When he gets in, I shake my head at him as he begins to pull out of the parking lot. He turns onto the main road and asks, "You like Thirty Seconds to Mars?"

"Love them."

He smirks at me and questions, "Really?"

"Yeah, why?"

"You just don't strike me as the type of girl who would like that kind of music."

He turns on the stereo and 'Northern Lights' begins to play when I ask, "And what type of girl is that?"

"First impression I got was that you're really quiet. I thought you were just shy, but the more we hang out, it seems like not much embarrasses you. When I look at you, I see this tiny little ballerina, so I figure you sit around and listen to Mozart and shit."

We both start laughing and I say, "Mozart and *shit*? I'm not *that* refined, so you can relax. But I've never been loud and obnoxious, so yeah, I'm quiet."

He quickly glances my way and grins at me before returning his focus to the road.

"So, where are we going?"

"Someplace I haven't been to in a long time," he says then reaches over and turns up the music. I lean back in my seat, and we don't say anything else. We just sit and listen to music. After a few minutes, he turns into a waterfront parking lot, and I am surprised at where we have wound up.

"The aquarium? I haven't been here since I was a little girl."

"Me neither."

"Why are we here?"

"To have a little fun. Come on," he says as he gets out of the car.

When we go inside, the place is full of kids and their parents. I feel as if we are the only adults that are here by our own free will because this place is a madhouse. We walk up to a huge underwater viewing window that greets you as you walk in. I go right up to the window and press my hand against the cool glass and watch as the fish swim by. I remember coming here on a field trip once before when I was in the fifth or sixth grade. Even though I grew up here, I never really did many touristy things unless it was through school. My parents rarely ever took me out to explore the city.

I look down to my side at a little boy, maybe around six years old, who is looking up at me. He has his hand on the glass just as I do.

"Hi."

"You're pretty," he says, and I smile down at him and

respond, “Thank you. You’re not so bad yourself.”

His face lights up with a huge smile when Ryan walks up from behind us and asks the little boy, “Do you think I can steal your girlfriend away from you, buddy?”

The boy looks up at him and laughs. I can tell he is embarrassed as he nods his head.

I say ‘bye’ to my new friend and follow Ryan as he navigates us all the way to the touch pool. I hesitate as he starts to walk up to the exhibit.

“Come on.”

I slowly walk up to the edge of the tank.

“You scared?” he asks.

“Kind of, yeah”

Pulling me up to the tank next to him, he dips his hand into the water and starts touching the orange and purple starfish.

“They’re not going to attack you, Candace,” he says with a smile.

“No way.”

“We aren’t leaving until you touch something in this tank,” he teases me.

I look around, and kids that are elbows deep in the water surround us. Pushing up my sleeve, I very slowly start to move my hand toward the water, but when I see a hermit crab crawling in the tank where I was just about to put my hand, I jump back and squeal. Several of the kids start laughing at me, and Ryan joins in.

“Really nice!”

“What?” he says through his laughter.

“You’re making fun of me.”

“You’re such a baby. Come here,” he says and takes ahold of my hand to pull me back up to the tank. He shifts his hand to grip the top of mine and I shout, “Wait a second!” when my hand almost hits the water.

I don't look at him, but I hear him laughing at me.

"Relax."

He moves our hands down to the top of the water, and I nervously start to shift my weight between both of my feet when I feel the cold water on my fingertips. I know I am bouncing up and down like a scared little girl, but I don't care. I am terrified of these little sea creatures, especially the spiky sea urchins. The few kids that are near us are giggling at me, and when I finally feel the course, rough texture of the starfish on my fingers, one of the little boys claps and screams, "You did it!"

I look up at Ryan, and he is laughing along with me at the excitement of the little kid.

"See, not too scary," he says as he takes his hand off of mine and goes to grab some paper towels to dry our hands.

We take our time exploring the aquarium and all the exhibits while laughing and having a fun time. After an hour or so, we head downstairs to the underwater dome. We walk through the small tunnel that leads into the concrete and glass enclosure. The room is a little dark because of the weather outside; the sun isn't out today to filter its light through the water. We find an open seat along the perimeter of the dome that faces the windows and sit down. I lean back and prop my feet up on the concrete ledge and watch the schools of fish swim by. This day has turned out to be really fun. I never go out like this with my friends, and I'm starting to wonder why. Being here has kept my mind free from the way I left things with my parents yesterday.

"What are you thinking about?" Ryan asks.

"Nothing really."

He doesn't say anything; he just sits back with me and stares out into the water. When we finally decide to leave, we stop and grab a coffee at the café before heading out to the car. It's a pretty cold day, so I basically use the coffee to keep my hands warm as we walk to Ryan's jeep. Again, he helps me step up inside the car, and I set the coffee down in the cup holder and shove my hands into my coat pockets.

"Damn it's cold!" Ryan says as he hops into the car and starts it. He turns up the heat and begins to drive.

Feeling tired, I rest my head on the back of the seat and shut my eyes. Our drive is quiet and peaceful. When I finally hear the car turn off, I open my eyes and wonder why we are parked in front of a grocery store.

"What are we doing here?" I ask.

"You said you don't have any food at your house."

"Yeaaah?"

"Well, let's go buy some food so I don't have to hear about you eating stale popcorn again," he says as he laughs at me.

He gets a cart and starts following me around the store. Feeling a little uncomfortable and embarrassed, I throw in a couple bags of lettuce and some apples.

"No wonder you were starving at breakfast, you eat like a rabbit."

I roll my eyes at him and continue grabbing food for the week. Once I purchase everything and we load the car, I give him directions to my house. When he pulls into my driveway, I become nervous. I don't like the idea of having him inside my house. I try to calm myself down, but I can't help feeling scared. Hanging out with him all day has been fine, but we have been surrounded by people. I don't like the idea of being alone with him in my home. Knowing there isn't really much I can say to make him stay in the car, I hesitantly get out and grab a few bags as he grabs the rest, and I unlock the front door.

"This is a pretty nice house for a college student," he remarks.

"Yeah," is all I say in response as I lead him into the

kitchen. Trying to keep calm and not overreact, I silently and quickly put everything away. When everything is in its proper place, I immediately start walking to the front door, and thank goodness Ryan follows without questioning my strange behavior.

As we are driving back toward the café, I feel bad for my rude behavior, so I soften it by saying, "Thanks."

"For what?"

"Today. I had fun hanging out."

"You should say 'yes' when I ask you to go running with me tomorrow morning."

"Is that you asking me or telling me?"

He turns to look at me and smirks, not saying anything. Giggling at his invitation, I say, "Okay then."

"Okay then," he repeats.

By the time we arrive back at the café, the parking lot has emptied out and the rain is now falling hard. Ryan reaches over and turns down the music before saying, "I didn't want to say anything earlier, but I can't help but wonder about what made you come home yesterday."

Being worn out from our day, and feeling more at ease around him, I don't hesitate much when I decide to answer. "I got into a fight with my parents. Some pretty nasty things were said, so I just left."

He shifts in his seat to face me and I do the same, as he asks, "You guys fight a lot?"

"My whole life. My mother is a difficult woman to be around. She doesn't approve of the way I want to live."

"What do you mean?"

"My parents are more concerned about their social standing than my happiness. So, having a daughter who wants to be a dancer and is unengaged is not a good look for them."

"That's pretty shitty."

“I’m used to it,” I quietly say and lean the side of my head against the seat.

“No one should be used to that,” he says in a soft raspy tone. “They should be proud of you. I’ve only just met you, but you’re pretty great from what I know so far.”

His words are so sweet, but at the same time, a little unnerving. What’s strange is that I can say the same about him. I have only known Ryan for a short while, but our friendship feels very natural.

“I had always hoped that somewhere beneath their hard exterior that they would be proud of me, but after last night, I now know that they aren’t. My mother actually said she was embarrassed by me.”

Ryan lets out a long sigh and leans in closer to me. I look down to see him reaching over and sliding his hand over the top of mine. When I look up at him, he is staring at me with a hint of sadness in eyes.

My heart starts to race, and I feel myself wanting to close off. It hasn’t really bothered me when he’s taken my hand in the past, but something about being alone with him now and opening up to him is beginning to overwhelm me. I sit up, pull my hand away from his, and start fiddling with the door handle. I hear the click of the locks and thank him with a shaky voice for hanging out with me. I hesitantly turn around to look at him when I get out of his car and give him an apologetic smile because I don’t know what else to do, but I need space, and I need to be alone before I start to really freak out. I dig out my keys from my purse and unlock my car door. I take another quick glance at him before driving away, and he is sitting there watching me with a confused look on his face.

Embarrassed by my moment of weakness, I pull away and start driving home. Anxiety begins to course through my body, and I cry. How can I be so weak and show it in front of

Ryan? I'm disappointed in myself for not holding it together better.

When I pull up to my house, I just sit in my car and continue to wipe the tears that are falling down my cheeks. I slowly inhale a deep breath and am able to gain a little bit more control over my emotions.

Why am I acting like this? I had such a great day, and Ryan has become a good friend to me. I know I need to just pull myself together because he will be coming over tomorrow morning to run, and he will think I'm a total basket case if I call and cancel on him after what just happened. *God, Candace, get your shit together. You can do this.*

chapter seventeen

After I lace up my shoes, I go to the kitchen to get some water when I hear the doorbell ring.

"Hey, you ready?" Ryan asks when I open the door.

"Yeah. Here, hold these." I hand him the waters and turn to grab my hooded running jacket off the couch. Zipping it up, I say, "Okay, I'm ready. Let's go."

I take one of the bottles of water and tell Ryan to keep the other. Locking the door behind us, we start off with a brisk walk through the neighborhood.

"I figured we could run around campus and through some of the surrounding neighborhoods. How are you with distance?" he asks.

"I'm good for around six or seven miles, but it's pretty cold out today, so I'm not too sure how long I'll last."

The morning is bitterly cold, and the sun has just started to rise. The streets are empty aside from a few other runners we see as we start walking toward the UW campus. We begin with a light jog for about a half-mile before we break into our run. The streets are wet and soggy with dead leaves that are piled along the curbs and scattered over the lawns. A slight mist is in the air, which isn't anything new, and it looks like we are due to have another rainy day. It has rained every day this month, and the news keeps talking about the city hitting the big 'four-oh' this next week when the yearly rainfall will reach forty inches.

When we finally hit the campus, the sidewalks are completely empty, and it's abnormally quiet.

"Next weekend Mark's band is playing another gig at the bar. You should stop by," Ryan says as we run through the quad that is lined with now-bare cherry trees.

"Thanks, but I have to work."

"Would you come if you didn't have to work?"

"Probably not," I answer a bit more honestly than I intended. He knows I don't go out much, well, ever. Jase is always teasing me about being a hermit around Mark and Ryan, so it shouldn't be any surprise to Ryan when I say that.

"Have you ever heard Mark play?"

Jogging up a flight of stairs, my breath is short when I answer, "No."

"Never?"

"God, don't make it sound like I'm such a bad friend, Ryan," I say sarcastically.

Ryan starts to laugh. "No, I'm not. I'm just surprised, that's all."

When I look over at him, he meets my eyes, and I say, "No, you're not," with a grin.

"So, why don't you ever go out?"

"I'm normally busy with either school or work. I've never gone out too much. In fact, the past few weeks have actually been a big stretch for me. But, Jase has been on my case, so instead of butting heads with him, I haven't been putting up much of a fight."

"I should thank him then."

"Why's that?"

"Because I really like hanging out with you," he says openly, and I immediately feel my face heat despite the frigid weather. I don't respond as we continue to run. If I'm being honest with myself, I really like hanging out with Ryan as well. He's been a great distraction for me since the fight with my parents.

"So, what are your plans for today?" Ryan asks after a while.

"I need to study. I was also thinking about going up to the studio since nobody should be there and working on my solo."

"Your solo?"

"Yeah, graduating seniors have to choreograph a solo and audition for our final production at the end of the year." I say as we begin to veer off into another neighborhood. "It's kind of a huge thing."

"Why's that?"

"It's the one time that agencies come out to watch. So if you get one of the solos, then you have a good chance at having a job after you graduate."

"Will it be hard for you to get a solo?"

"I honestly don't know. My piece of music isn't the best, so I'm having a hard time feeling it, and my instructor is noticing, which is never good. Plus, all the girls are insanely competitive." I say with labored breath.

The cold air is starting to burn my lungs when Ryan asks, "You doing okay?"

"My lungs are burning."

Looking over at me with a slight smile, he says, "No more talking, just run."

I smile back and nod my head as we continue to weave through the quiet streets.

We are making our way back to the house when the rain starts to fall. The drops feel like tiny pieces of ice on my face as we pick up our pace to get back to my house. Ryan turns to look at me, and I see that he's laughing.

Barely able to breathe at this point, I manage to huff out, "What the hell's so funny?"

"Us."

I stare at him until he continues, "Always getting stuck in this freezing ass rain."

Smiling in agreement, we start sprinting to my house as we round the corner onto my street. Running up the sidewalk and the few steps to the covered front porch, I lean over and grip my knees with my hands as I gasp for air. I begin to feel lightheaded when Ryan steps in front of me, placing both his hands on my shoulders. He walks me over to the large bench on the porch, and we both sit down. Still feeling slightly dizzy, I lower my chest down toward my knees and lay my head in my hands.

Ryan places his hand on my back, leans down to my ear, and says, "Slow your breathing, Candace." He begins to rub my back when he repeats, "Slow."

I take in one long, deep breath and let it out gently. When the dizziness begins to subside, I slowly lift my head up and lean back into the seat.

"Here," Ryan says as he unscrews the cap to his bottle of water and hands it to me.

My throat burns, so I'm only able to take in a small sip before thanking him.

"I shouldn't have pushed you like that by sprinting," Ryan says.

"It's fine, I just haven't been running very much since summer, and the cold air got to me. I'm okay," I say with chattering teeth. I look at him, his long hair dripping with water, and I know I would be a total bitch if I left him like this to drive home. So, with hesitation, I say, "We should go inside and dry off."

When we walk in, I show him to the guest bathroom and run to grab some of Jase's clothes that are in my room for him to change into. I leave him be while I go into my room and change into some dry clothes and tie my wet hair into a messy bun. When I walk out of my room, Ryan is sitting on the couch in the living room. He stands up and starts thanking me for joining him on his run. A huge part of me is relieved that he isn't trying to stay here and hang out. Being alone with him inside my house still makes me feel very uneasy.

"You still going to the dance studio after that run?" he asks while walking to the front door as I follow him.

"Yeah, honestly, I'm fine. I didn't eat before we left, so I'm sure that's why I got lightheaded. I'm going to fix something to eat, then study for a while before I head up there."

"I'll catch you later then?"

"Yeah," I say.

Once Ryan leaves, I make a pot of coffee and grab a breakfast bar. I go back to my room, pick up my phone, and call Jase. When he answers, he's concerned that something is wrong. I assure him that I'm fine and that I just miss him. He can't talk for long because he is out with Mark's family for brunch. I'm used to always having Jase around, but I am happy that he is so content with Mark. They have become very serious in these past few months; I know Jase really loves him. Both of them come back home tomorrow, so Jase and I make plans to hang out after Mark goes home.

Dancing was just what I needed today. After Ryan left, I spent the majority of the afternoon stressing about my parents rather than studying. I'm used to my father calling me after a fight and trying to smooth things over, but he hasn't tried contacting me at all. My mother and I said some pretty harsh words to each other, and I'm just not quite sure how we are going to move past this.

Going to the studio helped clear my head and relaxed me as it always does. I was able to focus on and choreograph several eight-counts for my solo. I am starting to get some direction with the piece, and it feels good to be making progress with it.

After I worked on my solo, I decided to stay a while longer to work on my center floor technique. I ended up being at the studio for a little over three hours. By the time I got back home, my head was clear, so I decided to make good use of it and get the schoolwork done that I couldn't focus on earlier.

Finishing up some research for a paper, I check my phone to see that it's past eight o'clock. I decide to call it a night and quickly change into a pair of pajama pants and a t-shirt. I pop a sleeping pill and walk to the kitchen to grab a quick bite to eat before heading to bed.

The doorbell rings just as I am opening the fridge. I'm beyond surprised when I open the door and see Ryan standing there with a pizza and beer.

"What are you doing here?!"

Giving me a slight smile, he steps around me and comes inside. "I ran out to grab some dinner and knew you weren't doing anything tonight, so I drove here instead of back to my place."

"Oh..."

"That a problem?"

He starts walking to my kitchen, and all I can mumble out is, "Ummm...no. I just..."

"Just what?"

"Just surprised that's all. Why didn't you just text me?"

He sets down the pizza and beer and starts opening drawers until he finds the one with the bottle opener. "Because I figured you would probably tell me you were studying." He pops the cap off the beer, hands it to me, and winks as I press my lips together and agreeably nod. He takes his beer bottle and clinks the neck of it to mine then takes a sip.

"Plates?" he asks, and I nod my head over to the cabinet they are in while I take a long sip of my beer. "So, how was the rest of your day?" he continues while he moves with ease around my kitchen.

"Good. I got a lot done actually."

"Great, let's eat then," he says as he stacks the plates and napkins on top of the pizza box and heads into the living room. "Do you mind grabbing the beer?"

"No problem."

Setting everything down on the coffee table, he plops down on the couch and watches me until I move to join him. The past two times he has been here made me very uncomfortable, but his playful attitude tonight is amusing me more than anything.

I am pleasantly surprised when I open the pizza box to see that he got a Hawaiian pineapple pizza. I look over at him and ask, "How did you know I like pineapple on my pizza?"

Leaning forward and grabbing a slice, he says, "I didn't. Like I said, I got this for me before deciding to come over."

"Oh."

He smiles at me before taking a bite, and I grab a slice and join him. Sitting here, eating pizza and drinking beer, feels a lot like the times Jase and I have done this—comfortable. Then I remember that it probably feels comfortable because I already took my sleeping pill, which always helps relax me. Enjoying his company, I brush it off.

"So, you know what I did with my day. What about you?" I ask.

"After our run, I went to the gym to do some lifting. Then later, I went to the bar to work. Had to sign off on a bunch of paperwork and inventory orders. That's pretty much it."

I grab another beer and hand it to him so he can pop off the cap. When I start to take a drink, Ryan suggests finding something to watch on TV. I grab the remote for him, and he starts flipping through all the channels before stopping on some old black and white movie. He sets the remote down and leans back on the couch, content with his selection.

"What the heck is this?" I ask facetiously.

"You don't know this movie?"

"Does anyone know this movie?"

He smiles at me and says, "Candace, it's a classic."

I shake my head at him, completely clueless.

"It's 'Double Indemnity' from the 1940's. It's a great movie."

"You watch a lot of these movies?"

He shakes his head at me in mock disapproval. "Sit back and just watch. You'll like it." I sit back into the couch, and he points to the TV as he continues. "See that girl? Her name is Phyllis and that guy is an insurance agent that she is trying to seduce."

"Why?"

"Because she wants him to murder her husband so she can collect the money from his policy."

"Oooh, I like her already," I tease.

Ryan laughs at me and says, "Just watch."

Kicking our feet up on the coffee table, we lean back and watch the movie.

"Candace...Candace, wake up."

Opening my eyes, I look up and see Ryan as he is whispering at me to wake up. I lie there, confused in my sleepy haze, and it takes me a moment to realize that I am lying on the couch with my head in his lap. The haze instantly disappears as I jump up, startled at the scenario. *What happened?* I must have completely passed out. Mixing my sleeping pill with the beer was a huge mistake.

"Are you okay?" Ryan asks as he stands up and takes a step toward me.

Feeling a bit flustered, I hold my hands out to gesture to him not to come any closer.

"I'm sorry, I didn't want to leave you without you locking the door behind me. You fell asleep, and I didn't want to wake you, so I let you sleep for a while."

"I'm sorry."

"For what?"

"Startling easily. I didn't know I fell asleep. I'm just...I was just disoriented." I put my hands down and feeling abashed, I apologize again.

"Candace," he says as he takes a step toward me and reaches his hand to brush back a lock of my hair off of my forehead. My body stiffens at his touch, and he quickly pulls his hand back.

"I'll lock the door behind you," I say to rush him out.

"Let me help you clean this up."

Looking at the pizza box and beer bottles, I say, "I'll do it. It's all trash anyway."

"You sure?"

"Yeah."

We walk to the door, and he turns back to look at me. He is standing so close that I have to look up at him. I have never noticed our height difference before now. I'm a little over five feet, so he stands much taller than I do. Looking me in the eyes, he quietly says, "I want you to feel comfortable with me."

There is something about the look on his face that's

telling me he feels strongly about this, and I whisper, "I know," because I think I feel the same way.

"Okay. So, we'll talk later?"

Nodding my head, I say, "Yeah."

I lock the door behind him after he leaves, and I let out a long sigh. I grab all the trash and dump it in the garbage can then go crawl into bed.

Feeling confused about Ryan, I have a hard time settling back down to sleep. My mind is all over the place, and I am not sure how to sort my thoughts out. Thank God Jase is coming back home tomorrow because I really need to talk to him. For now, I lie in bed, confounded by my thoughts as I stare into the darkness.

chapter eighteen

Being alone in the house all day is driving me crazy, so I decide to head over to Jase's even though his flight doesn't get in for another two hours. The quiet is just a reminder of how much I miss my roommate. It's almost as if I live alone because we hardly ever interact anymore. I do know that she will be coming back today, I just don't know when. Before this year, we were like sisters. Even though I never really went out with her and her other friends, we always made time for each other and would constantly call and text each other. Now—nothing.

When I get to Jase's apartment, I go lie down in his room. It has been a couple weeks since I have slept here, so his bed is a welcome comfort. I think it will always be a comfort to me. I still have trouble sleeping alone in my bed. Even with the sleeping pills, my nights are restless and filled with night terrors, and I often have flashes of that night when I close my eyes. The flashes aren't nearly as bad as the nightmares, but they are still a constant reminder of the turmoil in my life.

My new friendship with Ryan is not something I expected. Then again, that's what's got me so confused. How can I be so closed off to the world around me, yet feel comfortable with this new person? The fact that he has become good friends with Mark and Jase eases my mind, but the past few days have me questioning a lot.

I jump off the bed when I hear Jase walk through the door. I practically knock him over when I run into his arms. I didn't realize how much I missed him until now.

"I am so glad you're back."

"Everything okay?"

Letting go of him, I smile and say, "Yeah, I just missed you." I take his arm and pull him toward the couch as I say, "I am dying to know everything about your trip. Where's Mark by the way?"

"He just dropped me off. He has an early morning tomorrow, so he needed to go home, unpack, and get laundry done," he says while we sit on the couch.

"Sooo...?" I say and Jase just smiles at me. Nudging him in the arm, I demand, "Come on! Tell me. How was it?"

"Great, actually. His family is nothing like our families."

"Thank God for that," I tease.

"We had a great time. His parents were so accepting of me, which made me comfortable from the moment I arrived. His sisters are a little crazy. We went out with the two of them one night, and they got totally shit-faced, so Mark and I had to sneak their loud asses into the house so they wouldn't wake up his parents. It felt like high school." Jase laughs, and he seems genuinely happy.

"They sound great. I am so happy for you, even though I missed you."

"I missed you too."

"So, it seems you and Mark are pretty serious now."

"I really love him. I was a dick before and thought I had screwed everything up, but I'm glad he gave me another chance. He's pretty perfect for me."

I can't help but smile when I hear Jase talk like this. He has been through a lot to get to this level of happiness.

"Well, for what it's worth, I really love Mark too. He's been a good friend to me, and he has never questioned our friendship, which means a lot to me. He totally gets us," I say.

"I know. He really does, and that makes me love him even more."

I lean in and give him another tight hug and then he asks, "So tell me about your break? How did Thanksgiving go?"

Leaning back, I sigh. "It didn't. I left before the food came to the table."

"What happened?"

"Honestly, it was pretty bad," I say, and I continue to tell him all about the fight and what was said. He shakes his head, but I know he isn't shocked. He has gotten to know a lot about my relationship with my parents over the past three years.

"So has your dad called you?"

"No, which worries me. He always calls to try and brush everything under the rug."

"So, you've just been laying low then?" he asks.

I fidget when he asks, and he picks up on it immediately when he questions curiously, "What's going on? Why are you nervous?"

"Not nervous...confused really."

"Tell me."

"I actually spent the past couple of days with Ryan."

"Alone?"

I nod my head, and he looks a bit stunned when he asks, "How did that happen?"

"I guess he got my cell number from Mark, and he texted me. We wound up spending all of Friday together and then some of yesterday as well."

"What'd you guys do?"

“We grabbed breakfast, then we went to the aquarium, but I kinda freaked when I left to go home.”

“What happened?”

“We were alone in his car, and I was telling him about the fight with my parents, and when he reached over to hold my hand, I panicked.”

Jase turns his body to face me when I continue. “He had held my hand earlier, but it was different. We were at the aquarium, and he was trying to get me to touch the sea creatures at the touch pool, but the way he held my hand in the car was just...I don’t know. Anyway, I acted like a maniac. I couldn’t get out his car fast enough. I just left without really saying anything.”

“What did he do?”

“Nothing. He didn’t say anything. But I was really shaken and cried the whole drive home.”

“Because he touched you?” he questions.

“I mean...I felt panicky when it happened, but I think I was more upset because I felt that way. Am I making any sense?”

“Yeah. I just don’t like that you beat yourself up for having feelings,” he says, and he takes my hand in the both of his.

“I hate that there are these random moments that come out of the blue, and I can’t hold myself together. But that isn’t the worst of it.”

“What?”

“He surprised me at my house last night after I had taken my sleeping pill. We ate dinner and were watching a movie, and the next thing I knew, I was waking up with my head in his lap. I totally freaked, Jase.”

“What did Ryan do?”

“He just apologized, then I apologized, and then we had this weird moment when he was leaving. I just don’t know what to think."

Shaking his head in confusion, Jase asks, "Let me get this straight, so he comes over and you let him stay with you...alone?"

"I know, but he actually made it comfortable for me. I mean, we had a fun night, but before he left, he brushed some hair out of my face. I know this may sound stupid, but it felt extremely tender, and now I'm confused because he's my friend."

"Are you confused because he's your friend, or are you confused because it feels wrong?"

Jase is still holding my hand, and I lean the side of my head on the couch. Sighing, I say, "I know you don't understand, but it doesn't feel right. It just doesn't feel right to be having any feelings like this."

"So, you like him?" he quietly asks me.

Whispering back in hesitation, I say, "I don't know." I close my eyes and sit there for a moment. My thoughts are all over the place, and when I open my eyes back up, a few tears fall. "I just can't be feeling like this."

"Why not, sweetie? I mean, if Ryan makes you feel safe enough to be alone with him, why is it so wrong to feel something for him, if for only that?"

"Because...he can't even touch me without me constantly freezing up and being scared. I feel so pathetic and weak, and I hate it. I hate that I feel like this—every day. I try so hard, Jase." I feel myself cracking as I cry and continue to say, "Every day I do everything I can just to hold myself together, and when I think I'm finally getting past this, something happens, and I am reminded just how weak I am. And I don't know what to do. I just wish I knew what to do, but I don't." Jase pulls me into his arms as I cry harder, and he just holds me. "I just want to move on, I want to feel like I used to. I mean, it's been three months of hell. I just want to go back. I should have never gone to that party. All I want is to forget. Just forget everything."

"Three months isn't enough, sweetie. It's just not enough. No amount of time will ever be enough for you to forget, for you to go back completely." Jase pulls back to look at me, and I can't stop myself from apologizing. Shaking his head at me, he gives me a smile, and suddenly I feel a little stupid for my tears. I know he is trying to cheer me up and lighten the mood when he teases me by saying, "So, Ryan has a thing for my girl."

"Shut up," I tease back.

"Seriously though, I want to see you happy. And if hanging out with Ryan makes you feel good, then you shouldn't question it. Don't stand in the way of your own happiness."

Cupping my face with his hands, he gives me a kiss. Hopping off the couch, he pulls me up and starts walking to his room.

"What are you doing?" I ask.

"Sleeping. I'm so tired, and I've missed you."

"But I've got an early class tomorrow."

Jase starts getting ready for bed when he says, "Skip."

I stand there and laugh at him, but I comply because I've missed him too.

This week has gone by really fast. I did wind up skipping my morning classes on Monday to spend time with Jase instead. Aside from that, I have been really busy with the quarter coming to an end shortly. Ryan has been texting me throughout the week, and we went running again Thursday morning. We decided to make it a routine to run together on Thursday mornings before I go to school.

Yesterday, he had some free time before he had to go to the bar, so we met up for an early dinner at a sushi-go-round restaurant near my house. While we were eating, we made plans to go running again when I get off work today. So, I am quickly finishing up my end-of-shift routine so I can change before he gets here.

It's been a busy morning today, and I haven't had much time to stand around and think, which is good because I feel like I have been thinking too much lately. Jase told me to relax a bit, and that's what I am trying to do. I'm texting and hanging out with Ryan the way I would with any friend. But I'd be lying if I said that there wasn't something about him that intrigues me. Lately, I've been having that fluttering feeling in my stomach when he's around. I haven't had a relationship with a guy since high school, and I'm not sure that one even qualified.

I don't feel right even thinking about this. How can I? Plus, who would even want me if they even knew who I really was? I'm still a mess, and that damn bell above the front door reminds me of it every time someone opens it.

Jase brought up calling the detective the other day. He has never mentioned it before, but he said he never wanted to because he knew I wasn't ready. I'm not sure why he thinks I'm ready now. I'm not. I don't want to be. All I want is to lock that horrific memory up and burn it to ashes, not be forced to relive it over and over for others to hear. I told Jase to drop it, told him it would never happen, so he didn't say another word about it.

"Hey Roxy, I'm gonna go to the back to restock a few things before I leave, okay?"

"Yeah, thanks," she says over the hissing of the steamer.

I grab a box cutter and start opening boxes of flavored syrups and stocking the shelves. When I move on to the sugar boxes, I see Roxy come through the door with a huge smile on her face.

"So, that hot-ass guy is back and asking for you."

Sitting on the floor, surrounded by scraps of cardboard boxes, I say, "His name is Ryan."

"Well then, that hot-ass guy, Ryan, is here for you," she says teasingly with her hands on her hips.

"Thanks. Can you tell him to give me ten minutes?"

"You guys have a date or something?"

Standing up, I say, "What? No! He's just a friend."

"Mmm hmm." Roxy turns on her heel to walk back out to the front, and I pick up my bag and go to the bathroom to change into my running clothes.

When I walk out, Ryan is chatting with Roxy. He looks up at me as I'm walking over to him and says, "Hey."

"What are you guys talking about?"

"Your friend, Ryan, was asking about my tattoos." I silently thank her for leaving out the *hot-ass* part.

Ryan takes a step towards me and asks, "You ready?"

"Yeah, I just need to put my bag in my car."

Reaching out, he takes the bag out of my hand and starts walking to my car. I say 'bye' to Roxy as I follow him out.

I zip my keys up in the pocket of my running jacket, and we take off for our run from the parking lot. We head around the perimeter of campus before making our way through a few neighborhoods. I am mostly quiet as I listen to Ryan talk about work and the new bands that have been playing there during the week. Turns out that we pretty much have the same taste in music, and I find his reaction funny each time he discovers I like another one of his favorite bands.

We start making our way through some streets we haven't gone down before. I follow him and keep my pace by his side. My throat is beginning to dry out when I realize that neither of us brought any water, and I know we've already run at least three miles. I am more quiet than normal, and I'm sure Ryan notices when he turns his head and asks, "You okay?"

"I'm thirsty. We forgot water."

"No worries," he says as he picks up the pace, and we turn down another unfamiliar street.

I don't have time to question him when he slows down and starts walking up a driveway to a three-story building.

"What are you doing?"

"Getting you some water. Come on," he says while nodding his head toward the building.

I walk a few steps behind him, and he pulls out a key fob from his pocket. When he clicks the button, the garage begins to open.

"Do you own this building or something?" I ask.

Ryan turns back to look at me and grins. "This is my loft. I live here."

"Oh," I mumble, but I stop following him, not really wanting to go into his home. I try hard to control the anxiety that begin to race through me. I have been spending a lot of time with him and feel like he is trustworthy, but I can't seem to shake my nerves right now.

He motions for me to come, and I don't want him to think I'm some sort of basket case, so I swallow back my apprehension and follow him into the garage to the staircase leading up to the loft.

When we reach the top of the stairs, he unlocks the door, and we head inside to the large open space. The main room is completely open with a large kitchen along the back wall of exposed brick. The finishes in the kitchen are industrial and sleek, and two of the walls are lined with floor to ceiling windows. There are exposed beams on the ceiling, and the wooden floors are a rich wide-planked espresso. I wonder how he came to own a place like this; the square footage alone would cost a fortune.

"Here you go," he says as he walks back to me and hands me a bottle of water.

I take a sip and say, "This is a great place. How long have you lived here?"

"About five years."

He pulls his cell phone out of his jacket when it begins to ring. I can tell it's something about work when he starts talking. Telling the person on the other end to hang on, he puts the phone down to his side and tells me, "Make yourself comfortable. I need to take this call really quick. I'll only be a few minutes, okay?"

I nod my head, and he walks down the hall and into one of the rooms. I stand there in the middle of his house, not sure what to do. As I drink my water, I make my way over to Ryan's living room. It's filled with overstuffed furniture and a TV that is mounted to the wall above a large fireplace. I walk over to one of the windows near the corner of the room. I accidentally kick a stack of books, and when I bend down to straighten them back up, I see several large black photo mats. Leaning down, I flip one over and look at the beautiful black and white photograph that is a close-up of the curve of a woman's bare back. The lighting of the photo is exquisite.

I kneel down to flip through the others when I hear him walk back into the room. Before I can stand up he is at my side. I look up at him and say, "I'm sorry." Setting the photos back where they were, I stand up and he asks, "For what?"

"I wasn't snooping or anything, I just noticed these and was curious."

"Candace, I have nothing to hide. I told you to make yourself comfortable, and I meant it." He steps aside, sits down in one of the large, overstuffed chairs, and takes a swig of his water.

"Where did you get those?" I ask, referring to the photos.

"They're mine," he says.

"Yours?"

"Yeah. Sometimes I get bored and like to mess around with my camera," he says casually.

"That's pretty amazing for just messing around. You only shoot people?"

"For the most part, yeah," he says as he gets up from his seat and walks over to me by the window. He picks up the picture of the woman's back and looks at it as if he hasn't seen it in a long time.

"She a model?" I ask about the woman in the photo.

"No, just some chick I used to know." He sets down the photo and walks to the couch while motioning for me to join him.

I walk over, sit down next to him, and ask, "So, when did you get into photography?"

"When I was in college I took some art classes. So, one day I just decided to buy a camera and started taking pictures. Like I said, I pretty much have no clue what I'm doing. Just a little hobby of mine I mess around with every now and then."

"You ever do anything with them?"

"No."

"Maybe you should," I say, and he turns to look at me and repeats my words back to me quietly, "Maybe I should."

"You sure you don't want to come out to the bar tonight to see Mark play?" he asks.

"I told you, I have to work."

"I just picked you up from work."

"I know, but I have to go back. One of the girls quit and Roxy hasn't hired anyone to replace her, so I've been picking up extra shifts," I explain. "Plus, I'd probably be tired and no fun to be around."

"I can't imagine it not being fun to be around you," he says as he looks at me intently, and I begin to feel uncomfortable with his words. "You ready to finish the run?"

A smile crosses his face when he stands up and reaches out his hand to me. I sit there for a beat before I hesitantly place my hand in his. When I do, he gives me a slight tug and pulls me off the couch. He never lets go of my hand as he locks up and we walk down the stairs and out to the driveway. This closeness has my nerves twisted up, and I'm sure he can feel sweat on my hand. As we walk out to the street, hands still connected, he asks, "Wanna make it a long run, or are you ready to head back?"

I take a hard swallow before saying, "Long."

He gives me a squeeze before he unwraps his fingers from around my hand, and we begin to run.

chapter nineteen

School has been really busy. It's the last week of classes before finals. Aside from work, I have been buried in my books and getting everything wrapped up before the quarter ends. I'm going into all my finals with perfect grades, so I am sure I will still be able to maintain my four point GPA.

I did manage to meet up with Ryan Thursday morning for our run. I was starting to get really stressed out, so the run was just what I needed. Ryan was considerate and let me ramble on and on the whole time about my classes and everything that I needed to do to make sure I was ready for my exams.

But now that classes are officially over until January, I can start to wind down a bit. I only have three finals next week and a studio final. Everyone has learned the same routine, and we will perform in groups of four for our final grading. I have the dance memorized and perfected, so today when I go to the studio, I plan to just work on my solo. Ms. Emerson will be meeting me up there in a little bit to critique what I have so far. I am surprised that she offered to do this for me since she never gives anyone private instruction. So when she offered, I immediately said yes.

Ryan said he would meet me at the studio around four o'clock to grab a coffee before he has to go into work. I shoot him a quick text as I am heading out.

Leaving now. See you in two hours?

I'll meet you in the parking lot.

OK, catch you later.

When I arrive at the studio, Ms. Emerson is already there waiting for me.

"Hi, I hope you weren't waiting long," I say when I walk in and set my bag down.

Walking over to the stereo, she says, "Not at all. I just got here. Did you stretch at home?"

"Yes, but I need to warm my muscles up a little more." The cold temperatures make it hard to keep my muscles loose, so after my pointes are on, I slide on some leg warmers and loose long pants.

"Well then, let's do a little floor work before we begin." She flips on the music, and she joins me in the center of the room as we do a few adagio combinations.

I have never danced alone alongside Ms. Emerson. She is as focused as I am on arm placements and bodylines. We move gracefully together through the movements and repeat the combination a few more times before she asks for my music. I hand her the disc, and she gets the music set up as I take my spot on the floor in fifth position. When I hear the strings, I slowly relevè on my pointes and begin a series of chainès across the floor. I continue through my choreography, and when I get to the peak of my developè, I begin spotting my head as I go into a variation series of fouettès. I hear Ms. Emerson beating the counts by loudly clapping her hands. When I come to the end, all she says is, "Again." She clicks the remote, and the music cues back up.

I repeat my steps, and I focus in on the movements as I hear: "I need more, Candace...Hit that position, and hold!" *CLAP CLAP CLAP* "Piquè! Piquè! Come on! I need more from you!" I hear her stern voice through the loud music and follow her commands. When I come to the end, she repeats, "Again."

We go through this process countless times before taking a break only to continue repeating this routine over and over. I keep pounding out the moves harder and harder, but she continues to yell and demand. We do this for over an hour, and I begin to grow exhausted when she shouts, "Again!"

The music repeats, and I go through the steps over and again. "Pick it up, Candace! Hit! Hit!" She claps the counts loudly and continues, "I'm not feeling it! Come ON! Feel it! Watch that port a bras. Demi second, make it strong!" I focus on her commands, trying to keep my emotions tight, although I feel like I'm at my end. She's relentless. "Again. Last one," she says, and she starts the music again.

"This time...*feel* it, Candace. Really feel it. Let it out."

I nod my head and silently take my position again as the music pounds through the room. Making my way through the steps, my toes are aching, but I push through again. I can hear the frustration in Ms. Emerson when she yells over the music. "Feel it, Candace! You're dead behind the movements...Make that spotting stronger!" *CLAP CLAP CLAP* "Hit those fouettès...Smooth out that demi right there. I'm getting nothing! Feel, Candace!"

She shuts off the music, and I stop, standing in the center of the floor when she walks toward me.

Speaking softly, she says, "Whatever walls you have built this year, you need to break them down. I'm getting nothing from you. You feel nothing."

"Yes," I say breathlessly as I nod my head.

"We spoke about this earlier, but I'm not seeing any changes. This is a powerful piece of music. In my opinion, the best piece of all the girls, but you're wasting it. Whatever this is...fix it."

"Okay." And before I can say anything else, she turns to leave.

When the door closes behind her, I let out my pent up frustration and scream through my clenched teeth. Ripping off my pointes, I throw them hard across the room. I lie back on the floor, taking a few deep breaths and feel the tears welling up. My emotions are on edge after being so harshly berated for the past two hours. I squeeze my eyes shut and feel the tears as they roll down my temples and into my hair. I throw my arm over my head and continue to breathe in and out slowly.

Letting a few minutes pass, I grab my things and leave. I just want to go home, shower, and try not to think about this disastrous rehearsal. I slam the door open when I walk out, and I'm shocked when I see Ryan leaning up against my car. *Shit!* I completely forgot that he would be here. Quickly, I wipe the tears off my cheeks and try to pull myself together fast. But before I can start walking, he's standing in front of me with both hands cupping my face.

"What happened?"

"Nothing, honestly. Just a tough rehearsal." My voice comes out wobbly, and I hate that.

Ryan stares down at me with a clenched jaw. Taking his thumbs, he wipes my damp cheeks. The tender action breaks my strong façade, and I fall into his chest allowing the comfort of his arms as they wrap around me. He cradles the back of my head with his hand the same way Jase does when he hugs me, but this feels different. His hold is strong and tight, and I let myself soften into him. Aside from Jase and Mark, there is no one that I ever let touch me like this. I know it isn't much, but it's difficult for me. Being in Ryan's embrace feels safe, so I wrap my arms around his waist as we stand in the empty parking lot.

When I start to pull back from him, he asks again, "Are you sure you're okay?"

I nod my head, uncertain of how my voice might sound.

Ryan takes the bag off of my shoulder and drapes his arm around me. "Come on," he says as he starts walking me to his jeep.

I don't ask where we are going, and honestly, I'm too worn out to really care. He helps me into his car, and when he closes the door, I rest my head against the back of the seat and close my eyes. Ryan doesn't say anything; he doesn't even turn on the music as we drive. It's only a few minutes later when the car stops in front of his loft.

When we get upstairs, I sit on the couch in his living room while he gets me a bottle of water from the kitchen. He sits down next to me, and I gulp the water down quickly.

"Feeling better?"

"Yeah, I'm sorry. After being yelled at for two hours, I just..."

"Don't worry," he says as he puts his arm around me and draws me closer to his side.

Leaning my head back on the couch, I say, "No...It's embarrassing."

"Don't let it be," he says.

"Can I ask you a huge favor?"

"Anything."

"Do you have dry shirt I can change into? I've been dancing for the past few hours, and I'm sweaty and stinky."

He laughs at me and says, "You don't stink at all actually."

"Liar."

"I'll be right back." I watch Ryan as he head up the

stairs, to what I presume is his bedroom.

"You need socks?" he yells down.

"Please. It's cold," I say.

When he comes back down, he hands me his clothes and shows me to the guest bathroom. "Thanks. Just give me a few minutes."

"Take your time."

I turn on the faucet and wait for the water to run hot. I open the linen closet and find a washcloth. When I take off my clothes, I wet the washcloth and freshen up as best as I can. I slip on his old UW shirt and a pair of his pajama pants, leaving my dirty clothes folded on the side of the sink. His clothes are huge on me, and I have to tug on the ties of his pants to cinch up the waist and rollup up the waistband several times, but the pants still drag on the floor.

Walking back into the living room, Ryan is sitting back on the couch, flipping through channels on the TV. I sit down next to him, and he grabs the bun that is still secured on the top of my head and laughs. "This is cute," he teases me.

I swat his hand away. "Whatever."

"Come here," he says, and I lean back on the couch with him. "So, what happened?"

"I have this tough piece of music, and I'm having a hard time connecting with it. My instructor keeps telling me what I need to fix, but I don't really know how. It's frustrating. I can perfect my moves, but I don't know how to get into this piece."

"So she just bashed you the whole time?

"It's how she is. But the fact that she even came in to work with me is unheard of. She's extremely stern, but she's only trying to help me."

"I didn't like seeing you upset."

Looking up at him, I say, "It's not a big deal, really."

"I didn't like it." He says this intently as he looks down

at me, and I have to look away from him because when he says things like this, it makes me feel too much. I know Jase likes Ryan, but the other night Mark had mentioned that he has a bit of a reputation for hooking up with random women. It's hard for me to picture him that way because I don't see him like that, but at the same time, it makes me feel like I should be even more cautious around him.

"You want that cup of coffee?" he asks, and I am pulled out of my thoughts.

"That'd be great, I'm still really cold."

"There are some blankets in the trunk by the fireplace," he tells me as he walks into the kitchen. I hop up and grab a large blanket, wrapping it around me before I sit back down.

"How do you take it?" he asks from across the room.

"One sugar and really blond."

Ryan hands me my mug and sits down next to me with a grin. "You getting warm?"

"Trying too."

He picks up the remote and turns it to TCM. I shake my head and laugh at him.

"What's so funny?"

"You. I don't know anyone who watches the classic movie channel, aside from you."

"You want me to change it?"

Pulling my feet up on the couch, I say, "No, it's fine. I'm only teasing you."

He turns up the volume and we sit back and watch 'The Blue Dahlia.' He knows I'm only half paying attention because every now and then he will make commentary to keep me up to speed.

By the time the movie ends, Ryan has to get ready to go to work. I grab my clothes from the bathroom, and we head downstairs to his jeep. When he pulls in the studio lot, he asks me to come out tonight. When I tell him that I can't, he doesn't push.

"I'm sorry, but I'm just really tired and will probably go to bed early," I say. I know Mark's band has become the regular Saturday night house band and that Jase is often with him, but the thought of being in a crowded bar, and possibly crossing paths with Jack, is too much for me to think about. "Plus, I have the early shift at work tomorrow."

"Your boss doesn't strike me as the type who would mind if you came into work a little hungover," he jokes.

"You're probably right about that, but I've never drunk enough to have ever been hungover."

"Never?"

"Don't act surprised."

"I'm more relieved," he says

"I'm not even going to ask why. But, thanks for today."

"Any time."

"Tell Mark and Jase I said 'hi' when you see them tonight, okay?" I open the door and hop out of the car. Looking back at him before I close the door, I say, "Thanks again for being there today. It probably would have ended up being a crappy day if I just came home."

"Thanks for letting me be there," he says.

I close the door and get into my car.

When I arrive home, Kimber is sitting in the living room flipping through a magazine as I walk in.

"Hey," I say.

Looking at the clothes I'm wearing that are entirely too big, she asks, "What are you wearing?" I'm surprised that she is speaking to me.

"Oh, um..." I stutter as she nods her head. By the look on her face, she seems annoyed. She closes the magazine and starts walking toward her room.

"Kimber," I call out after her, but she just ignores me and slams her door shut.

I dump my clothes in the laundry room before I go into my room. I brush my teeth, take my sleeping pill, and slide into bed. I am still wearing Ryan's clothes, and can smell the warmth of his scent with a hint of amberwood as I start to grow tired.

chapter twenty

"What are you going to do for the next few weeks?" Ryan asks as we unload some firewood from his jeep. I figured since I was going to be alone for Christmas break, I could at least make it as festive as possible with a tree and wood for the fireplace. I called Ryan to go with me to the tree lot since his jeep is big and could hold everything I wanted to buy.

"I don't know. This is the first year that Jase isn't here with me. We normally spend most of the break together when I am not at my parents'."

"How is that going?"

Stacking the firewood in the garage, I say, "It's not, really. I spoke with my father for the first time since Thanksgiving a few of days ago, and he wants me to come over for dinner Christmas Eve."

"You haven't spoken with them for all this time?"

"No."

We walk out to grab another load of wood. Kimber and Jase both left as soon as they were finished with finals, so I have been picking up a lot of extra shifts at work this past week to keep myself busy. Ryan and I have been spending more time together. He continues to show affection with me by holding my hand or putting his arm around me while watching TV, but that's about it. I'm not sure about my feelings for him, but I'm pretty sure that he sees me as more than his friend. Sure, I'm affectionate with Mark and Jase, but they are non-threatening to me.

When Ryan and I were out getting coffee earlier this week, we ran into a girl that Ryan must have dated in the past. He seemed really uncomfortable talking to her in front of me, but she seemed more than comfortable with him. It didn't make me jealous, but it made me a little more guarded. Ryan is a good-looking guy, so I shouldn't be surprised that he has dated a lot of girls, I'm just not sure what *a lot* actually means. Part of me doesn't really want to know.

"So, you're going over to see them then?"

"Well, yeah, I don't really want to, but it's Christmas and all. I'm just a little scared about how it will all go. The last time I saw them, we said some pretty nasty things to each other, and I have never gone this long without talking to them."

"What are they so upset about?"

Back inside the house, I pour a glass of wine, and Ryan takes a beer from the fridge.

"Everything. Turns out I've been nothing but an embarrassing disappointment to them all along."

Ryan lets out an irritated sigh as we take our drinks and head into the living room. We sit down on the couch, and Ryan slides his arm around my shoulders, pulling me next to him.

"I'm sorry, babe," he says quietly, and I notice his term of endearment. I try not to act flustered, but he has never said anything like that to me before. It's things like this that he does that confuse me. The friendship that we have has been eased into pretty naturally; I have never questioned him about it, and I find myself liking it.

"Honestly, it's nothing that I didn't already know deep down, but it was the first time that it actually hit me that these were their true feelings toward me."

"I don't want you going over there." His statement catches me off guard, and I look up at him. I can see it written all over his face that he's nothing but serious.

"Ryan, I have to. They're my parents."

"I don't care. I don't want you going over there for them to treat you like shit."

Letting out a sigh, I lean back and rest my head on his chest. I'm not sure why this upsets him so much, but I can't not go see my parents at Christmas. "I have to go," I softly whisper. "It's Christmas, and I really should be there. I'm only going for dinner. That's all."

"Then I'm going with you."

I pull away from him and turn to look at him straight on. "What?"

"I don't want you going alone, Candace. I'll go with you."

I shake my head and say, "I don't think that's a good idea."

"Well, I don't think it's a good idea that you're going. So, we can argue about this, or you can just say 'okay.'"

I sit there looking at him, surprised that he would even care so much about this. But, he's right, I don't see him backing down, so instead of fighting him on this, I turn and lean back into him. "Okay."

"And I don't want you spending Christmas alone either, so why don't you come with me. I could use the distraction at the madhouse."

"What?! No. Thanks, but I'll be fine."

"I'm sure you will be fine, but I don't like the thought of you sitting here alone, so you're coming with me."

"Ryan, it feels weird."

"Why?"

"Because. It just does. I know you have a big family,

and I just don't want to intrude."

He shifts to face me, and says, "It's not an intrusion. My family isn't like that."

I look down and take a moment before saying, "Okay, but no gifts. It makes me uncomfortable."

"Why's that?"

"I don't know. It just always has. Please," I say in a serious tone.

"Okay. No gifts. But just so you know, I have a shit-ton for the kids," he says with a chuckle.

I smile and we sit back, kicking our feet up onto the coffee table. "So when did you start making all the rules?"

"When you started making me worry about you."

I don't respond to his statement; I don't know how to respond. The protectiveness of his words confuses me, but they make me feel good. Instead, I just sit there next to him and stare at the undecorated tree by the front window and worry about Ryan meeting my parents.

I have been on edge all day thinking about how dinner will go tonight. I'm nervous because the last time I saw my parents, it didn't go so well, and nothing has been discussed or resolved. I'm also nervous about Ryan meeting them. I know my mother will jump to conclusions and assume we are dating, and that will not go over well since I know she will be judging him and measuring him up to her unreachable standards.

When I see Ryan's black Rubicon pull up in front of my house, I slip on my coat and head out. He gets out of the car to help me into my seat. When we pull away, he must have picked up on my nerves when he says, "Relax."

Feeling the need to warn him, I say, "Ryan. You need

to know that—"

But he doesn't let me finish when he interrupts me and repeats, "Candace, relax."

"They're just very judgmental people."

"There is nothing that they can say that I haven't heard before," he says, and I wonder what he means by that. Is he referring to his parents? I know he is close with his mother, so I assume maybe his father has something to do with his statement. Ryan has never mentioned his dad. I figure his parents are divorced and he just isn't close with him, but I have never asked.

I start fidgeting and twisting my hands when he pulls into the gates of The Highlands. He reaches over and lays his hand on top of mine to calm me, but it doesn't help. When he pulls into my parents' circle drive and shuts off the car, I don't get out. We both sit there for a moment when Ryan asks, "You ready?"

"Yeah," I breathe out.

"Bunny," my dad beams as we walk through the door. His candor is not what I expected, and he pulls me in for a big hug. "You look beautiful, dear." He turns to Ryan and shakes his hand. "And you must be Ryan. Thanks for joining us. Come in."

Turning back to me he says, "Your mother is finishing getting ready. She should be out shortly."

We walk back into the kitchen and my father asks, "What can I get you two to drink?"

"A beer is good, Mr. Parker."

"Please, call me Charles."

My father hands Ryan a bottle of beer and pours me a glass of red wine.

"Why don't we go to the library and visit while we wait for your mother?"

As we are walking through the house, Ryan keeps a

supportive hand on my back, and I appreciate the gesture.

"So, Ryan, what is it that you do?" my father asks as we all sit down.

"I own a bar right off campus."

"Oh, how did you get into that type of work?"

"Long story short, after I graduated college, I couldn't seem to find a job with the economy, so I just sort of fell into this business deal. It's been working out nicely though, so I can't complain."

"What did you study in college?"

"Finance."

"Now that's a respectable degree," my mother says as she walks into the room, heels clicking against the wooden floor.

I cringe inside at her passive-aggressive statement. When she approaches, I stand to give her a quick embrace.

"Hi, Mom."

"Good to see you, darling. And Ryan, welcome."

Ryan stands to take her hand, and says, "Thank you for having me."

"Of course. It isn't every day that our daughter brings a man home."

I roll my eyes, and Ryan sits down next to me and squeezes my knee. I know this is going to end in disaster already. My mother's words are like poison, and I'm beginning to question why I even came.

"Ryan was just telling me about the bar he owns," my dad tells my mother.

"A bar?"

Before I allow my mother to make some snarky comment, I jump in, "So, when are the two of you leaving for Colorado?" My parents own a cabin in Aspen and go there every year after Christmas.

They begin to talk about what they have planned for

their trip this year, and I sit back and listen to them go on and on. It's pretty much the same every year.

As I take the last sip of my wine, my father says, "Bunny, why don't you show Ryan around. I need to talk with your mother about something. We will leave in about thirty minutes."

"Okay, sure."

I walk Ryan around the house and then outside to show him the view of the Sound.

"I'm sorry about that," I say.

"About what?"

"They can be a lot. They're pretty pretentious."

"Candace, no one has perfect parents. Everyone's flawed in some way."

We walk back to the covered patio and sit down on one of the benches. I tie my scarf tighter around my neck, and Ryan wraps his arm around my shoulders.

"So, you grew up here in Shoreline?" he asks.

"Yeah. In this very house. The Kelley's, who live across the street, have a daughter that's the same age as me. We used to be best friends when we were growing up."

"And now?"

"And now all I really have is Jase, Mark...and you."

"What about your roommate?"

"Kimber? We used to be really close, but not so much anymore."

"So what happened to all your friends from high school?"

"They've moved on. Applying to grad schools, getting married, making a life for themselves. Most of the kids here wind up becoming people like my parents. More concerned about their image and what social circle they are in. It's not me, so I never cared enough to stay in touch with anyone."

I feel Ryan squeeze my shoulder and pull me in tighter,

and I'm starting to feel uncertain about all this. Him. Having him here with my parents. Talking about myself. Him touching me. I pull away and stand up, needing a little space to try and calm my nerves.

"We should go back inside," I say.

Walking back into the house, my father calls from the library, "Candace, could you come in here?"

"Yeah, just a second," I holler back. I turn to Ryan and say, "I'll be right back. Make yourself at home."

"Do you want me to come with you?"

"No, it's okay."

When I walk into the library, both of my parents are waiting for me, and my father tells me to shut the door behind me. I do so, anxiously wondering what this is all about.

As I walk further into the room, my dad says, "Well, I just got off the phone with a friend of mine who works in admissions at Columbia. He owed me a favor and was able to pull some strings to get you a conditional acceptance for the fall semester."

"What?"

"This is wonderful news, isn't it, darling?" my mother says.

"I'm sorry, but what is this all about?"

"Well, we know that you've been busy finishing up at U-Dub, so your father and I thought we would help you out by taking care of this."

"Taking care of what?" My head is spinning, and I can't believe what I am hearing. Are they serious right now? "Honey, you look upset. You should be happy—"

Raising my voice I say, "Happy about what?! Happy that you don't trust me to make decisions for myself? Happy that I know you don't think I'm good enough? Happy that you feel I am so pathetic that you have to go behind my back to try and control me?"

"Candace, lower your voice please," my father says sternly.

"No! I can't believe you did this!"

"I would have hoped Thanksgiving would have given you something to think about, but clearly you are determined to make a fool out of yourself. And to top it all off, you bring home a boy that works in a bar. Honestly, I don't know what you're thinking."

"He owns that bar, Mother," I spat.

"It's not you. This path you're leading yourself down is not for you," my mother says.

"It's not for *you.* You're too goddamn judgmental to ever live like I do. I'm happy. I wish you could just see that and accept that." I look to my dad to try and grasp why he would do this. I always thought that he understood me, but he just stares at me with an unfaltering look. I slowly shake my head in disbelief and ask him, "Why?"

"Your mother is right, dear. We thought you would come to your senses, but clearly you are stuck in this fantasy of yours. You have a name to uphold."

My eyes start to blur, and when I blink, the tears fall.

"I just don't understand you. You should be thanking your father, not pouting."

"You are unbelievable, Mother!" I continue to yell as I say, "I'm not a child! You can't just step in and take away everything I have worked so hard for during these past four years! How can you call yourself a mother? You're nothing! You say you're embarrassed by me, well it goes both ways." When I stop to take a breath, I see Ryan rushing in.

Holding out his hand, he says, "We're leaving. Now."

"Excuse me, but this is a private matter," my mother says to him condescendingly.

Looking at Ryan and the anger in his eyes, I can't seem

to stop the tears that are falling. I'm shocked that he would care enough to come in here and stop this fight.

"Candace, if you walk out, it's over. Don't come back. We refuse to sit back and watch you ruin your life." I look at my mother and can't believe she even went there.

I shift my eyes to my father's. "Daddy?"

"We're done letting you play games, bunny. No more."

I look at the both of them, and I feel myself falling apart. My own parents, threatening me and trying to control me. Looking at them is actually making my stomach turn, so I do the only thing I know to do. I grab Ryan's hand and let him take me away.

His grip on me is tight as he walks us through the living room, grabbing our coats, and leading me outside to his jeep. He doesn't say a word, but the look on his face tells me he's pissed. He opens the car door for me, and I begin to feel lightheaded. I reach forward and brace my free hand on the side of the seat, trying to hold myself up and clear the haze in my vision when Ryan grabs me and pulls me into his arms. I cling to him tightly and start sobbing into his chest. I can barely grasp what just happened. But, I know I can't go back. They made that clear.

After a few minutes, I'm able to calm myself down enough to stop the tears. My breathing is still erratic, and I'm so embarrassed that Ryan had to see all of that. I can't even look him in the eyes, so I keep my head down when I finally loosen my grip on him and pull away. He kisses the top of my head before gripping my waist and helping me into the car.

The drive home is quiet. I'm still trying to process what happened back there. I never thought my parents would ever go that far. I don't need their money or their lifestyle, and the fact that they thought it meant that much to me that they could threaten me with it proves that they don't know me at all.

When we get back to my house, I am thoroughly drained. I curl up on the couch and kick my heels off and onto the floor. Ryan walks into the kitchen, and when he comes back out, he has a beer and a glass of wine. He hands me the glass, and I gulp half of it down quickly before setting it on the coffee table. Sitting down on the couch, he leans back on the side armrest, pulling me between his legs so that my back is resting on his chest. He wraps one arm around my waist while his other hand is threading through my hair. I can feel his steady breathing by the rise and fall of his chest.

This closeness that I feel with Ryan is a lot for me to process. Closing my eyes, I take a slow, deep breath and shift to my side, resting my cheek on his sternum. I listen to his heart as it beats rapidly.

"You okay?" His words are the first spoken since we left my parents house. I know I can't talk around the huge lump in my throat, so I just shake my head. Ryan rests his chin on the top of my head, and when I begin to cry again, he tightens his hold on me.

I feel safe enough with him to finally have this release. I've spent years making excuses for my parents, just brushing off and accepting their behavior. But, this...this cuts deep. My whole life I've been trying to make them proud of me, but I just can't be what they want me to be. I can't even think about trying to bottle up this pain, so I just let it out.

chapter twenty-one

Ryan stayed over for a few hours before leaving me last night. We barely spoke at all as he held me, but we didn't need to talk. I never feel as if I need to be anything I'm not when I am with him. I don't even want to think about what last night would have been like if he hadn't been there.

He told me I didn't have to go with him to his mom's house, that he would stay with me. But I really need the distraction. So, we are making the four-hour drive to Cannon Beach in Oregon to spend the next few days with his family. I'm nervous about meeting everyone. Ryan has a large family, something I have never been around. All I know is the dysfunction I grew up around with my mother and father.

"You're quiet over there," Ryan says as he drives through the tall, thick pine trees of the mountains.

"Just a little nervous."

"Don't be." He gives my knee a soft squeeze of reassurance.

On our long drive, I try not to worry too much about what they will think of me. Ryan does a good job of distracting me with conversation and listening to music. After a while, I decide to lean back and take a nap since I had a restless night of sleep.

When we pull up to the large, two-story, dark grey beach house with a driveway and street full of cars, I start wringing my hands and fingers together. He parks the jeep, steps out, and walks around to my side, opening my door.

Grabbing both of my hands, he says, "Don't be so nervous. Just relax."

I nod my head, but I worry they might think I'm weird or rude if I'm too quiet. I worry that I don't look nice enough, or maybe that I look too nice. Ryan helps me out of the car, and when I start smoothing down the pencil skirt of my black cap-sleeved dress, he starts laughing.

"Why are you laughing at me?"

"Because I've never seen you so wound up before."

He reaches in the jeep and grabs the bottle of Pahlmeyer Merlot that I bought for his mother. We start walking to the front door when I tug against his hand. Turning around, he cocks his head slightly and gives me a concerned look.

"Ryan...I don't do well around a lot of people," I hesitantly confess to him.

He places his hand on my shoulder and says, "My family will love you, but if you feel that uncomfortable, we can go. Just say the word."

"No, I want to meet them, I'm just..." I feel like I am stumbling over my words when he says, "Hey, I'm right here. No worries, okay?"

Letting out a sigh, I say, "Okay."

He takes my hand in his and starts leading me up the wet drive. When we walk in, I'm almost knocked down when two little boys dart through the foyer, chasing each other with plastic swords.

Ryan chuckles at the kids and says to me, "Come on," as he takes me through the house. The walls are filled with family photographs. It's a beautiful house, not extravagant like the one I grew up in.

Laughter echoes through the large house, and as we

turn the corner into the kitchen, I see three women huddled over the counter looking at a tabloid magazine. One of them looks up as we enter the room, and a warm smile crosses her face when she sees Ryan.

Stretching out her arms and wrapping them around him, she says, “Finally, you made it. We missed you this morning.”

Never letting go of my nervous hand, he embraces her with his free arm. When I start to loosen my grip to allow him his other arm, he tightens his hold on me.

After she lets go of him, she turns her attention to me, and Ryan introduces us. “Mom, this is Candace.”

“I am so glad to finally meet you, dear.” And just like she did with Ryan, she pulls me in for a warm hug, but I’m a little distracted by her word *finally*. Has Ryan mentioned me to her before a few days ago when he called to tell her he was bringing me? Before I can think about it too much, Ryan’s hand leaves mine as the other two women are hugging me and introducing themselves as his aunts. Little kids start flooding into the kitchen screaming for their Uncle Ryan. His mother starts calling off the names of all the children, but I can’t even focus on what she is saying because I’m overwhelmed. I look over to Ryan, and he’s holding two little girls, one in each arm. One of the girls is tugging on his hair while he is pecking kisses on the other one’s ear, making her squeal loudly. Seeing him like this makes me laugh at how fun and easygoing he is. Although he shows these traits around me, he has started to become more protective lately.

It’s a whirlwind as I’m introduced to all of Ryan’s cousins and their spouses, along with his two uncles. Everyone is talking and hugging me, and I know there is no way I will remember anyone’s name aside from his mother’s, which I’d already known.

All the noise and touching is beginning to overpower

me, and when I look to see where Ryan is, he is engulfed in a conversation with two of his cousins while he is still holding one of the little girls.

Needing some space to regroup, I turn to his mother and quietly ask, “Excuse me, Donna. Where is the restroom?”

She directs me to one that is on the other side of the house, and I quickly make my way through the chaos. When I shut the door behind me, I walk over, sit down on the lid of the toilet, and embrace the calm. I take a few minutes to compose myself when someone knocks on the door.

I stand up to go open the door, and when I do, Ryan is standing there.

“Everything okay? When I looked up you were gone.”

“Yeah, just needed a moment to myself.”

“Sorry about that,” he says.

“It’s okay. I’m just not used to...”

Ryan runs his hands down my arms and says, “I know. Do you need a few more minutes?”

“No, I’m fine.”

Holding my hand, he begins to walk me back to the kitchen where all the commotion has died down a bit. Most of the little kids are now watching a movie in the other room as a few of the guys sit on the couches, drinking and laughing about whatever they are talking about.

I turn my attention to Ryan when he hands me a glass of red wine, and I give him a smile. I appreciate that he does things like that for me without needing to ask, that he pays attention. I used to feel uneasy around him, but over the past month or so, that feeling has waned, and I have become more relaxed when we’re together.

“Come with me,” he says in my ear, and he leads me out of the room. We wander through the house as he shows me around. The house backs up to the beach, and the view is absolutely breathtaking. When we walk past the formal dining room, two of his cousins are sitting at the table chatting. One of the girls looks up at me and invites me to join them. I look to Ryan, and he says, "I'll just be in the other room helping my mom out."

I nod my head and walk over to sit down as he leaves the room.

Not remembering their names, I say, "I'm sorry, but with all the introductions, I can't remember your names."

"I'm Tori, and this is Jenna."

"So, you live in Seattle too?" Jenna asks.

"Yeah, I grew up there. What about you, where do you guys live?"

"We both live in Astoria, but my sister, Katie, lives in Portland," Tori says.

The three of us begin to talk and get to know each other. The two of them, along with Katie, are the daughters of Ryan's two aunts. They are all married with kids and live in Oregon. They told me that Ryan is the only one in the family that lives in Washington, that he moved there after high school to go to college and just never came back. They seem genuinely interested in me and ask a lot of questions about college and my dancing.

"Tori, Madison's sick," her sister says as she comes into the room.

Tori asks, "What's wrong with her?"

"She was upstairs throwing up. I know there has been a stomach bug going around at her preschool, so I'm hoping that's all it is. I laid her down in Ryan's room, and she's sleeping now."

"Well, just let her rest. As long as she isn't running a fever, I wouldn't worry too much. I think Aunt Donna actually has some leftover Pedialite from when Connor got sick."

Turning to me, she says, "I'm sorry, it's been so crazy

today, and I didn't meet you earlier. I'm Katie, Tori's sister."

"I'm Candace."

"So, Ryan finally brings a girl home. I can't believe it," she says.

I see Tori give Katie a wide-eyed, annoyed look, and Katie dramatically says, "What?!"

Jenna and Tori both shake their heads at her, and I'm beginning to feel awkward, so I just ask, "What do you mean?"

Surely he's brought girls home before. From what Mark has told me about what he's heard from Ryan's friends, he has been through a slew of women.

Jenna tells me that all the women in the family are constantly giving him a hard time for never bringing a girl home, that I'm the first one.

"Well, we're just friends. Honestly, I think he only invited me because he felt bad that I was going to spend Christmas by myself."

The three of them give each other curious looks when I say this, which doesn't do much for my comfort level. I feel like they know something I don't, so I just come right out and ask, "Am I missing something here?"

Tori shakes her head at Jenna as Jenna leans in and quietly says, "I don't think that's why he invited you."

"What do you mean?"

Before anyone has a chance to say anything, Ryan's mom walks in and jokingly says, "You girls look like you're up to some gossip." Looking over at me, she says, "I've been so busy all day, I haven't had a chance to visit with you. Let's go chat."

Donna's personality reminds me a lot of Ryan's. She's not intimidating and seems fairly laidback and casual. She has a cute short bob of light blonde hair, and is tall and slender. She's dressed casually for the day in black pants and a red cable-knit sweater.

I stand up and grab my glass of wine as I follow her through the living room where I see Ryan helping one of his nephews put together a puzzle. When he looks up at me as I pass through, he gives me an endearing grin as I smile back. His mother and I walk out of the room into a quiet study.

She makes herself comfortable on the couch with a cup of coffee in hand while I sit in one of the plush chairs. Setting my wine down on a little round table next to the chair, I thank her for having me as a guest.

"You are more than welcome. I have been wanting to meet you for a while now."

I am flustered by her words, especially after the conversation I just had with his three cousins. "A while?" I ask.

"Yeah, ever since he first called me to tell me about you, I've been wanting us to meet."

Not wanting to sound like I'm snooping, I just let her comments be. "Well, I'm glad we got to meet. Ryan's been a good friend to me. I feel like I'm imposing a bit, but he insisted that I come."

"You're not imposing at all! When you have as many people over here as we do, adding one more to the mix is nothing," she says with a giggle. "Ryan tells me you have a fairly small family."

"Yeah, it's just me and my parents." Although I say this, I'm not so sure that's even true after last night. I kind of feel like Jase is my only family now, and at the same time, I wonder how much longer I will have him. He and Mark are very serious, and I have no clue what will happen after we all graduate this year.

"I hope you don't mind, but Ryan has told me a little bit about your family dynamics. I just wanted you to know that Ryan and I have a close relationship and he talks openly with me."

"I don't mind. I figured the two of you had a tight bond. You guys are lucky. I never had that with my parents." I take a sip of my wine when I start to feel the lump in my throat return. I have always wished for that type of closeness with my parents, but it never came. And now we couldn't be any more divided.

"So, Ryan tells me that you're studying ballet at school. It sounds like such fun, to have the opportunity to turn a passion into a career."

I can't contain my smile when I respond, "I can't imagine doing anything else with my life. I've taken ballet since I was a little girl, so when I graduated high school, there was no doubt what I wanted to do next."

"That's great to have that desire and focus. Not a lot of kids your age do."

Donna and I talk and get to know each other. She wants to know me better, and I find her to be warm and very easy to talk to. We are deep in conversation when we hear Ryan yell from across the house, "Mom! You're slacking in the kitchen! I think the ham is done!"

Donna and I look at each other and laugh.

"Can I help you in the kitchen?" I ask.

"I have it covered. You go and enjoy yourself."

"Really, I'd like to help."

Donna looks at me, and I can see in her eyes that she probably understands why. Taking my hand, she says, "I'd love that."

Before we ate dinner, Ryan finally let the kids open their gifts. He wasn't kidding when he said he had a lot. He clearly spoils his nieces and nephews rotten, and it was fun for me to sit back and watch him. He's just so relaxed with them. Ryan sat on the floor with Zachary, his nine-month-old nephew, in his lap and helped him tear off all the giftwrap, and then laughed in amusement when all Zachary wanted to do was play with the paper, waving it around in his hands.

Dinner wasn't like any Christmas dinner I have ever had. The kids ate at the bar and breakfast table, with Jenna sitting next to Zachary who's in a high chair. And everyone else spread out between the formal dining room and the living room. We couldn't all sit together with there being eighteen of us. The evening was casual with loud conversation and lots of laughter. Ryan's family made me feel as if I'd known them all forever. I really get along well with Tori and Jenna. Katie has been upstairs with her sick daughter most of the day, so I haven't had much time to get to visit with her.

After a while, the commotion and noise start to overwhelm me. Needing to take a little breather, I offer to take Katie a plate of food since she missed dinner. Walking upstairs, I quietly knock on the door to Ryan's room. I crack the door open and Katie is lying in bed next to Madison.

"I brought you some dinner," I whisper.

Katie gets out of the bed, and I hand her the plate.

"Thank you so much, Candace. That's really sweet."

Looking over at her daughter, I ask, "How's she feeling?"

"She doesn't have a fever, just an upset tummy mostly. I can't get her to go to sleep though."

"Well, I have no experience with kids, but do you mind if I try?"

"God, pleeease," she chuckles. "She has books in her bag by the bed if you want to try reading to her."

"Thanks. Why don't you go downstairs and eat? I'll stay with her."

"Are you sure?"

"Yes, go," I say with a smile.

"Okay. Thank you."

Walking over to the bed, I sit down and Madison rolls over with a tiny groan.

I tell her that I'm a friend of her Uncle Ryan's, and she immediately starts babbling about him and asking me questions. When she begins to slow down, I reach over to her bag and take out two books. They're both ballerina princess books.

"You like ballerinas?" I ask.

"Mmm hmm, I wanna be one. Mommy says when I turn four that I can go to dance class."

"I think you'll make a beautiful ballerina." She smiles up at me and I say, "Do you know that I'm a ballerina?"

"A real one or pretend?"

"A real one."

"You wanna be my friend?"

"Best friends."

She giggles as I open one of her books and begin to read. It isn't long until she is sound asleep with her head on my lap. Not wanting to wake her, I keep still and allow her to sleep.

Setting the books down, I finally take a moment to realize I am lying in Ryan's bed. I look around the room that he grew up in. He has a couple of surfboards leaning against one of the walls and a large flat screen mounted on the wall facing the bed. Something about being in his room makes my heart beat a little faster. I don't want to be feeling this way, but I am. The way he was with me last night makes me feel as if I want to like him more. I have never felt this way about any guy in the past, and that scares me. I only wish he knew me before this year, before I was so screwed up.

Light filters into the room when the door opens. Ryan

walks in, looks at me, and laughs. "Are you stuck under Maddie?"

"I didn't want to move and wake her up. What time is it?"

"Past eleven. Everyone has gone to bed. I told Katie to go on to bed and that I would check on you and Maddie."

"I wanted to thank your mother before she went to bed."

"Don't worry about it. Here's your bag. I made a big pallet of blankets and pillows downstairs in the living room. Since Maddie is in my room, we're just going to sleep down there. We can watch a movie or something if you want." He sets my bag on the floor and walks further into the room.

"Oh...ummm..." I mutter nervously. I was supposed to sleep in this room and Ryan was going to stay on the couch.

Sensing my hesitation, he says, "Don't worry. I'll take the floor and you can have the couch."

I smile at him as he walks over and grabs some clothes from his dresser. "I'll be downstairs. You can use my bathroom to change."

"Okay," I say as I slowly slide out from underneath Madison, careful not to wake her.

I grab my bag and go into Ryan's bathroom. I quickly take my sleeping pill, brush my teeth and hair, and then change into a pair of pajama pants and a black cami.

When I walk downstairs, I see Ryan in the kitchen wearing only a pair of flannel pajama pants that are hanging low on his hips. I'm surprised when I see a half-sleeve of tattoos on his right arm that spans a few inches onto his chest.

When he spots me from across the room, he says, "Grabbing some water. Want a bottle?"

"No, thanks."

I notice all the blankets and pillows piled into a big

fluffy makeshift bed in the center of the living room.

"You mind if I take the floor?" I ask.

"You sure?"

"Yeah. It looks more comfortable anyway."

"Okay."

Suddenly feeling nervous about spending the night here in the same room as Ryan, I apprehensively walk over and sit down, sliding the covers over my legs. He walks across the dark room, the only light coming from the last of the burning embers in the fireplace. I try not to stare at his bare chest that is revealing the tattoos I never knew he had. He sits down next to me and turns the TV on.

"TCM?"

I laugh at him and say, "It's all we ever watch. Why switch now?"

"I think you're starting to like my movies," he teases.

"Maybe."

We sit back and start watching a movie when Ryan turns to me and says, "Were you okay today?"

"I was. You're really lucky; you have a great family."

"Well, everyone really likes you, especially my mom."

"She's really nice. We had some time to visit earlier."

His words are sweet, but at the same time bring sadness. I only wish it was my parents who felt this way. But being here today, with his big family, has made me realize just how cold my family is. You can't even compare the two. Feeling the emotions tugging at me, I lie down and lay my head on the pillows sitting next to Ryan. He starts playing with my hair, and it's only a matter of minutes when I begin to feel the effects of my pill and drift off.

Gasping for breath, I thrash up out of a dead sleep. My

breathing is loud, and I'm confused about where I am until I hear Ryan say, "Candace," as he jumps off the couch and is by my side in a second, pulling me into his arms. "You okay?"

My body is stiff, and I'm shaken, panicked by what just happened. I have no idea what I was dreaming about. I start taking deeps breaths.

"What happened, babe?"

"Bad dream," I quietly whisper through my erratic breathing. I have no idea what brought that on.

"Slow your breathing down, okay?"

I do as he says and concentrate on his heartbeat as he holds me against his chest. Wrapping my arms around him, he begins to stroke one of his hands up and down my back. Once I'm calm and my breathing has steadied, he asks, "Wanna talk about it?"

I don't speak; I just shake my head no. Truth is, I don't know what I was even dreaming about, and the last thing I want to do is try to remember it.

Ryan slides under the covers with me and lays us down, both on our sides facing each other. I look up into his eyes, and he is staring back into mine. Holding me tightly against his warm body, looking into his clear-blue eyes, my heart begins to quicken again, but in a completely different way. He brings his hand up and gently places it on the side of my cheek. My breath catches, and I am so close to him that I can hear his breaths as they begin to increase slightly. Everything about him is calling me. I'm too scared to even move, but at the same time, I want to move. He's all around me, and I still want more. Never taking his eyes off of me as we lie in the darkness, I grasp onto a thread of bravery and bring my hand up to cup his cheek as he is doing mine. Wrapped up in each other, his gaze slowly moves down to my mouth. I shouldn't be wanting to do what I know he wants to, but when his eyes flick back to mine, I keep my eyes locked on his as I nod my head, my timid way of letting him know what I want.

Lowering his head slowly, my heart begins to pound in my chest as he gently presses his soft lips to mine, and my eyes fall shut. My body starts to tremble under his arms, and he grips me tighter. His kisses are slow, but purposeful. When I begin to move my lips softly with his, he glides his hand from my cheek to the back of my head, weaving his fingers into my hair and holding me close.

He brushes his tongue across my upper lip, and a soft noise escapes my throat. I want this, and I want this with him, but I'm scared. I've never felt this way before, and I don't know what it is about him that makes me feel like this. I take my hand from his cheek, slide it under his arm, back up around his broad shoulder, and grip tightly. My heart is all over the place as our lips meld together.

Without breaking our connection, he shifts me onto my back. He begins to softly nip and suck, taking his time and not rushing our kisses. I slide my hands down his shoulders and hold tightly onto his muscular arms. When I feel his tongue brush across my lip again, I part my lips more and allow him to deepen the kiss. He dips his tongue into my mouth and caresses it against mine.

My emotions are running high, and I'm not used to the feelings that course through me. Suddenly, the thought creeps in that I'm too damaged for him to ever want to be with me. And what if I'm just another girl to him? I can't do this. I realize that I'm feeling too much, and he now has the potential to hurt me.

I push my hands against his arms, and he pulls back."I'm sorry," I barely whisper, keeping my eyes closed because I'm embarrassed to look at him.

He continues to hold me tightly in his warm arms. "Look at me, Candace," he breathes out.

I take a second before I hesitantly open my eyes and look into his. Supporting himself above me on one elbow, he takes his hand and brushes the back of his fingers along my face.

“I don’t want you to feel sorry for that.”

Another small noise escapes me as I nod. I can’t speak, because holding on as tightly as I am to keep my tears from falling is taking up all the strength I have. So, I wrap my arms around him, clinging to his warmth, to the belief that I didn’t just do something stupid—clinging to my hope that he won’t hurt me.

Leaning down and resting his forehead against mine, I can’t help myself when I tilt my chin up and gently kiss him. His lips fall slowly onto mine, pushing my head into the pillow. I cup his face between my two hands before he languidly pulls his lips from mine. Lying back on his side, he pulls me into him, and for the first time in my life, I let someone besides Jase hold onto me through the night.

chapter twenty-two

My legs are tangled with Ryan's, and he's lying behind me with his arm draped around my waist. His warmth is wrapped around me and although I feel nervous about seeing him after our kiss last night, I also feel relaxed in his arms as he sleeps.

My stomach is full of butterflies, and I haven't even opened my eyes yet. What does this all mean? I wish I knew where his head was at, what he's thinking. At the same time, I feel like I'm not guarding myself like I probably should be. What if that kiss didn't mean anything to him? What if that's something he just does with any girl? Did he feel what I felt?

Taking in a deep breath, I hold it and try to clear my head of all these jumbled thoughts. When I let out my breath, I open my eyes and see two round blue eyes staring into mine.

"Night night over."

"It's not over, Bailey," Ryan mumbles behind me in a sleepy raspy voice.

I look at Bailey, Ryan's two-year-old niece, and give her a grin.

"I eat bweakfast. Night night over," she says to me in her sweet toddler voice.

"Okay," I whisper to her as I start to wriggle my way from underneath Ryan's arm.

He pulls me back down and with his eyes still shut says, "Where are you going?"

"To go get her something to eat." I slide out from under the pile of blankets and walk to the dining room while Bailey follows.

Pulling out a chair for her at the table, she takes a seat and says, "I eat ceweal."

"Sounds good. Where's the cereal?" I say to myself as I walk into the kitchen and open the door to the pantry. I scan around and see a box of Cookie Crunch.

"How about this?" I ask her as I hold up the box.

A big smile covers her face, and I start opening and closing cabinets to find her a bowl.

"The kid's things are in the cabinet by the fridge," Ryan says from across the room.

I look over my shoulder at him as he is walking toward me. His hair has a messiness to it that just adds to his appeal. I shake off the thought and turn around to pour the cereal in the bowl.

I walk over to the table and set it in front of the little girl and then peel open a banana for her as well.

"Fanks," she says around a mouth full of cereal.

When I walk back into the kitchen, Ryan is starting a pot of coffee. The house is quiet and we are the only ones up.

"Want some?" he asks as he is opening the cabinet to grab the mugs.

I lean back against the counter opposite of him and nod my head. I don't know what to say to him, and I'm a bundle of nerves as I watch him move around the kitchen.

"Umm, I'm gonna sneak upstairs and get cleaned up." I need space to regroup and watching him move around wearing nothing but a loose pair of pajama pants is way too distracting for me.

"Here," he says as he pours the creamer in my coffee

and adds one sugar.

"Thanks." I take the cup, and avoid eye contact. *What am I doing? Why does this make me so uncomfortable?* Even the fact that he remembers how I take my coffee feels like too much.

It's always been difficult for me to connect to people, to let them in. Jase says it's because of the lack of affection I had when I was growing up. Maybe he's right. I've only ever truly let one person in—Jase. Guys have always made me feel awkward. I don't know how to respond to affection, and I wind up feeling embarrassed and shy. For the first time, I don't want to feel that way. Not with Ryan. Maybe it's because he has seen a part of me that no one besides Jase has.

Fighting with my parents has been my life. I am used to the chilled air that surrounds them. But having Ryan witness that, and then watching me fall apart, is something that no one has seen. I've always kept that hidden within me.

"Hey," he says, and I am snapped out of my thoughts. "You okay?"

No. I'm confused. I don't want to be, but I am. What happened last night? What did that mean?

"Yeah, I'm fine. I just want to get ready before everyone wakes up."

"Okay."

I turn and make my way upstairs and quietly sneak into his room, careful not to wake Madison.

I take my time showering and getting ready, needing to pull my thoughts together before going downstairs. Yesterday was overwhelming, being around Ryan's large family. I am so used to calm and quiet. I can already hear the kids playing as I slip on my jeans and one of my old UW sweatshirts. Wrapping my hair on top of my head in a messy bun, I hear a knock on the bathroom door.

"Come in," I say. When the door opens, Ryan walks in

and leans up against the sink right next to me. I look over at him while I'm swiping on some lip-gloss and start putting everything away. He watches me as I pack my things up, and when I pass him, he takes me by the waist and pulls me in.

"What's wrong?" he asks.

"Nothing. Really."

Cocking his head slightly to the side, he says, "You wanna get out of here for a while?"

Without thinking too much, I nod my head.

He takes my hand, but this time it's different. He laces his fingers through mine and leads me downstairs. Everyone is moving about, eating breakfast, and tending to all the kids. He walks us into the formal dining room where his mother and cousins are sitting. I see Donna's eyes go straight to our hands, and I quickly try to pull my hand away, but he grips me tighter.

"Good morning, Candace," she says as she stands up and gives me a hug. "How did you sleep last night?"

"Good, thank you."

"Hey, Mom, we're going to go to Indian Beach for a while," Ryan tells her.

"Oh, okay. Well, the girls and I are heading to Astoria for the day to do some shopping, so we won't be around. But the guys are going to stay here with all the kids."

"What are the plans for dinner tonight?"

"The kids really want Fultano's Pizza," she says.

"Text me when you're driving back, and we'll go pick it up," Ryan tells her.

"Thanks, dear." She leans in and kisses him on the cheek. "You guys have a good day."

We head out to the jeep and start driving towards Ecola Park to the beach. The drive is quiet as we weave through the lush trees on the narrow, winding road. The surroundings are absolutely stunning, considering the dark grey skies and rainy weather. When we make our way out of the canopy of trees, Ryan parks the jeep, reaches into the back seat, and grabs me a hooded raincoat.

"Here, wear this," he says as I take the coat from him.

When we get out of the jeep, I shrug on the huge coat and pull the hood over my head. The wind off the water is strong, and the chill is biting. He takes my hand again and starts walking us down the wooden stairs to the wet puddled sand and rocks. This place is beautiful in a dark and moody way. We are the only ones on the beach aside from a few surfers in wetsuits out in the water. I follow Ryan and we walk along the uneven stacks of black rocks toward a few logs of driftwood. We sit on one of the logs, and he wraps his arm around me as I shiver in the rainy cold. The view of the deep cliffs around us and the sea stacks in the water are awesome.

"This is amazing," I say.

"Yeah, I love it out here. I used to surf here a lot growing up."

I nod my head, remembering the surfboards in his bedroom.

"Candace," he says as he turns his focus on me. Looking into my eyes, he asks, "What's bothering you? And don't say nothing, because I know something is."

Looking away, back at the water, I try to find my words. If I don't talk to him, then the awkwardness will just continue. But, what do I say? There are a million things racing through my head, and I am finding it hard to hone in on just one. And what if he thinks I'm crazy for reading too much into a kiss that was probably something so casual to him?

"Candace," he says, and I turn to look back at him.

I let out a breath before admitting, "I just don't really know what we're doing." It's all I can say.

Shifting his one leg over the log, he turns to face me straight on. “Tell me what you want.”

What? Why can’t he just tell me what he wants?

Not wanting to look at him, I stare out into the water again when I confess, “I’m not good at this stuff, Ryan.”

“Come here,” he says as he tugs on my leg, and I shift my body slightly to face him. “I’ve wanted to kiss you since the night of the concert. I don’t know where your head is at, but whenever I’m not with you, I want to be.”

My heart begins to race as he says this to me. It’s what I was hoping to hear, but also what I was scared to hear.

When I drop my head, he says, “Talk to me, babe.”

“I just...I don’t do this well.”

“Do what?”

“This...” I stop talking when he cradles my face in his hands and moves me so that I’m looking at him.

“Whatever *this* is, I want it. I just need to know if you do.” His eyes are serious, and he never takes them off of me as he speaks. It’s intimidating and makes me anxious. Hearing him speak so honestly makes my stomach flutter. I’m scared. I’m happy. I’m all over the place when I finally look up at him. And with trepidation, I nod my head yes.

A smile breaks across his face as he pulls me in and kisses me. I wrap my arms around him, underneath his coat as his cold, rain soaked lips cover mine. He draws me in tight, and I melt into him. Pushing my fears aside, I focus solely on him. His hold on me is strong, which contrasts his gentle kisses. He’s in no rush as he takes his time, dragging his tongue across my lip and slipping it inside my mouth. When our tongues slide across each other, I tighten my grip on him. His lips are soft, and I can taste a hint of mint on him. He holds my head and guides me with him as we move with one another. I’ve never been kissed the way Ryan kisses me. He’s slow and deliberate, and I can feel that it’s more than just a kiss to him, which settles me because it's more than that for me too.

His hands still on my cheeks, he breaks our kiss, and I stare up into his eyes when he says, "Should we get out of here?"

"Let's stay." I'm in no hurry to go back to his house, and I don't want this moment to end just yet.

"Come here." He pulls me onto his lap, and I hook my arms around his neck. He is much larger than I am, so I fit perfectly in his hold.

"Can I ask you something?"

"Anything," he says as he turns his head to look at me.

"I never asked before because I didn't want to intrude, but...where is your father?"

He lets out a slow breath and shifts his focus out to the beach. "He died about ten years ago." He turns to face me again, and I feel awful for asking.

"I'm sorry, I shouldn't have asked," I say when I drop my head, feeling bad for bringing it up.

Lifting my chin to look up at him, he says, "Candace, you can ask me anything. I don't want you to feel like you can't, okay?"

"Yeah," I quietly sigh and turn my head away from him, still feeling like I shouldn't have asked him that.

After a moment he begins to speak. "My dad was an asshole." When I look at him, he continues, "He drank way too much and was never around, but when he was, he was a total dick. So, don't feel bad for asking, because I don't feel bad that he's dead."

His voice is hard when he speaks, and I have no idea how to respond to his harsh words. I want to know more, but I don't dare ask. Whatever is underneath this is something that seems painful, so I let it go.

I look up at the cliff that is behind us and notice a roped

off ledge. "Is there a trail up there?"

Turning his head to see what I'm looking at, he says, "Yeah, it's a pretty decent path if you want to go up there."

Needing to cut this intensity, I say, "Yeah, let's go."

He eyes my leopard rain boots and asks, "Those have enough traction?"

"We'll see." I giggle and hop off of his lap and grab his hands to pull him off the log.

He smiles at my laugh and leans down to give me a chaste kiss before bending down and grabbing me behind my knees, scooping me up over his shoulder. I squeal as he starts hauling me up the stairs while I hang upside down. I don't even think to tell him to put me down because I love this feeling of playfulness. I honestly can't remember the last time I have felt like this; I don't think I ever have.

We hike along the path and explore the area for a couple hours. I was apprehensive about coming on this trip with him, but I'm so glad I did. My discomfort has dissipated, and it feels like it always has with us—light and easy.

We start walking back to the jeep, thoroughly wet and windblown.

"You up for shopping?" he asks me with a smirk.

"Shopping?"

"Yeah, everyone is leaving tonight, so I need to get the kids hopped up on sugar before they go," he jokes. Opening my door, he helps me up into my seat before walking around to the other side. When he gets in, I ask, "Where are we going?"

"Seaside. There's a cool candy shop called The Buzz."

I laugh at his excitement. "Your cousins are going to hate you, you know?"

"I'm their uncle, it's my job to spoil the shit out of those kids to spite their parents."

He makes me laugh, but his love for his nieces and nephews is apparent. I get the feeling that is how they all are with each other. It feels so abnormal to be around them, but I know it's because I've never had that in my life. It's always just been me and my parents, and there was never any warmth between us.

Ryan reaches over, laces his fingers with mine, and holds my hand. I smile when I look over at him. I sit back, with our hands connected, and enjoy his quiet company as we drive.

Pulling onto the Broadway Strip of Seaside, there are throngs of people walking on the sidewalks, going in and out of the shops that line the street. When we find a parking spot, we walk to the candy shop. He leads me to the back of the store, and when I see what he is eying, I start laughing and say, "You cannot let those kids eat this stuff!"

"Watch me," he says with a devious smile.

I just stand there next to him, shaking my head as he tells the sales clerk to bag up chocolate-covered and peanut butter-covered Twinkies, chocolate covered bacon, and a chunk of peanut butter foam rock.

Looking over at me as he pays for the diabetic-coma-in-a-bag, he innocently says, "What?" as if he doesn't understand the absurdness of his purchase.

"Nothing," I say in a high-pitched mock defensive tone.

After grabbing lunch, we continue to shop around before deciding to head back. The rain has been constant all day, and we are both in desperate need of clean, dry clothes, especially since we decided to hike in the mud earlier.

Ryan's mom calls to let us know that they are on their way back to the house, so we stop by Fultano's to pick up a few pizzas for an early dinner before everyone leaves.

We arrive home before his mother and aunts do, so Ryan stashes the pizzas in the oven and offers to take the older kids upstairs to play to give their dads a little break. There is a large playroom that he takes the three kids into and has me shut the door behind them.

"Can you guys keep a secret?" he asks them.

Madison, Bailey, and Connor, his four year-old nephew, all say 'yes' in excited unison when Ryan pulls out the bag of sugary junk. I sit back on one of the couches in the room and laugh as Ryan and the kids dive into everything. Watching how he is with these kids, laughing and playing on the floor, is another reason for me to like him even more. I know he owns a successful business and works hard, but it's nice that he has this lighthearted side to him as well.

Ryan comes over to sit next to me with one of the pieces of chocolate covered bacon.

"Here," he says as he tries to hand it to me.

Pushing his hand away, I say, "Gross. I'm not eating that."

"It's surprisingly really good." He takes a bite out of it and holds the leftover piece to my mouth. "Just try it," he says, and I open my mouth and bite it out of his grip.

I'm amazed that it is actually good. The salt and smoke of the bacon blends well with the sweetness of the chocolate.

"Okay, you win. That was actually really good," I admit.

Ryan looks out the window that's over my shoulder then back to the kids.

"Guys, eat fast. Our mom's just pulled up."

The three of them giggle as they try desperately to scarf down the rest of the sweets. Ryan and I laugh while watching them in their simplicity of fun. We get up, and Ryan wads up all the wrappers.

Holding out my hands, I say, “Give them to me. I’ll hide them.”

The kids run downstairs and Ryan hands over the wrappers as I walk to his room. He follows me in and closes the door behind us. I walk into the bathroom and toss everything in the trashcan. When I walk out, Ryan is sitting on the edge of the bed.

“Come over here,” he says.

Walking over to him, he pulls me between his legs and slides his arms around my waist. Because of our height difference, we are almost level. Looking at me, he says, “I’m glad you’re here with me.”

I smile at him with my hands gripped on his shoulders. “Me too.”

Placing his hand behind my neck, he draws me in so he can kiss me. He keeps the kiss short then pulls me down to sit on his knee. The room is dark as we stare at each other with our foreheads resting together. Being like this with him, in this quiet room, is peaceful. Neither one of us speaks as we sit here together.

“We should go downstairs,” I whisper.

Whispering back, he says, “Not yet.”

We stay like this, me on his knee, foreheads together, when Connor comes bursting through the door.

“Busted!” he shouts.

I jump up, and Ryan turns to him. “What do you mean?”

“Bailey had chocolate on her face and Mom is blaming you.”

“Okay, kid, let’s go face the firing squad.”

When Connor starts running back downstairs, Ryan and I follow.

“What did you feed these kids?” Tori asks Ryan.

“I’ll never tell, and neither will they,” he jokes as the

kids start laughing uncontrollably. "Call it a going-home present," he says with a wink.

"Payback's a bitch. Just remember that, Ryan. One of these days, when you have kids, you'll see."

Ryan laughs at her, and I try to stifle my laugh as well. Watching their playful banter is pretty funny.

The house is quiet and still. Everyone left about an hour ago, and I have been curled up on the couch, reading one of my favorite childhood books I found on the bookshelf, since I got out of the shower. Ryan is upstairs, getting cleaned up, while I drink a cup of hot tea and read as the rain trickles down the large windows that look out to the beach.

"Where's Ryan?" Donna asks as she walks into the room.

"He's taking a shower."

She grabs a couple blankets and joins me on the couch. "Here, cover up. It's cold."

Draping the blanket across my lap, I set the book down and say, "Thanks."

She wraps up in her blanket and asks, "How are you doing, dear?"

"Good actually. I'm sorry I wasn't around much to visit with everyone. I hope no one thought I was being rude."

"No one thought that. Please, no need to apologize."

"It's just...I'm not used to being around a large group. It's a little overwhelming for me."

"You don't need to explain. Everyone loves you. It was a nice surprise to have you, and Ryan seems really happy."

"Oh," I say, not sure how to respond to her statement.

"Ryan said he went to meet your parents on Christmas Eve. I've been so busy, I haven't had a chance to ask him about it. How did it go?" she questions.

Looking down at my tea, I shake my head. "Not well."

She reaches over and places her hand on my knee. "What happened?"

I sit there, trying to figure out where I should begin. I've been so busy the past few days that I haven't had much time to think about our fight. Now that I am searching for the words, the finality of our fight plays back in my head. I swallow hard against the lump in my throat, and when I open my mouth to speak, I can't seem to get anything out. I close my mouth and stare into Ryan's mother's eyes.

"Oh, sweetie," is all she says when she scoots closer and wraps me in her arms.

How is it that this woman I just met yesterday seems to read me better than my own mother? Why can't my mother just love me? Why has she never loved me? My thoughts become too much, and I begin to weep quietly as Donna rubs my back. My mother has never comforted me like this, not even when I was a little girl. When I was younger, it was always the nanny who would lie with me when I got sick, or put Band-Aids on my knees when I would fall off my bike. Why couldn't I have had a loving family like Ryan's?

"Do you want to tell me about what happened?" she asks as she pulls away.

Wiping my tears, I decide to open up to her. "We got in a bad fight. It wasn't good. They told me they were done with me and not to come back."

"My God," she says quietly in shock.

"What's worse is that Ryan heard it all."

"Ryan would never judge you for that."

"I hope not, but it was embarrassing nonetheless."

"What were you arguing about?" she asks.

"The same thing we always fight about. They aren't happy with my choices. I'm not good enough. I don't measure up to the name they work hard for." Donna leans over to the end table and hands me a box of tissues. I pull one out and wipe the tears from my cheeks. "It's always been this way, but then at Thanksgiving my mother told me that I was nothing but an embarrassment to her."

"I'm so sorry, dear. No child should ever have to hear that."

"Hear what?" Ryan questions, and when I look up, I see him walking down the stairs. He crosses the room and comes to sit next to me on the couch as I face his mother. I try not to look at him as he wraps one of his arms around me.

"Candace is telling me about what happened the other night."

"Mom."

"It's fine," I say.

Covering my hand with hers, she asks, "Do you have any other family at all?"

"No. It's only ever been the three of us since my father's parents' passed away."

"What about your mother's family?"

"I've never met them. I have never known them to speak. I'm not even sure they know about me." Wiping my cheeks again, Ryan rests his other hand on my leg. He doesn't say anything, he just sits there, letting his mom and I talk.

She shakes her head as if she can't believe what I am saying. Leaning forward, she takes me in her arms again. The comfort I am getting, being held by both Ryan and his mother is almost too much for me, but I know this is what I've been missing my whole life. I wrap my arms around Donna as more tears fall.

Letting go of me, she says, "I'm glad you're here with us," as she brushes her thumbs under my eyes. "I'll let the two of you be," she says to Ryan then kisses my forehead.

When she leaves the room, Ryan pulls me back onto his chest.

"Don't cry, babe," he says softly in my ear.

"I'm tired. I don't want to talk anymore."

Ryan gets off the couch, and I follow him upstairs. Walking into his room, I go into the bathroom to take my sleeping pill and brush my teeth. When I walk out, he is still standing by the door. I crawl into his bed and don't even question him when he slides in behind me. He pulls me into him and curls himself around me. Neither one of us moves, we just lie there, snuggled up together. I've never had this before. But there is something about Ryan, about the way he makes me feel, that makes me want this—with him.

chapter twenty-three

"Morning, babe."

Lifting my head and looking up at Ryan, in the still-dark room, he has me tucked tightly against him. Trying to wake from my sleep, I let my head fall lazily back down on his chest. His thumb is stroking my shoulder, and I blink a few times before fully opening my eyes.

The room is cold, and I sink further down in the bed beneath the covers.

I hear Ryan chuckle under his breath as he says, "What are you doing?"

"I'm cold," I whisper.

"You're always cold."

I roll over onto my stomach and look up at him. "I know."

He reaches down, pulls me back up against him, and wraps the comforter around me.

Aside from Jase, I have never slept a full night in bed with any other man. I thought it would be weird; maybe it would be with anyone else, but with Ryan it feels safe.

We are supposed to be driving back to Seattle later today, and I'm not quite sure how Jase is going to react to this new development. He knows I'm here; I texted him after the fight with my parents to let him know I was going to be with Ryan, but I haven't spoken with him since I have been here.

"Why are you so quiet?" Ryan asks me.

"Just thinking."

"About?"

Snaking my arm around his waist, I say, "Jase. He and Mark will be back Saturday."

He rolls on his side and props himself up on his elbow. Looking down at me, he says, "Stop thinking," as he leans down and nuzzles his head in my neck, lightly nipping on the sensitive flesh. Goosebumps begin to prick on my skin. Raising his head, my hands holding his face, he says, "Do you know how beautiful you look right now?"

His words make my heart quicken, and I pull his face down to me and kiss him.

"Are you guys all packed up?" his mother asks as Ryan pulls out some cold pizza for us to eat.

We spent the morning lying in bed, dozing in and out of sleep, and just enjoying the calm of being alone.

Handing me a slice, he turns to her and says, "Yeah, I have to go to my office and get a bunch of paperwork done, and Candace has to work tonight."

The three of us sit together at the table, eating cold leftover pizza. I sit and listen to Ryan and his mother talk to each other. They have a natural flow and connection between them, and it's apparent that the two of them are really close.

"Candace, will you take a quick walk with me on the beach before you go?" she asks.

I look up at Ryan, and he smiles at me before getting up from the table. Turning to look at Donna, I answer, "Yeah. Let me go grab my rain boots."

The mist is light this morning, as we walk along the

firm puddled sand. The wind is kicking hard, and the waves are rough as they crash along the shore.

"I'm sorry if I pushed too much yesterday," she says, looking at me over her shoulder.

"You didn't. I don't ever talk about that stuff with anyone, but it felt nice to unload a little of it."

"I feel just awful about what you've been through, and I want you to know, that even though we just met, you can talk to me whenever you want. I'll give you my number before you leave. Call me, please."

I nod my head and say, "Okay."

"Everyone needs a parent they can depend on, including you, dear."

I'm taken back by her words. Donna has such a warm and maternal demeanor.

She stops and turns to face me when she says, "He hasn't always had it easy, you know? He doesn't let a lot of people in, but I know you're special to him, which makes you special to me. From what Ryan has told me, he's really lucky to have you."

We stand there, facing each other, and I'm at a complete loss for words. Where have these people been? Why are they just now in my life? Why couldn't I have met Ryan years ago? I could have possibly been saved from so much, and now I feel like I could destroy this if he knew my secret. Standing on this beach right now with his mother, I vow to do everything I can to bury this deep down. If he knew, he would never look at me the way he does now. He would be disgusted, and everything would crumble. I can't have that happen. I've lost Kimber, I've lost my parents, I've even lost myself; I can't lose anyone else.

When Ryan pulls up to my house, I quickly jump out to stretch after the long drive. Ryan gets my bag and walks me inside. He follows me back to my room as I go to put my bag away. I turn to look at him standing in the doorway. He's looking around my room as if he is taking in every detail.

"What?" I question, feeling a little too self-conscious of my belongings.

He walks right up to me and scoops me up in his arms. I love it when he holds me like this, I think he gets a kick out of how light I am and picks me up often. I wrap my arms around his neck and giggle as I look down at him.

"You've got a lot of ballet shit in here," he says, and I can't help but laugh at him.

"Yeah, I do."

Leaning my head down, we spend the next few minutes kissing each other. He is always so patient with his kisses, never rushing. It's perfect. He walks over to my bed and lays us down. He doesn't push to go any further than kissing, and I thank God for that because I don't think I am capable of doing anything else. He just holds me.

"What time do you have to be at work?" he asks.

"At seven. I have to close, so I won't be home till midnight."

"Come to my place tonight."

"I don't...I," I stumble over my words, not really knowing what to say, but stop trying when I hear Ryan chuckle at me.

"Why are you nervous? You've slept with me for the past two nights."

"Stop laughing at me," I say as I nudge him in the ribs. "And that was just a little different."

"Why?"

"Because your mother was there."

He starts laughing again, and I know he's not doing it to be rude, but I'm scared. This makes me nervous, and I don't know how to explain it to him. I'm sure most girls wouldn't have an issue with this. Most would be doing more than kissing like a couple of kids, but I don't know what I'm doing, and this scares the shit out of me.

When he realizes that I'm no longer talking, he shifts over me, and in a more serious tone asks, "What's going on?"

I shake my head, because what could I possibly say to a twenty-eight-year-old man that isn't going to sound completely pathetic.

"Talk to me."

"I don't know what to say," I tell him honestly.

"Say what you're thinking, babe."

"I told you that I don't do this well. I just...I don't." Taking a deep breath I close my eyes and continue, "I don't do this, I'm..." *Shit. Why can't I get my words out without sounding like an idiot?*

"Open your eyes. Don't hide from me." When I look at him, he brushes his hand through my hair and says, "We'll move as slow as you want. But, I want you in my bed tonight. I want you next to me."

"Okay," I whisper.

"I want you to talk to me though. I need you to tell me what is going on in your head. I'll never judge you." God, why does he have to say these things to me? His words pierce through me and melt me, but they also intimidate me. How can I be open with him when I have never opened up to anyone besides Jase?

He brings me out of my thoughts when he says, "I'll never hurt you. I just need you to trust me."

I nod my head at his words, but how can I trust him like that when I don't trust anyone?

"Come on," he says as he stands up and pulls me off the bed. "I have to run and take care of things at work. You'll come over tonight." He doesn't ask, he just tells me. Not allowing a response, he leans down and kisses me before leaving.

After I unpack, I call Jase. I need to talk to someone about everything, and when he answers the phone, I break at the sound of his voice. My emotions are all over the place, but Jase is my rock, and I really need him right now.

"What's wrong?"

"I don't really know where to begin. I wish you were here. I just really need you right now." My voice trembles as I try hard not to cry.

"Sweetie, you're scaring me"

"I think I may be getting in way over my head with Ryan."

"What are you talking about? What's going on with Ryan?"

Not sure where to begin, I just start rambling uncontrollably, and I'm sure I'm not making any sense. "He kissed me, and I kissed him back. We've been sleeping next to each other. He told me he wants to be with me, and I foolishly agreed. Now we're back home, and he wants me to spend the night at his place. And I just have no clue what the hell I'm doing. And you're not here. And I'm freaking out. And..."

"Whoa, you have to slow down," he cuts me off. "Go back. He kissed you?"

"Uh huh."

"What happened?"

"It was late Christmas night. We were lying down, and it just sort of happened. I don't know. We just kissed, then we fell asleep together."

"Well, how did you feel when you woke up?"

"Really confused. I mean, I know we've been hanging out a lot, but I feel like I don't know a whole lot about him. And then everything Mark told me about all the girls started freaking me out."

"But he told you he wants to be with you?"

"Yeah, we went to the beach, he just came out and told me, and then I agreed with him. We ended up sleeping together again. And then his mother was insinuating that he's talked to her about me in the past, and that kinda intimidates me."

"Why?"

"What do you mean? You know I have zero experience with this shit. I have no clue what I'm getting myself into. I have never felt this way about anyone before, and I'm scared."

"What are you scared of?"

"Everything. He hasn't done anything more than kiss me, but what happens when he wants to do something else? Knowing what Mark told me, I feel like I just can't handle this. I'm scared he's going to touch me, and then what?"

"Ryan doesn't seem like the kind of guy who would push you."

"What? How do you know?"

"Because, he told me how he feels about you."

"What?!" I squeal out. "When?!"

"He called me Christmas Eve to tell me what happened with your parents. He told me that he's been having feelings for you for a while and wanted to know if he was wasting his time."

“What did you say?”

“I told him I thought he should tell you. But I told him not to fuck with you if he wasn’t serious, that you’ve been dealing with a lot, and that I didn’t want to see you get hurt.”

I’m shocked. My heart is racing, and I don’t know what to say.

“Candace?”

“Yeah, I’m here. Why didn’t you tell me?”

“I’m telling you now.”

“Don’t joke with me, Jase.”

“Because if I told you, you would have never let this happen. You would have completely shut him out, and you need to start living again.”

“I have been living.”

“You’ve been existing. There’s a big difference.”

His words cut into me. I can continue to make excuses, but I know he’s right. Tears well up in my eyes, and when I sniff, Jase is right there with me.

“Don’t cry, Candace.”

“I’m scared.”

“I know. But it’s okay to feel that way. You have to feel this. You have to start opening yourself up again.”

“Am I going to lose you?” Wow, that came out of nowhere. But, I have been thinking a lot about what will happen after this year. Plus he’s with Mark now. What if Mark gets a job out of state? Will Jase go with him? What if Jase gets a job out of state? And where will I get a job?

“Never. I promise.”

“I want you to come home.”

“Two more days. Don’t cry. It’ll be fine.”

“Okay.”

When I hang up the phone, I take a deep breath and pull myself together. I throw a load of laundry in and repack my bag before heading out to work. I try not to think too much about all the possible outcomes of what I am getting myself into. I like Ryan, and Jase's reassurance gives me the push I need to move forward, to try to open up to him. That's all I can really do—just try.

chapter twenty-four

It's a little past midnight when I pull into Ryan's driveway. The lights are on up on the second floor. I grab my bag, walk to the side of the building, and up the flight of stairs that lead to his front door. I stand there for a while and think about what Jase told me earlier. Based on what he said, I shouldn't be nervous about Ryan, but I am.

Aside from everything else, this is new to me. The guy I dated in high school hardly counts as a relationship. We barely even knew each other, and he didn't care enough about me to really even pay much attention to me. It was a relationship of convenience; he served as a distraction from my home life, and that's it. Aside from graduation night, we never had much of a physical relationship. I am completely inexperienced, and I know it. The fact that I am almost twenty-three makes it even more embarrassing.

I am startled when Ryan opens the door.

"What are you doing out here?" he asks.

"Umm, nothing. I was just about to knock," I lie.

He takes my bag out of my hand and steps to the side so that I can come in. I walk to the living room but don't sit. I stand like an idiot in the center of the room, not sure what I should be doing. I don't know why I feel so awkward tonight. Ryan was right; we have spent the past two nights together, so why do I feel weird about a third? Maybe it's because I am in *his* home. How many girls have been here? How many girls have slept in his bed? God, why am I even thinking about this?

He sets my bag down by the stairs that lead up to the third floor where his bedroom is, and starts walking toward me.

"Did you eat?"

"I did before I went to work."

When he reaches me, he wraps his arms around my waist, and the touch alone is enough to relax me a little bit. I clasp my hands together behind his back and lean my forehead against his chest.

Kissing the top of my head, he says, "Better?"

"Mmm hmm," I hum.

"Good. I'm wiped, what about you?"

"Yeah." Driving back from Oregon and then having to work so late, I'm drained.

Taking my bag, we go upstairs to his room.

"The bathroom is right over there," he says, and he points past his large closet.

Closing the door, I lay out my clothes and turn on the shower so that I can rid myself of the smell of coffee. That's the downfall of working at a coffee shop: you leave work smelling like an old pot of coffee.

After drying my hair, taking my sleeping pill, and brushing my teeth, I walk back in the room at the same time Ryan is coming back upstairs holding two bottles of water.

"Here," he says as he hands me one of the bottles.

"Thanks."

Ryan wears a pair of pajama bottoms with no shirt, and when he crosses the room, I notice another tattoo that looks like scripted words that is inked on the side of his ribs. He walks over to the large king-sized bed and starts pulling back the covers. I hop up on the bed and slip under the sheets.

Ryan sits next to me, leaning his back against the dark leather headboard. When he lifts his arm to wrap around me, I can finally make out the words of his tattoo:

pain is a reminder
you're still alive

Laying my hand over it, I ask, "What's this for?"

He looks down at my hand and says, "A reminder." He takes my hand off the tattoo and holds it against his chest.

I then notice a jagged scar under the tattoo. I want to ask, but I don't. When Ryan sees what I'm looking at he says, "Like I said, my dad was an asshole." I shift my eyes to his when he begins talking again. "He was a drunk and liked to take his anger out on me and my mom. I took more of it than she did. The drunker he was, the worse it would get. He was like that for as far back as I can remember. It was all I knew. Then one night, I beat the shit out of him when he was wasted, and when he got in his car and left, he never came back. His car was found wrapped around a tree, and that was it. He was dead."

I'm sure my eyes are filled with horror as I listen to him speak because he pulls me tight and comforts me instead of me trying to comfort him. I am speechless; I can only tighten my grip around him to let him know how I feel. How could I have droned on about how shitty my parents are? I've had it pretty good compared to what he had to grow up with. And Donna, God, I had no idea. She is such a wonderful person. My heart hurts for what they must have gone through.

"You're the only one who knows that, outside of my mom and me," he tells me. He is only giving me more reasons to trust him.

"I feel really stupid. I'm so sorry about complaining about my parents."

"Candace, you're far from stupid. Your parents treated you like shit. They filled you full of misconceptions of yourself and fucked with your head. Anyone would be devastated. Don't dismiss your pain because you don't think it's worthy. It is."

Raking my fingers through the hair on the back of his head, I pull him down to kiss me. He slides down in the bed and hovers his body over me. He drags his lips from my mouth, across my cheek, and down my neck, taking little sucks along the way. I hold him close to me when he starts trailing kissing across my collarbone. Taking his face in my hands, I guide him back up to my lips. I begin to slip away to a place where nothing exists but us. His soft lips caress mine as we move at our slow pace. Taking one of my hands in his, he laces his fingers with mine and presses my hand into the mattress as I feel myself falling for him even more.

When Jase got back in town, we spent some much needed alone time together. Ryan has been busy this past week with work, and we haven't had much time to hang out during the days. In the mornings, we have been running together. Aside from that, I've been in the studio almost every day and picking up extra shifts at work.

Somehow I let Jase and Ryan talk me into going to Ryan's bar to hear Mark's band play tomorrow night. Still nervous about the possibility of seeing Jack out one of these days, the fact that I'll be there with Jase and Ryan was comforting enough for me to say yes.

Ryan is working late tonight, so Jase and I are spending the evening together at his place. After grabbing some tea and coffee at Peet's on the ground floor of Jase's apartment building, we head upstairs for the night.

Making ourselves comfortable on his couch, we talk for quite a while about Mark and Ryan. This is the first time that both of us have had boyfriends we can talk about, and I'm enjoying our newfound pastime for gossiping. But, the conversation takes a more serious tone when Jase asks, "Can you hear me out on something?"

"Sure. What's up?"

"I know I've brought this up before, but I want to bring it up again because you seem to be in a better place now."

"What are you getting at?"

"Have you thought about calling the detective from that night?"

"What? Why would I do that?"

"Because Candace, you know who did this, and the hospital has the evidence."

"I don't want to talk about this."

"What if he does this to someone else?"

"Drop it, Jase."

"Candace, think about it. If he could do what he did to you..."

"I'm serious, Jase. Drop it." My hands are shaking, and I cannot believe he even went there. Getting off the couch, I storm off to the bathroom and slam the door behind me. I have been trying so damn hard to not think about that night, and now when I close my eyes, I'm right back there. How could he do this to me? I turn on the faucet and splash cold water on my face, but the anger keeps coursing through me. Looking at myself in the mirror, I realize I'm crying, and when I see the tears, I get more pissed.

The door swings open, and Jase is standing there with guilt all over his face.

"What's wrong with you?!" I scream at him.

"Shit, Candace, I had no idea," he pleads. "I honestly thought you..."

"Would be over it by now?! I can't. He won't ever let me," I sob out. "I can still feel his hands all over me, and I hate it."

"God."

"All I have ever asked is for you to drop it, and now you bring this shit up?! Now?!"

"I thought..."

"I just can't. And God, Ryan would find out."

"He doesn't know?"

"No! He'll never know. He can't."

"Why?"

"Because I'd lose him. He'd run away. Who would want me?"

"You have to tell him."

"No, I don't. This is my secret, and I plan to keep it that way."

"Candace, I'm sorry. I didn't realize." His voice is hurt, and I feel horrible for blowing up at him like that.

"I'm sorry," I say then hug him. "I'm sorry."

"I never thought you'd be over it; I know you better than that. I just thought that you'd be in a little bit of a better place."

"Can we just forget about it?"

"Of course. Forgotten."

I decide to call it a night. Jase wanted me to spend the night, but I really need some space.

Seth's car is parked out front when I get home. As I walk past it, I notice for the first time that he has Greek letters on his back window; the same Greek letters of Jack's fraternity.

Oh my god.

Does Kimber know this? She'd almost have to know. I start to panic a bit, wondering if she's talked to Jack, and if so, what was said. Did he say anything about me?

I feel uncomfortable when I walk in and see Kimber and Seth watching a movie in the living room. I quickly walk through the room. Kimber doesn't say anything; she simply sits on the couch and looks at me when I walk to my room. This tension with Kimber hurts and the fact that Jase and I just had an argument, when we never argue, has me emotionally exhausted. God, I hate this.

Ryan seemed excited this morning on our run that I was finally going to come by his bar and hang out. After everything that happened with Jase last night, I am more apprehensive than ever, but I stuff it down deep because I know Ryan wants me at the bar with him tonight.

He's already there—he's been working all afternoon—and Mark drove with Chasten, the drummer, for a quick sound check. So, I'm getting ready and hanging out with Jase. The tension between us has dissipated and neither one of us mentions our fight.

Sliding my black boots on over my jeans, I say, "Okay, I'm ready."

"Finally," Jase teases as we start to head out.

I pull my hooded black raincoat over my plum satin swing top and lock the door behind me. When we get in the car, I text Ryan to let him know we are on our way.

"Mark is really excited that you're coming tonight."

"I feel bad that I've missed all of his shows," I say.

"Don't. He gets it."

Jase turns in down an alley, and I give him a look as he says, "We're parking in the back employee lot."

As we drive around the building, I'm surprised at the size. I had no idea he owned a place this big. Although it's dark and rainy out, I can see that the front lot and side streets are lined with cars.

Jase turns the car into a small empty spot in the back. When I get out and turn around, away from the car, my heart freezes—I can't breathe.

Holy shit.

I zone in on the blue chipped paint. I see those chips that expose the dark metal underneath almost every day. I'd know them anywhere.

When I take a step back, the heel of my boot snags on a divot in the asphalt and I trip, falling on my bottom. I begin to panic when I hit the ground. All I see is that dumpster, and I can't get up fast enough.

I can't even hear Jase as I see his lips move as he squats in front of me. Quickly, I pull myself up and Jase follows, grabbing my shoulders, he puts me back in the car. I lower my head to my knees and begin to sob uncontrollably.

When Jase gets in the car, I start screaming, "Get me out of here! Go! Get me out of here!"

He doesn't say a word as he starts the car. I sit up, with sobs wracking me. I'm still screaming when I see the back door open, and Ryan comes out. His eyes meet mine, and I can see the shock in his face as I'm crying and screaming at Jase to drive.

He rips out of the parking lot as I hear Ryan yelling my name.

Covering my face with my hands, I continue to wail.

Jase pulls the car into a gas station and throws the car in park. Getting out, he comes around to my side, opens my door, and kneels down beside me.

"Candace, I need you to breathe. Calm down, okay?"

But I can't. That night keeps replaying in my head. That dumpster. Jack ripping off my clothes. Digging my nails in the asphalt, trying to get away. It all flashes through me.

"Candace, look at me. What's wrong?"

Letting my head fall in my hands, I say, “That’s the alley. That’s the alley Jack...” I still can’t bring myself to say that word, but no words are needed when Jase pulls me into him and holds me.

“Oh God,” he mutters over and over as I cry.

My sobs begin to weaken, and fatigue overcomes me. I release my hold on Jase and fall back into the seat, thoroughly drained and exhausted.

“Let me take you back to my place, okay?”

My eyes sting from the mixture of tears and makeup, so I keep them closed and nod my head.

Walking into Jase’s apartment, I head straight to his bedroom and lay my head on his pillow. My head is pounding, and my body is weak. Jase lies down next to me and holds me.

“What can I do?” he asks hopelessly.

“Just make it go away,” I mumbled. If only he could, I just might have a fighting chance to be myself again. Instead I lie here, as I have so many times before: pathetic, weak, and broken.

Letting out a sigh of defeat, he tells me, “I wish I could. I would. I would do anything to take this away from you.”

I know that he would too, but hearing the pain in his voice brings on another slew of tears.

We both jump when there is a loud pounding on his door. I sit up when Jase gets out of bed.

“Stay here,” he says as he shuts the bedroom door behind him.

I soon hear Ryan’s loud voice demanding to know where I am and Jase yelling at him to give me space, when the door suddenly opens.

Still crying, I look up at Ryan, and he gently closes the door behind him and rushes over to the side of the bed where I am sitting. Kneeling between my legs, he holds firmly onto my knees. I hate seeing the pain and confusion in his eyes. I continue crying and repeating, "I'm sorry. I'm sorry, Ryan. I'm..."

Grabbing me behind my back, he slides me off the edge of the bed and onto the floor with him. "What happened, babe?"

Hiding my face in my hands as I cry, I keep apologizing. He pulls me tight against him, and I wonder what I could possibly say to excuse this breakdown. He's going to want to know, and I don't know what to do.

He takes my wrists and pulls my hands away from my face, "I need you to talk to me."

Looking down at my lap, I say the first thing that comes to my mind, "I just...I got myself too worked up and had a panic attack. I know you wanted me there tonight, but I couldn't."

"Why couldn't you just tell me?"

"I was embarrassed. This has happened a few times in the past, but only Jase knows that I have these."

He wraps me up in his arms, and I feel horrible. I didn't lie, but I still feel guilty.

When I'm calmed down, he backs away and looks me in the eyes when he says, "You could've come to me. Jase isn't the only one you have, you know?"

The hurt in his eyes is too much, and I have to look away, but he lowers his head to catch my dropping eyes. "I need you to trust me enough to talk to me." Nodding my head he continues, "I understand you and Jase, but I know how I feel about you." He takes a moment before softly saying, "I want you to need me more than him."

Feeling the need to defend myself, I say, "He's all I've

ever had."

Taking my hand in his, he places it against his chest when he tells me, "You have me now too."

I feel myself falling for him even more when I hear the sincerity in his words. Fisting his shirt in my hand, I wrap my free arm around his neck and hug him.

"Let's go home," he says into my ear, and I know that when he says home, he means his place, and I like that.

chapter twenty-five

School started back up this past week and so far, it seems that apart from my dance studios, classes should be fairly easy. Leaving my Technique Instruction lecture, I text Ryan to let him know I'm coming over a little earlier than planned since all we did was go over the syllabus.

The other day I was looking at the matted photos that I had seen back in November and when I asked to see more, he offered to show them to me this afternoon. I have been fixated on the photo I originally saw of the curve of a woman's back. I've been trying to not let my curiosity get the best of me, but I can't help but wonder who the women are in his photos.

When I arrive, the door is unlocked, so I let myself in. I don't see Ryan when I enter, so I call out, "Ryan?"

"Back in my office," he yells.

Walking down the hall to his home office, the door is cracked. I lightly knock before I enter.

"Hey, babe," he says as he leans back in his leather chair from behind his desk. "Come here."

I walk around his large desk as he scoots his chair back. He stretches his arms out and envelops me as I sit on his lap.

"How were your classes today?" he asks as he brushes my hair off my shoulder.

"Uneventful, but it's only the first week. Nothing but

going over the syllabus for the most part."

"I'm glad you're here. I've missed you," he says as he brings my head down so that he can kiss me.

I've been working more while Roxy rearranges the calendar to accommodate everyone's new class schedules. When I'm not working, I have been in the studio adding choreography and rehearsing my solo. Auditions for our final production are next month, so there hasn't been much time for Ryan and I to spend together.

"So, don't be mad, but..." I start when Ryan interrupts, "Oh, God."

"Just listen," I say. "When I was on campus today I ran into Stacy Keets who works at the Henry Art Gallery. She was telling me that one of her pieces got picked up for a gallery show next month."

"So, you want to go?"

"Yes, but I was thinking that you could submit one of your photos."

"Babe," he says as he cocks his head to the side. "Those are just a hobby that I hardly even take seriously. I'm far from having them displayed in a gallery of all places."

Rolling my eyes at him, I continue, "Well, I happen to love the few photos I've seen. They're a lot better than you think they are."

"You're cute," he teases.

"I'm serious, I think that you should at least submit something and see if it gets accepted. If not, nothing lost, right?"

"And if they are?"

"Then you can take me as your date for the showing," I say with a sly grin.

"If I say I'll think about it, will that suffice?"

"Yep."

Laughing at me, he buries his head in my neck and

starts nipping the curve of my shoulder, which he knows is my ticklish spot.

Giggling uncontrollably as he playfully assaults my neck, I manage to push him away and hop off of his lap.

"Show me all your photos so I can pick out the ones for you to consider submitting," I tease.

Rolling his chair back to the wooden credenza on the wall behind his desk, he slides one of the doors open and pulls out a stack of mattes.

"Here, boss," he says with a wink and then follows me as I start making my way to the living room.

"Want something to drink?" he asks.

"Yeah, anything hot."

Taking a seat on the couch, I cross my legs under me and make myself comfortable as I look at the first photo. It's a black and white image of a woman's neck and collarbone. It's backlit so everything is black except for the outline of the curves. Flipping to the next, it's another similar sensual photo. Then a photo of a naked woman lying on her back with her legs seductively crossed. I keep flipping, until my stomach is knotted up so tightly that I can't look anymore.

I set the stack facedown on the coffee table and stand up.

"I'll be right back," I say as I rush to the bathroom and shut the door behind me.

Seeing the one photo a few months ago seemed so harmless compared to all the ones I just saw. Who are all those women, and why is every picture so sensual? What is he doing with me? I could never be what those photos are, and I know he can't possibly see me in that way. I don't think I want him to see me that way. No, I definitely don't. It's not me. I'm...no, I can't even finish my thought.

Thoughts begin to flash quickly through my head, and I can't tell if I am overreacting. If he looks at women like that, then what is he doing with me? I have never really felt unsure of Ryan, but maybe I should be.

My thoughts seize for a moment when I hear Ryan tap on the door, and I wonder how long I've been in here going crazy. Apprehensively, I open the door.

"What are you doing?" he asks suspiciously as he takes a step in, and I take a step back. He can read my apprehension and gives me a confused look. "Babe, what's wrong?"

"Nothing."

Dropping his head, he lets out a breath of irritation at my lie.

"Is it the photos?"

I don't respond when he asks, but I know it's all over my face.

"Candace, you asked to see them. You knew what they would be of."

"I know, I'm sorry. I didn't think they would all be like that."

He walks in front of me and leans against the sink and says, "They're just pictures, that's all."

Sitting down on the closed toilet seat, I say, "But...they just seem so intimate."

"Babe, don't."

I look up at him and ask, because I need to know, "Did you sleep with them?"

"Yes," he responds honestly.

"How many have you...?"

"A lot."

"And you photograph them?" I say with a tinge of disbelief.

"No. I've only photographed a couple women. Most of those photos are the same person."

"Oh," I say as I drop my head, now more worried than

ever. I feel uneasy sitting here in front of him when he's just told me all of this. I can't help but think what those women must have meant to him. Did he talk to them the same way he does with me? Were they all in his bed, the bed I sometimes sleep in? And what am I to him?

He crouches down in front of me and says, "I know what you're doing, and you can stop. None of them meant what you mean to me. I never had or wanted a relationship with them."

"Then why?"

Holding my hands, he admits, "Because for most of my life I've been lost. I dealt with a lot of shit growing up, and I used women as a way to escape. But when I met you...you're just different. I wanted to know you, really know you. You're nothing like those women. Nothing. I've never looked at them or wanted them the way I do you."

"I don't know what I'm doing," I shamefully confess.

"I don't either."

"I mean...I haven't..."

"Been with anyone?"

When I cover my face with my hands, he grips me behind my waist and brings me down to the floor with him, sitting sideways between his legs. Holding me, knowing I must be embarrassed, he says, "Talk to me."

"Only once, but he was really drunk and it...well, it was pretty much over before it begun."

"Sounds like an asshole."

"He was, but it kept my parents off my back. They really liked him and his family, so we would go out every now and then, but that was about it. So, I can't help but sometimes wonder what you're doing with me." *Crap! Did I really just admit that?*

"Look at me," he says, and when I do, he continues, "I don't give a shit how inexperienced you are. In fact, I prefer that because the thought of another guy touching you pisses me off. That guy was a dick for treating you like you were disposable. But don't devalue yourself because of that. I won't rush you into anything. You know that right?"

When I nod my head, he says, "You're what I want. No one else, okay?"

"I just get scared, and I feel like you might start thinking you're wasting your time with me. I know you'd prefer that I stay every night here with you, but that's what scares me. I just need to move slow with this."

"You're not a waste of my time. You're worth every second."

Sighing with a mild feeling of relief, I smile as he leans down and gives me a slow, soft kiss.

When I let a giggle slip out, he breaks our kiss and asks, "What?"

"Can we get off your bathroom floor now?"

Laughing, he stands up and holds out his hand to help me up.

"Let's get out of here," he says.

"Where are we going?"

"Let's go hang out at Zoca's and get some coffee."

"Perfect."

Regardless of the rain, we decide to sit outside, drink our coffee, and listen to an insanely grungy street performer. Standing in the rain, he strums the somber chords of 'Something in the Way' by Nirvana as he sings the doleful lyrics. Listening to this stranger sing one of my favorite songs, I get lost for a moment at the familiar words.

"You know this song?" Ryan asks, and I pull myself out of my daze.

I turn to look at him, and respond, "It's one of my favorites."

"I used to listen to this a lot when I was younger."

"Hmm..."

"What?" he asks.

"I did too." When the corner of Ryan's mouth turns up in a small half smile, I say, "Go give him some money."

Snickering, he says, "What? Why?"

"Because I want him to keep playing, and he deserves to be paid." I say as I smile back at him.

He shakes his head at me in amusement when he walks over to the desolate man and drops a few bucks in his open guitar case. When he returns and sits down, he gives me a smirk. "Happy?"

Lifting my mug to my mouth, I murmur, "Mmm hmm," as I take a sip of my coffee.

"I've been wondering about something."

"What's that?" I ask.

"I need to know that you're okay with money. Since your parents aren't helping you out and you just work part-time at a coffee shop, I've been worried."

"Don't be. I'm fine. When I turned twenty-one, I gained access to my trust fund, and my parents resigned as trustees."

"I didn't want to overstep, but I needed to know you're okay."

"I am."

"Ryan, man! Where've you been?" a guy yells as he's crossing the street toward us.

Ryan stands up and walks toward him, clasping their hands together before leaning in for a quick hug as they slap each other on the back. "I've been busy keeping the bar going."

"Shit, man, last I heard that place was raking in the money."

“Something like that.”

The guy looks down at me and back to Ryan. “Sorry, I’ll let you get back to your friend.”

“No worries. This is Candace.”

He reaches out his hand, and I stand up and shake it, when he says, “I’m Gavin.”

“Hey.”

“Sit down and grab a drink, man,” Ryan says, and Gavin pulls up a chair to our table. Ryan turns to me and says, “Gavin and I’ve been friends since I moved here for college.”

“Oh, yeah?” I say.

“Yeah, this guy left my ass behind when he decided to buy that fuckin’ bar.”

“So what do you do then?”

“I work in promotions and marketing at Sub Pop Records.”

“Really? That sounds like a lot of fun. Working with anyone good?” I ask.

“Ever heard of Washed Out?”

“Yeah, I have their album actually.”

“Within and Without?”

“Uh huh. So they’re your client?”

“Yep, one of them. We’re trying to get a tour set up right now, but that shit takes forever. Before this guy got so tied up with work, he used to always come out and listen to all the bands play,” he says, nodding his head at Ryan.

“You should give me a list of some of your guys, and I can check the lineup and see if I have space for any of them to perform,” Ryan says.

“Yeah, man. That’d be great.”

“So, Candace, what do you do besides hang out with this loser?” he says while laughing at Ryan.

“I’m a student, actually.”

"U-Dub?"

"Yeah."

"What are you studying?"

"Dance. I'm a Fine Arts major."

"No shit?!"

"Yeah, man. No shit," Ryan jokes with a hint of possessiveness, and I have to laugh at his demeanor.

"Well, hey, I gotta run. I was actually on my way to a meeting, but I had to stop when I saw you."

"I'm glad you did. Sorry I've been out of pocket for the past couple months."

"No worries, but, hey, I'm throwing a party next month at my place. Everyone will be there. You should come by."

"I will. I'll call you next week."

"Oh, and if you're still around, you should come too," he says, cocking his head my way, "At least you have decent taste in music." He winks at me before saying, "Seriously though, it was nice meeting you."

Ryan looks at me and jokes, "Just ignore him."

"It was good to meet you too, Gavin."

"Take it easy, man," he says to Ryan as he starts walking off.

Turning to Ryan, I say, "So, why haven't you been hanging out with your friends?"

"I've been a little distracted for the past few months," he says with a grin, and I know he's referring to me.

Grinning, I say, "Well, don't let me keep you from your friends."

"Don't worry about my friends, I see most of them a lot 'cause they hang out at Blur to hear bands play."

"Oh." I feel like I have isolated myself from a part of Ryan's life because I never go to his bar. Maybe if I did, I would know his friends. Instead, there's this disconnect. Ryan knows my friends, albeit, only Jase and Mark, but he also chats with Roxy frequently when he stops by the coffee shop when I'm working. Although I've met his family, it would be nice to get to see him with his friends as well.

"I didn't mean how that came out," he says.

"No, I understand. You guys hang out, I just didn't know that."

Reaching over and taking my hand in his, he says, "Would you think about coming up again? We can just go together during the day. No people."

I stare at our entwined fingers, and I know that night bothers him. He hasn't mentioned anything since or questioned me about it, but I know it hurt him that I bailed with Jase and didn't turn to him. But, I don't know if I can ever go there again.

When I don't answer, he simply says, "Just think about it, babe."

"I will. I promise."

chapter twenty-six

Hey! You home?

On way now. Leaving gym.

Mind if I stop by?

Not at all. Be there in 10.

See ya!

"Hey, Roxy," I holler over the coffee bean grinder. "I'm heading out, okay?"

"Yeah, okay. Thanks for covering the shift this morning."

"No problem. Have you found anyone to replace Brandon yet?"

"I have another interview today," she says as she hands a customer their drink.

"Well, I'll be in tomorrow."

"Okay. See you then."

"See you," I say while putting on my coat and popping the hood over my head before heading out into the rain.

I've been taking over Brandon's shifts after he had to quit a few days ago. I'm not taking as many hours in school right now, so I have the free time. Now I need to run by Ryan's and pick up that photo so that I can submit it to Thinkspace Art Gallery. I didn't bother selecting photos when I was over there last Thursday. That sort of turned into a mess that led to confessions on the bathroom floor. Not my finest moment, but let's face it, those are few and far between these days.

But, I only need that one photo that originally caught my eye. When I walk into his loft, I can hear the shower running upstairs, so I go into his office. Sliding the door open to his credenza, I notice the mattes aren't there. I head back into the living room to look around, but I can't find them.

"Hey, babe," Ryan says while he's walking down the stairs. He's dressed, but his hair is still wet from his shower.

"Hey."

"What are you scrounging around for?" he asks as he cradles my cheeks and kisses me.

"Your mattes. I can't find them."

Kissing me again, he briefly pauses to say, "That's because they're not here," before covering my mouth with his again.

"Where are they?" I mumble against his lips.

Pausing again, he says, "I tossed them," and then he kisses me again.

I pull back in surprise. "What?! Why?"

"Because they made you uncomfortable."

"But I was looking for the photo of the woman's back so I could submit it to the gallery."

"I don't have it. I threw them all away."

Flopping down on the large leather chair behind me, I let out a defeated sigh.

Ryan sits on the coffee table in front of me, elbows resting on his knees, and asks, "What's wrong?"

"Nothing, I was just excited to submit that photo."

Leaning my head back on the chair, I mumble, "Maybe it was a stupid idea."

"Is it that important to you?"

"I just thought if you saw one of your pieces in a showing, that you would see the art in it."

Giving me a smile, he says, "It wasn't difficult to capture or enhance. I can recreate it if you want."

"We don't have time for you to find someone to pose. It needs to be submitted tomorrow by the end of the day."

"We don't need to find anyone. Let's go upstairs. I'll shoot *your* back," he suggests and I feel my face flush at the thought of him photographing me.

"No."

"No, what?"

"I'm not taking my top off for you to photograph me."

He leans in and rests his hands on my knees. "You don't have to take anything off, promise. It's an extreme close-up; you only need to hike it up a little."

His original photo was so beautiful; there is no way he could capture that with me.

Standing up, he takes ahold of my hand and lifts me out of the chair.

"What?"

"We're going upstairs."

I tug my hand away. "Ryan, no."

He turns around to look at me. "What's wrong?"

"It feels weird to me."

"Don't let it."

"You just can't say that and expect me to be okay," I say and fold my arms across my chest. "I'm not like the girls you took those pictures of. I'm..."

"No, you're not. You're nothing like them, which is why I threw them in the garbage." Cupping my face again, he kisses me before assuring, "I only want you. No one else.

The only photos I want are ones of you."

When we walk into his room, my heart starts beating faster. I sense the dampness on my palms and they begin to tingle with nerves.

Ryan goes into his closet and pulls out his camera. Walking toward the windows, he pulls the drapes shut and the room darkens. He takes my hand and leads me over to the bed.

"Just lie on your stomach."

I swallow hard against the lump that's lodged in my throat and lie on the bed, folding my arms beneath my head. Staring at him as he climbs onto the bed next to me on his knees, my body tenses when I feel him touch the hem of my shirt.

"I'm just going to lift it up a little."

Taking a deep breath through my nose, I close my eyes and feel his hand graze my back as he pulls my shirt up and tucks it under my bra.

"You okay?"

"Mmm hmm." My heart is still racing, and I'm very aware of myself.

The bed shifts, and when I open my eyes, Ryan is kneeling beside the bed, focusing on his camera and adjusting the settings. I take a calming breath and concentrate on what he's doing to take my mind off of how awkward and exposed I feel right now.

Holding the camera up to his eye, he sets the flash and starts fidgeting with the camera again. He repeats this a few times, then tells me, "I'm gonna take a few test shots to get the shutter speed right, okay?"

I nod my head and watch him as he leans in close to me, his camera up to his eye. The loud clicks of the camera startle me slightly, and my body tightens as I flinch. I'm hyperaware of everything around me as I lie here in the dark.

He reaches over me and picks up a pillow. "Here, lean up," he says and I push my chest off the bed as he places the pillow under me. "I just need a little more curve to your spine. Just lay down and relax."

He kneels back down and moves in close to me with the camera back up to his eye. "That's perfect," he mumbles, and I begin to hear the fast clicking of the camera. The flash pulses in pops of light in the dark room. And before I know it, it's dark and quiet again. The bed dips back down as he sits next to me, untucking my shirt from my bra and pulling it back down over my back.

Bracing his arms on the mattress on either side of my shoulders, he hovers over me and lowers himself to kiss my cheek.

"Thanks," he says with a soft rasp.

I shift to my side, and he lies next to me, pulling me closer to him. He lightly brushes his lips against mine before pressing into me. Weaving my fingers through his hair, I pull him even closer. My stomach starts to flutter, and an overwhelming need for closeness takes over. Being with him like this makes me want to open myself up. I feel safe in his arms and the feelings that come with it are intense. Feelings I have never had for anyone else before. I want to be close to him, but I'm so uncomfortable with myself. I worry I'll embarrass myself if he touches me in a way I can't handle. I worry that I'll be a disappointment to him.

Rolling me on my back, he begins to trail his warm damp kisses down my neck and along my shoulder. I grasp onto his arms and feel the flexing of his muscles under my hands as he moves across my collarbone. He reaches down, placing his hand on the side of my thigh, and squeezes as he starts to glide it slowly upward. My breath catches, and I quickly clamp my hand around his wrist. Pulling his head back, he studies my face, and I whisper, "Sorry."

"You don't ever have to be sorry."

I gently nod my head.

In a whisper, he says, "God, you're beautiful."

"So, you have to tell me what's going on with you and Ryan," Roxy says as we move around, making drinks for the line of people waiting.

"I don't really know."

"You like him, right?"

I look at her as I steam some milk for a customer's latte and she prompts me, "Right?"

Snapping the lid on the cup, I walk over and hand it to the girl who's waiting on the other side of the counter. Roxy steps next to me as she hands a drink to another customer. We walk back over to the machines and I finally admit, "I do."

When she looks at me, I clarify, "Like him. I do."

A sincere smile slowly creeps across her face and I become embarrassed. "Stop!"

"Oh, come on Candace! Give me a break here. I've known you for almost three years and you have never shown an interest in anyone. Let me enjoy this."

"You're embarrassing me."

"Sweetie, everything embarrasses you. Get over it," she says with a sincere smirk.

As we continue to fill drink orders, Roxy begins asking a multitude of questions, all of which I avoid answering. When the last drink is made and the shop calms down, we both take a seat and relax from the Monday morning rush.

"Well, even though you won't tell me anything, I'm happy for you."

"Thanks. Now will you stop?" I tease.

"For the time being, I'll stop," she says with a grin.

My phone chimes from under the counter. When I retrieve it, I see I have a missed text from Ryan.

Your photo from yesterday is almost finished. Touching up the lighting.

Getting off work in 30 min. Can I stop by?

Yeah.

"Ryan?" Roxy pries.

"Didn't you just say you would stop?"

Laughing, she teases me again. "So secretive."

"I'm going to the back to refill the syrup bottles. Yell for me if it gets busy."

"Yeah, yeah," she says as she waves me away.

It's nice to be able to joke around with Roxy again. The tension has definitely lightened in the past few weeks, and I know the reason for that is waiting for me at his loft right now.

I can't contain my smile when I think about us in his bed yesterday. The way my skin tingles when he kisses me, the way I soften when he holds me, the fluttering I feel when he whispers his words to me. Even though it's all so new, it's also so comforting.

I could tell he was disappointed when I didn't spend the night with him, but he understands that I don't feel comfortable being there every night. Although I love being with him, I'm still scared about moving forward.

When the bottles are refilled, I walk back into the store and put them back on the shelf. I start to gather my things and clock out.

As I'm walking out the door, Roxy can't help herself

when she says loudly, "Tell your hot-ass boyfriend I said 'hi.'"

I roll my eyes at her as I open the door to leave.

Leaning against Ryan's desk, he hands me the large matte, and I cannot believe how well the photo turned out. Everything is black except for the curve of the back—my back—which is a striking muted grey with a shadow cast along the spine—my spine.

I stand there, staring at the photo, every detail of the photo. When I do look up, Ryan is focused on me with a grin on his face.

"What?" I ask.

"You."

"Me?"

Stepping in front of me, he takes the matte out of my hands and places it on the desk behind me. He slides his arms around my waist and pulls me into him and says, "You're fucking amazing," and kisses me with an intensity I haven't felt from him before. I let myself fall into him as his lips tangle with mine. When he dips his tongue in my mouth, I can taste the coolness that is left over from the mints he's addicted to. I feel so connected to him right now, and I never want to lose this feeling. So, when he breaks our kiss, I can't help the moan that creeps past my lips.

He closes his eyes and rests his forehead against mine, and I can hear his heavy breaths. Placing my hands on his face, I move in to selfishly kiss him, to feel the warmth of his touch on me. Gripping my waist, he lifts me onto his desk as he stands between my legs. Holding the back of my head, he intensifies our kiss, and I let him take more control than I have in the past.

When his shoulders tense up under my hands, he pulls away. I know it's hard for him to stop himself when we are together like this.

"Do you know how hard it was to concentrate on touching up that photo of you?

As I shake my head, he tells me, "You're so fucking beautiful."

I believe him when he says those words to me. I might not feel that way in a day from now, or even an hour from now. But right now, in this moment—I believe him.

chapter twenty-seven

After studio ends, Ms. Emerson asks me to stay so that she can watch how my solo is progressing. Last time I rehearsed with her, it was a disaster. I'm beginning to feel the power of the piece when I dance. I know she wants me to focus on myself when I hear the music, but I just can't go to that place yet. Instead, I think about Ryan and everything he's told me about growing up and the violence in his house. It's been enough to help me better connect with the piece.

"Okay, Candace. Are you ready?" she asks as she grabs the remote to the stereo and takes her place at the front of the room.

"Yes." I walk to the center and place my feet in fifth position, waiting for the music to begin. When the strings begin to echo through the speakers, I slowly relevè on my pointes and begin my series of chainès across the floor. The low hum of the cello vibrates within my chest as I work through the movements. My heart thumps harder with the staccato brushes of the violins, and I'm spot on when I turn into my fouettè sequence. I flow through the progressions and the twinge in my stomach courses through my body as the music slowly fades into nothingness.

The room is quiet except for the breaths flowing in and out of my lungs. When I look over at Ms. Emerson, she's walking toward me. Standing in front of me, she says without any inflection in her voice, "That's better."

She says nothing else, and turns to walk out of the room. When the door closes behind her, I let out a puff of breath and allow myself the relief of a huge smile. Replaying her words, those two simple words, in my head, I spend the next hour dancing and feeling. Even though I am feeling someone else's pain, I'm still feeling.

When I leave the studio and get into my car, I decide to stop by the loft and surprise Ryan before he has to go into work for the night.

"Hey, babe!" Ryan says when he opens the door. "What are you doing here?"

"I wanted to see you before you left for work."

Picking me up in his arms, I laugh before he kisses me.

"I've missed you this week," he says as he sets me back down.

"Sorry. Auditions are in a few weeks, and then I won't be living in the studio."

"Candace!"

Leaning over to look around Ryan, I see Gavin walking over.

"Hey, Gavin. What are you doing here?"

"Just stopped by to bullshit with Ryan."

I look back at Ryan and say, "I'm sorry, I should have called before stopping by."

Gavin grabs my hand and pulls me inside. "Wanna beer?"

"Um, no."

Walking past me, Ryan says, "I'll get you a water."

"Thanks." I love that he knows exactly what I need without having to ask.

Gavin and I sit down in front of the TV where they have been watching *SportsCenter*.

Pointing the neck of his beer bottle to my head, he

jokes, "What's with the hair, grandma?"

"Don't be a dick," Ryan says as he hands me a bottle of water and sits down next to me, wrapping his arm around my shoulder.

I shake my head at their banter and unscrew the lid to my water. "I was in the dance studio all day," I say and then take a long drink of water.

"How'd that go?" Ryan asks. He knows I've been having a lot of bad studios and rehearsals lately.

"It actually went pretty well. My instructor complimented me on my solo."

"Really? That's great, babe."

"Well, actually all she said was 'that's better' but coming from her, that's huge."

"You coming out with us tonight?" Gavin asks me.

"Umm," I say, turning my attention to Ryan, wondering what Gavin's talking about.

"Gavin's just coming by the bar tonight with some friends, that's all."

"Oh," I say and turn my attention back to Gavin. "No, I've got plans."

I feel left out of Ryan's life with his friends. I know it's my own doing, so I try to not let it affect me. I know it's just me being over-sensitive, but I can't help the feeling of being left out.

"What are you doing?" Ryan asks.

"I'm going to Jase's to hang out. We haven't had a lot of time to see each other lately."

"Come with me to my office before you go," he says as he stands up and takes my hand.

"If you guys are gonna fuck, I'm out," Gavin says.

"Dude!" Ryan snaps at him.

Shrugging his shoulders, he says, "What? It wouldn't be the first time."

I look at him in disbelief when he says, "Just sayin'," as he leans back on the couch and turns up the TV.

Ryan starts leading me to his office, and when he closes the door, he turns around, placing his hands on the door, caging me in.

"Sorry about that. The guy has no filter."

The fact that he isn't denying what Gavin said is making my stomach turn. I want to run out of here, get some space, but I know he won't let me do that. I can't even look at him right now, so I keep my eyes focused on a stack of papers lying on his desk.

"Candace," he says quietly, and I turn my head and look to the floor.

He drops his head and sighs, "I'm sorry."

"Did you really do that?"

Our eyes meet when he looks up and by the look written all over his face and his creased forehead, I can tell he's ashamed to answer me.

He nods his head and says, "Yes."

I feel sick, and I look back down, not knowing what to say. Even though he didn't know me back then, it still hurts. It hurts to know that he has shared something so intimate with those girls. An intimacy that we don't share.

Tears begin to flood my eyes, and I look at him when I ask, "Is that what you want?"

He gently takes my face in his hands, and when I blink, I can feel the heat of my tears rolling down my cheeks.

"No. I was miserable then. None of them ever gave me what you give me."

"That's the problem, though. I can't give you what they could."

"You give me everything." Taking his thumbs, he wipes the tears from under my eyes. "You have more of me than any of them ever had. And when you're ready to move forward, I can promise you that it won't be like what I had with them. It was just empty with them."

He leans his forehead against mine and even though I feel upset about the way Ryan was before he met me, I'm also upset for me, that I can't give him what I want to. I can see the pain and regret in his face.

"I shouldn't be upset. I didn't know you then."

"You have every right to be upset."

Not wanting to drag this out, I wrap my hand behind his neck, draw his head to mine, and kiss him. I don't want to think about it anymore; I just want to have peace with Ryan.

"I've missed you," he mumbles over my lips, and when he does, I pull him closer to me and cover his mouth with mine. "Stay with me tonight?"

Parting our lips from each other, I whisper, "I can't."

"Why not?"

"I promised Jase I'd stay with him."

Ryan lets out a deep sigh, hanging his head down, and I know he's frustrated, but I don't ask. I haven't spent the night with him since last Sunday, and I'm sure it's bothering him.

"You have to work anyway," I say.

"I want you in my bed when I get home."

I release my hands from his neck and look down, feeling guilty, that I'm not giving him the closeness that he wants. I know he'd prefer moving this a lot faster than we are, but I feel like I'm pushing myself as it is.

"Ryan..." I whisper.

"I know," he says as he leans his forehead against mine.

I know he doesn't really understand my feelings of apprehension, and it hurts me that he's feeling this way because of me.

I cup his cheeks and pull up on my toes, pressing my lips into his, and when I do, he holds my head in his hands as well. We hold the kiss for a few seconds before pulling away.

"I should go."

"I'll walk you out."

We walk through the house and Gavin looks up and asks, "You heading out already?"

"Yeah, I gotta go."

"Good seeing you again."

I smile and turn toward the door with Ryan and say goodbye.

"Ryan's frustrated with me."

"What makes you say that?" Jase asks while chopping up the peppers for the stir-fry he's making.

"I just get the feeling that he is. I mean, we've been together for a few months and haven't done anything more than kiss. He has to be getting annoyed with me."

"But he hasn't said anything?"

"No, I don't think he would though."

"Do you trust him?"

Taking a sip of my wine and setting down the glass, I say, "Yeah, but I'm scared he's going to compare me. I mean, how could he not? It's only natural, right?"

"No, it's not. It's not like that. You're someone new to him, and he clearly loves you. He would be a total ass to compare you."

I widen my eyes when he says that Ryan loves me, and he catches the look on my face when he sets down the knife and questions me, "What?"

"God, Jase, you think he loves me?"

"Candace, have you seen the way he looks at you? Yes, the guy loves you." He scoops up the peppers and onions and dumps them into the hot skillet, shaking it around and flipping the vegetables. When he turns back around, he laughs. "Why do you look so surprised?"

"Because, I just...I mean..."

"Do you love him?"

"Jase!"

"Seriously. Do you?"

"At times when we are together I feel like I do. I mean...I think I do. Honestly, I am overwhelmed most of the time. But I'm scared. All I know is that I have never felt this way about anyone else."

"What are you so scared of?"

"Everything."

He turns around, picks up the skillet, and pours the stir-fry onto our plates. We walk into the living room and set them down on the coffee table to cool when he continues, "Explain to me what *everything* is."

I empty out my thoughts with Jase because I know I can tell him anything and he will never judge me. "I'm scared I might freak out on him, and he'll think I'm weird and won't want to waste his time with me. I'm scared I'm not enough for him. I'm worried he will somehow know what happened to me, and he'll be disgusted by me. And I'm scared of losing him, for whatever reason. What if this thing ends up badly and I'm left hurt?"

"If that does happen, you'll be okay. You're strong. I know you don't see it, but I do. You're the strongest person I know."

"I don't feel like it."

"You are. And everyone has fears in a new relationship. It doesn't make you weak; it makes you real. I was scared when Mark and I got back together. Scared that somehow I would screw it up again. That I would fall for him and then he would realize what a dick I was and leave. Scared that his family wouldn't like me. I was scared of a lot, but I still wanted him more than I wanted to give up."

"But everything that Mark was telling us. The stuff about all the girls. It's true."

"What did he say?"

I don't tell Jase everything, because what Ryan told me is private, and I want to keep it that way, so I say, "He said it was a rough time in his life, and he used women as a distraction. I asked him how many and he just told me it was a lot. But today when I stopped by his place, one of his friends was there, and he made a comment that's really been bothering me."

I pick up my plate and start moving the food aimlessly around as I continue, "So, Ryan and I were walking to his office to talk, and his friend made a remark about us having sex in there and that it wouldn't be the first time Ryan has done that."

"God."

"I know. So, when we were alone, I got upset, but then I felt bad for him. You should have seen the look on his face, Jase. It was horrible. I know he felt embarrassed, so I let it go and didn't say anything else."

"That's probably best. I mean, what is there really to say?"

"I know. It just makes me uncomfortable to think about that stuff happening at his place, and now I'm hanging out there."

"That sucks, but you can't think about all that. It's just going to eat at you."

I take a big bite of food, tilt my head back, and say, "I know," so that none of it falls out of my mouth.

Laughing at me, he jokes, "Is that how they taught you to eat at the country club?"

We both laugh and enjoy our dinner, dropping all serious conversation aside.

After dinner we simply hang out like we used to, watching trash TV and relaxing. We decide to call it a night around midnight. We lie down in his bed to sleep. We have been sleeping together for the past four years. I have always found it to be comforting, not sexual at all. Being able to have that closeness with Jase has really bonded us together. I know I can totally be free and open with him, and I need that. I don't have that with anyone else. He's seen me at my absolute worst, and has never abandoned me.

I've been studying and trying to get ahead in my classes this afternoon. Knowing that my audition is in a couple of weeks, I have been spending most of my free time at the studio. Kimber has been at her parents' house all weekend, so I have the house to myself.

I've been working on a project for one of my classes for the past few hours when Ryan drops by. I welcome the distraction as we hang out in my room and talk. I can tell something is bothering him, and I just assume it has something to do with what Gavin said yesterday at his place.

But before I can say anything, he says, "I need to talk to you about something."

Sitting on my bed, I cross my legs and say, "Okay," feeling a little nervous at the seriousness in his tone.

"Look, I get your relationship with Jase, and I haven't ever had any issues with it, but I don't like that you guys still sleep together."

"But, it's not like that."

"I know, but I still don't like it."

"But..."

He turns to face me, placing his hands on my knees, and says, "I know it isn't like that with you two. I get it. But I don't like the thought of you in bed with another man holding you. I want to be that guy. I want you to want me to be that guy, not Jase."

When I hear the crack in his voice, I know that this is really affecting him. Returning the honesty, I tell him, "I want you to be that guy, but I don't know how. Jase is so unthreatening to me because he's just my friend."

"Why do you think I'm threatening?"

My hands begin to fidget when I tell him, "Because you could easily walk away from me." I have to look away from him because the honesty I just put out there is too much for me.

He scoots right up next to me and says, "You think it would be easy for me to walk away? It wouldn't be easy, babe. And I doubt there is anything you could say or do that would make me want to walk away. It kills me that you're so scared of me."

When I look up at him, I confess, "You're the only person I've ever felt this way about, and I don't want to lose you."

He shifts on his knees and leans into me until I am lying on my back. He's supporting himself above me on his one elbow and wraps his other hand around my head, pulling me in for a slow kiss. I hold his face in my hands as his lips dance across mine. When he pulls back, he takes his time staring at me, and I get lost in his clear-blue eyes for a moment before he says, "You're not gonna lose me, babe. I love you too much to let you go."

The pounding of my heart is all I can hear as I try to digest his words, and I know that I love him too. I just can't bare myself that much to him, so I clench my need to say it back to him. The love I feel for him overtakes me, and I start to blink out the tears that fill my eyes. When I nod my head, he leans down and melds his mouth to mine, gliding his tongue across mine. I pull him down on me as I grab his hair with my other hand. I need to be close to him, to somehow show him that I do love him, even though I can't say the words yet.

He reaches down and skims the skin between my pants and my top with his knuckles, and I begin to quiver under his touch, but I allow it. I need to give him more. He flips his hand and begins running his palm up my stomach slowly. My breaths become short, and I try to focus more on his kisses than his wandering hand.

Holding him tight against me, I lean my head forward and nestle it in the crook of his neck. His hand stops right below my bra, and he keeps it there. I know I have to try, so I whisper with a tremble, "It's okay." Dropping his mouth on my shoulder, he grazes his lips across my sensitive skin, kissing and gently sucking as he covers my lace-covered breast with his hand. Pushing my head harder into his shoulder, I hold on tightly to him.

"God, you're perfect," he mumbles between his kisses, and when I feel his thumb skim across my nipple, a whimper escapes my mouth.

Lifting his head up, he says, "Don't hide from me, babe."

I slowly let my head fall back onto the pillow and open my eyes. A few locks of his hair have fallen over his forehead, and his eyes are locked on mine. Keeping his hand on my breast, I pull him down for a kiss. He hooks his finger under the lace of my bra and slides it across my bare skin. Our legs are tangled together, and when he starts to tug at the fabric, I get a flash of Jack tugging at my bra, and my body tenses up. "Please, don't."

Ryan doesn't say anything as he slides his hand from underneath my shirt and moves it to my head, threading his fingers through my hair.

"I'm sorry."

"Look at me," he demands, and when I do, he continues, "When we're together like this, I don't ever want you to be sorry for anything, okay?"

Nodding my head, he kisses me lightly, barely brushing my lips with his when he says one more time, "I love you, babe."

chapter twenty-eight

Sitting at my desk, I finish emailing a paper to one of my professors when there's a soft knock on my bedroom door.

"Come in," I say as I hit send and close the lid to my laptop.

Kimber opens my door and asks, "Can I come in?"

"Umm, yeah."

She walks in and takes a seat on the end of my bed, and I turn my chair around to face her, when she says, "I need to talk to you about after graduation."

I have hardly spoken to Kimber in months, so sitting here with her in my room makes me a little nervous.

"Okay."

"Well, I didn't know what your plans were."

"My only plan is to try and find a job. I've always had my heart set on New York, but I will go wherever I get an offer from. Why?"

"I was thinking that it might not be a good idea if you lived here after we graduate."

"Oh." I feel a lump forming in my throat and I want to cry, but I don't. We used to be so close, like sisters, and now she wants me out. How could I let things get this bad between us where she doesn't want me here?

"It's hard having you around and us not talking. I just

don't feel like we are even friends anymore. It's been five months, Candace."

"I don't know what to say."

"I wish you would just talk to me. But, honestly, I don't even know if it would do any good at this point. I don't want to continue walking around here with this tension every day."

"Okay," I say. I'm hurt and pissed at myself for causing this fracture between us and now I wonder if this is even fixable.

Neither one of us says anything else, and it's only when she leaves that I begin to cry. When I pick up the phone to call Jase, it starts ringing in my hand. Being upset, I answer it without looking to see who is calling.

"Hello," I choke out.

"Jesus, what's wrong?"

When I hear Ryan's voice I start babbling. "Kimber asked me to move out. She doesn't want me here. She doesn't feel like we're friends anymore. She'd rather I went somewhere else, and I don't know if I can fix this."

"Breathe, babe. I'm in my car heading to the gym. I'm right by your house. I'll be right there."

"Okay," I say before hanging up.

When Ryan arrives, we go back to my room. Sitting on the bed with his back against the headboard, he holds me in his arms as I curl up beside him, still upset.

"So, what happened?" he asks as he starts threading his fingers through my hair.

"What I told you. That's all that she said. I didn't say anything because, you know me, I just shut down."

"What the hell happened between you two anyway?"

Shit! What do I say?

Thinking quickly, I tell him the truth, but leave out what I can't have him know.

"At the beginning of the school year, I stayed with Jase

at his place for a while and Kimber thought I was avoiding her for some reason. But she didn't believe me when I told her it had nothing to do with her. So we got into a fight and she called me a liar. That was it. We've literally been avoiding each other ever since, and now so much time has passed that we're barely friends anymore."

"I don't understand you chicks, but I hate to see you so upset over this."

"I just miss her. We used to be close like sisters."

"Can't you just tell her that?"

"It won't do any good," I say.

"You know you can always stay with me."

"Yeah, I know."

Ever since Ryan told me he loved me a couple weeks ago, I have been more comfortable talking to him and opening up more. But I have yet to tell him I love him. Something about being that vulnerable still daunts me. He told me he knows I love him and to not worry about the words. I know I'm getting there; it's just taking a little while.

Quickly changing the topic he says, "Come to the gym with me."

I sit up and look at him bemused. "What?"

"Yeah, come with me. We haven't been running much because of your deranged fear of breaking your legs. You can ride the bikes, or if you're feeling risky, run on the treadmill," he jokes with me.

Smacking him in the arm, I say, "Stop laughing at me. And it isn't deranged. Seriously, what if I broke my leg before this audition? It would ruin everything."

Raising his hands in defense, he says dramatically, "I know. You've been telling me this all week."

Needing to get him off my back, I say, "Fine. I'll go ride the bikes. Let me go change."

When I walk out of the bathroom, Ryan is standing

there waiting for me. Bending down, he scoops me up, over his shoulder and playfully grabs my ass. I can't control my laughter as he hauls me through my house. I return the favor and grab onto his ass as he carries me out to his jeep. When he sets me down, I have to grab hold of his arms until the dizziness subsides. He opens my door and helps me up into the car before leaning in and kissing me.

When we arrive at the gym, I make my way over to the cardio machines and Ryan follows closely behind.

"What are you doing?" I say as I turn around to face him.

"Your ass looks hot in those tight pants," he says with a wicked smirk.

I roll my eyes and before I can turn around, he grabs me by said ass and pulls me against him. Swatting his hands away, he laughs as I make my way over and sit my ass on a bike.

"Now what the hell am I supposed to look at?" he complains.

"Go lift your weights and stop harassing the gym's clientele."

I spend the next half hour riding the bike and then decide to run on the treadmill. At least there's a bar I can grab onto if I fall. Ryan has been getting a kick out of teasing me about my fear of breaking anything that has to do with my legs.

I increase the incline and set the speed for a quick-paced run. I scan the gym until I spot Ryan by the free-weights. He's lying on the incline bench doing sets of chest presses. While he's focused on his workout, I take a moment to ogle over his muscular body. When his eyes flick to mine and he catches me gawking, he gives me an egotistical grin, which I shake my head at.

We spend the next hour going back and forth like this,

although I catch him a lot more than he catches me. Walking across the gym, he stands in front of my treadmill, leaning against it while I continue to run.

"You trying to kill yourself?"

"No," I say breathlessly, "Just building endurance."

His cocky grin returns, and when I side-step off the tether, I smack him and clarify, "Not for that! For dancing, you perv."

I take his hand as he helps me off the machine, and we walk over to grab some water. I drain my bottle quickly and toss it in the trash. After I towel off my face and neck, we head outside, and I welcome the cold drizzle that's falling.

On the drive back to my place, Ryan mentions the party that Gavin is throwing this weekend. Wondering if I still wanted to go, he assures me it'll be a small crowd, so I tell him yes.

We've hung out with Gavin several times in the past few weeks. He has since apologized to me for making that comment to me at Ryan's loft. I could tell he felt bad about it, so I brushed it off. He's very crass with his words, but he's really funny at the same time. The party, if nothing else, will at least be amusing with him there.

Walking into Gavin's house, Ryan is greeted by several people. Keeping a firm grip on my hand, he introduces me to a few guys before Gavin walks up and throws his arm around me.

"It's about time you guys showed up. Help yourself to whatever is in the kitchen."

"Hey, Gav."

"Hey, gorgeous. I can't believe you haven't left this ass-hat for me yet."

"If it weren't for your delicate language, I might consider it."

"Leave her alone," Ryan says as he pulls me away and into the kitchen to grab a couple of beers.

As he's opening my bottle, I notice a tall blonde eying him. When he hands me my bottle, he leans down and gives me a chaste kiss then leads me back to the living room. We sit on the couch and Ryan begins chatting with two guys that he knows. I sip on my beer and only catch bits and pieces of their conversation. I like that he never takes his hand off of my knee while talking to them; that he's always so aware of me.

I scan the room and spot Gavin who is talking with the blonde I saw in the kitchen. Her hair is long, about the length of mine. She wears her makeup in a sultry way, opposite of my simple mascara and lip-gloss.

When both she and Gavin turn their heads and look at me, I immediately shift my eyes to Ryan. Looking back at me, he squeezes my knee, and Gavin flops down next to me.

"What's up?"

"Were you talking about me?"

"God you're paranoid," he teases and nudges my leg.

"I'm gonna go get another drink." Scooting forward on the couch, I ask Ryan if he wants another beer.

"Yeah, babe. Thanks."

I grab his empty bottle and make my way into the kitchen, tossing them into the trash. Opening the fridge, I grab two more and when I turn around, the tall blonde is standing next to me.

"Hi, I'm Gina," she says politely and holds out her hand.

Sticking one of the bottles under my arm, I reach out my now free hand to shake hers.

"I'm a good friend of Gavin and Ryan."

"Oh. I'm Candace."

"They've never mentioned you before."

"I just met Gavin a few weeks ago," I say.

"So are you and Ryan...?"

"What?" I question, not quite sure what she is trying to ask me.

A grin begins to spread across her face when she leans in and says, "He's good, isn't he?"

I back away from her face and say, "Excuse me?"

"Oh, come on. Everyone knows what he's like."

What the hell is this girl's deal? Did he sleep with her? Thoughts start flooding my mind, and I just want to leave. Jealousy fills me when she says, "I'm a little surprised by you though. You don't seem to fit his type."

"Excuse me," I say as I start to walk away. I don't know this girl, but I hate her nonetheless.

"Oh my God. That's so cute," she says before I can get too much distance between us. When I turn around to look at her, she's laughing at me and says, "You think he loves you? Ryan doesn't know what that is. Trust me, I've been with him enough times to know that."

I feel sick and fire rushes through my veins, and if I wasn't so small compared to her, I'd slap the shit out of her. I set the beers on the counter and turn around. Walking through the living room, I pass Ryan and snap at him, "Take me home," and then make my way outside. My hands are shaking as a multitude of emotions runs through me: jealousy, anger, embarrassment.

"Candace," Ryan says as he rushes behind me.

I turn around, angry, and shout at him, "Did you sleep with that girl in there? Gina?"

He lets out a deep breath, and I shake my head and say, "Forget it. Just take me home."

I open the door before he can open it for me and hop up

onto the seat. It's one thing for me to hear about his past, but to have his past right there in my face, taunting me, is more than I can handle.

When we start driving, Ryan finally speaks up. "I didn't know she was going to be there. When I saw her, I didn't want to say anything to draw attention."

I don't respond. I'm too upset to respond, so I pull my knee up to my chest and shift my body toward the door, leaning the side of my head against the cold leather seat and stare out the window. I want to cry because I'm embarrassed and hurt, but I don't.

"Candace, say something."

I don't.

To be honest, I'm upset with that girl, not Ryan. I know Ryan has been nothing but open with me, so I can't fault him for that. But, it doesn't make it any easier. I wonder if everyone in that house thought I was just another girl like Gina. I hate that thought.

When he pulls into his driveway, I softly say without moving, eyes still looking out the window, "Ryan, I really just want to go home."

He doesn't say anything when he gets out of the car and walks around to my side. Opening the door, he takes my hand and helps me out. I don't protest because I'm too tired to argue with him. We walk inside, and he takes me upstairs to his room.

I stand in the doorway as he walks over to his dresser and starts pulling out clothes.

"Ryan, what are you doing?"

"You're not going home. Here," he says as he hands me a pair of his boxers and a t-shirt.

I stand there for a moment and watch him as he begins to undress, then I turn to go to his bathroom and change myself. Realizing I don't have my pills, I call out for Ryan to bring me my purse.

When he knocks on the door, I open it and thank him when he hands it to me. I quickly brush my teeth, and when I walk out, the lights are off, and Ryan is already in bed. He didn't pull the drapes shut, and the moon casts a muted light through the room.

When I slide under the covers, Ryan instinctively pulls me in, facing him.

"Talk to me," he says with a soft voice.

"I'm sorry. I'm not mad at you, and I shouldn't have snapped at you. I just...I don't like feeling the way she made me feel. It's embarrassing."

"She was nothing to me."

"When did you...I mean...How long ago?"

"August or so."

I sigh and close my eyes, not wanting to talk about this or think about this anymore.

Brushing my hair back with his hands, he tells me, "They were only there to distract me, but when I saw you, you faded everything I needed distracting from."

Opening my eyes, I look up at him and ask, "Did you love any of them?"

"No."

Hesitantly, "Do you love me?"

"I've only ever loved you."

He rolls on top of me, staring down into my eyes. I pull him down, and I kiss him with an intensity I haven't felt before. Crushing his lips with mine, tasting each other, and feeling each other, I grab his hair, keeping him close to me. He trails his hand down the center of my sternum, between my breasts, over my stomach, and when he reaches the hem of my shirt, I feel the heat of his hand as he slides it up, making my body shudder beneath his. When he cups me in his hand and squeezes, my body bows up to him, and he lets out a deep moan.

"God, I want you," he whispers.

Sitting back on his heels, he pulls me up to him. He reaches down and slowly begins lifting up my top. Raising my arms up, he peels the cloth off of me and tosses it on the floor. He takes his hands and slides them down my sides. "Babe..."

He lays me back down and grazes his lips down my neck and over the thin lace of my bra. I hold tightly onto the sides of his head when he covers my nipple with his mouth and drags his tongue across the fabric. I begin to feel the anxiety build inside my stomach. I can't do this.

When he hooks his fingers under the waistband of my shorts, I clench my eyes tightly shut, panic coursing through me. I choke back a silent sob, and when I open my eyes to stop him, I see a pained look on his face. He's sitting back and slowly brushing his thumb over my tattoo, staring at it intently. His touch is jittery on my skin, and when his eyes shift to mine, I can't take the panic that is still coursing through my body.

I quickly shift up to my knees and throw my arms around his neck, just needing to feel safe in his hold. It takes him a while, but he eventually wraps his arms slowly, almost hesitantly, around me. I grip him tightly, trying hard to not freak out in front of him, and I notice his body trembling under my arms. I don't say anything because I am still so consumed with anxiety and wondering if he can tell how scared I just got when he touched me like he did.

Silently freaking out, neither one of us moves. We cling to each other and let time pass.

Eventually, I feel my heart slow, and I begin to soften in his arms.

"Candace."

"Please, don't say anything."

And he doesn't as he lies us down and pulls the covers over us.

When we wake up the next morning, Ryan is really quiet and seems tense. I notice his eyes are a bit bloodshot, and I ask him, "Did you not sleep last night?"

"Not too much," he says while pouring me a cup of coffee to take with me before he drives me home.

We've barely spoken this morning, and he hasn't been his usual affectionate self with me. In fact, I feel like he's avoiding me. I'm feeling extremely self-conscious; not only because of what happened last night, but also the way he is acting today. I'm sure he's getting tired of me always pushing him away. From my run in with Gina last night, I can tell he's used to getting what he wants without having to wait.

"You ready?" he asks.

"Yeah." I'm surprised when he takes my hand as he walks me to his jeep.

When he pulls up into my driveway and parks, I turn to him and say, "I'm sorry about last night, and I get that you're mad, but—"

"What?" he interrupts. "Why would I be mad?"

Suddenly feeling very unsure of the situation, I say, "Because I keep pushing you away. You've hardly said two words to me this morning. So, I just figured..."

He turns away from me and gets out of the car. I watch him, confused, as he walks around to my side and opens the door. He reaches over me and unclicks my seatbelt, turning me toward him.

"Everything you give me is perfect. You have to stop feeling like this. I'm here with you, and I'm not going anywhere." He leans in to kiss me, and his words bring me relief. "I'm sorry if I've been a dick, I just didn't get much sleep."

"It's okay. I overreacted."

Helping me out of the car, he kisses me again before leaving.

When I walk inside, Kimber is studying on the couch, and I've never felt more awkward around her since she asked me to move out.

"Who was that?" she asks as I walk across the room.

Turning to her, I ask, "Who?"

"That guy you just kissed in the driveway. I wasn't spying or anything, but you're right outside the window."

I look out the large bay window then back at her. She looks sad when I say, "Oh, um, his name's Ryan."

"You dating?"

"Yeah," I say, and I can tell that she is upset. I'm guessing it's the same sadness I felt when I found out about her and Seth. I want to talk to her, to tell her all about him and how great he is, but I can't. We aren't like that anymore, and I know she's hurting more than me as each day we grow more distant.

"Well, I have to go get ready for school," I softly say and then walk out of the room.

Seeing her now, after yesterday, is awful. I hate knowing that I've hurt her this much. I feel like I've lost her, and it's hard to be in the same house as her when we both feel the way that we do.

When I pick up my phone, with apprehension, I type out my text.

Can I stay with you?

I hold my phone with nervous hands and wait for the reply.

Of course babe.

chapter twenty-nine

After I had texted Ryan about staying with him, he came over later that night when I got off work to help me pack a few bags. Thankfully, Kimber wasn't home. It was hard enough trying to pack when I was so upset. But I know I need a little time away from this house so that emotions can settle.

I thought it would be weird staying with Ryan, but he's been able to keep the weirdness away. I know he's happy that I ran to him instead of Jase. But after knowing how he feels about Jase and me sleeping in the same bed, I knew I couldn't stay with him.

My sleep has been a little more restless lately and filled with night terrors since I stopped taking my sleeping pills last week. Taking them was always hard for me; a daily reminder of why I need to be on them and it was only becoming worse. So I hoped that enough time had passed, and I wouldn't need them anymore. I haven't had another nightmare though, which has been a relief. My restless sleep worries Ryan, but I just told him it's because of stress with school, graduation, and my issues with Kimber. I know it's a lie, but I told him that regardless.

Jase and Mark have been spending more time at the loft as well, now that I'm there. They tend to come over, or at least Jase does, when Ryan goes into work at night. They have both been scouting out firms to start applying to in a few months. I try not to think about what graduation will mean for Ryan and I. He hasn't ever said anything or asked, so if it's been on his mind, he doesn't want me to know. Truth is, I could wind up staying if this is where my job is. I have no idea where I will wind up, but for the moment, I want to enjoy being right where I am.

Ryan makes me happy, and I desperately need that. I still have my moments where I think I'm going to see Jack at school, or that he's going to walk into the coffee shop. And I know he's the cause of my restless sleep. Every time I take off my clothes, I'm reminded of him, of that night. He left a scar on my breast where he bit me so hard that he broke my skin. I can still remember the pain that shot down to my belly. Ryan has never seen it because the few times he's taken off my shirt, I never let him take off my bra. But he's seen my tattoo; the foolish tattoo I got when I thought it was time to abandon my cautious ways and have a little fun. Who knew fun would have left me battered, lying on a street by a dumpster? But, when I'm next to Ryan, he takes almost all of that away from me. I only wish he could take it all away.

"Candace Parker, please take the stage." My name echoes throughout Meany Theater. Nerves course through me, as they do every time I walk across this stage. Walking to the center, I find my spot and posture myself in fifth position. The thump of the spotlight being turned on is loud as it casts its glow down on me. And as it does, like all the times in the past on this very stage, my body relaxes and I am free when the music begins.

I let go, and do what I have been training for during the past six months. My body knows exactly what to do as I work the floor. The comforting sounds of my ripped satin pointes gliding across the stage, and the thuds of my boxes only add to the peace I feel when I am on this stage. I know I don't have to concentrate on my turnouts and port a bras, my body does it for me.

One haunting beat after another, I feel it pouring out of me: the pain, the darkness, the weakness; it's all there on the smooth black floor beneath my feet. My spots hit hard and sharp, and I know my lines are perfection when I feel the pinching in my back. My ankles are warm and loose when I move into my fouettè combination during the peak of the music. When I flow out of it, naturally leading with my heel to further push my turnout, I progress through the piece. The return of the staccato brushes of the violin pushes the music to its drop into silence.

The spotlight thumps off, and I can finally see the panel of instructors as they are taking notes. There are nine of them. I've been with them for the past four years, dancing in their classes and learning from them.

None of them look at me, and when I hear the voice of Sergej through the speakers announcing the next dancer, I walk off the stage and hope it isn't the last time I will grace it alone.

My heart races the whole drive back to Ryan's. I can't get out of the car fast enough when I pull into his driveway. I run up the stairs and burst through the door, throwing my bag on the wooden floor. When I see Ryan walking down the hall from his office, I run like a child and jump into his arms, wrapping my legs around his waist.

"I take it you kicked ass?" he asks through his laughs.

I can't wipe the cheesy smile off my face. "I totally kicked ass. It was amazing!"

My legs are strong around his waist when he takes his hands off of my hips, places them on my cheeks, and kisses me. I slam my mouth onto his as he pushes me up against the hallway wall, but we don't stay connected for long because I cannot stop talking and laughing, telling him each detail when I know he has no clue what the hell I'm saying, but I don't care and I know he doesn't either. He just watches me in my excitement with his beautiful smile.

He never moves me from the wall, and I keep my lock around his waist as he lets me ramble on.

"I'm so proud of you, babe. I wish I could have seen you," he says when I finally stop talking.

"I know. I'm sorry. Auditions are always closed," I say as I run my fingers through his hair.

"When will you find out?"

"March first."

"Next week?"

"Yeah, Friday."

Pulling his head in, I kiss him again, and he begins to mumble over my lips that don't want to stop. "I've got news too."

Still not willing to break my lips from his, I mutter, "What's that?"

"Thinkspace Gallery called."

I snap my head back as a new wave of excitement begins to flow through me. "And...?"

"They accepted your photo."

"Your photo?!"

"No, *your* photo, babe," he says softly and he rests his head against mine.

I smile at his words. I can't help myself. He knows how tense I was when he took that picture that he refuses to take credit for it.

"Congratulations," I say when he changes our pace and slowly presses tighter against me, tenderly pressing his lips over mine. I rake my fingers through his hair, and I am overcome with happiness. Happy about having a great audition, happy that Ryan's photograph will be displayed in an art gallery, and happy that I am sharing this moment with him. Everything about Ryan floods my being, and I want no one else.

He pulls back and looks into my eyes and when he does, I see it all. I see it clearly; he loves me, and I know I'm safe.

"What is it, babe?"

Brushing my hand down the side of his face, I give him a part of me that I've been holding tightly to.

"I love you."

I know he's been waiting a long time for me to get here, but I know it's okay when I look into his clear eyes and see the lines appear at the corners when his smile grows.

"You'll never know what those words just did to me," he says and he carries me over to the couch, where we proceed to make out like a couple of kids. This might not be typical for anyone else our age, but it's us, and I love us.

I'm not sure where I am when I wake up. I try to sit up, but I'm paralyzed. Looking up, I see the dark sky filled with tiny sparkling specks of stars.

"Ryan?"

There's no answer in the stillness. When I roll my head to the side, I see a rust covered wheel and lock. It's familiar. I inhale the damp summer air.

Wait. It's supposed to be winter.

"Ryan?"

Where is he?

I focus my attention back on the rust, and when I finally realize why it looks so familiar, I jerk my head back to the stars, but they're gone, and my heart stops.

His taunting laughs fill the silent night as his devilish eyes peer into mine.

"Ryan!"

Leaning in, his hot breath on my face, his voice a quiet firm growl, "Shut the fuck up."

He strikes my cheek with the back of his knuckles, and my face burns when the tears begin to prick out. Trying with everything I have in me, I can't move. I'm frozen on the rough concrete as he stares down at me—laughing. He starts to unbutton his pants, and I begin to lose control and shriek for Ryan, but no one is here to help me. My heart is pounding in my chest so hard my ribs ache. The terror singes through my veins, and I scream, "Please, not again."

"This time, you're gonna fucking like it," he sneers as he pulls my shirt up and rips my bra down. All I can do is dig my brittle nails into the cement. My blood-covered hands shake and sting as I cry helplessly on the ground. His mouth is all over me as I beg him to stop.

I turn to find the dumpster, but it's no longer there. I need that dumpster to take my mind away and it's not fuckin' there!

My stomach convulses with each button he pops open on my jeans.

"Get off of me!"

Ripping off my underwear, he slides his hand between my legs, and I begin shrieking out violent sobs. Gripping my upper arms, he holds me down as I keep screaming through my labored breaths, "Get the fuck off of me!"

Panic and confusion hit me hard when I see Ryan's face above me instead of Jack. Suddenly, I feel my legs moving, and I begin to kick in a frenzy to get out of his tight grip. When I look back up, I see Jack again. He dips his head and licks up my throat.

"God, please stop!" I wail.

"Candace, wake up."

Thrashing under Jack's grip, I'm no longer paralyzed, and I'm no longer being pinned down.

I hear myself screaming as I shuffle back in a panic, trying to escape. I feel myself fall on my hip. Not able to get to my feet, I clumsily continue to shuffle on my hands, desperate to get away.

All I hear is Jack laughing at me.

When the wall hits my back, his hands are on my shoulders, and I scream, "Don't fuckin' touch me!" as I curl into a ball, covering my face with my hands. I continue to scream the same thing over and over until I no longer hear Jack, but Ryan.

Ryan!

"Candace, open your eyes."

But I can't. I don't know what's happening, what's real. My breathing is erratic, and I am engulfed in fear. I'm still sobbing. I don't know how to stop.

"Candace, please. Look at me. It's only me here with you."

My arms are stiff when he touches my wrists to move my hands away from my face. I don't want him to see me—not like this. When he moves my hands, I turn my face away from him, wanting to somehow disappear.

"Babe, please don't hide from me."

Trying to take in some air through my cries, I choke on my breath, and when I do, he pulls me close, and I just fall into him. His arms are so tight around me, and I know it's only him.

I don't know what I was thinking not taking my pills anymore. How could I be so stupid to think I was strong enough to be okay without them? Now I'm consumed with worry and dread. What the hell is Ryan going to do or say? What am I going to do or say? What do I do?

God, what do I do?

I'm curled up tight in Ryan's lap, and he is stroking my hair with his fingers. I'm so embarrassed. But, he doesn't give me a choice from eluding this when he leans back to look at me.

Closing my eyes, he says, "You have to look at me. Please."

When I feel the heat of his hands on my face, I blink my eyes open and slowly shift my eyes to him. His expression is worried as he scans my face.

"You okay?"

I nod my head.

"What happened?"

I drop my head and rest it on his chest as he rubs my back. I just want to hide and not have to look at him.

With hesitation, I ask, "Can you please call Jase?"

"What?" he says in disbelief, and I don't blame him. "Shit, Candace, no."

A new round of tears begin to flow, and I hear the desperation in my voice when I urge, "Please."

"Candace, no. You can't always run to him. Need me for change. Talk to me."

"I can't," I cry out.

"Yes, you can."

"No, I can't. Please. I just can't"

"But you can with Jase?"

I'm sobbing now, but Ryan never lets go of me.

"I want you to need me," he says.

"I do."

"You don't; you cling to him for everything." He takes my hands and presses them against his bare chest, over his heart. "Look at me," he demands, and when I do, he tells me,

"Cling to *me.* Love me enough to *need me*."

"I can't...I..."

"Why?"

I know he's not going to drop this, and I begin to get angry. Angry that I'm even in this position right now.

"Because, you'd leave me."

"Not happening, babe."

"Ryan, please," I plead.

"I'm not leaving you. Nothing you could say would make me want to leave you."

"I'm just too fucked up."

"We're all fucked up," he says. "I want you to let me in."

I know there is no way out of this. But how? How do I do this?

He grabs my hands again when I try to cover my face as my cries quake through me.

"I can't! You'll never look at me the same. You'll run away."

When I say this, he slides his hand around the back of my head and pulls me against him as he sighs out. I cry in his chest as he says, "I promise you, nothing will change the way I look at you. Nothing will change what you do to me when you're next to me. You make my heart beat in a completely different way—nothing will ever change that."

I finally wrap my arms around him, hanging on with everything I have. "I'm so embarrassed," I confess around my cries.

"God, babe." I can hear the pain in his voice. "Please, don't be."

I have never said the words. Not ever. Not to anyone. Not even to myself. Maybe I foolishly thought if I didn't say it, then maybe it wasn't really real.

When he strengthens his hold on me, I let it out on a

whimper, "I was raped."

Releasing a heavy sigh, he lays his head on top of mine, and I continue to cry. I feel so weak and tired, like I'm drowning. I keep treading water, but I can never seem to get my head high enough out of the water to take in a full breath of air. I've been drowning since that night. There are times I feel like I can make it, but then I'm pulled right back under.

Ryan says nothing as we sit here on the floor. I feel guilty for the lies and mistruths I've told him to try and hide this. When my sobs soften into whimpers, I speak.

"I've been lying to you," I say quietly.

"I don't care. It doesn't matter."

"I feel horrible."

"Candace, don't do this. You have every right to lie."

But I need to tell him.

"I can't go to see you at work because..."

"Shhh..."

"Because it happened in your parking lot. By the dumpster. That's why I freaked out. I didn't know where I was until I saw the dumpster."

When I tell him this, I feel a breath thud in his chest. I loosen my hold and pull back. I break when I see the tears streaming down his cheeks. Looking into his eyes, as the tears begin to fall from mine again, I cry, "I'm so sorry."

"Don't ever fuckin' say that again. Don't ever be sorry for anything again."

"I'm just so far from what you thought."

"You're not."

"I am. Every day is a struggle. Everything. I'm scared every day." I drop my head for a moment, and when I look back up at him, I finally admit what I've been feeling for the past six months. Ever since that night, the night Jack left me broken and desperate. The night he took everything from me: my trust, my peace, my security, my faith—my light. He took it all and left me with nothing.

"I'm fading." I feel the heat of my tears as they linger down my cheeks. "He took all my light, and I've been fading ever since."

Cradling my face in his hands, he says, "You're not fading. I won't let you."

I nod my head, fold myself into his arms, and let him hold me.

"That's why Kimber is mad. I didn't go home after it happened. I stayed with Jase and never told her why. She knows I'm lying."

Ryan doesn't say anything. He simply lets me talk and get it all out. I love him even more for that because I need to get it out.

"I've been taking sleeping pills, but I stopped last week. That's why I haven't been sleeping." I take a second before continuing. "I dream about that night—about him. All I see are his eyes." I confess as I weep out, "He made me watch him."

Ryan doesn't say anything as a new slew of sobs wrack my body. He just bands his arms tighter around me and I finally speak again, "So, I take pills to keep him away."

"Babe, why did you stop taking them?" he asks as he brushes my hair back behind my shoulder.

"Because every night when I take them, it's only a reminder of what happened. I just want to forget, but I can't."

"Have you told anyone?"

"No. Only Jase and Mark. Jase was with me in the hospital. Mark only knows because he walked in and saw my face. It was pretty banged up."

"Your parents?"

"God, no. It was because of them that I went out with that guy at all."

He pulls his head back and looks at me in disbelief.

"You knew him?"

I nod my head and he asks, "But you didn't do anything?"

"No."

"I wanna fucking kill him," he says through gritted teeth.

It takes a while, but when I finally feel Ryan's tense chest relax, he pulls back and looks me in the eyes as he says, "This changes nothing for me. Okay? Nothing. No one will ever love you like I do."

When he leans down and gently kisses me, I release my worry. Worry of him leaving, of him being disgusted, worry of him running away from my dark side. I relax in his arms, knowing that we have no more secrets.

chapter thirty

"He knows."

"You told him?" he says in surprise.

"I didn't really have a choice," I tell Jase. "I had another nightmare last night."

"What happened?" he asks as he shifts on the couch to face me.

"I freaked out with him in the bed. It was humiliating. So, I had to tell him."

Jase reaches over and grabs my hand, holding it tightly when I continue. "I've never said it before. I never wanted to say the words. I mean, I have silently in my head, but never out loud."

"Are you okay?"

"Yeah, I think so."

"What did he do?"

"I mean, what could he do? He listened and assured me that it doesn't change anything with us. I was scared he'd want to leave. I wouldn't have blamed him."

"God, Candace, I'm sorry, but he needed to know. I'm glad you told him," he says with sincerity.

"I told him I loved him." A grin spreads across his face and I say, "Don't embarrass me, Jase."

"I won't. I swear."

Taking my hand from his, I grab my glass of wine from

the coffee table and take a sip when he asks, "Do you know what he's doing for your birthday?"

"Jase, you know I hate parties and presents. It's all awkward and uncomfortable. Plus, I haven't told him it's my birthday."

He laughs at me and says, "You're so weird."

"Seriously, we have never done anything before, why start now?"

He takes a swig of his beer, then suggests, "Let's at least get together. We can go do dinner at Mark's. No birthday cake. Promise."

"Fiiine," I whine and then give him a tiny smile. "I'll let Ryan know. And no presents. It's just stupid."

"None."

We sit together on his couch and continue to drink and catch up on what's been going on in each other's lives. It's Friday night, and Ryan is at work. One of Gavin's bands is playing there tonight, so he and his friends decided to make a night out of it. He wanted to cancel when we woke up this morning, but I told him that it would make me more uncomfortable if he didn't go because of me. Plus, Jase and I had already made plans to get together, so Ryan agreed, although with much hesitation.

I nearly finish the bottle of merlot by myself and am drunk for the first time in my life. Maybe it was just everything that had happened yesterday that has me wanting to drink way more than I normally do. I'm barely coherent when Jase calls Ryan to come pick me up.

"Youuuu take me home," I slur out, and then burst into a fit of giggles.

"I can't. I've had too many beers. He'll be here in a bit. He just left the bar."

I lie down on the couch and close my eyes when the room begins to sway in a hazy way. Jase is talking to me, but it sounds like an echo at this point. When there is a knock at the door, I pop up on my knees, looking over the back of the couch as Ryan walks in.

"You're heeeere!" I scream and throw my arms into the air.

"Shit, man, what the hell did you give her?" he laughs out.

"She inhaled a bottle of wine," Jase tells him.

Pointing to Ryan, I shout, "You'rrre hot!" and then burst out into another fit of uncontrollable laughter.

"Okay, party's over, babe," he says as he walks toward the couch shaking his head humorously at me.

"Noooo!" I pout as I jump up to my feet on top of the couch and feign authority.

He grabs me behind my knees and throws me over his shoulder as I continue to giggle.

"Alright, let's go."

I reach down, grab his ass, and squeal, "Niiiice!"

"Oh yeah. You like that?" he says through his chuckles, and I can hear Jase laughing as well.

Looking up, I wave to Jase, "Byyyye, buddy!"

"Call me tomorrow when you sober up."

"Bye, man. Thanks for calling me," Ryan says before hauling me to the elevator.

When we get inside, he sets me down, and I turn to the buttons and laugh while I swipe my hands over them, lighting each one up.

"Woohoooo!"

"Shit, babe! Do you know how long it's gonna take us to get to the lobby?"

"A looong, looong time," I say extremely slow.

He holds onto my hips to steady me and then smiles down at me. "You're so fuckin' cute when you're drunk."

"I'm druuuunk?!"

"Yeah, just a bit."

Slinging my arms around his neck, I hang my head back and look up at him. "You'rrre so tall."

"I don't think so. You're just really small."

"I like it!" I chirp out. "It's sexxxxy."

"You think so?"

"Ooooh yeaaaah." Lifting high on my toes, I slightly lose my balance and give him a sloppy kiss before cracking up in giggles.

He wipes his mouth and mumbles, "That was interesting."

While the elevator slowly makes its way down to the lobby, stopping on every floor, I decide to make myself comfortable on the floor.

Sitting in the corner, Ryan looks down at me and smirks as he leans against the wall.

"Can we some cake?" I mumble out.

"Babe, you're missing some words in there." The elevator dings again, and this time, the doors open to the lobby. "Come on," he says and he scoops me up, cradling me in his hold. I wrap my arms around his neck and say, "I wannn cake."

"It's the middle of the night. You have ice cream in my freezer. Just eat that."

"I told Jase nooo cake for my birrrthday, But I wannn some."

Setting me in his car, he says, "Birthday, huh? Why am I just now hearing this?"

"It'sss Thursdaay."

"Hmmm." He reaches over me to fasten the seatbelt, and I lay my head down on the center console.

When he gets into the car, he brushes my hair back. "How're you feeling?"

"Sleepy."

"Just close your eyes."

My head grows heavy, and I begin to drift while Ryan strokes my hair during the drive back to his place. He carries me inside and up the stairs to his room. Sitting me down on the edge of the tub, he goes to get me my clothes.

"Here. Do you want me to help you change?"

"No. I can do it," I say, not wanting Ryan to see me without my clothes on.

"Okay. I'm gonna run downstairs. I'll be right back."

"Okay."

I slip into my pants and cami, brush my teeth, then go to slide into bed. I don't open my eyes when I hear Ryan come back in and change.

"Candace," he whispers.

"Hmmm..."

"Babe, where are your pills?"

"Purse."

When he returns, I take my pill and some aspirin with the bottle of water he set on the nightstand. I roll over into his arms and curl up.

"Thanks," I whisper in the darkness.

"For what?"

"Staying."

Turning on his side to face me, he pulls me in flush against him. "I told you, I'm not going anywhere."

"I know, but that was before..."

"I love you. I wanna be that person you can bring anything to; the good and the bad."

"I love you, Ryan."

He kisses me slowly and then tucks my head under his chin. "I love you too."

Time passes and I hear Ryan's breaths as they slow into a soft rhythmic pattern as he falls asleep. My head is woozy, and I try to fight the sleep that is threatening to take over. My dream last night fills my head and haunts me. I don't want to close my eyes because I'm afraid Jack is on the other side. I toss and turn in my restlessness. Reaching over, I grab Ryan's phone to see the time is almost two a.m., and when I roll back over, Ryan is awake.

"What are you doing?" he asks in a sleepy rasp.

"Nothing."

"How are you even still awake?"

I lay my head on his chest and don't respond.

"Babe...?"

"I don't want to sleep just yet."

"Why?"

"I'm just...I'm scared I'll have another bad dream."

He kisses my forehead and says, "Try not to think so much about it. It's just you and me. Think about us. If you could go anywhere, where would you go?"

"Back to Indian Beach with you." I think about that morning; him telling me that he wanted to be with me, us kissing in the cold rain.

"Close your eyes and go back there. You and me sitting on the driftwood."

"Talk to me," I request, and he does. He replays our morning on the beach and tells me everything he was feeling. Confessing how nervous he was and how much he was already falling for me. His words chase away the fears of Jack, and I drift off before he finishes talking.

I've had more free time to spend with Ryan since my audition last week. We've started running again, and I even let Ryan photograph me. He said he wanted to get a few shots of my legs. He's been working on them for the past couple days while I'm in class. He showed them to me this morning, and they are incredible. It's pretty amazing what he can capture and enhance. I love that we can do that together. The way he looks at me when he takes my picture, it's an intimacy I haven't ever felt before.

When I get back from work, Mark's car is already parked in the driveway. We decided to have my non-birthday dinner here at the loft tonight. I told Ryan to not make it a big deal, and explained how my mother would always throw these extravagant birthdays for me, but how they were really her way of one-upping her friends.

My parties had more of her friends there than mine, and we never got to do what I wanted. They were always so formal when all I really wanted was a simple white cake and to play silly games. Instead, for my sixth birthday, I had a tea party at the country club. We all wore frilly dresses and fancy hats. So, ever since I left home, I prefer to do nothing for my birthday since the day only holds dismal memories for me.

When I walk in, I am happy to see the guys watching TV and drinking beer. I love each of them in very different ways and smile when I see them sitting there.

I walk in and give Jase and Mark a hug and a kiss and when Ryan motions me over, I go sit on his lap.

"I missed you," he says quietly in my ear and runs his nose down my neck. "Mmmm...coffee," he jokes.

I laugh and hop off his lap. "I'm gonna take a quick shower. I'll be back."

"Pizzas will be here in a few minutes," Mark calls out to me when I start up the stairs.

"All right."

After I shower and dry my hair, I decide to take it easy and throw on my pajamas. When I hear the doorbell ring, I hurry downstairs because I'm starving.

When I turn the corner, I see Ryan hugging his mom.

I'm surprised when I say, "Donna?"

"Candace," she says with a smile.

I walk over to her, confused, and give her a hug. "What are you doing here?"

"I wasn't going to miss your birthday. But I'm a little disappointed that I had to hear about it from Ryan when you and I talk every week."

When I look over at Ryan, he gives me a wink and a chaste kiss.

"Sorry, I...I don't normally do anything for my birthday, but I'm so happy you're here," I say and hug her again. "I can't believe you drove all this way."

"It's a few hours, dear. Hardly a chore." She takes my hand and walks us into the living room.

I introduce her to Mark and Jase, and they all exchange hugs.

"Mom, what do you want to drink?"

"A glass of wine will be good."

"Me too," I say.

"You're not gonna get drunk, slap my ass, and tell me how sexy I am, are you?" he teases.

"Ryan!"

I look at Donna with an apologetic look while Ryan is laughing at my expense in the kitchen.

"I didn't...I mean it wasn't..."

"Honey, we've all been there," she says with a hint of laughter.

Ryan walks back in, hands his mom and I our glasses of wine, and sits down next to me while his mom and I chat. Ever since Christmas, she calls me once a week to check in. At first it was a little uncomfortable, but we've grown close. She knows that I've been staying here with Ryan and how I feel about him. She's never once been judgmental or snarky like it was with my mother when she would call me. The relationship I have with Donna is one that I have been needing, now more than ever. She's nothing but supportive and encouraging, and I love her for that.

When the pizza arrives, we all sit around the living room and eat straight from the boxes. Ryan and I share the box with the pineapple pizza. I love that I can spend a night like this, in my pajamas, with people I care about.

Mark and Ryan gather all the boxes and take them to the kitchen when we are done. When they come back in, Ryan is holding a cheap grocery store birthday cake.

"Don't get upset, but you told me in the elevator that you wanted cake, so here it is."

He smiles at me as he sets it on the coffee table and Mark hands everyone a fork. We all sit on the floor, around the table, and eat. We don't bother cutting it; we just eat straight from the cake. When I can't take another bite, I throw my fork in and lie back.

"I'm gonna die," I moan out in discomfort.

"I don't get how you can be so tiny when you eat like a horse," Mark teases.

"Because I work my ass off."

"Please, you twirl around on your toes," he chuckles out.

"Oh yeah? When I find a pair of pointes in size Yeti, I'm gonna make you wear them, and then you can see what a workout it is."

"I'd pay to see that shit," Jase says.

Ryan and Donna clean everything up while Mark, Jase, and I continue to tease each other.

When we decide to watch a movie, Donna calls it a night. She's tired from the drive, but we will have all day tomorrow to hang out. While Ryan gets her situated in the guest bedroom, Jase, Mark, and I get comfortable on the floor and turn out the lights. We pull the pillows off the couch and chairs and huddle under blankets. Ryan returns and slides under my blanket, and we cuddle as we watch 'The Breakfast Club.'

By the time Allison throws the bologna and cheese on the statue and proceeds to make a sandwich out of Captain Crunch and Pixie Sticks, Jase and Mark head out. Once they're gone, I roll over and face Ryan, the only light being the flicker of the TV. I tangle my legs with his and snuggle in close.

"Thank you."

"For?"

"Your mom and the cake," I say with a grin.

He kisses my nose and says, "Anytime."

I slide my hand under his shirt and run it up his smooth back. "I love you."

He doesn't say anything; he only kisses me. It's all I need as I melt into him. I can taste the sugar from the cake and he caresses his tongue with mine. I grip onto his shoulder and wrap my leg around his hip. Grabbing onto my thigh, I tangle my other hand in his hair. He rolls on top of me and runs his palm up my side, under my shirt.

We've done this before, and I let myself relax because I know that he knows when to stop with me. I trust him, and I know he would never push me. I feel warm under his touch, letting him wrap me up in it. He makes my heart beat faster, and I just want to be close with him. I love what we have together, and I love him.

It's been two weeks since I told him my secret, and he hasn't once looked at me differently. When he said to me that it didn't change anything, I didn't believe him at first, but now, all I can do is trust him and what he says.

Ryan runs his soft kisses up my neck and then pulls away. "Come on," he says as he holds out his hand for me. "I want you in my bed, under my sheets."

I smile up at him before he grabs me and takes me upstairs.

chapter thirty-one

Donna insisted we go to Common Grounds for breakfast while Ryan goes to the gym. She said she wanted to see where I worked, so when Ryan left, we got ourselves ready and I drove us to the coffee shop.

The place isn't too busy when we arrive. We walk up to the counter and I introduce Donna to Roxy.

"So, you're Ryan's mom?" she says with a smirk, and I know she wants to mention his hot-ass, as she does every time his name comes up, but thankfully, she keeps her couth.

"Yes, it's so good to meet you."

Donna doesn't look fazed at all by Roxy's unique style and her cobalt-blue hair.

"Likewise. So what are you girls up to today?"

"We're just here for breakfast," I tell her.

Donna and I give Roxy our order and when she hands us our drinks and muffins, we make ourselves comfortable on one of the cozy small loveseats.

"Thank you for driving up here. It really means a lot me," I tell her as I sip my hot tea.

"Well, I'm glad Ryan called me to tell me it was your birthday."

"Sorry, if it was last minute notice, but he didn't even know until last week."

She gives me a warm smile and says, "Well, I'm happy

to be here. It's so good to see the two of you. I've never seen him so happy. All he seems to talk about when I call him is you. So, I take it you guys are getting more serious?"

It's not awkward for me to talk to her about Ryan. We talk about our relationship almost every week. Even though I haven't known her very long, she gives me the maternal support I've never had. She's been easy for me to let in.

"Yeah, I mean we love each other. I try not to think about it too much, but I sometimes worry about what will happen after I graduate."

"Well, have you thought about where you want to go?"

"I don't have a whole lot of choice in the matter. I have to go where the job is, and I have no clue what company will offer me a spot. That's what's so unnerving."

Swallowing a bite of her muffin, she asks, "What does Ryan say?"

"We haven't talked about it. I've never mentioned it."

"You have to follow your dreams. I don't see Ryan standing in the way of that."

"I really do love him."

"I know you do," she says as she reaches for my hand.

"I don't know if I could ever leave him."

"Don't let your dreams fade away. Whatever happens, I know you two will find your way through it."

I smile at her words and hope that she's right. I know Seattle has a few outstanding ballet companies. I've expressed interest in a couple; I just hope that one of them will offer me a spot, but at the same time, I've always dreamed of New York. Ever since I was a little girl, I've been fantasizing about dancing in the city.

"Well, dear, Ryan told me to not get you anything, but..." She reaches in her purse and pulls out an old weathered box. "I didn't wrap it, so technically, it's not an official present."

When she places the box in my hands, I look at her in disbelief. “Donna, I can’t.”

“I’ve had it for years, dear. It’s just an old, dirty book, but I saw you reading it at Christmas, so I thought you wouldn’t mind having a copy.”

I open the box, and I know it’s the original publisher’s box. Pulling out my favorite book from my childhood, I open it up to see the publishing date is 1935.

Shaking my head, I say, “But this is a collector’s edition. How...?”

“When I was a little girl, I loved this book. My grandmother bought this for me when she found it in a rundown antique shop. I bought a current published version for the kids that I keep out, and when I saw you reading it, I figured you would appreciate having this version.”

When I start to shake my head again, she places her hand on top of one of the original prints of Frances Hodgson Burnett’s book, ‘A Little Princess,’ and says, “Like I said, it’s an old book that has been sitting at the top of my closet for years, doing nothing but collecting dust.”

Tears prick my eyes when I think about what this book was for me when I was growing up. In a way, I felt a lot like the girl, Sara. She believed herself to be a princess, and even though her world was falling apart at the hands of someone else, she pulled through, despite the cruelty she suffered. I hadn’t read it in years, but when I saw it at Donna’s house, I read it again and found it to be just as meaningful as an adult as it was when I was a child.

I set the book in its box on my lap and lean over to hug her. “I can’t tell you what this means to me. Thank you.”

“Thank you for accepting it.”

When she sits back, she smiles and says, swiftly taking the focus off of her non-present, “So, tell me, when do you find out about your audition?”

Placing the cover back on the box, I say, "Today, actually. It should be posted this afternoon around five."

"Either way, I am so proud of you."

Hearing those words from her, every time she says them, fills little empty places in my heart. I never got to hear those words from my parents, so hearing them now does tremendous things to me.

"Tell me about this production. How many dances will I get to see you in?"

"You're coming?" I ask.

"Are you kidding me? I can't wait to see you dance."

Again, filling up little pieces of my heart.

Smiling, I tell her all about the three ensemble pieces I will be dancing. While I talk, she asks questions and is sincerely interested. We continue to enjoy each other's company and relax in our slow lazy morning. When we finish up, we decide to walk around the block and into some of the little boutique and fragrance shops. We both buy a few things here and there as we hop from store to store.

When I look at the woman Donna is, it's hard for me to imagine what her life used to be like with Ryan's father. Ryan told me that the night his dad died, he had beaten Donna pretty badly, smashing a coffee mug into the back of her head. Ryan was just coming home from a party and walked in on it. He said he lost all control of himself and started throwing punches. His dad managed to grab a knife from the counter and that's how Ryan got the scar on his ribs.

Once his dad died, Donna was determined to put that life behind them. Seeing them now, you would never know the hell they lived with. I know that Ryan still deals with the memories of it all. He told me that he's scared that he'll wind up like his father, and that's why he's never wanted to get serious with a girl. So he got pretty good at shutting down when he was with women. I hate to think about him being like that; I can't even picture him as that person because all I have ever known is the way he's always been with me.

Leaving the last store, we make our way back to the loft so that Donna can pack and start driving back to Cannon Beach. It's a little after twelve by the time we get back, and Ryan is waiting on us.

"Damn, that was a long breakfast," he says when we walk through the door carrying all of our shopping bags. Walking over to us, he kisses his mom and then me before taking the bags and setting them on the table.

"Sorry, time got away from us. If I didn't have to go home, I would have spent the whole day with her."

Ryan throws his arm around my shoulder and teases his mother. "Well, thanks for bringing her back, I'm sick of sharing her."

"Ryan!" I say as I nudge him playfully in the gut.

"Sorry, babe, but it's the truth," he says, then starts facetiously ravaging my neck.

"Okay, kids. I've seen enough. I'm going to go pack," Donna says, as she's already halfway down the hall.

"Ryan, that tickles," I chuckle out, trying to wriggle out of his arms, but it only encourages him. Picking me up off the ground, he carries me to the couch and lays me down. Softening his kisses, he asks, "Did you have a good time this morning?"

"Uh huh," is all I can manage to say when he licks the hollow of my neck.

"Ryan, we should stop."

"Why?" He says this without taking his lips off of me.

"Because your mom is about to leave, and you should go spend a little time with her before she goes."

He lets out a sexy groan and pulls away. "Okay, but I'm not done with you," he says as he starts to walk away.

I give the two of them some alone time to visit while I

start unpacking my new purchases. After hanging up my new dresses in Ryan's closet, I put my new bottle of perfume on the bathroom counter. When I look around his room and see my things, it makes me happy to be sharing this space with him, but it also reminds me that I'm not at home with Kimber. I've been so wrapped up in Ryan these past few weeks that I haven't thought much about her, but now I wonder. Wonder how she's feeling about everything, wonder if she's mad that I left again, wonder if I can mend this fracture between us.

"Candace," Ryan hollers from downstairs.

"Coming," I say, and when I get to the door where Donna is standing with her bags, I suddenly feel a twinge of sadness creep over me. A part of me doesn't want her to leave. She's become someone special to me, and having her near brings a peace that I've been missing all my life.

I don't say anything when I reach her, I just let her hug me, and when I feel the tears puddle in my eyes, I pull back. When she sees my sadness, her face pains. I blink, and the tears roll down my cheeks.

"Dear," she says softly before pulling me back into her arms, and I feel Ryan's supportive hand on my back.

"Come see me, okay?"

When I let go of her, I nod my head, not able to speak around the knot in my throat. Ryan wraps his arms around me from behind, and I lean back into him.

"When is your next break?"

Ryan answers for me, knowing that I don't like to talk when I get like this. "She has the last two weeks of this month off before her last quarter."

Looking at me, she says, "You and Ryan come visit, okay?"

As I nod my head, she picks up her bags, and Ryan says, "Mom, let me take those out for you."

"That's okay. I've got it. Stay in here with her."

"Thanks for coming, Mom. Call me when you get home."

"I will, and call me when you find out about the solo."

"We will," he responds.

When the door closes, Ryan turns me around in his arms and holds me until I can compose myself enough to pull away.

Cupping my head in his hands, I look up at him when he asks, "You okay, babe?"

"I hate that she lives so far away. I really like having her around."

Wiping my tears with the pads of his thumbs, he says, "I know you do. We'll go visit her when you're on your break."

I rest my head back against his chest, and I take a moment before saying, "My parents never even called me."

He runs his hand up the back of my head and grips me close when I add, "I mean...I knew they wouldn't, but it still hurts."

"I know it does."

I inhale a deep breath and let it out when he says, "Come on, let's go grab something to eat before we go to the campus."

"Sounds good. Give me a few minutes to freshen up?"

"Of course."

We have a long lunch at Eastlake Bar and Grill before driving to UW. We park and walk to Meany Theater. Walking up, I can see a crowd of fellow dancers walking inside to see if their name is one of the two that will be listed. I feel the butterflies in my stomach and turn to Ryan, "Can we just go for a walk first?"

"What? Don't you want to find out if you got it?"

"Yeah, but not around everyone else."

Holding my hand, he turns the other direction. By the time we walk through the quad and back to the theater, the crowd has dissipated, and we walk inside. My palms start to sweat when I see the white sheet of paper taped to the wall. When I step closer, I let out a loud sigh in disbelief. Shaking my head, I turn to Ryan and say, "I can't believe it."

"Believe it."

My rapid breathing slowly turns into laughter, and I sling my arms around Ryan's neck as he picks me up. Wrapping my legs around his waist, I squeal out, "I really can't believe it!"

Looking up at me, he smiles, wide and gorgeous. I lean my head down and kiss him, but it doesn't last long with my excitement. When I look up, I see Ms. Emerson and Sergej walk through a set of double doors. I jump out of Ryan's arms and try to reel in my emotions, but I can't seem to wipe the cheesy smile off my face.

When they walk past me, Ms. Emerson stops to face me. I notice a small twitch in the corner of her mouth as she gives a slight nod of her head before turning and walking out the door. Spinning around to Ryan, I can't contain myself, and I cover my face with my hands as I feel a weight being lifted from my chest that I never knew was there.

"Come over here," Ryan says, and I walk to him, straight into his embrace. "You're amazing, you know that?"

Looking up at him, I confess, "Because of you."

"No, babe. It's all you."

Today has been a mixture of emotions, and after I finish brushing my teeth, Ryan slides his arms around my waist from behind and starts kissing my neck. We watch each other in the reflection of the mirror, and when I turn around to face him, he picks me up and sets me on the edge of the sink. Tilting my head back to look up at him, he says, "You're fuckin' gorgeous."

He makes me laugh as he leans down to kiss me. My legs wrap around his waist, and I twine my fingers in his hair when he picks me up. When we fall into bed, he trails his kisses down my neck, and my body starts to shiver. He slowly pulls back and gazes down at me with an intensity burning in his eyes. Sliding my hand up his chest, I wrap it around his neck and pull him back to me.

Our kisses are slow and with a passion I haven't felt before. I thrust my tongue into his mouth and taste him, throwing myself into our kiss. His arms band tightly around me, and I've never felt so safe. My mind blurs, and I begin to lose myself in his touch.

When he lifts my back off the bed, I'm barely thinking when I pull off my top as he lets out a low groan. Lowering me back down, he shifts his hips between my legs and drags his head down to my breasts.

We've never moved quite like this before, but a part of me doesn't want to stop. What I feel for this man is more than I ever thought I was capable of feeling. For a while, I thought I would never truly laugh again, but with Ryan, I'm my happiest. He gives me what I have been desperate for. Feeling him on my fingertips is enough to take me over, and I now want more.

Dragging his mouth from me, he pants, "We should stop."

I'm not sure I want to though. I know I will never love anyone the way I love him; he's all I want.

"Don't."

"Babe," he says in heavy breath, searching my face.

When I look up in his eyes, I see all I ever want to see. He loves me in a way I never thought I could be loved.

"I don't want you to stop."

"I need you to talk to me."

I can tell he's unsure, I see it in his face.

"I don't want to stop tonight."

He closes his eyes and drops his head to mine. "Please tell me this is okay." When I nod my head against his, he says, "I need to hear you say it, babe."

Cupping his face in my hands, I say, "It's okay. I want this, with you, I just...I don't know if I can."

There is a worry in his eyes that I don't want him to have. Although I'm scared, I know I want him.

I take his hand with my trembling one and place it back on my breast and whisper, "Just touch me."

He leans down and kisses me, long and slow while he slides his hand underneath my bra strap and slips it off my shoulder. I've never taken my clothes off in front of him before, and I feel the anxiety pool in my belly as he slides the other strap down, kissing my bare shoulder along the way. Pulling the fabric down, my pulse quickens, and in a moment of nervousness I confess, "I'm scared. I've never..."

Sweeping my hair back, he assures me, "It's just you and me. You're all I'll ever want."

He wraps his arms around me and unhooks my bra, dropping it on the floor. When he looks down at me, he sees my scar.

"He bit me," I say on a hush.

I hate that I have Jack's mark on my breast. It torments me to look at. It surprises me when Ryan leans down and kisses the scar.

"God, you're perfect," he breathes against my skin.

He drags his kisses down my stomach then sits back on his heels. Taking my hand in his, he places it over his scar on the side of his ribs. With words unspoken, I hear what he's telling me. We're both still alive, together, and we're okay. Brushing his scar with my thumb, I bring my hands to his stomach, feeling his defined lines under my touch as my fingers slide up, around his neck, and tangle into his hair. I pull him down and lose myself in him.

My legs begin to quiver when he hooks his thumbs inside the waistband of my pants. He strokes his knuckles across my belly before gently tugging down. When I lift my hips, he pulls off my pants and underwear, tossing them aside. I watch as he removes his pants, and when we are both naked, he lowers himself back on me and my whole body is trembling. He pulls the covers over us, and I start to wonder if maybe I can't do this. I want to, but I'm so scared. I have nothing good to associate with this, and I'm not sure I can.

Holding himself up on his elbows, he says, "Babe, you're shaking."

"What if I can't do this?"

"Then we stop."

Nodding my head, I am filled with nerves.

"We'll move as slow as you need. You just tell me when to stop."

"I don't want you to stop."

Giving me a smile, he leans down and kisses me. I wrap my arms around his neck and part my lips for him. He slides his tongue across my lower lip before he dips it into my mouth. We meld together as I run my hands down his neck and over his chest. His muscles are hard and cut beneath my hands, and I've never really taken my time to explore him until now. He's a lot larger than me, and I feel tiny underneath him, sheltered. I take my lips from him, skimming them across his tattooed covered shoulder to his neck.

I need him when he grazes his hand over my breast and takes me in his mouth. I let out a soft moan when he slides his tongue over my nipple and gently sucks. My body heats, and I arch myself into him.

"Ryan," I breathe out.

He drags his damp lips up my neck before saying, "You sure?"

When I say yes, he takes a moment to make sure we're safe and protected. Resting his forehead against mine, he says, "Tell me that you want this, that you want me."

And when I say, "I want you to make love to me," he reaches down and slowly starts to push into me. I tense up at the touch, having never experienced it in this way.

He pulls back slightly and says, "Are you okay?"

I nod my head and whisper, "Yeah," before he continues to ease himself inside of me. Letting out a gasp of breath, he drops his head in the crook of my neck.

"Fuck, you feel so good, babe."

My legs are tense around his hips as he holds himself in me. Clenching my eyes shut, I can feel the few tears that have escaped and are rolling down the sides of my face. Tears of nerves and tears of overwhelming love.

"Open your eyes, Candace. Look at me."

"Don't make me look," I softly plead. I'm afraid if I watch him, it will remind me too much of watching Jack. I'm scared.

"Baby, please open your eyes. I need you to be here with *me*. It's only me."

When I cautiously open them, I can see the concern in his eyes.

I focus on him and gradually begin to soften myself into him and relax. He takes his time as he starts to gently move inside of me. The room begins to fill with our soft moans and breaths of pleasure, never taking our eyes off of each other. He wraps me up in his strong arms, and I cling my hands around him as we slowly move together.

"God, I love you," he sighs.

I lean my head up to kiss him, needing more of him. "I love you," I whisper against his lips.

He's all around me, and my breathing grows heavy as the air thickens.

He takes my hand and laces his fingers with mine, holding on tightly to each other as he pushes himself deeper inside of me. Grabbing behind my knee, he pulls my leg up around him then runs his hand up my thigh, gripping onto my hip. I'm overcome with the closeness I feel with him on top of me, with him inside of me.

I push my hips against his hold, needing to move with him. Letting go, he runs his hand up my side and into my hair, threading, and gently grabbing. The pleasure he gives me runs from my thighs through my core and up my chest where my heart is enduring most of the intensity. I can no longer keep my eyes open when I begin to feel a swarm of sensations deep inside. I realize I've never felt this before, and my legs clench apprehensively to his hips.

"Relax, babe."

I hang on tightly around his neck as the feeling begins to build. When my hand jerks in his, he says, "Open your eyes. Stay with me."

They flutter open, and I see the want in his gaze. His face is heated and flushed, and when a whimper escapes me, my breath catches.

"Baby, let go for me."

`I lock my eyes with his as I fall and begin to shudder beneath him, giving him every piece of me as the intense pleasure radiates through my body. I feel myself pulse and tighten around him as he buries his head in my neck, grunting my name, and I feel his release.

Wrapping my legs tightly around him, I try desperately to hold back the tears that are threatening. I'm completely overwhelmed with emotions. To me, that was my first time. He's what I have always needed. Being with him like this, together in this special place that only we share, I know I'll never love anyone the way I love him.

When our breathing slows, he lifts his head, and brushes my hair back. I can feel the tears roll down my temples.

"God, baby, what's wrong?" he asks, as he brushes my tears away with his thumb.

I shake my head to let him know I'm okay. When I'm finally able to speak, I hand my heart over to him and bare, "Being with you...that's all I want."

Dropping his head to mine, he confesses softly, "You're the only one I've ever done that with. You're the only one I've ever made love to."

And with that, I pull his lips back to mine.

chapter thirty-two

Waking up, I am wrapped up in Ryan. Last night was incredible, being with Ryan in a way I never thought I could. I gave him all of me and have left myself entirely vulnerable to him. When he tells me he will never leave me, I believe him.

I gently ease my way out of his hold, careful not to wake him. I find my clothes that are strewn across the floor and quickly slide them on before walking to the bathroom. Brushing my teeth, I notice a necklace on the counter between the two sinks as I rinse the toothpaste out of my mouth. When I turn off the faucet, I pick up the thin, delicate silver chain that has a flat bar that horizontally connects the chain together. I see that the bar is etched with tiny letters that scribe: *And though she be but little, she is fierce.*

He had to have lain this here last night after I feel asleep, because I would have noticed it yesterday. Carrying the necklace in my hand, I open the door and see Ryan awake in bed.

He smiles at me when I hold up the necklace. "What's this?"

"Well, it's definitely not a birthday gift, because that was two days ago."

I can't help but laugh as I slip back into bed with him.

"I love it," I say as I hand it to him so that he can clasp

it around my neck.

When he does, he crawls over me, forcing me down on my back. He drops soft kisses along my collarbone and back up my neck to my ear where he whispers, "Do you know how beautiful you are?"

"Mmmm," I softy moan.

"You were amazing last night."

Tangling my hands in his messy hair, I enjoy the shivers he sends through my body as he licks and kisses me while peeling off my clothes.

Last night was a first for me, and I know Ryan was being cautious, but lying here with him now, I am calm under his touch. I know he senses it, and when he removes my pants, he softly nips his way up my thigh. I watch as he makes his way up my stomach, and when he peeks up at me, I grab his face and pull him up to my lips.

He must have already been awake when I woke up because I can taste the mint when I slide my tongue over his. When I graze my teeth across his lip, he pulls back and says, "All I want is you, every fuckin' piece."

I melt into him and give him myself. We take our time now that my nerves are more settled and get to know each other in a whole new way. Ryan's lovemaking is slow and intent and when we can't hold on any longer, we lose ourselves entirely to each other.

Being curled up with Ryan in his sheets, I've never felt more secure. Folded up in his arms, we stay in bed for the rest of the morning.

Ryan went into work this afternoon to take care of some things so that he could stay home tonight. While he's gone, I drive over to Jase's place to hang out for a while. I know I need to tell him everything that's happened since seeing him the other night. When I get there, Mark is there too.

"Hey, what's up?" Jase says from the kitchen.

"Not much. I'm so glad you're home. Ryan had to go into work for a few hours, and I had nothing to do."

"Is he not working tonight?" Mark asks.

"No, he's taking the night off to hang out at the loft."

"So...?" Jase hints.

"What?"

"You never called. Did you get the solo?"

"Oh! God, I'm sorry I forgot to call. Yes, I got it!"

"That's awesome!" Mark says, and when Jase walks in the living room with beers for all of us, he sets them on the coffee table before giving me a hug. "Congratulations, sweetie."

"Thanks."

"Is Ryan's mom still in town?" Mark asks, and then takes a swig of his beer.

"No, she left yesterday. But hey, I have to tell you something, but you can't embarrass me and get all crazy, okay?"

"Shit, this sounds good," Mark teases, and when I eye him, he says, "Sorry."

"Promise. We both do," Jase says.

"Okay, so last night..."

"Holy shit! I knew it!" Jase yells.

"What?" Mark and I ask in unison.

"Oh, come on. It's written all over her face," he says to Mark while gesturing to me with his hand.

Mark looks at me and gets a wicked grin on his face.

"What did I just say about embarrassing me?"

"Candace, you're always getting embarrassed. Spill it," Mark says with a hint of laughter.

"Seriously, guys."

"Okay, serious," Jase affirms. "I had no idea you were even thinking about going there."

"Well, yeah. I mean, we love each other and I've been wanting to, but I've always been too scared. It's not like I've had anything good to associate with sex."

"So, how do you feel about it now?" Jase asks.

"Happy. He's what I've been missing my whole life."

Leaning in, Jase hugs me and whispers, "He's lucky to have you."

"Thanks."

"So what kind of lover is he?" Mark asks with gossipy intent.

"Mark!" I say in shock. "I'm not telling you."

Jase starts to laugh and when I narrow my eyes at him, he defends, "What? You know that Mark thinks Ryan is hot. He's not gonna stop asking."

Mark shrugs his shoulders, laughing. "Gross," I say to him.

"Why's that gross?"

"Cause he's my boyfriend."

"So! I let you sleep with *my* boyfriend," he says, tipping his head at me and lifting an eyebrow.

"That's different," I argue.

"Candace, it's not that different," Jase chuckles.

"Aren't you supposed to be on my side?"

Jase and Mark laugh at my childish remark, and I give them an equally childish eye roll.

The three of us continue our playful bickering and hang out for a couple of hours. I never reveal anything to Mark even though he keeps pestering me. Jase, being as levelheaded as he is, just laughs at Mark's crooked curiosity.

When I get back to the loft, Ryan still isn't home, so I decide to get some schoolwork done. I have two exams next week before the end of the quarter that I need to prepare for. Spreading out my books and notes on the coffee table, I make myself comfortable on the couch. I lose track of time as I flip through my books and study some of the dance terminology that I need to know for one of my classes.

When I notice the grey, misty sky beginning to darken as the sun sets behind the clouds, I wonder why Ryan isn't home yet. Picking up my phone, I call him and he sounds stressed when he answers.

"Babe, hey."

"Hey, I didn't think you were going to be working this late."

"I wasn't, but one of our distributors stopped by today and notified me that we are now a COD contract. When I went back, I saw that Michael hadn't been paying the fucking invoices. So, I've been going through the back logs making sure there aren't any outstanding."

"Have you found any?"

"No, but this shit pisses me off. I need a manager who is more organized. This shit's a mess in his office."

"I'm sorry."

"It's fine. Just been a long day. I'm about to pack up and leave."

"Have you eaten anything yet?"

"Yeah, I had one of the bar girls run out and pick up some food."

"Okay, well, I'll see you in a bit."

"Love you."

"Love you too."

When Ryan gets home about a half hour later, we decide to camp out downstairs and watch a movie. We change into our pajamas and Ryan pours me a glass of wine then gets himself a beer. Moving the coffee table out of the way, Ryan lights the fireplace while I throw a pile of blankets and pillows on the floor.

Wrapping up in the blankets together, Ryan puts on one of his old black and white movies, and I can't help but smile in amusement when he does.

"What? You wanna watch something else?"

"No," I say and I settle my head on his chest, getting comfortable. "I love watching these with you."

"I thought you hated them. You're always making fun of me."

"I know, but secretly, I've always loved it."

Kissing the top of my head, he wraps his arms around me as we watch 'Out of the Past.'

About halfway through the movie, I remember that I need to run upstairs and take my sleeping pill. When I return to Ryan, I curl in beside him and he rolls over to face me.

"I need to run into work tomorrow and sign off on a few things Michael is redoing tonight."

"Okay."

"I was thinking you could come with me."

"Ryan..." The last time I went there I totally panicked. The last thing I want to do is go back just to be reminded of what happened.

"I know, but I hate that you can't come up there to see me. I mean...it's where I work, babe."

"I understand what you're trying to say, but I just...I can't."

"I know, I just think if you tried...we can go in the morning, before we open. You and me. We'll park in the front."

Letting out a deep breath, I close my eyes. I want to be able to go up there and see Ryan. I'd love to hang out with him and his friends and see where he works. And it bothers me that I've never seen Mark's band play. I'm just not sure if I'm ready to push myself that far yet. I know I can't avoid that place forever since Ryan owns that bar.

He cups my cheeks with his hands and whispers, "If you're not ready, I get it. It was just a thought."

I open my eyes and look up at him. "Ryan, it just takes me back farther than I want to go. There have been times I've wished that I would've just died that night."

He releases a hard breath and tucks my head under his chin as he holds me.

I know what he's trying to do, and a part of me loves that he pushes me and doesn't baby me. The fact that he thinks I'm strong enough to go there shows me that he views me in a way I want to truly be—strong. But another part of me is terrified to stir up those memories again. I love Ryan, and I know that he cares for me. I want to show him that I can push myself.

"Okay," I whisper softly.

"What, babe?"

Pulling my head up, I say, "Okay, I'll try," when he looks at me.

"Are you sure?"

"No, but I'll try."

Cradling my face in his hands, he says, "Do you have any idea how amazing you are?"

"Ryan, I'm not saying I will. I'm only saying I'll try."

"And that's all you need to do. The fact that you're even willing to is one of the reasons I love you so much. You're so unbelievably strong."

Before I can deny his words, he captures my mouth with his.

I'm a bundle of nerves as I drink my coffee and wait for Ryan to finish getting ready. I had agreed to make an effort to go with him to the bar this morning. The place doesn't open for a few hours, and he wants us to go when no one else is there.

When he comes downstairs, he takes my hand and reassures me that all I have to do is say the word and we'll come back home. But I don't want to be that person. Ryan sees me in such a strong way. I wear his necklace that he gave me that is engraved with the word 'fierce.' He chose that Shakespearean quote for a reason. If he believes that about me, then maybe I should try to believe that about myself as well.

My stomach is in knots as he drives, and I don't say a word. His hand is laced tightly with mine, and I turn cold when I see us approaching the building. He does as he promises and parks along the curb in front of the bar. I know there is no way I could handle being in the back lot with that dumpster.

I'm lost in my thoughts and don't even notice that he's gotten out of the car until I turn to see that my door is open and Ryan is standing there with his hand on my knee.

"Just try," he says as he takes my hand and helps me out of the car. I'm not familiar with the front of this building, so I don't find it terribly difficult to walk with him. I keep telling myself not to think about what is on the other side.

When we get to the door, he takes his keys, unlocks the door, and opens it for me. When I step inside, I am surprised that the place looks completely different than what I had envisioned. The interior is dark and masculine. There is a huge rich mahogany bar that runs the length of one of the walls with exposed brick and wooden shelves that hold a variety of liquors. On the opposite wall there is a fairly large platform stage. Sleek leather bar stools flank the high top tables that are scattered throughout the place.

I follow Ryan as he walks me down a small hallway that leads to stairs.

"My office is up here," he tells me before he takes me up.

Still holding my hand, we walk up the wooden stairs. When we reach the top he tells me he's going to get the papers from Michael's office. When we walk in, I instantly turn around and stumble into Ryan. Behind Michael's desk is a large window that looks over the back lot.

"Babe?"

"I want to go."

Reaching around me, he picks up a folder from the desk and walks me out, shutting the door behind us. We walk into the office across the hall, and he tosses the folder onto his desk. I'm shaking when he turns to me, running his hands up and down my arms.

"I'm sorry, I didn't think."

I don't even need to explain what's got me startled, he just knows.

Leaning against the edge of his desk, he pulls me between his legs and hugs me. I lay my head on his chest and listen to his heart while I focus on slowing mine down to match the rhythm of his. I don't speak because I'm trying not to get myself worked up.

After a few moments, I look up and over Ryan's shoulder. His view is out the front of the building. I watch the mist collect on the glass and slowly trickle down.

"You okay?"

I nod my head and lean it back down on his chest, letting out a slow sigh.

"I hate seeing that dumpster." His arms tighten around me, and I find myself continuing to talk. "It's weird because I also love it in a messed up way. It's all I had to focus on."

“I’m so sorry.”

“When I dream about that night, it’s always taken away from me. There’s nothing to distract me.”

“I wish I knew his name,” he says with spite.

Ryan has asked me once to tell him who the guy was, but I refused. I know he’d only kill him if given the chance. It doesn’t matter anyway; what’s done is done, and it can’t be fixed.

When I look up at him, his jaw is tightly clenched. Sliding my hand along his jawbone, I lift up on my toes to reach his mouth and give him a soft kiss. I hate that he feels this way—helpless.

He pulls me closer to him, and I feel him relax under my hand.

“I’m glad you’re here,” he says when he breaks our kiss.

“It isn’t anything like I’d thought.”

“How’s that?”

“I don’t know...I didn’t expect it to be so nice.” I chuckle, realizing how rude that just sounded.

“Wow. Thanks, babe,” he says, with mock annoyance.

I smile up at him. “No, that’s not what I meant. I like it. I should have known it would be nice like this by the way your loft is.”

“It’s okay. Let me just sign these papers and we can go, all right?”

“Okay.”

I watch him as he stands over his desk and finishes signing the orders. I’m relieved that I can be here and not be having a total freak out. Of course, we are here alone, which helps, but realizing that I can come here feels good. I don’t fight the smile that starts to spread across my face. When Ryan sets his pen down and turns to look at me, he grins, and asks, “What?”

"I thought this would've been a lot harder."

"Thank you for doing this," he says as he runs his hands down my arms.

"Thanks for pushing me."

When we leave and get into his jeep, I know I just did something huge. I did it, and I was okay. I've been avoiding this place for months, and it feels slightly empowering that I don't feel that same level of fear. It isn't completely gone, but it's a big step for me.

chapter thirty-three

"Why don't you come with me?"

"Because I just rehearsed for an hour on top of my two-hour studio. I've also been getting painful cramps in my calves.

"When did that start?"

"This week. I upped my calcium and have been using Tiger's Balm, but I don't really want to put anymore strain on my legs right now."

"Okay, well, I'll be back in a couple hours. I'm gonna run after I lift," he says as he's mixing his protein shake.

"I'm going to go pop by Jase's while you're gone since I won't see him much during the break."

He takes a gulp of his shake, sets it down on the kitchen counter, and brings me into his arms.

"Text me when you're on your way back, so I can be here waiting for you," he says in a sexy low voice as he grabs my ass and sets me on the countertop.

When he leans in to kiss me, I push against his chest. "Don't kiss me after drinking that crap."

"What?" he says as he chuckles.

"That stuff is nasty. I don't know how you can stand it."

Laughing at me, he ignores my words and plants a big kiss on my mouth. I try to turn my head to the side when he kisses me, but his hold is tight, and my outburst of giggles makes me too weak to push him off. He tastes like chocolate dirt.

"Ryan! Gross!"

He releases me, takes a few steps back, all the while laughing, and then picks up his cup and chugs the rest of his shake.

Wiping my mouth with the back of my hand, I jump off the counter and jab my finger in his ribs as I walk out of the kitchen.

He follows behind and locks up as we head out to our cars.

"See you later?" he asks as he opens my car door for me.

"Yeah, I'll text you when I leave."

"Love you, babe," he says before he leans in and nips me on my neck.

"Love you, too." I slide into my car, and he shuts the door before I start backing out of the driveway.

When I hit the elevator button in the lobby of Jase's apartment building, I'm caught off guard when the door slides open and Kimber is standing there. She looks equally shocked to see me.

Stepping out, she says, "Hey. Where have you been?"

When I called Ryan to stay with him, I only planned on a week or two, but it's been over a month since he came over to help me pack my bags.

"With Ryan."

"You living with him now?"

"Um, no...I mean, kinda." I shake my head and gather my thoughts. Being honest, I tell her, "I could tell you were upset after we talked, and I was upset too. So, I thought I would give us both a little space. I didn't intend on being gone this long."

"Whatever," she says softly as she hangs her head and looks to the floor. "I guess it doesn't really matter." That's all she says before turning to walk outside.

"What are you doing here?" Jase says when I walk into his apartment.

"Just thought I would stop by. You busy?"

"No," he says as he scans my face. "What's wrong?"

Upset from seeing Kimber downstairs, I let out a sigh and fall onto his couch.

"Was Kimber just over here?" I ask him when he sits down next to me.

"I didn't want to say anything because I didn't want to upset you."

Looking over at him, I say, "I'm not upset."

He cocks his head and says, "Sweetie, I can tell when you're trying not to cry. You get all squeaky."

Taking a deep breath and puffing it out, he continues. "She texted me a few days ago wanting to know where you were. When I called her, she was upset. I felt bad, Candace. She was my friend too, and I have felt real shitty about how I've treated her."

I wipe the tears from my cheeks as I listen to him talk, and I feel like a horrible person for causing all of this.

"She asked if she could come over and talk. Candace, she's really upset. She misses you."

Trying to stop the tears, I begin hiccupping back my breaths. Jase scoots over and wraps his arm around my shoulder.

"Do you think you could talk to her now? Be honest with her?"

"I can't. Her boyfriend is in the same fraternity as Jack."

"What? How do you know that?" he asks as he looks at me with surprise.

"I saw the Greek letters on his car one day."

"Did you say anything to Kimber?"

"No, why would I?"

"Are they friends?"

"I don't know. I never brought it up because I didn't want to draw any attention to him."

Jase leans his head back on the couch, and I feel envious that he can still be friends with her.

"I'm not upset. I understand that she's your friend. I'm sorry I ever put you in that position."

"Sweetie," he says as he rolls his head to the side to look at me. "I love you. Even though I haven't been a good friend to her, I would have done that to anyone for you."

I smile at his words. There isn't any way I could ever express exactly how much they mean to me. Jase has always been so selfless with me, and I try to give back to him what he gives to me.

"So, what did she say?" I ask.

"She just talked about you. How hurt she is. How much she misses you. She wanted to know what's going on in your life. I told her about Ryan and that you're really happy with him."

As I nod my head, he adds, "If you won't talk to her, then I think you should at least start spending some time back at your place."

"Yeah...okay."

I sit back on the couch next to him and rest my head against his shoulder. After a few minutes pass, Jase switches topics and asks me about the gallery show at Thinkspace on Friday night. Ryan's photograph will be on display and up for sale. Jase and Mark are going along with some of Ryan's friends as well. I haven't told Jase that the photo is of me. I don't want anyone to know, and Ryan doesn't either.

"So what time should Mark and I be there?"

"It starts at eight, so anytime around then."

"Sounds great. And when are you guys heading out to Oregon?"

"We're going to leave the next morning. I'm not sure when we'll be coming back. Ryan wanted to leave it open. He's taken the week off, so we will just play it by ear."

"Mark and I will be around, so when you get back, let us know."

"I will." Sitting up on the couch, I turn to look at Jase and say, "Hey, you wanna go down to Peet's and grab a coffee? We can walk around some of the shops."

"Yeah, let's get out of here. Give me a second to throw on another shirt."

We spend the next couple of hours shopping around the vintage stores on Fremont after stopping by Peet's. While we roam around, I think about what Jase said. I know I need to talk to Ryan and let him know that I should go back home. I never intended on staying at his place for as long as I have. We just kind of fell into it. I love him, and I love being there, but I have my own place and a friend that I sort of abandoned, even though we aren't really talking and haven't been for months. I can't tell her about Jack. After telling Ryan, I don't ever want to go through that again. Plus, I'm not even sure of Seth's connection with Jack. It scares me to think what Kimber would do, being that she is, in a way, linked to him. I don't know what I can do to salvage my relationship with Kimber, but I do know I should at least try.

I've been gone most of the day, so when I return to the loft, Ryan is more than eager to have me back. We spend the rest of the day being lazy and listening to demos from bands that are trying to get spots at Blur. I know I need to talk about going back home, but I know Ryan isn't going to like that idea very much. I've spent most of the evening putting it off.

Ryan pulls me out of my thoughts when he says, "Something's been bothering me today." When I walk across the room to Ryan, who's sitting on the couch, he holds out his arm and tugs me down onto his lap. "I've never seen you dance."

"Oh...yeah, I guess not. But you will in May when we have our production. You'll see me a lot. I have three ensembles plus my solo."

"It just bothers me that there is a huge part of your life that I've never seen."

"Well, I can grab some videos at the studio of past performances. They have also recorded some of our studios this year. Would that suffice for you, watching me on video?"

Grabbing me behind my waist and neck, he flips me back onto the couch and just before he buries his head in my neck, he says, "Nothing about you will ever suffice for me. I'm always gonna want more."

So I give him more, right there on the couch. Truth is, I feel the same way. I don't think I'll ever get enough of him. Tonight, he's more playful with me and being able to giggle while we make love, I realize that he's finally giving me pieces of myself that have been missing for a long time. I relish in the closeness we have.

Ryan wraps us up in a blanket as we lie in each others' arms on the floor. Stroking his hand lazily up and down my back, we chat about random nonsense and continue with our fun banter from this morning. But I know I need to be honest and talk to him about what's been on my mind all day.

With hesitation, I say, "Ryan, I ran into Kimber today.

She was leaving Jase's when I walked into his building."

"Did you guys talk?"

"She just asked where I've been, and I could tell she was hurt. Jase told me she reached out to him and that she's really upset."

"I'm sorry, babe. I know how much this bothers you. Have you thought anymore about talking to her?"

Ryan and I had discussed Kimber the week before. He felt that maybe she wouldn't react the way I initially thought she would since I'm in a better place now. If she could see that I was happy, she might be less likely to be reckless with her reaction. I agree with him, but I also didn't tell him about Seth being Jack's frat brother. I haven't told Ryan anything about Jack because I know how much he hates him and worry about what he might do if he ever found out.

"I just can't. I don't trust her enough to not do something."

"I don't know what to tell you to do. Just try talking to her and see if you guys can move past this rift."

"I think it would help if I went back home."

"Candace..."

"Ryan, I was only supposed to be here for a week or two. I never intended on moving in like this. But, we are about to graduate, and I'd like to see if this is fixable. I can't do that if I'm not there."

"I still want you here."

"And I'll still be here. Just not *every* night."

He releases a deep breath and says, "Okay. We can go tomorrow and take some of your things back."

Sliding my hand over his cheek, I tell him, "Thanks for understanding," before pressing my lips into his.

The next day, Ryan helped me pack up my things and take them back to my house. He insisted I leave some of my belongings at his place, so I did. It was strange being back home after being away for so long. Kimber was home when we got there, so I introduced her to Ryan, but they really didn't talk.

Ryan wanted to stay here with me that night, but I thought it would be best if he didn't for the first night I was back. If Kimber was uncomfortable, I didn't want to make it worse. He wasn't happy with it, but he understood.

Tonight is the gallery showing at Thinkspace. I wanted to look nice, so I had gone out and bought a dress. Standing in front of my mirror, I smooth down the sheer nude lace of my sleeveless pencil skirt dress. The lace is offset by the black satin underlay and has a bateau neckline. Although the necklace that Ryan gave me doesn't go with the dress, I wear it anyway. I love the quote and that those words make him think of me, something I haven't thought about myself for a while.

When he comes to pick me up, he has an effortless style about him that I find alluring. Ryan often dresses in simple t-shirts and dark jeans. Even though his closet is filled with nice dress clothes, he never wears them. But tonight, he wears dark charcoal slacks, a sports coat, and a white collared dress shirt leaving the first few buttons undone. His clothes are tailored to him perfectly and accentuate his broad shoulders and chest that 'V' down to his narrow hips. Ryan spends a lot of time in the gym, in addition to running, and his frame is near perfection. His dark hair is slightly messy, like he just ran his hands through it, but in a sexy way.

"We need to skip this whole thing tonight," he says as he approaches me and slowly slides his hands from my neck to my shoulders down my arms. He pulls me tight, grazes his nose up my bare neck, and kisses me behind my ear.

Cinching up my shoulders from the ticklish spot he kisses, I laugh. “Ryan, stop.”

“I’m serious. Fuck everyone. I just want to stay here with you,” he whispers in my ear.

“The deal was, if you got your picture accepted, then I got to go as your date. So, whether you like it or not, I’m dressed and ready to go.”

“Okay, but tonight, you’re sleeping in my bed. I didn’t like not having you next to me last night.”

“Ryan.”

“I know, I get it. I understand the whole Kimber thing, but I’m taking you home with me tonight.”

I slip on my knee-length black wool coat before we walk out into the cold misty night. When we arrive at Thinkspace, a chic and contemporary art gallery in the heart of the city, I look over at Ryan and say, “I’m really proud of you, you know?”

“Babe, the only reason that photo is on display is because you’re in it. You’re perfect.”

I don’t even try to convince him of his talent because I know he would simply deny it. So, I let it be as we walk through the open doors. I immediately spot Stacy Keets, the woman that originally told me about this showing.

“Candace.”

“Stacy, hi,” I say as I give her a hug.

“That dress is amazing.”

“Thank you.”

“And this is...?” she asks as she glances to Ryan.

“Ryan.” I say.

“Ahh, ‘Nubile.’ Beautiful photograph,” she says as she shakes his hand. “I’m Stacy Keets. I work at the Henry Gallery.”

“Ryan Campbell.”

“Well, your piece is great. I saw a couple eying it a

minute ago. Do you have more pieces?"

"A few. It wasn't ever something I intended to show anyone or have displayed, but Candace insisted."

"I'm glad she did. I'd love to see more of your work." Looking at me, she asks, "Do you still have my number?"

"Yes, I do."

"Give me a call," she tells Ryan. "We have some wall space opening up soon, so if you're interested, we can discuss the possibility of displaying some of your pieces."

"Will do. I'll have Candace give me your number."

Turning to me, she says, "And I owe you a congratulations. I heard about your audition from Sergej."

Sergej has been dating Stacy since I met her over two years ago. He has instructed my partnering studio since I first came to UW. He's originally from Russia, but moved to the States and danced for a company in New York before retiring and relocating here to teach.

"I hope it was all good."

Lowering her voice, she tells me, "He thinks people will be fighting for you to sign with their companies."

"I can only hope."

"No hoping. I'm looking forward to seeing you perform in May."

"Thank you. I'll be sure Ryan calls you," I say.

"Enjoy your night."

"You too, Stacy," Ryan says as he starts walking us to the bar.

Mark and Jase are already drinking and mingling when we walk over. I knew they would have a good time and they'd know several people here with them being architecture majors and art snobs.

"Hey, man," Mark says when he spots Ryan.

We all stand around and visit. After Gavin and his friend Chris arrive, I excuse myself and take a glass of wine from the bartender. Jase and I separate from the group and start to stroll through the gallery, looking at all the pieces. I know Ryan is here merely for my sake, so I don't mind that he spends the evening with his buddies. When we find ourselves in front of Ryan's photograph, which he'd titled 'Nubile,' Jase says in a quiet voice, "You're beautiful." He speaks to the photograph, not me. I stand there for a moment and only respond when he slightly turns his head to wink at me.

"How did you know?" I ask.

"Because of what he titled it." He turns to look back at the photograph and adds, "It could only be you."

I don't know how I would live without Jase. He's my rock. He's always stuck by my side and has been my strength when I had none left. I step closer to his side and hold his hand, and when he looks over at me, I tell him, "I love you, so much."

"I love you too, sweetie." He squeezes my hand and we continue through the gallery, admiring all the art on display. We don't speak with anyone else; we just spend our time together and enjoy each other's company. Eventually we find a bench and take a seat to give my feet a break in my platform heels.

"There you are," Ryan says from behind me.

Jase takes my empty wine glass and excuses himself to give Ryan and I time together.

Sitting down next to me, he says, "Where have you been?"

"Just walking around with Jase."

"I heard someone bought your photo," he tells me, and I'm so excited for him.

"Really?"

He doesn't respond, he just smiles at me and takes my hand. "Walk with me."

Sliding my hand into his, I follow him through the gallery and down one of the halls to a roped off area.

"What are we doing back here? We're gonna get in trouble."

Laughing at me, he says, "You're so cute."

We turn to go behind a wall, far from everyone else. He turns to me, pressing my back against the wall, hands on either side of me, caging me in. He doesn't even need to say anything when I reach for his face and bring him down to me. He's eager and passionate, and I know if he had it his way, he would take me right here against this wall.

"We should go," I say breathlessly between our lips.

He pushes himself against me as I grasp his shoulders, and I know it's *really* time to go.

"Ryan."

When he finally drags his lips off of me, he takes my hand and walks us out of the back exit, not saying goodbye to anyone.

When we arrive at his place, he opens my door and scoops me out of the car, cradling me with his arm behind my knees. Kicking the door shut, he carries me up the stairs to the front door and once we are inside, straight up to his bed.

He lays me down and runs his hands down the length of my body slowly, down my thighs, wrapping around to the backs of my knees and then slides past my calves. He slips off my heels and I hear them as they clatter onto the floor. Standing by the edge of the bed, Ryan stares down at me as he takes off his shoes and socks and shrugs off his jacket.

My heart is racing as I watch him, and when he lowers himself on top of me, he gently kisses me. The rushed intensity that I felt earlier is gone.

"I love you so fuckin' much."

Brushing my fingers through his hair, I smile and study

his face, the way it looks right now in this moment.

"I love you, too."

"Make love to me, babe."

I know what his words mean. I've always let him be in control, not feeling confident enough in myself. But I love this man, and I want to give him what he wants, which is to give myself to him in a way I haven't yet.

Wrapping my arms around his neck, I nod as he pulls us up to our knees. I kiss him and caress his tongue with mine. Sliding his hands up my back, he catches the zipper and slowly pulls it down, loosening the lace on my body. One by one, I unbutton his shirt, and when I hit the last one, I run my hands up his cut stomach, over his chest, around his shoulders, and down his arms, sliding the shirt off. He covers my mouth with his, and when he does, I let the lace fall off of my shoulders. I sling my arms back around him and he lays me down, slipping my dress the rest of the way off.

His lips and tongue slowly drag against my heated skin as he makes his way up my legs, dropping kisses here and there along the way. He grabs onto my panties and starts pulling them down, taking his time as I lift my knees to help him. Leaning back over me, he runs his hands over my knees, up my inner thighs, and my breath hitches when he pushes his palm over my sex and up my stomach. I catch his hips with my legs, wrapping them around his waist, pulling him firmly against me.

He takes one of my legs and pulls it down from his hip as he unhooks his pants. When they land on the floor with the rest of our clothes, he leans over to the nightstand and puts on protection.

He reaches behind my back and pulls me up, sitting back on the bed as I'm straddling his lap. When he unhooks my bra, the last piece of clothing between us, I lift up on my knees, wrap my arms around him, and gently slide myself on top of him. I feel my body instinctively tighten around him when he enters me, and I have to drop my head in the crook of his neck with the profound pleasure that is coursing through my body.

His breaths are heavy, and when I lift my head and look into his blue eyes, I slowly begin to move. Giving myself to him as never before, I lace my fingers through his hair and fist it in my hands. I can't help the moan that escapes me, and I don't even try to hide the waves of pleasure I feel from being with him like this.

"God, I love you," he says through his panted breaths, and when my hips rock into him, his head drops to my chest.

Grazing his hands along my sides, he begins kissing my breasts, and I start to feel the intensity building. Our moans become louder as they fill the room. When he grips me tighter in his hold, I rock into him again, clinging to him when he says, "Look at me, baby. I want to watch you come."

Leaning my forehead against his, our eyes lock onto one another. My body begins to shudder and clench around him, and when I hear Ryan moan my name, I know he's right there with me. Never taking our eyes off of each other, we ride out our pleasure until we have nothing left.

He's hot to my touch, and I can feel the sweat beading down my back when he slowly begins to kiss me. Laying us down, I brush a few locks of his hair from his damp forehead.

"'I love you' will never be strong enough for what I feel for you."

Pulling the covers over us, he wraps me in his arms, still inside me, and I know I'll only ever have this with him—I'll only ever want this with him.

chapter thirty-four

"I can't find shit in here," Ryan says from deep within my closet.

He offered to help me pack since I didn't get much sleep last night. I was so wrapped up in the moment that I forgot to take my sleeping pill, and I kept waking up all throughout the night. I'm starting to wonder if I'll ever be able to sleep without them. My dreams weren't terribly vivid, but when my mind would begin to drift, Jack would find me.

Ryan suggested that I should talk to someone about what happened, but I quickly shut him down, same as I did with Jase when he brought it up months ago. Sitting around and hashing out what happened when all I am trying to do is move on doesn't sound like it would be beneficial at all.

"Just grab a few pairs of jeans."

"Which ones? You have like fifty pairs in here."

Laughing at his dramatics, I say, "It doesn't matter."

He walks out of my closet and puts them in my suitcase while I am going through my dresser.

"Could you grab everything that is sitting on my bathroom counter?"

"Yeah."

When I dig back in my top drawer to find my wool socks, I come across something I haven't seen in seven months. Pulling it out, I look at it, and I'm immediately taken back to that sterile hospital room. Jase was with me, never letting go of my hand, while the nurse scraped Jack's bloody flesh from under my nails. I can still feel the stinging of my eyes as my salty tears flowed effortlessly.

I stash Detective Patterson's business card back in the drawer and close it when I hear Ryan walk out of the bathroom.

"Is this everything?" he asks.

"Umm...yeah," I say as I continue to stand at my dresser, but when my voice comes out shaky, Ryan doesn't miss it.

"Babe," he says, and he walks over to me. Placing his hands on my arms, he continues, "I'm sorry about last night. I should have made sure you took your pill."

I don't correct him when he assumes my mood shift is due to my lack of sleep.

"No, it's not your fault. It's fine."

Kissing my forehead, we move around my room and finish packing my bags. I put in my dance DVDs that I picked up from the studio the other day.

"Okay, I think that's everything." I zip everything shut and Ryan grabs both bags off of my bed, and I lock up as we head out.

I sleep most of the drive to Oregon, but Ryan wakes me up as he exits the highway.

"Where are we?" I say, still groggy.

"Portland."

"Why?"

"Because I want to stop by Voodoo Doughnut. I'm starving."

"Do we really need to drive all the way into the city to get a doughnut?" I groan.

Looking at me with all seriousness, he says, "Yes."

Giving him a half smile, I shake my head. We drive

through the city and when we find a parking space, we walk, and get in the line that wraps around the building.

Standing in line with a variety of sugar-crazed Portland hippies, we finally make our way inside the artsy grunge doughnut shop. I stand next to the glass display and stare at the insane doughnuts that rotate on the round trivets. I look over at Ryan and ask, “You’re really going to eat one of those?”

“You are too. What do you want?”

“None.”

“Okay, then, I’ll pick for you.”

Shaking my head, still feeling tired, I let him choose for me.

Looking down at me, he gets an evil grin and says, “I’m getting you the cock and balls doughnut.”

“Ryan!” I elbow him in the ribs and start looking at the menu behind the registers.

He’s still laughing at me when the girl behind the register starts taking our order.

I carry the pink box and set it on one of the tables outside. I pull out my doughnut that is covered in Fruit Loops, and Ryan takes his creepy voodoo doll-looking doughnut with a pretzel stick that is stabbed through the heart. I laugh at him when he bites off the head and winks at me.

We take our time as we get wired on sugar and laugh together. When the light mist starts to thicken into heavier drops, I toss the remainder of my doughnut that I’m too full to finish, and we head back to the car to resume our drive to Cannon Beach.

We get to his mom’s house about an hour later, and it’s close to dinnertime. I am so happy to see Donna, and she is sweet enough to help Ryan unpack my bags when she sees how tired I am. Ryan explains to her that I had a rough night, and she goes downstairs to get me some hot tea.

Running his hands up and down my arms, he asks, “Are you hungry, babe?”

“No, I’m just so tired my head hurts,” I say as I rest my forehead on his chest.

“Why don’t you change and lie down?”

When I get into bed, Donna knocks on the door and sets the tea down on the nightstand along with a couple of aspirin.

“Ryan said you had a headache.”

“Thanks. I’m sorry to come and just crash.”

“Sweetie, please. Don’t worry about me.” As she closes the blinds she tells me that Ryan is eating a quick dinner and will come up when he’s done. I take the aspirin along with my sleeping pill, and after a few sips of the hot tea, I doze off.

Waking in a haze in the middle of the night, Ryan is wrapped around me. I roll over to face him, and when I do, he begins to stir.

“Everything, okay?” he whispers as he tucks me closer to him.

“Mmm hmm.” I weave my legs with his and close my eyes again, drifting easily back to sleep.

“How are you feeling?” Donna asks as she sits down with me on the couch and hands me a cup of coffee.

“Much better, thanks.”

“Hey,” Ryan says as he comes down the stairs, already dressed for the day.

“Good morning,” his mom says when he walks over and sits on the couch with us.

“So, you two are going to have the day to yourselves. Marci called me this morning and I have to drive into

Portland to go over and sign off on some tax documents. While I'm there I'm going to meet with a friend of mine for a late lunch, so I won't be home till around six or so. But I have no plans for the rest of week. This just popped up yesterday."

"Don't worry about it, Mom. I was going to see if I could convince Candace to hop on a surfboard with me."

"What?!" I say as I jerk my head to look at him.

"I just checked the weather and the waves should be pretty good at the beach we went to the last time you were here."

"That water's going to be freezing, Ryan."

He laughs at me and says, "That's why you wear a wetsuit, babe."

His mother interjects and says, "Well, have fun with that, Candace," dripping in playful sarcasm. "I need to go get ready. I'll see you guys later tonight."

Ryan and I head up to his room, and when I get out of the shower, I wrap a towel around myself to go grab some clothes.

"Fuck, babe," Ryan says as I walk into the bedroom.

"Don't start," I say as I lay my hand on his chest, keeping him from coming any closer. "Your mother is downstairs."

"I don't care who the fuck is downstairs when the only thing covering your wet body is that towel."

"That's why I'm getting my clothes."

I quickly grab my clothes and run back into the bathroom before Ryan can strip the towel off of me. Once I'm dressed and walk back out, he says, "Tori has an extra wetsuit in my closet that should fit you okay."

"What?"

"Surfing. You and me."

"I'm fine with trying anything new, but that water is

freezing."

"I promise, when you're in that wetsuit, you'll be fine. Tori loves to surf, so she has her wetsuit here and some swimsuits in my closet."

When we get to Indian Beach, the wind is just as strong as the last time we were here. The mist is thick, and the skies are dark and heavy with clouds today. I grab one of the blankets that Ryan put in the car before we left the house and wrap it around me when I get out. Ryan unhooks the boards from the top of the jeep, and we head down the wooden stairs to the wet and rocky beach. I stop and watch the rough waves as they crash along the shore. If ever there was a time I worried about breaking a leg, it's now.

Holding out his hand for me, he says, "Come on."

I shrug off my blanket, toss it on the stairs, and follow him out.

"Ryan, I'm going to hurt myself."

He chuckles and says, "No, you won't."

"That water looks rough. There's no way I'm getting up on that board."

"You're getting up, babe."

When we get to the water, he drops the boards on the ground and starts telling me everything I hope I need to know to not kill myself. He shows me how to pop up on the board, and I have no problems showing him I am fully capable.

I take the hairband from my wrist and tie my hair up on top of my head, as Ryan straps the cord around my ankle.

When he stands up, he gives me a quick kiss and says with a big smile, "I fuckin' love that you're doing this."

"You know I'm willing to try almost anything, but don't get your hopes up. I don't think I'll be able to get up."

Grabbing me and pulling me up against him, he leans down to my neck and says, "If you get up, I'll get up for you later," and then starts sucking on my neck.

I smack his arm and push him away as he's laughing.

"You're so gross!"

"Pick up your board. Let's go," is his only response.

I ended up having a pretty great time with Ryan in the water. When he wasn't trying to get frisky with me, I managed to get up on the board a few times. After several hours, we decide to head back to the house. I've been wrapped up in blankets since we got in the car to try and get warm again.

When we get back to the house, I run upstairs to take a shower while Ryan makes us sandwiches.

I turn the water on and step into the large glassed-in shower when steam begins to fill the room. My body is freezing and even though the water is scalding on my skin, I'm still shivering. I close my eyes and let the water wash over me as it slowly starts to warm me up.

I'm startled when I hear the door open.

"What are you doing?!" I squeal when Ryan closes the glass door behind him and wraps his arms around my waist.

"It's time to ante up, babe." Dipping his head under the running water, he pushes me against the cool wall, and slides his hand back through his wet hair.

Running my hand up and around his neck, he lowers his head to mine and kisses me. He easily pulls me up, and I wrap my legs around his waist, locking my ankles. The air is thick with steam, making my breathing labored as Ryan nibbles playfully along my neck and ear.

I've been wishing that there was someone just like him,

and now that he's found me, I feel like he has the power to pull me though this madness that has been consuming me.

His wet hand lingers down my neck to my breast, and he presses into me harder. Dropping my head into the curve of his shoulder, I breathe, "I want you."

"I don't have anything with me in here."

"It's okay. I've been on the pill for a while. I trust you."

He pulls his head back and gives me a confused look. "When did you get on the pill, babe?"

"I've been on it. I got it..." I drop my head for a second and when I look back up at him I tell him, "I got on it after what happened."

He goes on to assure me that he's always been safe and that he's never had unprotected sex. I know he would never hurt me, and I trust him, so I don't hesitate when I reaffirm that I want him.

As his bare flesh touches mine, a ragged breath leaves his chest.

"Fuck, babe, you feel so good."

I love knowing I can give this to him, that he can have me completely, with nothing to separate us. We proceed to spend a lengthy amount of time in the shower making love to each other.

After we eat lunch, we decide to spend the rest of the day being lazy in bed. I pull out the DVDs that he had asked for, and as we lie in bed, we watch a production from last year. I show him the two ensembles that I had lead placements in and one of my duets with Maxim.

As he's watching one of the ensembles where I have a standout solo, a hint of a smile appears, and for some reason, that tiny gesture has the biggest effect on me. I scoot down in the bed and nestle my head on his chest as he watches me dance.

"I don't know shit about dancing, babe, but you're amazing," he says as he continues to watch.

I can't help but laugh at him and wrap my arm snuggly around his stomach. When the clip changes to my duet, I know it won't take him too long to make one of his possessive comments, so I close my eyes and just wait for it.

"Hmm..." is all I hear him say for a while, and then it comes. "I don't like that dude's hands all over you."

"Ryan, his hands have to be on me for all the lifts."

"His hands are on you for more than just lifts, Candace."

A giggle escapes me and he says, "I'm serious, his hands are all over you."

"He's gay!"

"I don't give a shit. I still don't like it."

He is really unbelievable, but I love him all the same, so I simply laugh it off.

When the video ends, he tells me again and again how amazing I am, then proceeds to tell me how incredibly turned on he is, so we get a little playful before opting for a nap in the middle of the day. Having this time to be with him like this is making the thought of graduation that much harder. I love him, and I'm pretty sure I would never move away from him. I push all that aside for the moment and simply relish him.

Ryan and I decided to spend the rest of the week at his mom's. Both of us have enjoyed the down time. I love spending time with Donna. We have made a couple days out of shopping and dining. But it's the best when we stay home for dinner, and I can help her cook and clean up. It feels very comfortable and normal, and I crave that feeling at this point.

Ryan took me surfing again, and another day we took his jeep to Long Beach in Washington. We had fun driving up and down the sand along the water. We spent the day out there, building a small fire pit and wrapping up in blankets. I could have spent hours in his arms, staring out at the ocean.

I can't help but feel like part of his family when I'm with him and Donna. I'm sad to be leaving today, but so happy we got to have this week together. As I'm finishing getting ready in the bathroom, Ryan is packing our bags.

When I slip on my sweatshirt, my jeans tug down enough so that I can see a hint of my heart. I don't like what this tattoo reminds me of, and for some reason, I don't think Ryan likes it either. I've never asked him, but sometimes when we make love he covers it with his hand.

I shift my pants down slightly to look at it in the mirror. I've considered having it removed, but I've never done anything to look into what that would involve.

When Ryan opens the door, I quickly yank my shirt down and turn to face him.

Cocking his head, he questions, "What are you doing?"

"Nothing."

He steps over to me and places his hand over mine, which is still holding onto my top. He only looks in my eyes as he lifts my hand and exposes the heart.

I know he's curious, so I admit, "I don't like it."

He lowers my hand and shirt. "Why?"

"Because it's not me. I was trying to be someone different, and it only led to bad things."

He looks confused and asks, "What do you mean?"

"I got it in a moment of rebellion, I guess. It was stupid, really. I got it and started acting foolishly, which led to...umm..."

Ryan stops me so I don't have to finish. "I get it. But, babe, nothing you did led to that."

I can't look at him because I know if I'd never behaved that way, if I'd never led *him* on, it wouldn't have happened. When I walk out of the bathroom, he follows and grabs my arm.

"Wait. You know that, right?"

When I look at him, I know he can read it all over my face. And by the look on his face, he hadn't known that I felt the way I do.

"Come here," he says as he sits on the side of the bed and pulls me next to him. "Tell me you don't think that."

The way he says his words almost make me feel stupid. Like somehow I don't understand, but I do.

When I don't speak, he says, "Babe, there is nothing you could have possibly done to deserve that."

My throat begins to tighten when the tears come, and I begin to get upset at myself for showing this weakness. I shift away from Ryan and begin choking back breaths to stop the crying, which is actually making it worse. He pulls me back to him, but I keep my head turned away.

"Shit, babe. I had no idea this is how you felt."

My voice trembles when I say, "Please, don't."

"I need you to talk to me about this. You have it all wrong. What that guy did was fucked up, babe, and you didn't do shit to deserve what he did to you."

I don't even bother trying to stifle the tears, and I'm pissed that I can't hold myself together. I yell at Ryan through my cries, "You don't get it, Ryan! What I did was stupid, and I completely led him on. It wasn't right, and I knew it, but I did it anyway."

"What the fuck could you have possibly done, because I know you, Candace, and I know you couldn't have led him on that much. But that shit doesn't even matter because you could've stripped down in front of him, and you still didn't deserved to be raped."

"Don't say that fucking word, Ryan!" I sob out and then begin crying uncontrollably.

He pulls me into his arms and begins apologizing when I lose control and tell him, "I didn't even really like him, but I was stupid and lonely, so I would let him kiss me, knowing that I didn't like him. And I fucking hate my mother for this, because if it wasn't for her being such a bitch, I never would have gone out with him."

Ryan tries to get me to stop, but I continue. "You just don't get it. I did lead him on, and I pissed him off. I never should've acted like that. I should've just been honest."

"This isn't your fault," he says sternly, and I snap back, "Yes, it is!"

Not releasing his hold on me, he says again, "It isn't your fault, Candace."

Turning into him, I fist his shirt in my hands and cry, "But it is."

He doesn't say anything else. We wind up lying down in bed for a while until I calm down. We lie face to face, and with my eyes closed, I finally speak. "It's been seven months, Ryan."

"I know, babe."

"I just want it to go away."

"I know. But it's never going to get easier if you keep blaming yourself. It kills me that you feel this way. It fuckin' kills me that I can't take this away from you."

I close my eyes for a while, and when I feel myself start to drift, I ask, "Can't we stay another night?"

"Anything you want."

chapter thirty-five

On the drive back to Seattle, Ryan suggests that we talk to Jared to see about changing the tattoo. He thinks that it will help if I don't have to look at the heart every day just to be constantly reminded about everything, give the tattoo a new association.

I hold Ryan's hand the whole drive home, feeling like I need him close. I hate that he saw me so weak when I try to be so strong. I push myself so much with him, and then last night, I fell apart. I know he loves me regardless because he has never wavered, but I want to prove to him that I'm not this sad, pathetic girl, but I'm as fierce as he believes.

When we get back to my house, he carries my bags in for me. Since we didn't come back yesterday like we had planned, Ryan has to go into work tonight. Feeling a little needy, I tell him I don't want him to go.

"Baby, I have to. It's Saturday night, and I've been gone all week."

I fold myself into his arms and stay quiet.

"Come with me," he says, and when I look up at him, I ask hesitantly, "What?"

"You don't even have to be around everyone. Stay with me in my office."

Knowing how he just saw me last night, I know what I need to say.

"Okay."

He's right; I can just be with him and not around all those other people. I went there the other week, and I was fine. I can do this. I *need* to do this.

"Really?" The stunned look on his face tells me he wasn't expecting the response I just gave him. The look makes me smile, and I'm glad I don't have to be alone tonight.

"Just park in the front, okay?"

"Of course. You'll finally get to hear Mark play."

"Oh. I didn't even think about that. Could you do me a favor?"

"Sure."

"They've been kinda embarrassing me lately with...things. Um...could you just text them or something and tell them to not make a big deal about it."

Smiling at me, he holds my face and kisses me hard with intent. Keeping his hold on me, I let him control the connection and when it's broken, he says, "I love you so much. You're always surprising me."

As we walk into Blur, Ryan has a firm grip on my hand. When I was here the last time, it was empty, but tonight it's packed. I never expected this many people to be here.

"Where's Max?!" Ryan shouts to someone I can't see. I feel really overwhelmed with the amount of people in here, all of whom tower over me. I wrap my free arm around the arm that is holding my hand, and hold tightly onto him

"Right here, boss," a low voice calls from behind us. Turning around, I come face to face with an extremely large man with a shaved head wearing a black shirt that reads 'BLUR' in white.

Ryan shouts over the noise, "Max, hey, this is Candace."

Max looks down at me, and the warm smile that covers his face doesn't really match his overwhelming appearance. Whereas Ryan is muscular with long, strong, athletic cuts, Max is big, bulky, and very intimidating, but he has a soft smile.

"Nice to finally meet you," he says and shakes my hand.

"Nice to meet you, Max," I have to practically yell.

"You want to help us get upstairs?" Ryan says.

Probably noticing the tension written all over my face, Max says to me, "Not good with crowds?"

I shake my head, and he puts his arm around me, tucking me tightly to him with Ryan still holding my hand on my opposite side as he pushes his way through everyone. Feeling a bit uncomfortable with the closeness of being in Max's hold, I cling myself tighter to Ryan. He looks down at me, and all I know to do is give him a slight shake of my head, and by the look in his eyes, I know he understands what I'm trying to tell him. When we get to the back stairs, Ryan tells Max, "Thanks, man."

"No problem, boss. Let me know when you guys are ready to come down, okay?"

"Yeah."

We walk up the stairs and when we get into his office, he asks, "You okay?"

I nod my head, when he assures me, "Max is a good guy. I've known him for years."

"It's just uncomfortable," I say.

Walking us around his desk, he pulls me down on his lap when he sits in the chair.

"Is it always this busy?" I ask.

"On Fridays and Saturdays, yeah." When his cell

buzzes, he pulls it out of his pocket and says, "Mark and Jase just got here." Setting it down on his desk, he tells me, "I love that you're here," and then kisses my shoulder.

When there is a knock on the door, Ryan says, "Come in."

"Hey, guys," Jase says as he walks in. When he demands a hug, I get up off of Ryan's lap and walk over to him.

He folds his arms around me and leans in close to my ear, whispering, "I'm proud of you."

I sigh and squeeze my arms a bit tighter around him. Pulling back, I ask, "Where's Mark?"

"Downstairs. He said he'd find you before the band goes on."

"Oh, okay."

"Are you coming down to watch?"

"I...well, Ryan has some work to do, so I was just going to stay up here."

Jase tilts his head and shakes it.

"What?"

"Candace, at least go down for a couple songs."

"Did you see how many people are down there?"

"Yeah, sweetie. The same amount that are always here, and nothing has ever happened."

Looking over at Ryan, he shrugs his shoulders in agreement, and says, "I'll have Max stay with you."

I flop down on one of the chairs in front of Ryan's desk and think for a moment before saying, "I don't want everyone touching me."

"If Max is with us, trust me, you'll have breathing room."

"He's right," Ryan assures.

I take a moment before saying, "All right."

Ryan smiles at me as he picks up the phone and pushes

some buttons before saying, “Hey, Mel, send Max up to my office.”

I turn around when the door opens and Mark bounds in excitedly. “Hell, I thought it was a lie. I can’t believe you’re here.”

“Tone that shit down,” Ryan says to him as I stand up and give Mark a hug.

“I just wanted to see you before I go on. You coming down?”

“Yeah.”

“Awesome. Well, I gotta go. Love that you came.” He leans down, kisses my forehead, and then heads out at the same time as Max walks in.

“Hey, Max, Candace is going down with Jase. I don’t want you to leave her side, got it?”

“What about the door?”

“I’ll get Chase to take care of it.” Ryan gets up from his seat and walks over to me. “You want me to come down with you?”

“No, it’s fine. I haven’t talked to Jase all week, so...”

“Are you okay with Max?”

“Yeah. It’ll be fine.” Even though it makes me uncomfortable, I know Ryan is protective over me and wouldn’t leave me with anyone that’s less than completely trustworthy.

“Okay. Let me take care of a few things, and I’ll come down in a bit.”

Nodding my head at him, he leans down to kiss me. When we walk out into the hall, Ryan calls for Max to come back to his office.

“Stay here, I’ll be right back,” he tells me and then walks into Ryan’s office and shuts the door. It’s only a short minute when he walks back out and leads me back downstairs into the throngs of people. Holding me safely under his arm, he moves us across the busy room, and I see him nod his head at some people who are sitting at a table. They quickly grab their drinks and free up the seats for us.

"Shit, Max, why have you never helped me out like that before?" Jase jokes.

"Because you're not the boss' girlfriend," he responds with a condescending kiss in the air.

I laugh at Max as he sits down next to me, and Jase leaves to go to the bar and grab some drinks.

"So how long have you worked here?" I ask.

"About three years. Ryan and I go to the same gym, so we were friends before he hired me."

"Here we go," Jase says when he returns with a bucket of beers. Popping the top for me, he hands me a bottle.

Max sits silently beside me as Jase and I start talking about this past week. I tell him everything that we did, and we talk a little about Donna when Mark's band takes the stage. When they start playing, I am impressed with their sound. It reminds me a lot of the Silversun Pickups.

"They're really good," I yell over at Jase.

"Yeah, I know. I knew you'd like them," he yells back.

We continue to sit there and drink our beers while listening to the band. I can't believe it took me so long to come here. I feel happy and relaxed being here with Jase and finally getting to hear one of my closest friends play. The room is chaotic and noisy and I have no concept of time, but when I feel Ryan's arms wrap around my waist from behind, I know I've been down here for a while.

He nuzzles my neck and gives me a nip before saying, "You having fun?"

"Yeah. I had no idea how good they were."

"They've really been bringing in the crowds since they started playing here. Been trying to figure shit out because they aren't sure if they are still going to play after this summer. A couple of the guys are graduating with Mark, so we'll see."

A girl in a tight black tank top with the word 'BLUR' written across her chest, like Max's, approaches the table with a beverage tray in her hands. She sets the tray on the table, and while she is placing our empty bottles on it, she says, "So this is the girl that finally took you off the market," while looking at me. She doesn't give my stomach a chance to knot up when she gives me a warm smile. "I'm Mel." She reaches over to shake my hand and continues, "It's great to finally put a face to the name. Ryan never shuts up about you."

She laughs as she rushes away, not giving Ryan a chance to say anything.

He leans down to my ear and tells me, "She's worked here for years, you'll like her."

When I give him a side stare, he says, "Don't worry, she's married."

I shake my head and turn my attention back to the stage as I lean back in Ryan's arms.

It feels good to finally be here in Ryan's world. It's always felt weird to me to not be involved in such a big part of his life. I guess it must be the same way he felt about never seeing me dance. Finally being able to link these two missing pieces, I feel more connected to who he is.

For the past several weeks, Ryan has been good with me only staying with him a few nights a week, and although he complains, I know he understands. Kimber and I still don't really talk that much, but she has asked about Ryan and I have opened up to her a little about him. She is still dating Seth, even though she says it's not too serious. She told me he was accepted into graduate school at UCLA, so there is no reason for her to get too attached. She's convincing when she says that they are both just having fun together at this point.

I talked to Roxy the other day about changing my tattoo. She wanted to know why I wasn't happy with it, so I just told her that I wanted it to be more of a reflection of who I am now. She didn't really understand, and of course, I didn't expect her to. But I came to the decision to simply have the heart shaded in. I didn't want to add to it to make it any larger than what it already is. I like that it's tiny. I didn't realize until I fell in love with Ryan how full my heart could actually be, so having the empty heart on my hip filled in only makes sense. Ryan loved that idea and went with me yesterday to get it done.

I was a nervous wreck, the same as I was when I first got it. Jared was quick, and it didn't hurt too bad. Ryan held my hand through the short process, and now I have a solid black heart instead of the empty outline. Even though it's the same, it feels very different to me. I love Ryan for helping me transform something that was filled with such bad memories into something that now makes me happy when I look at it. I think of him when I see it, and I love that he was able to give that to me.

While I was going through my drawers and getting rid of old clothes, I ran across Detective Patterson's card again. I held it in my hands and thought about how I first met Jack and how quickly it spun out of control. I'm not even sure if too much time has passed to call. Not that I would call. I don't really know what to do about it all. I have always just assumed I would leave it be and move on.

But then the thought crept into my head that if he did that to me, then he has the potential to do it to someone else. What if he already has done it to someone else? What if I wasn't the first? What if there is a girl out there just like me?

I wondered if he was seeing anyone; if he had a girlfriend now. She has the right to know what kind of guy she's with. But the thought of having people know what happened to me, having to talk about it, I'm terrified it could break me. Even though Ryan assures me that I did nothing wrong, I still feel responsible for sending Jack over the edge and leading him on.

After a while, I give up on thinking too much about it all and slip the card back into my sock drawer. If I was going to do anything about it, I should have done it already. I need to just let it go, but for some reason, I can't bring myself to throw the card away.

chapter thirty-six

Ryan and I jog up the steps of my house after our morning run. It's still early out, and the sun is just starting to rise behind the grey clouds that blanket the city. Once inside, we each grab a bottle of water and go back to my room so I can clean up.

Shutting the door, he walks up behind me and starts planting kisses on the back of my neck. I reach up and wrap my hand behind his damp neck. His kisses make me shiver, and he grazes his lips over my ear and says, "I want you in your bed."

It may sound weird, but we haven't ever had sex in my bed, but then again, Ryan rarely spends the night here with me and the few times that he has, Kimber was home, and it made me feel uncomfortable with her in the next room. But she is gone this morning, and the way his kisses are affecting me, I don't want to say no.

Turning around in his arms, I start tugging up his shirt. He reaches over his head and pulls it off at the same time I take mine off. We stumble over to the bed and when we collapse on it, we are a tangled mess, fumbling to get each other's clothes off. Running my lips down his neck and along his broad shoulders, I taste the salt on his skin. I knot my fingers in his sweaty hair and pull him down on me.

My body bows into his when he grinds his hips into me,

pushing himself deep inside me, and we begin to move together. Reaching behind my back, he pulls us onto our sides, and I wrap my leg around his waist pulling him closer to me. We lie face-to-face, flushed and panting, as he grips tightly onto my thigh.

We don't speak, and with our foreheads connected, we keep our eyes locked while he takes his time with me. Never rushing. Never in a hurry.

I'm alone for the day while Ryan is at work. Tonight, Blur is hosting a concert for one of Gavin's bands and they are expecting a huge turnout. I agreed to go since Mark and Jase will also be there. My car is still over at Ryan's house from last night. When we left for our run this morning and found ourselves here, I told him I didn't need to go back for my car. I would just stay here for the day.

It's nearing the end of April, and I decide I should start sorting through my belongings and slowly start packing. I still don't know where I'm going, but with graduation a little over a month away, I need to start getting organized. New York has always been my dream, but I know I'll never be able to leave Ryan behind—I'll never *want* to leave him. Plus, Seattle has produced many world-renowned dancers and choreographers. Pacific Northwest Ballet is here in Seattle and is internationally recognized as one of the elite. Even if they're not interested in me, I know if I stay here, I can still have a successful career.

After I pack up a box of books, I start thinking more and more about Ryan and how I never thought I would have what I found with him. Jack destroyed everything in me, and to be able to trust someone again is something I didn't think would ever be possible. Is it selfish of me to not want to save someone else from that theft? I know that it has probably been too long, but maybe I should just call and get some information on what could be done. Hell, for all I know, I could even remain anonymous. But, I will never know if I don't call.

Opening the top drawer of my dresser, I fish out the card that I was given now eight months ago. I keep telling myself that it's just a phone call; I just want to ask some questions.

Picking up my cell, I swipe the screen and with nervous fingers dial the number while my heart beats at an insanely rapid rate. After several rings, I am half relieved when I get the detective's voicemail. I leave him a quick message with my name and number and set the phone back down. All of a sudden I consider the possibility of Jack finding out. If I did do anything, would he come after me? Would he try and hurt me? I resolve that it's probably best if I don't say anything. I shouldn't be calling and talking to Detective Patterson. I really do need to move on and just let it be.

"Babe, you ready?"

"Yeah, I just need to grab my jacket," I say as I walk back into my closet.

"So, it's going to be busy. A lot busier than the past few times you've been. You sure you're okay with that?"

"I mean, if it's too much then I can always go upstairs until you're ready to leave."

He takes my hand and laces his fingers through mine, pulling me to him, and suggests, "Or we could just stay here and break in your bed a bit more," as he nuzzles my neck.

I smile at the memory of being with him this morning and give him a kiss. "I think we should go now and break in the bed later."

Nipping my lip, he walks us out to his jeep.

When we pull up in front of the bar, there is a line wrapped around the building. Max spots us from the door and is standing next to me when we walk in. The music blasts through the bar as Ryan and Max lead me to the side of the bar that curves around to the back wall. We told Mark and Jase to meet us here and see them waiting for us. When we approach them, Gavin and several of Ryan's friends are there as well. Jase orders me two shots, and I feel relaxed over in the corner with our group of friends. We all drink and laugh and eventually Mel comes by to chat with me a bit while the guys are busy talking about things I couldn't care less about.

Mel has always been really sweet to me. She's a little older than I am and reminds me a lot of Roxy. Her husband is a drummer for a band that just got signed to a label in L.A. I've only met him once when he was in town during a break in recording his album. She decided to stay here in Seattle so that she could have the support of her family instead of being alone in L.A. where she doesn't know anyone. Personally, I think she isn't too happy in her marriage and that's why she stayed.

A few hours later, the band returns to the stage after taking a short break and begin to play a cover of the Imagine Dragons' 'Radioactive.' Ryan tells me he needs to run upstairs to grab some inventory sheets to give Mel before we leave. Holding my hand tightly, he tries to lead us across the bar. The door has been busy, so Max is back at his post outside.

Bumping shoulders through the crowd, Ryan wraps his arm around me and we slowly walk through the swarm of people. I stumble a little when I suddenly spot Kimber out of the corner of my eye. I had no idea she was even here. My body jerks and freezes when I think I'm seeing things. Running his nose along some girl's neck, when he turns his head back to the stage, I know I'm not losing it. I see Jack's face. My vision begins to tunnel as panic shrieks through me, and I start tugging in the opposite direction that Ryan is going, pulling back against his arm that is around me. My eyes are locked on Jack, who doesn't see me from across the room.

"What are you doing?" Ryan hollers over the crowd as I keep stumbling back. When he shifts his body, I fall out of his hold and tumble onto the floor.

In shock and terror, I keep trying to shuffle back when Ryan picks me up. He turns to see what I'm staring at and looks back at me as I attempt to turn my back and run. He grabs me around the waist, not letting me escape and leans over my shoulder, yelling over the music, "Babe, what's wrong?"

Trying to peel his grip from me, all I can do is shout, "It's Jack!"

"Who?"

"Get me out of here!" I scream in a panic, jerking to get out of his grip. "I can't breathe! Get me out of here!"

Tucking me tightly against him, he moves us quickly to the door, yelling at Jase to follow, but Jase is too far away.

When we finally make it outside, my breathing is labored and my whole body is shaking. I run to Ryan's car, wanting to get as far away as I can from Jack. Aside from my dreams, I haven't seen him since that night.

"Babe, what the fuck happened in there? Who the fuck did you see?"

Leaning my back against his jeep, I grip onto Ryan's shirt as I start to cry and gasp for breath.

"Jack is in there. We have to leave."

"Who's Jack?"

"Him! Jack is..." I'm cut off when I hear Jase holler my name as he runs toward me, and I'm sobbing hysterically.

"Candace, what happened?"

All I can say between my panting breaths and tears is, "Jack's inside."

"Oh, shit!"

"Who the fuck is Jack?!" Ryan yells and Jase tells him, "The guy that attacked her."

Ryan snaps his head to me, grabs my shoulders, and says in a low stern voice, "Get in the car. Now." He reaches in his pocket and hands his keys to Jase and yells, "Get her in the fucking car!" And then he takes off back to the bar while I sob uncontrollably.

"What's going on?" I hear Mark ask Ryan as they pass each other. Ryan says nothing as he goes through the door.

Jase turns around and yells at Mark to go in after him.

"What the hell is going on?" he asks.

"Jase, he'll kill him," I cry out and he turns back to Mark. "Jack is in there! Ryan's gonna fuckin' kill him!"

"Shit!" Mark yells as he starts to run back in, and I see Max following right behind.

"Jase, you have to go get him!"

"Sweetie, get in the car," he says softly.

"What?! No!" I thrash in his arms and wail, when he wraps his arms over mine, locking them down and lifts me up into the jeep. He stands outside the car with the door open, and I lower my head to my knees and cry. Rubbing my back, he assures me that Mark's going to get him.

My mind is racing, and I can't seem to focus on anything in particular aside from what Ryan is doing inside. I cry as Jase keeps reassuring me and trying to calm me down. When I hear Ryan's voice, I sit up and watch him as he walks over. His hands are covered in blood, and blood is splattered across his face. When he walks past Jase, he quietly demands, “Keys.”

Jase hands them over and quickly leans in to kiss me and says, “Call me.”

I nod as he closes my door, and I turn to look at Ryan as he gets in the car. He doesn’t say anything and neither do I. He starts the car and begins to drive. His jaw is clenched hard, and his breaths are slow and heavy. Ryan’s grip is tight on the steering wheel, and his knuckles are cut open and covered in blood.

Neither one of us speaks the whole drive to his loft. His breathing has slowed and softened by the time he shuts off the car. My tears haven’t stopped flowing. Getting out, he walks in front of the jeep to my side, opening my door. When I shift myself to face him, he drops his head to my lap and grabs onto my hips. Weaving my hands through his hair, I fist them closed and lean my body over his. I know he’s crying when I feel his back begin to heave.

I let go of his hair when he pulls back. The pain in his eyes is almost unbearable. Wiping my thumbs across his cheeks, I brush the tears away from his bloody face. I look over him, and I know it has to be Jack’s blood because Ryan doesn’t have a scratch on him. I don’t ask what happened because I don’t think it really matters.

He takes my hand and walks me inside and up to his room. While he’s in the shower, I grab my purse and take my sleeping pill. I can’t stop crying as I change into a pair of his boxers and a t-shirt and wait for him in bed. He walks out with a towel slung around his waist and goes to throw on his boxers. Getting into bed, he scoops me in his arms as I continue to cry.

All I can see is Jack. He’s there when I close my eyes; he’s there when they’re open, staring into the darkness of the room. I cry because I don’t know how to get him out of my mind. I just need to be close to Ryan, to feel safe and to know everything will be fine.

I lay my hand on his cheek and turn him to me. Pressing my lips against his, I pull back for a moment and whisper, "Make love to me," before kissing him again.

"Baby, you're crying."

"I don't care." I bring him to me and begin running my kisses down his neck. Ryan doesn't move, so I pull away and look at him. "Kiss me."

"Candace, you're upset."

"I need to be close to you right now. I want to get him out of my head, and you're the only one who can do that for me."

He rolls on top of me and lets out a sigh, resting his head against mine. "Are you sure, babe?"

"Yes," I say through the tears that won't stop.

I cling tightly to him as he slips his hand under my shirt and squeezes my breast while kissing my neck. I reach down and tug on his boxers, just wanting them off.

"Candace."

"Please, Ryan."

He pulls down his boxers, and I lift my hips so that he can remove mine. I quickly pull off my top, and when he slides into me, I close my eyes, letting the tears seep out. Ryan has a thing about watching me when we make love, but tonight, he never asks me to open my eyes. I cling to his body as he pushes into me unlike any time before. Without words, he continues to thrust inside of me until we both find our release.

When he rolls off of me, he pulls me snug against him, and he reaches down to grab my hand, holding it tightly. He never lets go of it, and I suddenly feel bad for using him like I just did when he's also so upset.

"I'm so sorry. I shouldn't have done that."

"Don't be. You take whatever you need from me."

chapter thirty-seven

The ringing of my phone wakes me up, and I climb out of bed to dig it out of my purse. Not wanting to wake Ryan, I step out into the hall, closing the door softly behind me. I don't recognize the number, so I answer with a hesitant, "Hello?"

"Is this Candace Parker?" a man's voice asks.

"Yes. Who is this?"

"Detective Patterson, ma'am. I got your message and was returning your call. How can I help you?"

The anxiety slowly builds in my stomach as I'm caught off guard by the phone call, especially since last night's events. A flash of the girl's face that Jack was with crosses my mind, and I decide that maybe this is what I need to do.

"Oh, yeah. I...umm, I'm not quite sure where to begin."

"It's okay. Did you have a specific question you wanted to ask me?"

I walk further down the hall and sit down at the top of the stairs. "I guess I was just curious about what would happen if I wanted to press charges; if it was too late...or..."

"Well, I have your file here. It seems the hospital went ahead and had your rape kit sent over to the criminal lab where it is being stored. That, along with the eye-witness report, well, you have a solid case."

"Umm, so there was someone there? I don't

remember..."

"Yes, ma'am. Let me pull up his statement." It takes a few seconds before he continues, "Okay, according to his statement, he heard screaming in the alley. When he came into view, you were knocked unconscious. He was the one who called 911 and waited with you until the ambulance arrived."

My hands begin to tremble as I think about someone being there with me. It makes me almost feel embarrassed just thinking about someone seeing me like that—beaten and naked. That night begins to replay in my head: the screaming, the weight of him on top of me, his grunting, watching his fist before he slammed it into my face.

"Umm..." I mumble out in a shaky voice and wipe away a few tears that are now rolling down my cheeks. "Do you know who? I mean..."

"Give me one second." I hear him tapping the computer keys when he continues, "Last name is Campbell. Ryan Campbell. Seems he owns the building where this happened."

Suddenly the air is sucked out of me, and the sensation of pinpricks overtakes my body as I turn cold.

"Ma'am?"

The phone slides out of my trembling hand and tumbles down the wooden stairs. I'm frozen and I'm shocked. *Ryan?* I begin to wonder who the man is in the other room; the man I trust. *Why didn't he ever tell me? Was this all a game to him?* My stomach churns, and I feel like I'm going to be sick. How could he lie to me, deceive me?

I start taking deep breaths as I reach my hand up, grab onto the banister, and pull myself onto my wobbly legs. I need to get out of here.

Gently easing the door open, I quietly pad across the room and pick up my purse. I look down at Ryan, who is still sleeping, and I feel pieces of my heart crumbling and falling hard into the pit of my stomach. I'm so embarrassed. No wonder he was so patient with me; he knew all along. *How could I be so stupid? How could I have let my walls down like this?*

I fumble with the necklace around my neck, and suddenly, everything feels like a lie. If he truly ever thought I was fierce, it was just a product of his deceit. I clench the bar of the necklace and yank on it, breaking the delicate chain. I look down at the engraving, and I feel like an idiot for allowing another man to strip me bare.

When the tears begin to fall, I set the necklace on the nightstand, and I turn my back and leave. Quickly running down the stairs and out the door, I run to my car as fast as I can and throw it into reverse. All the wounds I've tried so desperately to mend are slowly starting to rip open as I start putting together all the pieces. The way he looked at me the first time he walked into the coffee shop. He knew me. He never pushed me because he knew exactly who I was. It was all a lie. It was all a sick game, and I was the fool who fell in love. *What the fuck is wrong with me?*

As soon as I get home, I run into my room and shut the door behind me. Still trying to make sense of everything, I fall onto the bed and cry. I cry for a long time. I've never felt so hollow, so completely hopeless. When I can move, I roll over and grab my pillow to bury my head in it while I sob. Gasping for breath, I smell the remnants of his scent that linger on my pillow. I jump out of the bed and frantically start ripping the covers and sheets off, slinging them across the room.

"Candace?"

Startled, I turn to see Ryan walking into my room and closing the door behind him.

"Get out," I seethe.

"Babe, what's going on?"

Holding my arms out in front of me, I tell him, "Stay away from me."

His brows are knitted together as he looks at me in confusion. "Baby, what happened?"

I begin to cry harder and back myself against the wall. "You know exactly what happened. You know exactly who I am!"

Standing in the middle of my room, he doesn't say a word as his face slowly turns to shock, and I know he knows exactly what I mean.

"How could you?!" I scream.

Shaking his head, he says, "Babe, let me explain."

"Explain what?! That you've been lying to me this whole time? That you've just been using me? Why?!"

"No! It's not like that. I didn't know."

"How could you not know? God, I'm so fucking stupid."

"I didn't know when I first met you. I didn't know until I saw your tattoo."

"What?!"

"Babe, please let me explain."

"Get out!"

When he doesn't move, I scream, "Get the fuck out! I don't ever want to see you again." My legs can no longer support me, and I fall to my knees, sobbing—breaking.

"Just leave me alone."

"I'm not leaving," he says as he moves and kneels down in front of me.

"I fuckin' hate you. You made me fall in love with you, and it was all a goddamn lie."

"God, Candace. Please let me explain."

When he reaches out to touch me, I snap. "Get out! Get the fuck out!"

He jerks around when Kimber bursts through the door. Our eyes meet, and she turns to Ryan and demands, "Get the fuck out and away from her before I call the cops."

He turns back to me and pleads, "Babe, please. I love you so fuckin' much. Let me explain. Don't do this."

"I didn't do shit, Ryan!" Covering my face with my hands, I wail and scream, "Just go. It's over!"

"I'm serious. After the shit from last night, you better get the fuck away from her and leave. Now!"

All I hear through my cries is Ryan's voice echoing when he screams, "Fuuuck!" from across the house and then the slamming of the door as he leaves.

I fall into Kimber's arms when she rushes down to her knees in front of me. She holds me in her arms as I cry harder and harder. It's been so long since Kimber has hugged me, and her touch is almost too much for me. Ryan just took everything, and I feel like dust, like at any second I could be blown away into nothing. I grasp tightly to Kimber, desperate for her. I can't lie to her; I need her too much.

"I'm so sorry. I'm so sorry that I've been lying to you."

"Candace—"

I cut her off and let everything out. Everything I've been hiding.

"I didn't want to lie to you. I love you, but I was scared. I was scared you would tell someone, and I was afraid to trust you."

"Sweetie—"

"Jack raped me. That night of the party, he raped me. And I stayed with Jase because I didn't want you to know. I didn't want anyone to know, and I was scared you would go to Jack and do something stupid. So I hid from you. I lied, and I hurt you. I lost my best friend and I'm so sorry."

"Candace, you didn't lose me," she says as she begins to cry. "I've always been here."

"I'm so sorry."

Kimber doesn't say anything as we both cry. I don't know how long we are on the floor, but when exhaustion hits, I lean my head back against the wall and release a hard sigh. When I look back at Kimber, I apologize again.

"Let's get off the floor, okay?" she says and then stands and helps pull me up. We walk out to the living room, and I sit on the couch as Kimber gets us some water. Sitting down next to me she asks, "Candace, what happened?"

"With Jack or Ryan?"

"Jack."

"He got pissed at me that I led him on and when I ran from him, he..." I don't finish my thought, because I can't, and I know I don't need to. "I was taken to the hospital, and I went home with Jase. I couldn't come back here because Jack had banged up my face pretty bad."

"Fucker," she hisses.

"Kimber, you can't say anything."

"Ryan beat the shit out of him last night."

"I know, I was there. That's Ryan's bar, he owns it."

"Is that why you were fighting? I don't understand."

Shaking my head, I start to cry again. "God, it's so messed up."

"Candace, I know you didn't think you could, but you can trust me. I love you."

"The thing with Jack happened in the back lot of Ryan's bar. I didn't know it, and I didn't know him when we met. But I spoke with the detective this morning, and he told me that Ryan had witnessed it." Hanging my head down, I struggle to get my words out. "I don't know what to think. He knew me all along and never said anything. God, I broke down like an idiot and told him what had happened to me and he already knew."

"That's fucked up," she says as she hugs me.

"I fell in love with him. How could he make me fall in love with him? I feel so stupid."

"You're not stupid. He lied to you. He's a dick face."

I can't help but chuckle through my tears at her words. I've missed her words so much.

"I wish I would have known," she tells me. "I wish I could have been there for you. I had no idea. I thought you were mad at me, and I couldn't figure it out. I couldn't figure any of it out, so I just gave up trying. Then I just got mad at you."

"I'm sorry."

"I don't know what to do. I mean, last night was the first time I've hung out with Jack, but he's one of Seth's friends. They're frat brothers and all."

"You can't say anything. Please, Kimber."

"I won't. I promise. I just don't know what to do."

"I don't know."

"Are you pressing charges?"

"No."

"Why were you talking to a detective?"

"He was at the hospital. He gave me his card. Jase had tried a couple times to get me to call him, but I didn't. I came across it the other day when I was starting to pack my room and I...I don't know, I guess I wanted to see what my options were. I don't know."

"You can't let him get away with this, Candace. He has a girlfriend, you know?"

"Kimber, I just can't. This year has been a nightmare, a never-ending nightmare, for me. I thought I was stronger. I thought Ryan was real. I don't know, Kimber. I feel so lost. More lost than before."

There's a knock on the door and Kimber gets up to answer it.

"Hey, Jase," she says as he walks into the house and

straight towards me.

"I've been trying to call you, sweetie. What happened?"

I must have forgotten my phone when I rushed out of Ryan's place.

"He lied to me."

Sitting down next to me, he asks, "What do you mean 'he lied?'"

I start to cry and he takes my hand. "Remember when the detective told us there was a witness to what happened?"

"Yeah."

"It was Ryan. Jase, he saw it and never told me."

Kimber sits down on the other side of me as I lean into Jase's arms, and I hear Kimber tell Jase that I told her everything. And for the first time in a long time, the three of us hold each other. I'm so hurt and so lost, but at the same time, I feel like I'm finally back with the people who I have always considered my family.

When Jase pulls back, he wants to know how I found out, so I tell him about calling Detective Patterson and everything that he said.

"What did you say to Ryan?"

With a new slew of tears breaking free, I say, "I ended it. Jase, I don't know what to do. I just don't know what to do. How could he do this to me?"

"I don't know, sweetie."

"You're gonna have to go over to his place. All my things are there and my phone. I left it all there."

"Don't worry about any of that. Jase will take care of it," Kimber assures me.

"I'll go over there when I leave here. But I don't want to leave you like this."

I lie down, rest my head in Jase's lap, and let him console me. I listen to him and Kimber talk about everything while Jase answers all of her questions. I don't say anything.

I just lie there until the tears dry up and I have nothing left in me. I never thought I could feel as low as I do right now. I didn't think it was possible, but I feel like the depths of my despair can't sink any lower. If ever I wanted to lose myself and disappear, it's right now. I'm so empty and nothing Jase or Kimber can do or say could take away the stabbing pain inside me.

When Jase leaves, Kimber takes me into her room, and I crawl into her bed. I tell her I can smell Ryan on my sheets, and she goes into my room, grabs all of my bedding, and tosses a load into the washer. When she comes back, she lies down with me like we used to do and pulls the sheets over us, hugging me from behind. I've missed this, having her, my best friend, my sister.

chapter thirty-eight

These past two weeks have been such a daze. I'm miserable. I can't sleep. I can't eat. I try to keep myself consumed with school, but I can't even focus. Ryan calls me every day, and each time he does, it's just a reminder of how alone I am. I can't even read his texts. I delete them as soon as they come through. When Jase went over there to get my belongings last week, he came back and suggested that I talk to Ryan. But I know there is nothing he could possibly say to lessen this pain. I gave him everything I had to give. I bared it all to him, and the whole time he was lying to me. I feel so betrayed and so used. And the most sickening part of it all is that I still love him. I hate myself for that. I don't know what's wrong with me; I don't understand how I can still feel this way about him after everything.

Mark and Jase still talk to him and see him. I told them that I understand. After all, Mark's band plays at his bar. I can't expect them to not be his friend. But I've been keeping my distance from them because I can't help but feel hurt at the same time.

When Roxy kept asking about Ryan and why she hadn't seen him around, I just didn't have the energy to deal with it, so I quit. I know it was a total overreaction, but all I really want to do is escape from everything. I'm trying hard to be strong and put the pieces back together, but Ryan didn't leave me with pieces—he left me with ashes.

Since I no longer have anything aside from dance to distract me on the weekends, I'm home alone most of the time. Kimber is at her parents' this weekend. She wanted me to come with her, but just the thought of pretending to be happy around her family was enough to exhaust me. Jase called earlier to try and get me out of the house, but I told him I wasn't feeling well. I know he didn't believe me, but I don't care.

He's worried that I'm not taking care of myself, and I guess he should be. I know I look awful. It's only been two weeks and my clothes are all loose on me, but I can't rid my stomach of the knots that consume it. Ms. Emerson has been riding my ass again, and I know I need to pull it together and quick because our production is a mere two weeks away.

When the doorbell rings, I drag myself to the door. I look out the living room window, and I can't swallow against the lump in my throat when I see Ryan's black Rubicon. Leaning my head against the door, I say, "Go away."

"You won't return any of my calls, babe. Please, let me talk to you."

I turn away and start walking back to my room when I hear a key slide into the lock and then the door opening.

Snapping back to face the door, I yell, "What are you doing?!"

"Jase gave me a key."

"Ass," I mumble under my breath. "Ryan, please go. I don't want to talk."

"I can't *not* talk to you. It's killing me."

"It's killing *you*? What about me?" I can barely get the words out over the sob that starts to threaten. "Ryan, I can't do this. I can't even look at you. Please, just go."

"I can't stand to see you like this."

"Then go! I will do almost anything to make

you leave."

"Just let me talk to you. Please, babe, just let me talk."

"Fine, say whatever you need to say, then leave me alone."

He motions for me to sit on the couch and when I do, he sits next to me. I can't control the tears that free fall down my cheeks. Seeing his face and being next to him is too much for me. If I had never loved him so much, then he never would have had the power to destroy me like he did. More than anything, I want to cling to him, but I don't. I know I can't ever allow anyone to get that close to me again. I can't give another person the power to hurt me like he did.

"I'm worried about you," he says as he looks me in the eyes.

I turn my head so I don't have to look at him. "Don't."

"When was the last time you've eaten?"

"Ryan, don't. Just say what you need to say."

He reaches for my hand, but I pull it away as he says, "I love you. I know you don't believe me, but I do. No one has ever affected me the way you do, babe. I swear to you...I swear I didn't know. I didn't, Candace. Not at first." When I hear his voice crack, I look up at him and see the tears that fill his eyes, and I have to look back down.

"When I saw you at the coffee shop I thought it was you. I thought you were *that* girl. But then I kept thinking, 'What are the chances?' I didn't know because you looked so different than from that night. And then I found out that you were friends with Mark. Every time I saw you, I felt myself being drawn to you in a way I've never felt before. I had myself convinced that my head was playing games with me, and I honestly did not think you were that girl. It wasn't until I saw your tattoo when we were in bed. That's when I knew. When I found that girl, I saw her tattoo—*your* tattoo."

"Ryan, please," I whimper, but he doesn't stop.

"When I saw it, I broke. I didn't want you to be her. I had already fallen so hard in love with you and realizing that it was you fuckin' killed me. Everything started making sense to me. How scared you always were with me when we first met, how afraid you were when I tried to touch you. Everything made sense. But, I didn't know how to tell you. And then you told me you loved me, and I know how hard that was for you. I just couldn't hurt you," he says, now crying.

"But you did. You lied to me. I let you see all the parts of me that weren't pretty, but you knew all along. And when I finally opened up to you, you already knew." Lowering my head into my hands, I cry. I cry hard. "You let me give everything to you. You had to have known that you couldn't hold on to that secret forever. I would've eventually found out, and you still let me fall for you like I did. I feel so stupid and used, like you just felt sorry for me or pitied me."

"I never pitied you, babe. I have only ever loved you. I just didn't want to hurt you."

He reaches out to hold me, but I push him back and stand up from the couch.

"I can't do this. You can't say those things to me."

Standing up and taking a step toward me, he says, "I know I fucked up. I fucked everything up so bad. I know all you wanted was someone you could trust. I wanted to be that for you, and I fucked it all up. But, I didn't know what to say; I was scared. You'll never know how fucking sorry I am."

"I knew better. I knew I shouldn't have let you in like I did. But, I can't see you anymore. You have to stop calling and texting. I need you to just not exist for me because I can't do this. It hurts more than I thought anything possibly could."

"Candace, please."

"Just go."

He doesn't move. He just stands there. A part of me never wants him to move, but I know he needs to. I can hardly bear to see the pain in his eyes and the tears running down his cheeks.

"Please, you have to go. I can't do this," I plead with him.

Looking at me through his tears, he chokes out, "You have to know how much I love you."

"Please, Ryan," I say with closed eyes. I just need him to go because I can't take the excruciating pain any more. My eyes stay closed until I hear the click of the door as it closes behind him. I know I shouldn't, but I can't stop myself from watching him get into his jeep. I feel like I need to scream for him to come back, but I don't. I just let him drive away.

My heart hurts so bad, I swear it feels like I'm dying. I can't take this anymore. I know I can't live like this. I can't do this on my own. I've tried so hard. But I just can't do it anymore.

It's been just over a week since Ryan walked out of my house, and I finally hit my bottom. I finally had to surrender, and I knew I had to stop clinging onto people. I had to stop running to Jase. He would never be able to save me. And I no longer had Ryan to cling to. But even if I did, he wouldn't be able to save me either. I knew it was up to me to pull myself together and get help because all I wanted to do was fade away.

The first time I went to see Dr. Christman was the day after I saw Ryan. We decided that I would see her twice a week. During our first session, I basically told her everything that had happened since August: Jack, Kimber, my parents,

Ryan. I told her about how I grew up and why I didn't seek therapy earlier this year when everything was falling apart. I really like Dr. Christman. She's helping me to see that what Jack did wasn't my fault. I still harbor guilt about it, but not as much as I used to. She's helping me learn how to tolerate my emotions and not avoid everything that I consider my triggers, like my fear of crowds or my thoughts of Jack.

Today is our fourth session. When I walk into her office and sit in my usual seat on the couch. "Hello, Candace. How are you feeling since we met earlier this week?"

"Okay, I guess."

"And what does that mean? What's 'okay'?"

"I've been trying to eat better, which I think is good. But, I haven't been sleeping well, so I've been really tired."

"What do you think is keeping you up?"

"It used to be Jack, but lately it's been Ryan. He keeps flashing through my head, and when that happens, I get really upset. I know I need to move on, but it's really hard."

"It's only natural that this will take time. You loved him, and that doesn't go away just because he hurt you. But it sounds like he also helped you. Would you agree with that?"

Shifting on the couch, I say, "I suppose. But, it really just seems like a façade. Like everything I thought he was helping me through wasn't real because the whole thing was a lie."

She flips a page over on her tablet and begins taking notes before asking, "But was it a lie? We know he held onto the secret of who he was to you, but were the feelings a lie?"

"I don't know. I mean...they felt real."

"If Ryan would have told you from the beginning who he was, if he was honest about that, do you think you would have let yourself feel what you felt for him?"

Taking in a deep breath and letting it out slowly, I say,

"Yes."

"So, was it all a lie then?"

I shake my head and say, "I get what you're saying, but I can't go back."

"I'm not saying go back. There was a betrayal, and you have every right to guard yourself against that, but don't dismiss your feelings as a lie. He was able to show you that you are capable of loving, and trusting, and having faith."

"I just don't know how to move past him."

She sets her pen and tablet down and leans back in her chair. "Well, that takes time, just like any loss we suffer. What is one thing you think you can do to help that process?"

"I don't know. I guess...I guess I need to stop spending so much time thinking about why I can't go back to him and just focus on the fact that I was already with him and it just didn't work. When I think about why I can't go back, it's like I'm trying to convince myself that I shouldn't, when I really need to focus on the fact that it just isn't an option. He's my past, and I need to start focusing on what I'm going to do about my future."

"And what about your future can you focus on?"

"My dancing. I have my performance this weekend, so hopefully offers will start coming in this next week. I need to focus on making New York happen. It's always been my dream."

She picks up her notepad and begins to write as she says, "I think you have a good plan."

We continue on to discuss issues about Jack and some of the paranoia I still feel about him for the rest of the session. After making my follow-up appointment, I stop by the house and grab my dance bag to spend the rest of the day rehearsing and focusing more on the thing I do have control over, which is my career, not Ryan.

When I get home, I decide to start taking more control, like Dr. Christman suggested. I can't keep avoiding situations that make me nervous and uncomfortable. I know I can't keep hiding from my emotions because I'm too scared to deal with them.

I take out my phone, scroll down to Roxy's name, and tap her number. After several rings, she answers.

"Candace, hey."

"Hey Rox, do you have a minute to talk?"

"Hun, I always have time for you. How are you?"

"I'm doing better, actually. I wanted to call and apologize for my behavior and walking out on you. I've been going through some stuff, and I was out of line."

"I've been worried about you. We used to always talk, but I feel like you've somehow gotten lost this year, and I wish I knew how to be a friend to you."

"You are a friend. And I love you. It's been a rough year, but I think I'm getting on the right track. It feels that way, at least."

"That's good to hear."

"But, I was calling because I wanted to know if you've filled my position yet."

"Your position will never be filled."

"So, I can come back?"

"Always, hun."

"Thanks, Rox. Can you get me on the schedule for next week?"

"Of course. Stop by in a couple days, and I'll have the schedule out."

"Great."

"And Candace..."

"Yeah?"

"I'm glad you called me. You know you can always call, anytime."

"I do know. Thanks again. I'll stop by later this week."

"Sounds good."

"Okay, bye."

"So, tell me how things have been going?" Dr. Christman asks as she pulls out her notepad.

"I called my boss and got my job back. She put me on the schedule for next week."

"What made you decide to do that?"

"You suggested that I stop avoiding situations that spike my emotions. Work has always been that place for me. It's always been a place I feared Jack walking into."

"What do you normally do when your anxiety peaks at work?"

"I go to the back room and restock."

"And what are you going to do now when you start to feel that way?"

"I know I need to stay out in the shop."

"Just remember that a spike in emotions is okay. They will spike, but they will come down again and you will be okay."

"When I get anxious, I feel that there will be no coming back down. I feel like everything is about to spiral out of control."

"That's very common after the kind of trauma you've been through. It's normal to be afraid of feeling, but whatever you're feeling, you need to understand that those feelings will not be permanent. Instead of running from your feelings, I really would like for you to stay in them. Try not to shut down. Think about your anxiety level, and when it gets high, I want you to see that you're still okay."

I nod my head and say, "I think that doing something like that at work is a good place to start. I'm not alone, and sitting here with you thinking about it, I can rationally say that nothing would happen. That I would be okay."

"Good. And how has your sleep been lately?"

"Restless."

"Are you still on your sleeping pill?" she asks.

"Yes. Honestly, I'm too scared to wean off of them."

"That's okay. You're making progress in other areas, and so we will keep focusing on that before approaching your nightmares."

After the session is over, I head over to Common Grounds to pick up my schedule for next week. When I walk in, I see Roxy behind the counter. She walks around it and comes to give me a hug.

"I'm so glad you decided to come back. I've missed you. I've been stuck working with Sarah, and all she talks about is her stupid dog."

I laugh at her and say, "Thanks. I'm so sorry for—"

Cutting me off she tells me, "Forget it. I'm just glad you're here, hun."

I walk to the back room with her, and she gives me the schedule for next week. It feels good to be back here. Even though Dr. Christman helped me to see that this place is a trigger for my irrational feelings, I feel like this will be a good starting point for me to try to overcome them.

chapter thirty-nine

"So how are you and Kimber doing?" Jase asks me as we stand in the long line to buy our caps and gowns for graduation.

"Really good. We've both been busy getting everything wrapped up for graduation. But we spend several evenings a week hanging out."

"So are you excited about tomorrow night?"

"You have no idea. Excited and super nervous," I say as the line slowly moves forward. Tomorrow night is our final production, and I have been living and breathing dance for the past few weeks.

"Well, Mark has been dying to see you dance."

"I wasn't sure if he was going to be able to make it."

"Yeah, Ryan has a new band that alternates Saturday nights."

Looking down to the ground, I am a little caught off guard by the mention of Ryan's name. I know Jase is still friends with him, but he makes a point to not mention him around me.

"Sorry," he says.

I look back up at him and tell him, "It's fine, Jase. I know you're friends."

"So, can I go there?"

Letting out a sigh, I nod my head and he says, "He

misses you. He hasn't been the same since."

"Neither have I. But, it's done. It's been almost two months."

"So, that's it?"

"In case you haven't noticed, I've been pretty busy trying to sort my own issues out," I tell him.

"I know you have. And I'm proud of you."

We take a few steps as the line continues to creep forward. "I just need to be alone right now. I realize how much I was clinging to people. I did it with you, and I did it with him. In a way, I guess I'm glad this all happened. It forced to me to finally find the will to try to pull myself out this hell. But, I had to do it alone."

"I understand. I really do. So, how is everything going with all of that?"

"We've been talking a lot about the attack. Dr. Christman really wants me to stay in the moment, feeling the power of those emotions without shutting down. The more we do those exercises the less scary it is talking about it."

"That's really good. I'm really glad that you're doing this. I always felt so helpless. I never knew what to tell you."

Grabbing his hand, I tell him, "You always said the right things to me. You always made me feel safe."

He kisses my forehead and asks, "How are your night terrors?"

"I'm still taking my pills. She told me that the more I can cope with my anxiety and triggers during the day and realize I'm okay, then the night stuff should work itself out naturally. But for now, I still take them."

He slings his arm around my shoulder and kisses my head. "You're pretty amazing, you know that?"

"Stop embarrassing me. So, tell me about you. Any job offers yet?"

"I have an interview at Dean Allen on Monday."

"That's great! So, you're definitely staying in Seattle?"

"Yeah. It's home for me. I love the city, and Mark is staying, so it only makes sense. What about you? I know you were thinking about the Pacific Northwest Ballet."

"That's when I thought I could never leave. But, I'm really hoping for New York. I think I can go now and be okay. I'll miss you like crazy, but if I got the opportunity, I'd have to at least give it a shot, you know?"

When we finally make it to the front of the line, we get fitted for our purple caps and gowns. I hand over my paperwork to order my honor cords and stole. Jase laughs at me and all the bells and whistles I have to wear. I just shake my head at him. I was still able to maintain my perfect four point this year, which makes a solid four years.

"Want to grab a coffee before we go?"

"Yeah, that sounds good."

While standing in line for our drinks, I spot Kimber from across the room. I shoot her a quick text letting her know we are here, and I see her start heading our way.

"God, this place is packed with every douchebag around!" she snaps as she joins us.

I laugh at her as we walk over to take a seat at an empty table. "Did you order your cap and gown?"

"No, did you see that line?"

"Kimber, you have to get it ordered today. It's the last day."

"Come with me," she begs in a whiney voice.

Taking a sip of my drink I say, "Too late, I just did it."

"Jase?" she says in a singsong voice, but her face drops when he tells her, "Sorry, I went with Candace."

"You guys are hookers! Why didn't you call me?"

"Because you were in class," Jase tells her while I laugh. She's going to be one pissed off chick when she has to stand in that line alone.

"Well, stand with me anyway."

"I can't. I have rehearsals in an hour. I have to run home 'cause I forgot my dance bag."

"You guys are really sucky friends, you know?"

"What are you doing tonight?" Jase asks Kimber.

"Aside from standing in that long ass line, nothing. Why?"

"Come out with Mark and I."

"Drinking?"

"When do they ever not drink?" I butt in.

"Then I'm in! I'll call you when I can find my way out of this fuckin' crazy ass vortex," she complains as she stands up.

"Where are you going?" I ask.

"To go get my cap and gown. Alone."

Jase and I laugh at her when she walks off.

"Well, I better run too. I gotta get to the studio."

"Okay, well I know tomorrow will be busy for you, but if we don't talk before then, I want to wish you luck now, sweetie. I am so proud of you, and we will be there to watch you."

"Thanks, Jase. Love you."

"You too."

"How have you been dealing with the blame?" Dr. Christman asks after I sit down on the couch.

"I don't know. I guess I still feel responsible in a way. I can't get past how my actions led to his actions. I know his actions were wrong, but I still feel responsible for leading him there."

"You can't hold your past responsible for your future."

"What do you mean?" I ask.

"You can't hold the past Candace responsible for the future Candace. You're holding your future self responsible for something your past self didn't know anything about. You can't judge your past behavior because of the way things turned out. You had no way of knowing what would happen next. It's only because you *do* know that you judge your past self."

"I struggle with that. I get what you're saying, but I can't seem to see past all the poor choices I made."

"Well, we will continue to work on that. For now, let's transition and talk a little about tonight. How are you feeling?"

"I feel good. I feel like everything you and I have done has really helped me finally connect to this piece the way I always should have. I used to use Ryan's pain to draw on, but I feel strong enough now to pull from my own."

"That's wonderful."

"I just have to remind myself that it's all right to feel it. It's just a feeling and it will go away, and I will still be okay."

"And the more you can deal with these emotions in a rational manner, the more your sleeping should start to improve. The goal is still to wean you off of the pills." She flips the page of her notepad and continues taking notes.

"I know. I'm just scared."

"But you just said that your emotions will come back down and you will be okay."

"The day stuff seems so much easier than the nightmares. They are so real to me." I don't have the vivid nightmares when I take my pills, but even on the pills my sleep is still restless and filled with night terrors. I'm terrified that if I stop taking them, the bad dreams will start up again.

Crossing her legs, she asks, "So, tell me, what do you think is causing your restless sleep?"

"At this point, it's a lot of things. I still feel like I'm mourning the loss of Ryan. I miss him. A lot. I miss what we had. I wonder what he's doing now. If he's seeing anyone. If he ever thinks about me. I know I shouldn't, but I do."

She leans forward, resting her elbows on her knees. "There is no right or wrong way. These thoughts are completely normal. Do you feel like you need more closure?"

"I don't know." I feel a lump form in my throat, and my eyes prick and sting with tears. "It's weird because he lives a few minutes down the street from me, but it feels like he's a world away."

"I want you to think about what you might need to bring you more peace over this situation."

"Okay."

I look at myself in the mirror. I have finished dancing my ensembles and am applying the last of my makeup before I take the stage for my solo. Adding a few extra bobby pins to my bun, I stand up and make my way backstage. I focus on keeping my muscles warm as I wait for my call.

I feel nervous, as I always do, but I know the nerves will fade as soon as I hit the stage. When the curtain drops, the dancers clear the stage, and I walk to center stage and place myself in fifth position. My heart is pounding, and I'm anxious for the curtain to rise. I know I've worked my ass off for this moment, now I just need to nail it.

The heavy velvet curtain begins to rise as I hear my music start. The heat of the lights sinks into my skin, as I feel the weight of everything I have been working so hard for in the tension of my muscles. Sliding into my chainès across the stage, the music is loud and it fills the auditorium. When I feel the vibrations of the low cello in my chest, I let myself fall into the tortured piece. The music pulses throughout my body while I take myself to my dark places as I begin my footwork across the stage. I know every seat is filled, but right now, it's just me in this room as I glide effortlessly, always leading with my heel to show off my perfect turnout.

Everything about this year floods through me. I no longer need to take from anyone else; I only take my pain, my brokenness, my suffering. It pours out of me. Everything Jack did to me, and all the torment of losing Ryan. I let my heart bleed as I move through my piece. I throw it all out there and finally allow myself to truly experience this piece—I finally feel it.

When the staccato violins enter the piece, I hit my fouettès one by one with a double pirouette on every second and sixth count. The applause rises as I finish and slide out. The spots are sharp on my piquès and I know I've nailed the routine when the music hits its second high then drifts away.

The crowd is almost as deafening as the music was. I stand and pas marchè to center stage. With a strong port a bras, I take the final curtsey of my college career. Ms. Emerson catches my eye as she walks onto the stage, looking as stoic as ever, and hands me a bouquet of long-stemmed pink roses. I thank her, and I can barely hear her over the applause when she says, "I knew you could do it," and then steps aside, giving me a reverence, and I curtsey one last time before the curtain drops.

I stand there for a moment while dancers for the next ensemble run and rush all over the stage and around me. I soak in the moment and then walk off stage, back to the dressing room. I'm overcome by the congratulations from my fellow dancers and friends.

When the show ends, I wash my face and change into my old yoga pants and UW sweatshirt. I tie my running shoes and throw my bag over my shoulder as I make my way out of the building. Everyone is coming over to the house tonight for drinks to celebrate. Nothing big, just hanging out as we usually do. When I turn the corner, I have to do a double take when I see Donna standing there against the wall.

"You were amazing, dear," she says as she walks toward me.

I haven't spoken to her since Ryan and I broke up. She has called several times, but I knew it would hurt too much to answer. Donna filled a place in my heart that was only hers to fill. She's the mother I'd always wanted—the one I'd always needed.

"What are you doing here?"

Pulling me into her arms, I savor her embrace as she says, "I told you I would be here." Leaning back, she adds, "I couldn't miss seeing you dance. You were beautiful. I knew you were amazing, but I just had no idea you were that amazing."

"Thank you," I say as a smile breaks across my face. "I still can't believe you're here."

"I tried calling a few times, but—"

"I'm sorry. I know you called. It just...It hurt to lose Ryan, but it hurt to lose you too."

"You didn't lose me. I love you, dear. You will always have me whenever you need me. I know Ryan hurt you, and I understand it might be easier if I'm not around, but please know that I am always here for you."

Her words hit where they always hit: deep inside. My chin quivers as I try not to cry, and I go in for another hug. When she wraps her comforting arms around me, I let the tears free. "I'm glad you came. I've missed talking to you." When I step back, I add, "But you're right, it hurts. You were the best gift Ryan ever gave me, but I need the space right now."

"Of course. I understand."

"I'm sorry."

"You have absolutely nothing to be sorry about. I am so proud of you. You will do amazing things. Just keep following that strong heart of yours."

"Thank you, Donna. Really...thank you for everything."

"Well, I better get going. Congratulations."

I smile at her one last time as she turns to walk out of the building. Another pang of loss eats me from the inside and I cry. I don't fight it; I just let it envelop me. After a few minutes, I walk outside into the cold rainy night and welcome the chilling drops that plunk down on me and mix with my hot tears. I keep telling myself it'll be okay, because I know it will be. I have to believe in that.

chapter forty

A few days after the production, the calls started coming in. I was offered placements in five companies. Pacific Northwest Ballet here in Seattle was one of them, but when the call came from the American Ballet Theatre in New York, one of the most respected ballet companies in the world, I couldn't say no. My dreams of dancing full-length classics such as Swan Lake and La Bayadere at the Met are about to come true. I can hardly believe it. Life has been a total whirlwind since I accepted their offer.

Graduation is in two weeks, so I have been busy packing up my room and researching apartments in New York City. I found a flat in a walk up that is close to Lincoln Center, where I will be dancing every day. I rented a storage unit here in Seattle to store some of my furniture and the boxes of things I don't need or won't have space for. Once I'm more settled I will figure out what to do with everything.

Everyone is out of town for Memorial Day weekend. I stayed behind because I just had too much to do. Kimber is still seeing Seth even though he is moving to California for grad school. She says they aren't in love or anything, just having fun. They went to Whistler for four days while Mark and Jase went to Vegas.

It's Saturday night, and while everyone is on vacation, I am sitting on the floor of my trashed room, trying to sort through all of my things, deciding what to throw away, what to take with me, and what to leave behind in storage.

My phone rings and when I pick it up, I see it's Kimber calling and that it's already past midnight. Swiping my phone, I answer, "Hey, Kimber."

"Candace, hey." Her voice is shaky and slow.

"Is everything okay?"

"Yeah. Uh...Candace, Seth just got a call from one of his fraternity brothers, and I need to talk to you about something."

My mind immediately goes to Jack. Why else would I care about any news from Seth's frat house?

"Okay. What's up?"

There is a long pause before she speaks.

"Jack's dead."

I swear my heart stops when she tells me this, and I have to remember to breathe.

"What?"

"Yeah. It happened earlier today. A drunk driving accident."

"Oh." I don't know what to say. I feel numb.

"Look, I can come home if you need me to. I just wanted to tell you before you saw it on TV or something."

"No, I'm fine. Really." For some reason, I feel tears threatening, and I rush to get off the phone. "You guys have fun. I'm about to go to bed. I'll talk to you later."

"Are you sure?"

"Yeah. Bye."

When she hangs up, I set the phone down. I feel the tears run down my face, but I don't make a sound. *Jack's dead.* I keep saying it to myself over and over. *He's dead.* The more I say it, the more my emotions well up. I want to shut down, but I know I need to force myself to feel whatever it is that is brewing inside of me.

When I choke back a breath, that's when I begin to cry. I'm not sure why I'm crying. I'm so confused. I don't know what I'm feeling, but it feels a lot like sadness. But why am I sad? Shouldn't I be happy? But I'm not happy. He's dead. God, what's wrong with me? I shouldn't be feeling sad for the guy who raped me. I should be relieved—relieved that I don't have to be scared of him anymore. I begin to sob, my emotions overtake me, and I know for sure: this is hurt and sadness.

I pick up the phone to call Jase, but it just goes to voicemail. I hate that I'm feeling this way. I lie on the floor in the middle of my messy room, and curl into a ball. I try to slow my breathing, but everything about Jack starts flashing through my mind: meeting him for the first time at the club, dancing with him at Remedy, kissing him in his car. Why am I thinking this way? I should be thinking about the asshole that raped me, broke me, destroyed me. He ruined my life, and I'm sobbing on my floor because I feel bad for him.

I need to run away. I know I shouldn't, but I just need to escape. I throw on my running shoes and walk outside. It's the middle of the night, and the streets are quiet. It's raining, but I don't care. I just walk. I walk and cry as the drops fall from the sky. I don't know how long I've been walking or where I'm even going. My running shorts and t-shirt are soaked through, and my hair is drenched in a bun on top of my head. I wander through the streets, unable to calm myself down.

When I turn onto yet another street, my vision blurred by my tears, I start walking up stairs—familiar stairs. When I knock on the door and no one answers, a fresh wave of tears break free. I feel so alone.

Hearing the click of the lock, I look up as the door opens, and my stomach clenches when I see his clear-blue eyes staring at me. I start sobbing and fall into his chest. He quickly wraps his arms around me, and I cling desperately to him. It's been months since I've touched him. I melt into him, and he reaches down, slipping his arm behind my knees and scoops me up, cradling me in his arms as he walks me inside.

When he sits us down on his couch, I remain in his arms, curled in his lap. I lay my head on the curve of his shoulder as he holds onto me tightly, as if he's scared I'll slip away. When my cries soften into short breaths and hiccups, he asks, "Baby, what happened?"

I lift my head and look at Ryan. He reaches up and strokes my cheek with his knuckles.

Shaking my head, still confused, I tell him, "Jack died tonight."

He lets out a deep breath and leans his forehead to mine. When he does, I let out all my thoughts in a blubbering mess. "I'm sorry. I didn't know where to go. I'm so confused. I don't know what's wrong with me."

"Slow down, babe."

"Should I be happy? Or relieved?" I ask, desperate for someone to tell me how I should be feeling.

"Well, what do you feel right now?" he asks as he tucks a lock of my hair behind my ear.

"Sad. And hurt. I don't know why. It's like all I can think about is Jack when he was good. Or when I thought he was. But I know he wasn't. I know I should hate him. But, if I'm sad, does that mean I don't hate him?"

"I think you're just in shock. I think you need a little time to sort this out in your head."

I lay my head back down on his shoulder, when he says, "Let me go get you a towel. You're freezing."

I nod my head and scoot off his lap and onto the couch. He returns with two big towels and wraps one of them around my shoulders. Sitting next to me, he pulls me back into him.

"You need anything to drink?"

I lean back forward and let my head hang down. Wrapping my arms around myself, I shake my head no. Ryan's hand runs up my back and onto my shoulder as he tugs me back.

"Talk to me."

I sigh and say, "I'm sorry. I didn't even realize I was here until I was in front of your door."

"I'm glad you're here." He cups my cheek with his hand and says, "I've missed you so much."

His words hurt. They hurt because I know how he feels. I've missed him too. I've been trying not to. Trying so hard to not think about him, but he's always been there. Without even thinking, I reach up and run my hand down the side of his face as I feel my own face scrunch up, and I start to cry again.

"Baby, don't cry," he says as he brushes his thumbs over my cheeks.

Being here, in his house, on this couch where we've made love, and in his arms, I just want to go back to when it was all good. When I didn't know about the lies. When I was safe and we were so in love. But, I can't. I can't go back there again and make myself that vulnerable.

He leans down and presses his lips to my forehead, and I have to force myself to not take more. Pulling back, I shake my head and say, "I can't."

"Babe."

"I can't. It hurts so bad, I just can't"

"I swear to you, I will never hurt you again."

"But you swore you wouldn't hurt me before and you did."

Lowering his head slightly to look into my eyes straight on, he affirms, "I love you. God, I love you so much."

He moves his head in slowly. I can smell his sweet minty breath. I've missed that smell. His lips barely skim mine when I pull back slightly.

"I'm moving," I say on a hush.

Lifting his head up, he looks at me with his brows knitted together.

"I got a job. I'm moving to New York in two weeks."

He looks down and shakes his head slowly as I say, "You can't kiss me." My cries begin to intensify. "If you do...I'll never want to leave you."

"Then I'll come with you."

"Ryan...I just can't. I'm too scared you'll hurt me again. I just need to be on my own. I've been working so hard to pull myself out of the hell I've been living in."

"I know you have. I ask Jase about you all the time. He's told me how well you're doing. I just wish I could be around to see it, babe." He chokes on his words and drops his head. When he looks back up at me, his eyes are rimmed with tears. "All I ever wanted was for you to be okay, to be happy."

"I'm okay," I affirm.

We sit there while time slowly passes. I thought I would always be with Ryan. I thought he was it for me. I wanted him to be it for me. A part of me stills does, but I push that part deep down, because it hurts to feel it. I love Ryan. Despite everything that happened, I still love him. I'm not sure how long it will take for these feelings to fade, but I really wish they would because missing him is excruciating.

"Do you think you could drive me home?" I ask after a while.

"Yeah," he whispers, and I know he doesn't want to.

He helps me into his jeep and drives me the few minutes to my house. When he pulls into my driveway, he asks, "Can I walk you in?"

“Ryan,” I sigh out.

He nods his head, understanding that I don’t think it’s a good idea.

When I grab the handle to open the door, he says, “I’ll never love anyone the way that I love you.”

I turn my head back to look at him, and I know my face is reflecting the pain that is wracking me as my tears fall. I nod my head, my only way of letting him know I feel the same way toward him. I can’t speak. I don’t know how. My sobs start to break through when I open the door and walk away from the only person I never wanted to walk away from.

Leaving Ryan last night was the hardest thing I have ever had to do. I sit up in my bed and look at the chaos in my room. All my belongings are strewn all over the place. I feel like this room is a reflection of how I feel inside: chaotic. I need order in my life. I resolve to pull my life together and move forward, starting with this room.

I spend the day packing and sorting. By late afternoon, I can finally see the floor again when I stack all of the boxes along one of the walls. When my phone chirps at me, I read a text from Roxy.

Drinks?

When and where?

Prime. 7:00?

Perfect.

I hop in the shower to wash all the grime from packing off of me. After drying my hair and putting on a little makeup, I slip on a pair of dark wash jeans and a short-sleeved black peplum top.

When I walk into Prime, I am relieved to see that it's not too busy. I still tend to get nervous around crowds, especially since I don't have Jase or Ryan with me, but Roxy is already there, with her newly platinum blonde hair, waiting for me with a martini in hand. I smile at her appearance as she places her bright red lips on the glass and takes a sip, while all of her colorful tattoos are exposed on her sleeveless arms.

"Hey, hun," she says as I take a seat next to her at the bar.

"You been waiting long?"

"No, just got here."

I order a glass of red wine and Roxy asks, "So, are you all packed?"

"Pretty much. I spent all day working on my room."

She scans my face and says, "It shows. You look like shit, girl."

"Thanks," I chuckle.

The bartender sets my wine down in front of me, and I pick it up to take a long sip.

"Thirsty?"

Setting the glass down, I open up to Roxy about last night.

"It's really over with Ryan," I sigh.

"What?"

Resting my elbow on the bar, Roxy does the same when I start, "Yeah. I saw him last night. It was awful."

"What happened?"

"Nothing, really. I mean nothing was really said that wasn't said months ago. He did say that he wanted to go to

New York with me."

"God, he really loves you."

"I really love him too. But I can't go back there again. Besides, New York is my dream, and if I didn't go, I would always be wondering 'what if.'"

She leans back and takes another sip of her drink. "That's understandable."

Last week I decided to tell Roxy about Jack. My therapist told me that the more I deal with it, the easier it will become, and the less power it will hold over me. She's right. It was hard, but not unbearable. I did it, and I was okay.

"Jack's dead," I slip out.

Almost choking on her martini, she shouts, "What?!"

"God, you're loud."

"Sorry," she says, and then whispers, "What?" in exaggeration.

"Yeah, last night. Car wreck. Kimber called and told me. I went for a walk to try and calm myself down, and I wound up at Ryan's house. I shouldn't have gone there. I know it only hurt him to see me again, just to have me walk away."

"Why didn't you call me?"

"I don't know. I was a mess."

"Shit," she says as she sits back and downs the rest of her martini.

"I'm ready to move on though. I'm ready for New York."

She shakes her head at me, and I ask, "What?"

"I don't think you are."

"What's that supposed to mean?"

"Nothing. Forget it. I'm happy for you. I'm gonna miss the crap out of you."

"I'm going to miss you too."

"You think you'll come back?"

"I honestly don't know. I have no idea where my life is going to take me. But I think I am finally ready to explore it on my own."

chapter forty-one

I take one last look around the room that has been mine for the past three years. The walls are bare and everything that is mine is now in boxes sitting in storage. I dropped my car off at Kimber's parents' house last night. They are going to keep it in their garage until I figure out what I'm going to do with it. I already shipped out my boxes, and they should be waiting for me to pick up when I arrive in New York later tonight.

"You ready?" I turn to see Jase walking into my room, and he sits down on my stripped bed.

"I'm sad," I say as I sit down next to him and lean my head on his shoulder.

"Me too. I can't believe you're leaving."

"I know. Me either." My chest aches knowing I will soon be leaving everything I know and hopping on a plane to go where I don't know a single person. Jase has always been my rock. He's my best friend, and I swear he's the breath that kept me going this year. I'm scared to not have him.

Jase is moving in with Mark next week. They both got jobs here in the city and since Mark's roommate is moving out and he'll have the place to himself, he asked Jase to move in.

Kimber also got a job at a local magazine working in the marketing department. She told me she refuses to get another roommate, but that's just her being stubborn. She told me she didn't want to live with anyone if it wasn't me.

"Hey, guys. We need to leave soon," Kimber says as she stands in my doorway. She looks around my room and shakes her head. "This shit makes me sick." She walks over and sits on the other side of me. I still feel so guilty for wasting all that time not speaking to Kimber. I wish I could get every second back.

"Have you even told your parents where you're going?" Kimber asks.

"No. I haven't spoken with them since Christmas Eve. And when I never heard from them on my birthday or graduation, I figured, why bother?"

"That really sucks ass," she says.

"Yeah."

She wraps her arm around me and Jase does as well. Kimber is the first one to break down and start crying and I follow shortly after.

"I'm going to miss you guys so much."

"We are too," Jase says. "Come on, girls, we need to head out."

Jase stands up, walks over to my two large suitcases, and starts wheeling them out of the room. Sitting alone with Kimber, I say, "I'm so sorry that I didn't trust you enough to talk to you. You're my sister, and I shouldn't have avoided you like that."

"Candace, you have already apologized enough for all of that. It's okay. It's in the past."

"I hate that I'm leaving just as we are talking again."

"I know. Me too." She gives me a squeeze before standing up. "We'd better go."

The drive to Sea-Tac Airport is a quiet one. No one speaks, and the somber mood is thick in the car. I sit in the front seat with Jase and grip his hand the whole way there. I never thought I'd leave him. I never thought I'd be strong enough to. I keep reminding myself that this has always been my dream. This was the goal all along. I just got really sidetracked this past year.

Ryan keeps breaking through my thoughts. I tell myself moving will lessen the pain I feel every time I think about him. I know once I get to New York that I will be busy learning the ropes at ABT and learning a lot of new choreography. I'm already jittery thinking about it.

When Jase pulls the car around to the departures drive, I can feel the fear in the pit of my stomach. I tighten my hold on Jase's hand, and when I do, he looks over at me. "You're going to be fine. Everything is working out the way it should."

I nod at him, unable to speak, and he smiles at me. He pulls up to the curb, and the three of us get out of the car. I turn around to hug Kimber and breakdown at the same time she does.

"I love you," I choke out and I feel her nod her head in response. We hold tightly onto each other and when we finally loosen our hold, I turn to Jase and just fall into him and cry. His arms have been home for me. He's everything to me, and my heart breaks to think about not having him. He kisses the top of my head and says, "I'm so proud of you. I'm going to come visit you in a few weeks, okay?"

I pull back and nod my head. As soon as I accepted my offer in New York, Jase booked a ticket to come visit me at the end of June. So, I only have a few weeks until I see him again.

We all say our goodbyes and cry a little more before I grab my bags and wheel them to the luggage counter to check them. Once they are checked, I make my way through security and walk to my gate. My mind is consumed, and a part of me wants to hop in a cab and run back home. I start doubting myself, and I'm not sure I can do this alone. Maybe I should have taken the job in Seattle. If I did that, everything would be different.

I sit down on one of the chairs facing out the window. My plane is already here, and I watch as the carts drive up next to it with everyone's luggage. My insides are twisting with anxiety. I think about how everything has changed in the past two months, ever since the morning the detective called. It took me a while to understand why Ryan did what he did. Dr. Christman helped me sort out all of my thoughts and I know, in Ryan's mind, he only did it because he didn't want to hurt me. I know he never meant to deceive me, and in my heart I have forgiven him.

Going to New York has always been my dream, but now that it's actually happening, I'm suddenly questioning if it still is. Would I be this sad if it was? Shouldn't I be happy? I wonder if I should even be doing this. Maybe I'm just stuck on the dreams of my past. Dreams change; maybe mine has. I thought I had everything planned out, but this year took me in a completely different direction. Meeting Ryan and falling in love was the last thing I ever expected. The last thing I thought I ever deserved.

I've been working so hard in therapy, but now I think this whole New York thing is just something I'm forcing, to try and prove to myself that I am strong enough to do it, to stop clinging and be independent. But what if what I am actually clinging to now is the dream? A dream that really isn't my dream anymore. Because when I close my eyes it's never there. It's Ryan. What if the choice that takes the most strength is not the choice to get on that plane, but the choice to know that I shouldn't get on that plane? I snap out of my thoughts when realization suddenly hits me. *What am I doing?*

Grabbing my purse, I stand up and start pushing my

way through the crowds in the terminal. I run by the security check and find the exit. I fly down the escalators and when I run out the sliding doors, I hail the first cab that I see. I hop in the back seat and give the driver the address.

Pulling out my phone, I go through my call history and find the number I'm looking for. I tap it and after a few rings a woman answers, "PNB. How may I help you?"

"Is Peter Kirchner available?"

"May I ask who's calling?"

"Candace Parker."

"One moment please."

Butterflies swarm in my stomach as I wait. I'm on hold, hoping that I still have a chance to sign with them.

"Ms. Parker, this is Peter. How can I help you?"

"Hi, Mr. Kirchner. I was actually wondering if it was too late to be considered for placement in your company."

"What happened to the American Ballet Theatre?"

"It wasn't the right choice for me."

"Why don't you come in on Monday, and we can get all those papers signed? We would be honored to have you."

"Thank you. Really. I will see you Monday."

"See you then."

When the cab stops, I hand over the money, get out, and start walking up the drive to the stairs that lead to his front door. I ring the bell and immediately start crying, feeling a total overload of emotions.

When the door opens, my breath catches, and he takes one look at me and asks, "What are you doing here? I just got off the phone with Jase. He said he dropped you off at the airport."

"I can't go. I'm so sorry. I can't do it."

"What do you mean you can't do it?"

"Because...I love you too much to leave. And I miss you. And I made a huge mistake by leaving you. I'm so sorry," I cry out.

When he wraps me in his arms, I know this is where I belong. This is my dream.

"Baby, you didn't make any mistakes."

"I did. And I know I hurt you. But, I'm so sorry. I can't go because I can't leave you. I don't want to leave you."

Pulling me inside, he closes the door, and he walks me over to the couch. When we sit down, he says, "I can't let you give up on your dream. I can't."

"But, it's not my dream. I was just hanging on to it because I was scared to see that it really wasn't what I wanted. It's you. It's always been you."

When he crushes his lips to mine, I wrap my hand around his neck and climb onto his lap, straddling his legs. Ryan bands his arms around me and holds on tight. He pulls away for a moment and tells me, "I've missed you so much, babe. You have no fucking idea."

"I love you. I'm sorry I've been so stupid and wasted all this time when all I really wanted was to be here with you."

"You have nothing to be sorry for. I fucked up. I hurt you, and you'll never know how much I regret it."

"I don't blame you, Ryan. I did, but I don't anymore. I just want to be with you."

He cradles my cheeks and wipes my tears with his thumbs. "I don't ever want to lose you again."

"You won't. I'm yours."

Our affectionate kisses are laced with passion, making up for lost time. Picking me up, I lock my ankles around his waist as he carries me upstairs. He lays me down on his bed and crawls on top of me. I've missed this bed, being wrapped up with him in these sheets, smelling his scent all around me, feeling his warmth.

He reaches back, pulls his shirt off over his head, and

tosses it aside. I look at the tattoo that's on his ribs and read the words again: *pain is a reminder you're still alive.* I sit up and brush my fingers across his scar and over the words. I tilt my head back to look up at him and he says, "I couldn't breathe without you."

I reach up and run my hand along his jaw. "I need you."

And with words unspoken, he presses me down with his weight wholly on top of me, and I soften into him. I let my arms float above me as he takes his time peeling off my shirt. He slides his hands from my neck, over my breasts, along my stomach, and when he gets to my pants, he unhooks them and pulls them off, along with my heels. When he removes his pants, he lies down next to me, and I wrap my leg around his hip as we are face to face.

We move slowly as we reclaim each other after being apart for these past two months. Our hands explore, and I relax into the heat of his body. I feel the peace that had been missing since I left him return to my heart, and I'm whole under his touch.

Ryan unhooks my bra and drops it to the floor with the rest of our clothing. He trails his lips over my sensitive flesh and licks my nipple with his hot tongue before covering it with his mouth, sucking gently. My head rolls back into the pillow as my body lifts and presses into his, needing more. When he reaches down and drags his hand between my legs, feeling what he does to me when we're together, I release a moan. His touches are intimate and exactly what I need right now.

Shifting between my legs and running his hands up my knees and down along my inner thighs, he looks down at me, "God, you're so beautiful." I reach up and bring him to me, melding my mouth with his. When I feel him enter me, he parts my lips with his tongue and licks slow and deep, freely exploring each other's mouths. My arms wrap around his neck as his hips roll over me, pushing himself deeper inside. Our breaths are labored, and our moans fill the room.

He rolls us over, and I'm spread across his lap as he sits up to keep our bodies close. He wraps his hands around my shoulders as I slowly begin to roll my hips into him. We take our time with each other. I love that Ryan can be this way with me, open and vulnerable, never rushing. He's the only one who can make me feel so safe when I bare my entire self; he's the only one I want to.

With one of his hands on my hip, guiding me, and the other on my cheek, I wrap mine behind his head and weave my fingers into his unruly hair as my body begins to climb.

He doesn't even need to ask as we look into each other's eyes. I know he likes to watch me. My body begins to quiver beneath his hands as my hips rock into him, and I grip his hair in my fists. "Let go, baby." I drop my forehead to his as his blue eyes pierce mine, and I fall apart in his arms. A carnal moan escapes the both of us as he pushes himself deep inside of me and finds his release too, gripping his fingers tightly onto my body.

I fuse my lips with his, never wanting to let go as he lays us down on our sides, bodies still connected, facing each other. I've missed this so much, and I don't even try to hold back my tears. I love this man from a place inside that I never knew existed. He's saved me in a way I never knew a person could be saved. He holds me close, and it's only when I sniff that he pulls back from our kiss. "Babe."

Looking at him, I take my time before saying, "I never want to know what life is without you."

He reaches down and pulls the sheets over us as we tangle our legs. "You won't ever have to."

We continue to hold each other and kiss until we drift off together.

I wake from our afternoon nap, and the mist from earlier is now coming down harder. I lay in Ryan's arms for a while as I watch the raindrops trickle down the windows. I never knew home until now. It's with him, in this house, in this bed. My mind and body are free of doubt. This is my dream. He is my amazing.

Looking back over my shoulder at him, his eyes still closed as he sleeps, I know I will never love as powerfully as I do with him. I reach down, grab his discarded t-shirt, and shrug it on as I make my way to the bathroom. I flick on the light and before I can close the door, I see my necklace lying next to his sink. Walking over and looking down at it, I see that he got the chain fixed from when I ripped it off my neck. I run my finger along the etched letters: *And though she be but little, she is fierce.*

Looking up, I see that my toothbrush is still next to the other sink along with a bottle of my perfume. Warm arms slowly snake around my waist as his lips press into my neck. Our eyes meet in the reflection of the mirror. "I could never let you go."

He picks up the necklace and clasps it back around my neck where it belongs. I will never be close enough to him to satisfy me. Maybe it was supposed to be like this all along; maybe I needed the pain of losing Ryan to make me finally pull myself out of the madness. Maybe I just had to lose him for a moment to keep myself from fading.

Every 2 minutes, someone in the U.S. is sexually assaulted. Approximately 2/3 of assaults are committed by someone known to the victim. And only 46% of assaults are reported to the police.

You just read about Candace who suffered from Post-Traumatic Stress Disorder, Flashbacks, Sleep Terror Disorder, and Nightmares.

These are only a few of the effects one can experience after being sexually assaulted.

There is help.

National Sexual Assault Hotline
1.800.656.HOPE

National Sexual Assault Online Hotline
ohl.rainn.org/online/

Visit http://www.rainn.org to find more information and resources.

FALLING

a novel by

e.k. blair

coming soon

Sometimes it takes someone else to show us what we are truly capable of becoming.

Suffering from years of violent abuse, Ryan Campbell has learned how to keep people from getting too close. But when you shut yourself off, people get hurt along the way. Never caring much about others, Ryan creates a world in which he doesn't have to feel.

When Ryan meets Candace Parker, all of his walls slowly begin to crumble. Not sure of the truth of who she is, he feels his mind is playing tricks on him. Unable to force out the thoughts that consume him, Ryan is haunted by visions that torment him every time he looks at her. He finds himself swallowed by guilt and blame, but he's unwilling to turn his back on the one person that could possibly save him.

You've heard Candace's story in 'Fading,' now hear Ryan's.

acknowledgements

Deciding to write a novel did not come easy. There was a lot of self-doubt before I actually typed my first word. I never could have anticipated the power of this journey. It took the support and encouragement of many people to make this book a possibility.

It was my husband who first told me that I should write a book. I honestly thought he had lost his mind. But he saw something in me that I never knew was even there. He believed in me when I first started stumbling through the prologue. It was his encouragement that kept me going, and before long, I became unstoppable. I am so lucky to have such an amazing man in my life that provided me the freedom I needed to immerse myself in this book. He took on all mommy and daddy duties, along with all the cooking and cleaning while I typed my heart out. *I would thank you from the bottom of my heart, but for you, there is no bottom.*

This story would not be as beautiful as it is without Gina Smith. She has been with me from the first days of creating the plot for a book I didn't know the story to. I quickly deemed her my 'Creative Assistant.' She sparked the ideas for many of the scenes and helped me create the hauntingly romantic love story between Candace and Ryan. I could not have written this book without her guidance. We have clocked many hours on the phone and on the computer doing massive research to ensure that I was accurate in what I was writing, even down to map-questing drives to calculate timing. I will forever be indebted to her. Being able to share the love for my story and the love for my characters with her was such an amazing experience. I couldn't imagine ever writing a book without her by my side.

My editor had her work cutout for her. Lisa Christman, from Adept Edit's, is such an amazing person. An honest friend is hard to come by, but I found one in her. Brilliant and amazing. She not only encouraged me through this whole process, but she guided me in the right direction with my characters. Candace was not an easy person to write, but Lisa made it a possibility. I will never forget all your pep talks and comforting words when stress was getting the best of me. Thank you for taking this book so seriously, but also knowing when to use your humor to get me through all the editing. You will never know how hard some of your editing comments made me laugh and what that did for my stress. You really stepped up to the plate and delivered. You are such a dear friend, and I love you!

Thank you to the Haborview Medical Center in Seattle, Washington for guiding me and educating me. Making sure I told a true story was so important to me, and you made that a reality for me. Thank you Rene Langston for sharing your knowledge and assisting me with the hospital scenes. You kept me on track and made sure every detail was addressed down to the HIPPA laws. You also motivated me in so many ways to follow this dream and make it a reality. Your enthusiasm kept a smile on my face.

To include remarks about everyone who contributed to this book would be entirely too long, so here are the Cliffs Notes: My mother for enrolling me in my first dance class and giving me the freedom to grow in my love for the art. My father and step-mother for the constant support and excitement during this journey. All my beta-readers for opening your hearts to this story and helping me polish the book. Your hard work did not go unnoticed. You all were the cheerleaders I needed to get to the finish line. Maxim Malevich who shot the amazing cover. No other photo could ever measure up. You are absolutely brilliant. Sarah Hansen for hunting down Maxim when all I had was a photo and a dream to have it grace my cover. You made it happen, and I can't thank you enough for turning the photo into an amazing cover. To my Indie Chixx writing group for helping me learn the ropes in this crazy world of self-publishing. The support you girls give is amazing. And to all of my friends and family who gave me the motivation I needed during the madness of writing this novel. This story was a hard one to write and countless tears were shed. I could not have done it with you all!

Thank You!

e. k. blair

Facebook:
https://www.facebook.com/EKBlairAuthor

Twitter:
@EK_Blair_Author

Made in the USA
Charleston, SC
30 June 2013